Praise for

WHAT LIES BEYOND THE STARS

"A uniquely riveting vision of the inferno of our
present world joined to a redeeming promise of the
magic of love calling to us from within. Adam Sheppard
is truly a hero of the modern world."

— **Jacob Needleman**, author of *I Am Not I* and
The Heart of Philosophy

"Michael Goorjian's new novel—a deep exploration of
love lost and found across time—is a wonder to behold. If you
believe in the possibilities of dreams coming true, you'll love
this thrilling journey of hope and spiritual connection."

— **Gay Hendricks, Ph.D.**, co-author (with Kathlyn Hendricks)
of *Conscious Loving Ever After*

"Haunting, original, riveting, poignant, insightful,
and passionately romantic, *What Lies Beyond the Stars* is
the visionary and transformational love story of the 21st Century.
Michael Goorjian has created unforgettable characters who
illuminate how our humanity can triumph when we open
our minds and hearts to the magic and mystery of life
itself. I'll always remember this book and reread it
again and again . . . and so will you."

— **Stephen Simon**, film producer of *Somewhere in Time*
and *What Dreams May Come*

WHAT LIES BEYOND THE STARS

A NOVEL

MICHAEL GOORJIAN

VISIONS
HAY HOUSE, INC.
Carlsbad, California • New York City
London • Sydney • Johannesburg
Vancouver • New Delhi

Published and distributed in the United States by: Hay House, Inc.: www.hayhouse.com® • *Published and distributed in Australia by:* Hay House Australia Pty. Ltd.: www.hayhouse.com.au • *Published and distributed in the United Kingdom by:* Hay House UK, Ltd.: www.hayhouse.co.uk • *Published and distributed in the Republic of South Africa by:* Hay House SA (Pty), Ltd.: info@hayhouse.co.za • *Distributed in Canada by:* Raincoast Books: www.raincoast.com • *Published in India by:* Hay House Publishers India: www.hayhouse.co.in

Cover design: Michael Goorjian and Amy Rose Grigoriou
Interior design: Pamela Homan

Wild World
Words and Music by Cat Stevens
Copyright (c) 1970 Cat Music Ltd. and BMG Rights Management (UK) Ltd., a BMG Chrysalis company Copyright Renewed
All Rights Reserved   Used by Permission
Reprinted by Permission of Hal Leonard Corporation

Library of Congress Cataloging-in-Publication Data

Names: Goorjian, Michael A., 1971- author.
Title: What lies beyond the stars / Michael Goorjian.
Description: First edition. | Carlsbad, California : Hay House Inc., 2016.
Identifiers: LCCN 2016028076 | ISBN 9781401942687 (softcover : acid-free paper)
Subjects: LCSH: Self-actualization (Psychology)--Fiction. | Man-woman realtionships--Fiction. | Self-realization--Fiction. | Psychological fiction. | BISAC: FICTION / General.
Classification: LCC PS3607.O59255 W48 2016 | DDC 813/.6--dc23 LC record available at https://lccn.loc.gov/2016028076

Tradepaper ISBN: 978-1-4019-4268-7

10 9 8 7 6 5 4 3 2 1
1st edition, October 2016

Printed in the United States of America

And we came forth to
contemplate the stars.

— Dante Alighieri

Part 1

BENEATH
THE FOG

CHAPTER 1

AN ENTANGLED
PREDICAMENT

SAN FRANCISCO, September 2011

Adam sat in a straight-backed chair by the window, watching the fog bleed through the distant row of cypress trees. His room was small but charming, like something van Gogh might paint. There was a single bed, a side table, Adam's chair, and not much else. Miss Ferguson stood directly behind Adam. At five foot one, she was a few inches taller than he was seated, but it was enough for her to assess his view out the window.

"Mmm. A wee bit off." With a good heave-ho, the stout Scotswoman pulled Adam and his chair a few inches back and to the left.

There were two factors Miss Ferguson considered critical whenever performing this morning task. The first was making sure Adam faced the coastline, which was about a half mile beyond the barricade of windswept, old cypresses that lined the back of the hospital property. Both Adam's room and the solarium had partial ocean views, but if some less attentive member of the staff set Adam's chair at the wrong angle, Miss Ferguson inevitably would find poor Adam later in the day with his body twisted and his neck craned toward the coast.

It was Miss Ferguson who had first picked up on this peculiarity. Adam's primary doctor, Dr. Agopian, was very appreciative of her "meaningful discovery," as he had called it, and had even made a note in Adam's file. It was an interesting clue. Despite the eternal blanket of San Francisco fog, Adam Sheppard had spent every day since arriving at the hospital, close to nine months ago now, seated by the window like a diligent sentry, searching the ocean as if for some invisible presence beyond.

The second crucial factor in positioning Adam's chair was to place him at just the right angle so that in the afternoon, if the sun did, in fact, break through, it would not blind him, or worse, hit the glass in such a way as to create a reflection. Miss Ferguson didn't think unintentional mirror-work was appropriate therapy for a case like Adam Sheppard.

With the chair now properly set, Miss Ferguson crouched next to Adam and gently touched his wrist. "Okay, handsome. Everything is just as you like it."

Miss Ferguson had never married, but she imagined she might have addressed a husband with the same gentle whisper she liked to use with Adam Sheppard.

"Adam dearest, I need to tell you something important. This new nurse, Eve, will be filling in for me the rest of the week, so you won't be seeing my lovely face until next Monday." She paused for a moment as if listening, and then continued. "I know, I know. You're going to be missing me, dear, but we're all fond of Miss Eve, aren't we? You remember that perky blonde, don't you now?"

Miss Ferguson brushed a stray hair from her eyes and leaned in a little closer, searching her patient's face for a response she knew she would not get. Since Adam Sheppard had been admitted to the Presidio House, he had not spoken a single word—not to Miss Ferguson, nor to any staff, nurses, or psychiatrists. Not even to kindly Dr. Agopian. As Adam's chart stated, he was semifunctional and nonresponsive. He avoided eye contact as well as any other attempt to engage him. There was a bumpy patch when he had first arrived—a series of nightly manic outbursts violent enough to require restraints and heavy sedatives—but once Adam had settled in at the Presidio House, he'd quickly disappeared into himself.

Miss Ferguson gave a snort. "Ha! Your name is *Adam,* and her name is *Eve.* Now don't you be getting any funny ideas while I'm gone."

As Miss Ferguson continued her one-sided conversation, Adam's gaze remained fixed on the window over her shoulder. It wasn't that Adam Sheppard had fully checked out; Miss Ferguson was sure of that. She had handled comatose patients back at San Francisco General and was familiar with that unmistakably vacant look. Adam Sheppard was still inside there somewhere; he was simply in another room, down the hallway, or up in the attic, or perhaps down in the basement with a flashlight, searching for some foundation of reality he had lost touch with.

"All right then, handsome, we're all done for now." Miss Ferguson started to get up, but stopped. She decided to try something, a little test of sorts. She slowly leaned toward Adam until her face was directly in his line of vision. After a moment, just as he had done every time before, Adam leaned away from her until his eyes found the window again. Miss Ferguson sighed. She liked to imagine the day when Adam's eyes would suddenly focus on her, and he might say something like, "Why hello, Miss Ferguson. Don't you look bonny today?"

Miss Ferguson didn't know exactly what it was about Adam Sheppard, but more than any of the other patients at the Presidio House, he was special to her. He was 39, only 10 years younger than she was; however, his face was so boyish that he could easily pass as her son. *He is handsome,* she thought, *in a puppy-dog sort of way.* His messy, brown hair with its stubborn cowlick gave him that perpetual sleepy kid look. But there was also something sensual about him, about his lanky body without an ounce of fat. His most singular feature, the one that really tugged at Miss Ferguson's heartstrings, was his eyes. Those sad, sad eyes, forever searching for whatever he had lost out there on the horizon.

She had a sweet spot for Adam, no doubt about it, but Miss Ferguson knew she would never do anything inappropriate with a patient. As a nurse's assistant, she had a stellar reputation at both S.F. General's Mental Health Crisis Unit as well as here at the Presidio House, the hospital's long-term inpatient rehab facility. For 25 years she dealt responsibly with patients afflicted with every imaginable mental condition, from severe paranoid schizophrenia to bipolar disorder, not to mention extreme brain trauma cases— including one woman so convinced she was a parking meter that she almost died from eating loose change.

There was just something different about Adam, something strange and serious, as if the air around him was a little thicker. "Like that feeling you get when you're inside a windy, old church," she had once confided to Dr. Agopian. "And all the jibber-jabber in your head slips away a wee bit, and you feel yourself getting quiet and respectful."

A noise from the hallway reminded Miss Ferguson that it was time to move on.

"You have yourself a delightful week, dear." Miss Ferguson picked up Adam's charts off the bed, took his electric razor from the nightstand to the bathroom, and walked to the door. Like other nonviolent inpatients, Adam's door was left unlocked during the day. He was free to leave his room, walk around the common areas, and even go outside on the grounds. The Presidio House had an "open-environment policy," as Miss Ferguson often reminded Adam.

"Toodle-oo, handsome."

$$\diamondsuit$$

Despite the open-environment policy, Adam Sheppard knew he wasn't going anywhere anytime soon. What no one, including the extremely attentive Miss Ferguson, could see was that in reality (in the fullest sense of the word) Adam was *chained* to this room.

Chained not only by the chemical restraints of lithium, Depakote, and Zyprexa but also by a complex web of smaller, less obvious attachments firmly binding him to his straight-backed chair by the window. Thousands of steel-gray fishing lines were fastened to his body with sharp, barbed hooks, some secured to flesh, while many, over time, had burrowed deep inside him, into the core of his being. There were those chains administered to him at an early age, laid on by parents, schoolteachers, textbooks, and classmates. Chains introduced through the glow of a television screen, and coated in corn syrup, greased with real-butter flavoring. There were chains attached during puberty—messy, embarrassing chains held in place with self-doubt and fears of rejection. On and on they had piled through life, an endless array of restraints bequeathed by friends, neighbors, co-workers, and bosses, slipped down his throat with the aid of a therapist's prescription notepad. And, of course, there were all those new virtual chains, downloaded on demand, accessible instantly with free-roaming Wi-Fi.

This predicament, a deadly twist on Gulliver's Lilliputian dilemma, was no laughing matter. Struggling against his bonds had become unbearable, and despite all Dr. Agopian's efforts, Adam knew he could not survive his situation much longer. Freedom meant destroying himself in the process, and time was running out.

Since an outward struggle was futile, Adam's only hope was to become still, to give in to the tension of his bonds and inconspicuously turn inward. It was inside himself where he had discovered a way out, a temporary doorway through which he could slip unnoticed. Free from the imprisonment of his body, Adam could drift out into that coastal fog beyond his window and make his way back to the place "where skies grow thin"—the cliffs of Mendocino. Standing there at the edge of the world, he could look out to where hushed stars met restless waters, where two opposing forces pulled apart a seam in the fabric of time and space, opening the gateway to a hidden domain. It was from that infinite direction that *she* had come, and into which she had returned.

For Adam it was this unknown realm beyond the horizon, just visible from a high cliff's edge, which offered his only hope of freedom from his barbed entanglement. All that was required now was to take that first impossible step forward.

CHAPTER 2

RENE ADIKLEIN

Three years earlier . . .

"Adam. Wake up. *Adam!*" A hand smacked his shoulder.

Adam bolted upright in his chair. He had fallen into one of those mind loops again, an "Adam moment," as Jane, his wife, had dubbed them. Adam moments had been happening a lot lately, and in increasingly random places.

Like here, wherever the heck "here" was. Adam tried to orient himself. He remembered staring at the man seated in front of him, at the back of that bald head—that impossibly shiny head reflecting a yellow light from somewhere onstage. *There was something hypnotic about that light, which must have been the trigger,* he thought. It had reminded him of some long-forgotten place. *A place with sunlight,* Adam again recalled, *sunlight flickering on something metal.* The memory came with a "Did I remember to turn off the stove?" sense of urgency, but it was still too elusive to bring to mind.

Staring at the disco-ball head in front of him, Adam once again dug into his own head, into that mental filing cabinet of childhood memories, overstuffed drawers he had been meaning to organize. Again he tried to zero in on that nagging lost memory, but his

efforts were interrupted by an annoying string of computer code:
`- case CM_FILTERHIGHPASS: hrgn[2] = CreateEllipticRgn(x11,` `y11, x12, y12): break`; something he'd been working on earlier.
Adam gave his head an Etch A Sketch shake, attempting to wipe
away the lingering bit of code. He had to get back to the source
of that flashy yellow light before it slipped off again. *Something
happened to me there,* Adam thought. *Something I need to get back to
before I forget again.*

"Dude!" This time the hand gripped Adam's shoulder and
shook it. Adam looked over. It was Conner, or Cogan or maybe
Ken—one of the new 3-D landscape animators Blake had just
recruited. "Adiklein! Adiklein's going on," Adam's slaphappy
neighbor shouted over the applause.

Adam got to his feet with everyone else and looked around.
He was fifth row center in the Moscone Center's main auditorium.
Surrounding him were several thousand of San Francisco's top
tech-industry professionals, entrepreneurs, innovators, hackers,
bloggers, and wannabe billionaires. Everyone who was anyone in
tech was there, and they were all going apeshit for the person
about to speak.

Adam glanced down at the laminated pass hanging around
his neck.

TED TALKS 2008 VIP ADMISSION
Adam Sheppard – Lead Programmer
Pixilate Gamehouse,
Virtual Skies Social Gaming Division

Right. Blake arranged the tickets. Adam's present reality continued to render itself around him. Down the aisle, past all the
other Pixilate programmers and designers, Adam spotted his part-
ner/boss/best friend/savior, Blake Dorsey. Less than 15 years ago,
Blake and Adam had started Pixilate Gamehouse together, and
now with over 40 employees and one of the top-selling games on
the market, they were, as Blake liked to say, "killing it." Just four
months earlier, Pixilate had been acquired by Virtual Skies Media

Group to head up its new social gaming division. Blake had been approached directly by Rene Adiklein, Virtual Skies' legendary leader, the same man who was about to speak.

The lights dimmed slightly, and the crowd reacted with a cheer. Adam tried to join. "Whooo-hoo!"

That sounded fucking pathetic, he thought. Adam never had been any good at the crowd thing. It always made him feel like an alien pretending to blend in with real human beings and doing a crap job of it. *I just need to engage in life more,* Adam thought. "Engage with the present moment" was one of his therapist's favorite catch phrases. According to Dr. M., dissociative disorder was an issue for many programmers, not just Adam.

Adam really did want to be more present. After all, here he was at the epicenter of human innovation, about to imbibe the messianic words of one of the industry's loftiest high priests. *Anyone in tech would die to be in your shoes.*

"Whoo–hooo!"

Up on stage, the giant projection screen read:

TED TALKS PRESENTS
INNOVATIONS IN NEW MEDIA TECHNOLOGIES
Rene Adiklein
VP Marketing Strategist—Virtual Skies Media Group

Defying his 72 years, Rene Adiklein bounded onto stage like a teenage pop star. People were often taken aback by the man's youthful vitality. One prominent blogger once described him as "Silicon Valley's Mick Jagger." His signature slate-gray suit fit his slim frame impeccably. His shirt, carnation pink, was fastened at the collar by a round, black pin with a gold *A* (a design Adiklein had created himself). But the most distinctive aspect of Rene Adiklein's appearance was his shoulder-length, salt-and-pepper hair, which he wore slicked back to accentuate his cheekbones and long, slender nose, giving him the appearance of a bird of prey.

"Thank you. Thank you. *Merci beaucoup.*" Adiklein flashed the crowd a quick smile while adjusting his headset microphone.

Thanks to his Swiss upbringing, Adiklein's accent was French with a punchy hint of German. Not so thick as to be difficult to understand, but just enough to be irresistibly charming.

Like every other geek in the room, Adam knew the basics of Adiklein's rise to prominence. He had begun as a marketing consultant, promoting everything from Humvees to energy drinks, from pharmaceuticals to luxury airlines. He was so successful that at one point it was rumored that his clients numbered no fewer than 40 Fortune 500 companies. Then, during the mid-'80s, Adiklein started spending more and more time in the business parks of Silicon Valley, apparently sensing the immense impact technology would soon have on commerce.

At first he stayed behind the scenes, a name you might have heard whispered about in the tech industry, but unless you were Bill Gates or Larry Ellison, Adiklein was not someone you actually met. During the '90s many of the big tech firms began paying ungodly amounts to consult with the marketing guru before launching a new product, to fix a company's image, or to understand future consumer trends. He became known as the "Oracle of Silicon Valley," not for his profound understanding of technology itself, but because he had a more-than-profound understanding of the inner workings of those quickly becoming obsessed with technology, which soon turned out to be pretty much everyone on the planet.

The cheering crowd showed no hint of quieting. Finally Adiklein raised a hand, signaling that he was going to begin.

"Today is a very special day. For today I have decided to reveal a particular secret of mine, long shrouded in mystery."

As though following the diminishing curve of the audience's applause, the word *mystery* landed perfectly in the silence. Adiklein let it hang a moment before theatrically pulling a folded sheet of paper from his breast pocket. "On this paper I have written a *code*." Adiklein paused for a moment as he sized up his audience.

Adam marveled at how deftly his new überboss handled such a large crowd. Given Adiklein's reputation for avoiding the spotlight, Adam assumed he would be more at ease speaking to smaller groups, in boardrooms or at country clubs.

"A code that is a *key*," Adiklein continued. "A key that can unlock forces capable of shaping the very world around us. A *seed* from which the gardens of our social behavior arise."

He smoothed the paper between his slender fingers. "There are countless codes programmed into each and every one of us. Unconsciously dictating our needs, our desires. We're encoded for sex, violence, love, wealth, food, alcohol, drugs—you name it. But if you dig down deeply enough, you will find that there is, in truth, a single underlying code that is the root of them all.

"And I am here today to tell you that the men and women you learn about in your history books are those who have discovered this *première règle,* and used it to define the world we live in today. It is the skeleton key that unlocks every one of your dreams—success, power, influence, and market dominance. Every door will open to the man or woman who controls this one code."

Folded paper in hand, Adiklein made his way forward to the edge of the stage. Then, as if dropping a small nuclear bomb, he added, "The code consists of a single word."

Adam glanced around at the crowd. Amazing. In less than a minute, Rene Adiklein had 2,000 people completely enraptured.

"So. Can you guess the word?" Adiklein paused for effect, but not long enough for some asshole to break his momentum. "No? Okay, how about I give you some hints, yes?" Adiklein strolled across the front of the stage, the folded paper held casually in his hand by his side.

"Without this *one thing,* we die." After a beat he called out, "Food, maybe? No. How about air?" He shrugged. "No, too easy. What I have written on this paper is the single most valuable commodity on the planet! That's right. At this very moment, wars are being fought all over the world just to gain control of this, right here!"

He waved the paper in the air. "Oil, maybe? Gold? Money? Land? No, no, no!" Adiklein's voice rose with intensity. "All that means nothing—zero, *rien du tout*—to the man who controls this one thing! The. One. Thing!" Adiklein pivoted back to the podium, set down the folded paper, and picked up a small handheld remote. With a click he triggered his PowerPoint presentation.

Adam's chest tightened as he realized that all the lights in the auditorium were dimming. Even the giant projection screen behind Adiklein faded to black. Sitting in complete darkness was unnerving enough, but sitting in it with 2,000 other people was even creepier. A wave of murmurs confirmed that Adam wasn't the only one uncomfortable. Then the strains of symphonic music began rising out of the void, building quickly to a crescendo of Twentieth Century Fox proportions. There was a sudden burst of light before one giant word appeared on the screen:

ATTENTION

The lights came back up, accompanied by the sound of laughter and applause. On stage Adiklein was laughing as well. After taking a sip of water, he continued. "So. Do I have your attention now?"

More laughs. "Are you *paying* with your attention?" He put out a hand like a doorman accepting a tip. "Thank you very much. I'll take it!" Again the crowd laughed.

"Yes, I'll take it because I understand that your attention, it is the only thing of value you have to offer me. That is right. The more I keep of your attention, the more I keep of *you*."

Adiklein's thumb clicked the remote, triggering on the screen behind him an image—a glossy advertisement showing an infant lying in a crib, wide-eyed, looking up at its adoring mother. "From the moment we are born, what is the first thing we need?" Adiklein raised his eyebrows expectantly, then answered for everyone, "That's right, our mother's attention."

More images—babies and toddlers being held, fed, played with, loved. "We are *starved* for attention, right? We *cry* for it."

The next image was a European fashion ad: a gorgeous brunette in a miniskirt, teetering on high heels on a cobblestone street. Adolescent boys, a grocer, and an old man on a bike all stare googly-eyed. The model has the classic *I-couldn't-care-less-about-any-of-you* look on her face.

"Why does the woman wear the lipstick, the uncomfortable high heels, the short skirt when it's freezing outside? What is she after here?" Adiklein stabbed the air with his index finger. "Attention."

Another slide, this time a James Bond look-alike getting into a new Maserati in front of a country club. Valet attendants, country club members, and nearby golfers all look on in envy. "Why does a man work himself to death so he can buy the shiny new car, the club membership he never uses, the expensive watch?" Adiklein cupped a hand to his ear, and this time some of the crowd shouted along with him. *"Attention."*

Next on the screen came a barrage of red-carpet photos from Hollywood movie premieres. "We all want to be famous, right?" Adiklein waited for a response, but only got chuckles. Provoking the crowd, he added, "Oh, come on. Yes, you do! Fame is the new religion. You've all been raised to worship it."

Adiklein cued the next series of images—more tabloid photos, but now the tone shifted from glamorous to gruesome. Ugly paparazzi shots of rock stars, politicians, and reality TV stars looking needy and psychotic. Turning on the audience, Adiklein demanded, "Why? What for? What kind of imbecile would desire this kind of madness!" Adiklein continued quickly, not waiting for a sing-along. "Because of that massive hole inside of each and every one of us that can only be filled with *attention, attention, attention.*"

The screen displayed even darker images—a skinny, awkward schoolgirl being bullied, a pimple-faced boy posing with a gun, news coverage of a school shooting.

"Why does the outcast, the *nobody* bring the gun to school? Shoot his teacher, shoot his classmates? Shoot himself? Why? Why?"

The answer this time came from a piece of live news footage on the screen as a somber newscaster turned to his co-host, saying, "Yet another tragic case of a disturbed young man crying out, saying, 'Look at me, notice me, give me your attention.'"

The news footage froze on a haunting image of the teenage killer, and then slowly faded out. From the darkness Adiklein said softly, "Without attention we disappear. We become nothing. We cease to exist."

Once again Adam felt a tickle of panic creep into his chest. It wasn't just sitting in the dark with 2,000 people, or even Adiklein's provocative comments; it was that damn yellow light still wriggling beneath the surface of his mind, aching to be remembered. Adam found himself groping in his pocket for his emergency Xanax. Before he could distinguish the pill from a compressed piece of lint, the lights came back up. Techno music swelled as a dramatic overhead image of downtown San Francisco filled the screen.

"The business world is no different." Adiklein's tone was now brighter as well. "In our sector of Internet technology, computer software, and social media, we are equally dependent on this same lifeblood. This same attention." A new series of images gracefully dissolved one into the next, idyllic scenes of a rising tech company: funky office spaces, fresh-faced programmers, inspired designers, development meetings, product unveilings, investors cheering.

"We have our own words for attention, don't we?" Adiklein yelled out, "Ten thousand hits! *Attention.* Twenty thousand clicks! *Attention.* Users, visitors, friends, followers, traffic, eyeballs, views, likes—all these are quantitative expressions of attention. If your site isn't sticky enough, if what you're blogging about isn't provocative enough, if what you're developing doesn't reach through the damn screen and *grab* attention, then, like the baby whose mother loses interest, your business will quickly die." The series of images ended with a grim shot of an abandoned office space, the remains of a start-up gone bust.

Adiklein coolly set down the remote and moved to the front of the stage.

"Attention is the currency of the day. A plain and simple fact. Now for the real question . . ." He took a long pause before asking, "If I am good enough to earn some attention, *what do I do with it?*

"I don't just slip it under the mattress." Playing the greedy miser, Adiklein pantomimed hiding away his cash. "No, no, no. I must invest it, I must learn to work with the attention I've collected, so it can grow.

"You see, the more I appreciate the nuances of this new form of currency, the more I begin to see the incredible things it can do for me. I see that attention is more dynamic than a dollar bill or a gold ingot. It is alive! And if it is alive, it must eat—no? Of course! Just like I do with my little doggy, I must learn how to properly feed the attention I've gathered, so it will grow and grow, and more importantly, so it will remain obediently by my side. Perhaps I can even learn to feed it the *right kind of food* to encourage it to depend on me." Adiklein smiled, and then returned to the podium to take another sip of water.

Adam wondered what exactly Adiklein meant by feeding attention the right kind of food. Blake had recently told Adam about the first time he met Adiklein at one of the acquisition meetings with Virtual Skies. "Half the time I had no fucking clue what that dude was talking about," Blake said, "but I know it was brilliant!"

On stage Adiklein adopted a more casual, improvisational tone. "Okay then, let's have some fun, shall we? I'd like to take an example from something we're doing over at Virtual Skies." Adiklein smiled, knowing that any details about the inner workings of Virtual Skies would be like manna from the heavens to this crowd. Back in 2004 Adiklein had stunned the tech world when he began working exclusively for Virtual Skies Media Group, a then-floundering new media company. But as it subsequently skyrocketed to success, everyone knew it was Adiklein's doing. Within five years Virtual Skies had a record-breaking IPO launch, as well as its own spectacular new building, the Virtual Skies Tower, right in the heart of downtown San Francisco.

"Earlier this year, as you may have heard, Virtual Skies acquired a young company named Pixilate Gamehouse to head up our new social gaming division."

A cheer erupted from the programmers surrounding Adam, who quickly joined in. Blake Dorsey, a natural at crowd stuff, contributed a piercing, two-finger whistle followed by some frat-worthy fist pumps. Adiklein smiled. "Sounds like some of you might be here today, yes?" Adiklein put his hand up to shield his eyes and leaned forward beyond the stage lights to search the crowd.

Out in the audience, Adam noticed just offstage was a man with a headset, looking irritated by the audience interaction. According to gossip, Adiklein had put TED Talk's production team through the wringer. Just getting him to agree to the 18-minute format had been tough enough. He had reportedly also refused to hand over a copy of his speech until moments before the audience entered the auditorium.

"Yes, Pixilate." Adiklein smiled proudly. "Very successful in the gaming world. Their online multiplayer, you probably all know, is . . . um . . . *The Blood of Love*? *The Blood of* . . . something? Help me out, guys . . ."

Blake Dorsey shouted, *"Lust 4 Blood!"*

"Yes! Thank you, Blake! *Lust 4 Blood.*"

To the headset guy's chagrin, Adiklein said, "Stand up, Blake. Please."

Seemingly surprised, but not in the least bit shy, Blake immediately did as he was told.

"Blake Dorsey, everyone, founder and managing director of Pixilate. If you don't already know his name, you soon will. One of my rising superstars."

As the audience gave Blake a generous hand, Adam caught Adiklein giving Mr. Irritated Headset a look, as if to say, *I am Rene Adiklein and I will do whatever I want, fuck you very much.*

Cameramen were struggling to get a good shot of Blake, who had jumped onto the armrests of his chair à la Roberto Benigni.

The crowd ate it up. Blake Dorsey was arguably the hippest geek in the room. For one thing, he broke with the techie dress code of tee shirt, jeans, and hoodie. Instead Blake dressed like a rock star—motorcycle boots and hand-tailored suits over tight designer tee shirts. He had sandy-blond hair and Abercrombie & Fitch good looks. He was that rare popular guy in high school who, for whatever odd reason, wasn't afraid to be seen hanging out with a nerd.

That was actually how Blake and Adam became friends, but it was in college, not high school. And when the two formed Pixilate together, Adam provided the programming genius while Blake became the company's public face. His enthusiastic smile was a passport of likability, whether he was talking up angel investors or presenting demos at gamer conventions. Occasionally spiteful bloggers accused Blake Dorsey of being a slick, conceited prick, but for most everyone else, including the crowd at the Moscone Center tonight, Blake was just plain hard not to like.

On stage Adiklein gave a parental shake of the head as he watched Blake high-fiving the programmers seated around him.

"Well, Blake, it looks like you have your gang of *wunderkinder* here with you." Then Adiklein shouted, "What the hell, all of you over there, stand up! *Allez, allez,* stand up! I want the world to meet the geniuses of Pixilate Gamehouse!"

As Mr. Irritated Headset groped in his breast pocket, presumably for cigarettes, only to remember he had quit, Adiklein smiled contently. What he had just done was so inappropriate for a TED Talk that it would be the talk of the blogosphere for months.

As the cheering died down, Adiklein continued. "Two and a half million registered players to date! Not bad, eh? But do I care about profits? *Pffff.* No! I measure success by how much *attention* is being earned—number of players, average hours played. But most important, I look at the quality of attention, because not all attention is valued the same. I want attention that is young, that is hungry like a baby bird waiting with its mouth wide open, eager to discover our next amazing new product or service."

$$\diamond\!\!\!\diamond$$

During the VIP reception, Blake and the other genius nerds from Pixilate buzzed around in euphoric bliss, working their way through the swarm surrounding Adiklein, attempting to get as close to him as possible. Adam, however, opted for leaning against a marble pillar near the buffet. Glaring up from the table next to him was an epic array of catered deliciousness. Adam could eat none of it. He had forgotten to bring his Zantac.

Adam knew he should be mingling and networking, engaging in the now! This was a party, after all. He should at least appear to be having a good time.

A couple of young hackers noticed Adam and looked as if they might walk over to chat. He was something of a legend in the programmer world. But before the two geeks could get any closer, Adam stuck in his earbuds. Wearing earbuds, whether he was using them or not, had become his go-to strategy for warding off unwanted human interaction. It was surprisingly useful, especially in San Francisco, where one easily could be accosted by a panhandler, a religious fanatic, and an environmentalist all on the same street corner.

A new current of excitement was forming in the room, a small eddy quickly building into a whirlpool second only to the one encircling Adiklein. At the center of this new vortex was a young Hollywood couple known to invest in start-ups. Adam watched as the unstoppable smile of Blake Dorsey penetrated the eye of this new storm where he began effortlessly chatting up the investors. Later Blake would inform Adam that the celebrities were "full-on gamers and huge fans of *Lust 4 Blood*. Dude, *they* were starstruck meeting *me*! Seriously, she was totally flirting with me, and he was talking movies, as in *Lust 4 Blood, the movie!*"

"Wow." Adam did his best to sound enthusiastic.

"'Wow'? Come on, dude! At least pretend like you're lovin' it! By the way, did you know that Adiklein never forgets a name? Like even if he meets a hundred people at a party, he can remember every single person's name. Total badass!"

Adam really did want to be "lovin' it." He and Blake had a huge hit game; they were working at Virtual Skies, for the one and only Rene Adiklein, with a future that looked unlimited. Yet along with the success, something else had risen up inside of Adam. A dark, panicky something. That niggling feeling of having forgotten something important. *Was it sunlight? Sunlight flickering off metal? And was someone else there, someone important?* Something was lurking just below the conscious surface of Adam's mind, ready to pull him into another mind loop. But this one, he sensed, had no end.

CHAPTER 3

CLUTTER IN THE CAVE

Propelled by a surge of morning commuters, Adam emerged from the Embarcadero BART station into downtown San Francisco. Like being caught in a school of fish, the collective biomass carried him up the escalator and out onto Market Street where, protective earbuds in place, he flowed with the sidewalk current toward Fremont Street. There he waited for the light to change before crossing Market and heading directly toward the new heart of San Francisco, the monolithic Virtual Skies Tower.

Dubbed "Techie Heaven" by *The Wall Street Journal*, the building also had received other not-so-positive nicknames, including "The Tower of Babel" (*Wired* magazine) and "The Giant Dildo" (*SF Weekly*). Eighty-one stories of fritted blue glass glittering beneath an intricate latticework of brushed steel. Like a gemstone cocooned within a web of descending gray fog, the new tower was now officially the tallest structure in San Francisco.

Staring up at it from the corner of Fremont and Mission, Adam waited for the light to change. The sky was unusually clear this morning, and he could see all the way to the top of the Tower. It was dizzying. The intricate pattern of steel latticework did something strange in the light, creating the illusion that it was vibrating, shifting like a Tesla coil; but instead of pulsing energy outward, it seemed to be sucking energy into itself. At least that's what it looked like to Adam, but then again, he'd worked 16-hour days for the past two weeks.

Way up at the crown of the Tower, Adam could just make out the crystal-blue glass pyramid twinkling away in the morning light. *There's something strange about that tip of the spear,* Adam thought for the hundredth time. *What's it for, anyway? There's nothing actually inside of it, just like the Transamerica Pyramid, just empty space.* He wasn't sure why, but the thought of it up there always disturbed him.

The empty glass pyramid was just one resut of the many unusual circumstances surrounding the new Virtual Skies Tower. Originally conceived as part of the city's much-needed new Transit Terminal, the inclusion of a business tower was intended to provide additional funds for the project. To appease the Joint Authority the new tower was designed with 10 percent of its usable space devoted to public use. The building's lobby would be directly linked to the new Transit Center's rooftop park, and would showcase restaurants, retail outlets, and dramatic multicultural art installations, as well as high-speed elevators that would shuttle tourists to the Tower's rooftop, where they would find themselves in an open, glass crown with a grand 360-degree panoramic observation deck.

Everything had been approved, and construction was ready to begin, when one of the Tower's key investors mysteriously pulled out. The city was screwed, since it had already begun to demolish the old transit terminal. That was when an angel named Rene Adiklein fell into the picture.

At the time, Adiklein had just begun working with Virtual Skies Media Group to help reboot their company's image, but what he now offered the company's founders left them dumbstruck. He not only proposed to work for Virtual Skies exclusively, but promised to introduce them to the most exclusive private investment firm on the planet: Blanchefort and Rhodes. B&R was prepared to boost Virtual Skies' liquid equity and provide an impressive line of credit, hinging on one small condition: Rene Adiklein would run the show. The company founders would need to fall in line with Adiklein's directions—from marketing strategies to who they hired and fired, to how they diversified and which start-ups they acquired. As a face-saving measure, Adiklein would take the modest title of VP of marketing, though he would be firmly in charge.

The founders of Virtual Skies took less than a day to agree to terms.

A week later City Hall received an offer from Blanchefort and Rhodes to fund the new transit tower. There were, of course, several concessions the city would have to make, including a substantial redesign. Gone would be the cultural center, the art installations, and all public access to the building. Instead of the observation deck, the building would be crowned with a specifically designed glass pyramid, strictly ornamental. The city's choice was clear: Give up control of the Tower, and you get a new Transit Center. Retain control, and it won't get built.

Over the next few years, with the Transit Center on its way to completion and the city's newest skyscraper reshaping San Francisco's skyline, Virtual Skies Media Group, under Adiklein's direction, was also rising to the pinnacle. The company's headquarters would not only have amenities to rival the extravagant campuses of other well-known tech firms in the greater Bay Area, but more importantly, Virtual Skies wouldn't be stuck way out in Cupertino or Mountain View; it was right smack in the middle of the city! *Forbes* magazine called the decision "A masterstroke for Virtual Skies Media Group."

The light changed at Fremont and Mission. Adam crossed the zebra stripes, broke from the main current of foot traffic that turned up Mission, and continued along the rear facade of the Tower on Fremont. Lately he'd fallen into the habit of using the building's lesser-known back entrance. It was quicker, and the elevators on that side were far less congested.

For the first few months, Adam had entered through the Tower's more glamorous front entrance. To get there he would head up Mission with the rest of the crowd, to the escalators leading to the Transit Center's rooftop park. Then, as early-rising tourists veered right, Adam turned left toward the massive cast-iron gates and arched sign that read: Virtual Skies Media Group. It looked like the entrance to a Hollywood movie studio. Adam could feel the envious eyes of the public as he walked toward the security guards.

After presenting his ID, Adam would leisurely stroll through the Virtual Skies private park—past the day-care center, the wood-and-glass structure for yoga classes, the organic gardens, the fountains, the miniature outdoor amphitheater, and the sculpture garden—finally arriving at the Tower itself. His pulse would quicken as he entered the main lobby. Like the floor of the New York Stock Exchange, the Virtual Skies lobby had the electrifying feel of big things taking place here. Overlooking the lobby, mezzanine levels contained the health club, a full-service spa, multifaith worship rooms, and the building's primary eatery, simply named The Commissary. Serving 11 different cuisines, this not-so-unassuming cafeteria had reportedly received an unofficial Michelin star.

At first Adam felt as if he and his colleagues had relocated to a luxury resort in the Bahamas. He'd always enjoyed amenities at work—an espresso machine, a fancy refrigerator, a pool or ping-pong table—but sleep-pods and acupuncturists? It was all a bit much. Even worse were the Virtual Skies employees, who seemed to possess the same creepy, casual self-importance, as if they were all on the verge of saving humanity. *I just make games,* Adam wanted to say. So it was with relief that he had found the Tower's back entrance, which allowed him to bypass all of the bustle and the posturing.

Adam arrived on the 33rd floor and was greeted by the new promotional displays for *Lust 4 Blood Expansion Worlds*. The seven-foot cardboard stands depicted two sexy teenage vampires standing in a misty redwood forest, sucking each other's necks. Adam passed reception and cruised down a hallway past the executive offices—finance, legal, marketing, sales, and, of course, Blake's corner office. Adam peeked in, but, as usual, Blake wasn't in yet. His secretary, Cory, was at her desk eating what looked like a quinoa salad. Cory was a hot burlesque chick, who this week was sporting black-and-pink hair, lots of mascara, and a sleeveless top with a short, black skirt that revealed provocative tattoos crawling up her arms and legs. Adam always got nervous around Cory, so he moved on before she noticed him.

The farther he went into the bowels of Pixilate, the darker it became. They had been given the entire 33rd floor—which was at least 50 times the size of the garage Adam and Blake had started out in—but due to all the windows, a design team had been hired to modify the work environment. Spiraling inward, windows disappeared until finally the hallway ended in a large, gothic archway made of hard foam, which matched in every detail the entrance to level 19 of the original *Lust 4 Blood* game, *Grotto of Lost Souls*. On the arch's keystone hung a sign decorated with fake spiderwebs that read:

THE CAVE

Plunging into the dark abyss, Adam's eyes adjusted to take in a cavernous maze of cubicles, each displaying a garage-sale array of the occupant's paraphernalia: action figures, promotional toys, gamer swag, posters, giant candy jars, vitamin bottles, economy-size TUMS bottles, dead processors, motherboards, and soldering equipment. Adam worked his way to the far end of the Cave, past the testers, audio engineers, 3-D animators, and programmers, all the way back to the deepest crevice of seclusion, where his own collection of clutter awaited him.

As an original founder, Adam really should have had his own office, but in the chaos of the move, and with the addition to management, it just made sense for him to remain in the bull pen. "For now at least," Blake had said, "let's keep our genius engine master easily accessible to all the new blood." Adam had essentially created L4B, the original game engine that ran the *Lust 4 Blood* series. It was revolutionary in the world of computer graphics, and no one understood its source code and various modifications like Adam. Along with complex new techniques in computer graphics, Adam was also unparalleled in his nuanced understanding of the game's level design. His fingerprints were on every landscape, every tree, every rock, every fang puncture hole, every blood splatter, every shadow effect, and every algorithm lurking beneath.

Adam's cubicle had its own unique assemblage of clutter. Waist-high stacks of books barred entry for more than a single thin human. Decorating his walls were magazine clippings and color printouts of exotic places all over the world—the pyramids in Giza, a Tibetan monastery, the temples of Angkor Wat, India's Ajanta caves, and the ruins of an old Armenian church in the Caucasus mountains. Not places he'd been to, at least not yet, but he definitely planned to get to them once the pressure to keep producing new versions of *Lust 4 Blood* eased off a little.

Just after 10 A.M., Blake strolled into the Cave. "All right, geniuses!" Blake shouted. It was rare for him to make an appearance in the Cave, especially before noon. "Expansion teaser hits the web at twelve midnight!"

A halfhearted cheer sounded from the Cave's nooks and crannies.

"*And,*" Blake continued ominously, "you can forget that bullshit you've been hearing about pushing the launch date."

This news was met by a chorus of full-throated groans.

"Mitch, wherever you're hiding, you're a total douche for leaking that crap; we're slated for December fourteenth, and we're sticking to it!" Blake clapped his hands like a basketball coach. "Chop, chop! Instant user gratification, that's the name of the game. And that means eighteen-hour days, nights, weekends, and P1s flying at you people!"

Blake continued on through the Cave until he reached Adam's corner.

"Yo, dude." Blake perched himself on the edge of the cubicle.

At first Adam didn't notice him. His earbuds were in, and he was engrossed in something on his laptop.

"*Yo! Adam!*"

Adam looked up with a jolt. "Hey, Blake." He half shut the lid to his laptop.

Blake raised a suspicious eyebrow. "You looking at porn?" Leaning over, he pulled back the lid to expose an open image search window. No porn, just pictures of ocean cliffs.

"Research." Adam's voice was tentative.

"Porn would have been more interesting."

"What's up?"

"Your text from last night. Said you've got something tasty to show me?" Blake rubbed his hands together, the same greedy gesture he'd been using since they had met in college.

It took a moment for Adam to reshuffle his thoughts. "Oh, yeah. I was having trouble sleeping last night so I started messing around with a mobile app idea."

"Oh." Blake's enthusiasm dropped 15 degrees. "Not that web 2.0 shit?"

"That changed in March with the 3G. Apple opened it up to third parties. I downloaded the SDK; you can do some pretty cool stuff with it. Your own graphic user interface, your own icon—"

"I know everyone's talking mobile," Blake interrupted, "A waste of time to me." Blake pulled out his Jesus-phone to deal with a text that had beeped in. For years Blake had been a BlackBerry guy, which was annoying enough, but now that he had an iPhone, having a conversation with him was nearly impossible.

"I just thought it could be something fun to go out with the Expansion," Adam suggested.

"We don't do mobile. Even if we did, there's no real market yet. Too limited a platform, bro."

"Maybe we could just show it to Adiklein. I think he might actually like it—"

"*Asshole,*" Blake said under his breath. It took Adam a moment to realize that Blake was referring to his text. Blake looked back up with a smile. "Dude, I thought you were going to tell me about the other thing?"

Adam looked lost.

"*Zombies,*" Blake whispered.

Click. "Oh, right. *Zombies*," Adam said wearily.

Again with the greedy hands, Blake added, *"Zombieees."*

Adam sighed. One of the reasons Virtual Skies acquired Pixilate was to create games for MyStar, Virtual Skies' social media site. Blake already had a team porting a version of *Lust 4 Flesh*, and they had half a dozen other knockoffs in the works. But Adam had recently shown Blake a concept for how to take advantage of existing social networking aspects of the MyStar platform that could be easily integrated into a gaming environment. The zombie theme had been Blake's contribution.

"You haven't shared it with anyone else have you?" Blake whispered before giving a quick conspiratorial glance toward the other programmers. Adam saw that Blake was playing mischievous comrade, a role he took on whenever Adam got moody.

"No, it's safe. Not even on the network." Adam pointed down at the external drive under his desk. "I just haven't been able to focus on it with the Expansion coming out; half these new guys don't know what the hell they're doing." Adam shrugged wearily. *"Zombies* isn't exactly at the top of my list."

"Dude, we gotta move on that shit. Seriously. It doesn't have to be perfect. Just good enough to show Adiklein the integrated social networking concepts."

"But I'm going to have to totally rewrite L4B's renderer, the memory management needs to go, there's a ton of stuff to do—"

"Adiklein doesn't give a shit about your engine mods, just the social networking stuff. I'm telling you, it's going to blow his mind. And now that we're part of V-Skies, money is no object." Blake leaned in. "Blanchefort and Rhodes? Those motherfuckers run the world, dude. Seriously. And they are *right up there*." Blake pointed at the ceiling.

The only part of the Tower not occupied by Virtual Skies was the top two floors, which Blanchefort and Rhodes had taken for their new West Coast offices. The building's design had included a separate garage and elevators bypassing the rest of the floors. Other than B&R employees, the only person with access to the top floors was Adiklein.

"Seriously, dude," Blake continued. "We need to deliver eye-balls. It's why Adiklein bought us."

Adam did his best to show some enthusiasm. "Okay, I'll try to get back on *Zombies*."

Blake's phone beeped again. With a one-handed palming move, he checked the text while Adam tried to catch his eye.

"If you change your mind about the mobile app idea, I did a quick mock-up with some basic functionality."

"Total jackass." Blake shook his head at his phone. "This PR guy is a complete tool." He looked back at Adam and smiled. "Of course, dude, I'll totally look at it. Send it to me, and I'll check it out." Blake went back to his texts as he walked away, but then he stopped and half-turned back to Adam. "Oh, tell Jane that I'll do my best to make this dinner thing she e-mailed me about. What's it for again?"

"Birthday party."

"Nice. Chandler or Madison?"

"Mine."

"Cool. Wish them a . . ." Blake stopped texting and looked up. "Oh, shit, your birthday? Dude, I totally blew it. I just told Adiklein's office I'd go to this VC thing the same night. Shit!"

"Don't worry about it; it's not a big one."

"No way, dude. I missed your birthday last year, and that's not going to happen twice. Tell Jane I'm coming, okay? Now rock those zombies!" With that, Blake headed back through the Cave, tapping on his phone all the while.

As much as Adam sometimes resented Blake, his anger never lasted long. Throughout the years Blake had done so much for him. Without Blake, Adam knew his life would be a hopeless mess.

Swiveling back around, Adam clicked the mouse to awaken his screen. Today's work would be mechanical: fixing bugs, problem solving, cleaning up one little wrinkle after another. He would hold off on the zombie game for at least a day or two. That code would require a completely different level of concentration, a kind of personal sacrifice Adam offered up to his screens only on rare occasions.

As he was about to dive in, he noticed the open search window on his laptop. He stared at the words: **Ocean cliffs.** He had told Blake it was research, but that was a lie. *Why was I looking at cliffs?* he wondered. *Something to do with that flickering yellow light?* Adam gave his head another Etch A Sketch shake. There was no point in trying to figure it out now. Swiveling back to his monitors, he took a deep breath. Then, as he had done countless times before, Adam disappeared into the glowing screens before him.

CHAPTER 4

Lucid Larry,
a Ukrainian Vampire,
and Dr. M.

They met in the fall of 1990, Adam's sophomore year at San Francisco State University. Adam wasn't a nerd in the traditional sense, but he was odd enough to fall into the nerd category by default. Throughout his freshman year, other students avoided him as if he were contagious. And he did always seem to be ailing from one thing or another—allergies, asthma, stomach problems, eczema, or a head cold that never seemed to go away. Then there was his fashion sense, which didn't help matters. His uniform was a pair of tan corduroy pants and a puke-green Windbreaker zipped up to his neck. As a result, no one came close enough to learn much about Adam beyond his name.

That changed when a stoner named Blake Dorsey entered the computer lab 10 minutes late and, relieved to find someone still without a lab partner, sat down next to Adam. "Blake Dorsey, professional gamer, future billionaire," Blake said, sticking out a hand to shake. He seemed utterly oblivious to Adam's status as a social untouchable. "I bet you're a total hacker, huh?" Blake flashed a wicked smile.

Assuming the question was the setup for a humiliating prank, Adam responded, "Uh, not really. I've never really—"

"Yeah, you are! Total hacker!" Blake laughed, violently shaking Adam's hand. Turning serious, he added, "Just to warn you, I suck at Pascal and 8086 Assembly. Was raised on an Apple II, toyed with a neighbor's GS once. But if you wanna make video games, gotta hop on the PC bandwagon, right?"

"Right." *Maybe this isn't a prank,* Adam thought. *Maybe this guy, crazy enough to wear flip-flops and Bermuda shorts at SF State, isn't repulsed by me like everyone else.*

"By the way, dude, I'm totally unbeatable at *Sonic the Hedgehog.*" Again Blake flashed his award-winning smile. "In case you ever want to challenge me."

Back then Adam had no serious interest in video games, and he was by no means a hacker. But encouraged by his *Odd Couple* friendship with Blake, and with no other social life to maintain, Adam did more than just learn how to code. By the end of the first semester, he had devoured DOS, Pascal, and 8086, and was even digging into C, a programming language that wasn't even taught at the university. To impress his new friend, Adam began to make simple PC games—mazes, puzzles, Dungeons & Dragons–style adventure games, and arcade knockoffs. Blake loved them all. He made a few games himself, but nothing as advanced as Adam's.

After the semester break, Blake walked back into the computer lab to find a floppy disk waiting for him with the words *Lucid Larry* written on it. *Lucid Larry* was a game Adam had spent his entire break working on, and it was light-years beyond anything he had created so far. Modeled after SEGA's *Sonic the Hedgehog,* which Adam knew Blake loved, *Lucid Larry* was an adventure game in which Larry—a pelican wearing an ugly, green jacket—ran through a forest collecting orange peels while avoiding stinging nettles and dragonflies. Occasionally magic doorways appeared in the side of redwood trees, allowing Larry to enter a dreamlike world superimposed over the game's normal environment. In that dream landscape, nothing harmed Lucid Larry, and if the player continuously hit the Jump button, Larry began to fly up into a night sky, where strange and unusual creatures floated about.

"Holy shit. Holy shit. *HOLY SHIT!*" Blake said the first time he got Larry to go through a magic doorway and float up into the stars. While Blake pounded on the space bar to keep Larry afloat, Adam noticed his own hands were shaking. To complete the game in time, he had worked for days without much food or sleep.

"Dude! This is insane!" Blake yelled after finishing the last level. "How the fuck did you pull off side-scrolling?"

"Find Poland?" Adam asked, his brain woolly.

"No, dude, *side-scrolling*. It's just like a real console game! You realize that's never been done before? Not on a PC, not even on Apple IIGS! How the fuck did you do it?"

Adam had a tough time finding the words. "I had to rewrite . . . Well, basically, I tricked the graphics card."

"Dude, you could sell this shit! I mean it. You could go straight to Origin or Sierra On-line with this!"

"Well, I was just thinking we could play it. I mean, I don't know how to sell stuff."

"Dude, selling stuff is easy. I'll totally help you if you want. Right now everyone's drooling for PC games, and they all suck. Not this, though. This is totally rad!" Blake turned back to the game. "Of course, we might want to tweak it a little before showing anyone . . ." Blake started scanning through the levels. "Make the design elements a little sexier. Maybe add some more bad guys, a little more action."

Adam nodded happily through his haze of exhaustion. "Sure, Blake."

They agreed to meet back at the computer lab the following night to start reworking the game—changing the orange peels to gold dollar signs, adding a few alien spaceships to the night sky for Lucid Larry to zap, and so on. Once the game was sexy enough, Blake would approach game distributors, and if they were interested, negotiate a deal.

Adam had seemed excited by the prospect of having Blake as a partner, but the next night Adam never showed up. Nor did he show up for the next class or for the rest of the semester. Blake never saw Adam Sheppard at San Francisco State University again. His brilliant lab partner simply disappeared without bothering with explanations or good-byes.

Thinking back on that period of his life, Adam still felt terrible for leaving his friend hanging like that. Blake was a popular guy who had reached out to and befriended him, and helped him discover something he was good at. Blake was willing to help Adam make something of that talent, but Adam had ditched him without a word.

Thankfully two years later the *Odd Couple* lab partners ran into each other at a Longs Drugs—Adam picking up medication, Blake picking up condoms. Adam apologized for his sudden disappearance, mumbling something about his stepmother and having to drop out of college. Quick to forgive and forget, Blake was more interested in what Adam was up to now, and if he was still interested in programming games. Blake explained that he had landed a job at Softools, a company in San Rafael that created boring office software, but agreed to let Blake develop a few games on the side.

Adam was doing nothing at the time besides caring for his stepmother, who had suffered a stroke, so he eagerly accepted Blake's offer to program some games. Blake even talked his boss into hiring Adam. And at first, the owners of Softools seemed impressed with him, but after two months, Adam got fired. It was due in part to his unusual work habits; Adam sometimes didn't leave the office for days on end, and at other times, he didn't show up at all.

Adam felt bad. Not for himself but for Blake, who had gone out of his way to get him hired. Blake, however, refused to give up on Adam and devised a way for him to work freelance from home. That way he could just focus on the programming side of things. Blake handled everything else, and sometimes worked on the games as well, usually at the inception phase, nudging Adam's ideas in more commercially viable directions.

Their arrangement proved to be surprisingly effective. Soon Blake was able to buy himself a faster, new car, and Adam a faster, new computer. With his more powerful rig, Adam began to play around with 3-D graphics, trying to simulate the first-person perspective of some of the new console games. "Each portion of the height map is transformed into a column of pixels," Adam explained to Blake at one of their midnight meetings at Biff's diner in Oakland. "Then it draws them using the corresponding color from the texture map."

"Screw Softools. This new one is going to be too badass to share with those losers," Blake said, gulfing down a steak fry followed by a swig of Corona. "Look, it's time for us to take a chance and go big. Tomorrow I'm telling Softools that I'm leaving. We can still port some of our old games to Amiga and Apple IIGS, just to keep some cash coming in. Meanwhile I want you to go balls-to-the-wall building out this code. I'm talking night and day." Blake gave Adam a serious look. "Every cell in your body, Adam, focused on this."

"What kind of game you thinking?" Adam had a few ideas, but he also knew that Blake had a better sense of what gamers really wanted.

"Not just a game, Adam. I've got an idea that is going to blow people away. A friggin' *franchise*."

Adam sneezed. His allergies had been especially bad this year. "What genre?"

"Something no one's even touched. No more tired spaceships and played-out aliens, no more D&D fantasy rip-offs. No, this game is going to be scary and bloody and sexy all at the same time. We're going to introduce the gaming world to a new kind of hero."

Adam waited.

"Vampires."

"Vampires?"

"Yeah, baby. You heard me. Vampires."

Blake explained that his inspiration for what would become the original *Lust 4 Blood* came by way of a hot Ukrainian chick he had been dating. Blake had met the brooding waif in San Francisco at Café du Nord, where she and her coven of friends drank cheap red wine, listened to Morrissey, discussed the latest Anne Rice novel, and reveled in their collective ennui. At first Blake assumed it was all a joke, a sort of extended Halloween, but as he was exposed to the depths of Goth subculture, he saw its appeal—not to mention its potential as the basis for a video game. Dangerous, misunderstood, rebellious, sexy, and violent—vampires seemed tailor-made for the American teenager.

Building out the first *Lust 4 Blood* game took 11 months. Blake put a team together under the new company name, Pixilate. There were two level designers, a graphic artist, a story consultant (the Ukrainian vampire), and Adam. The team worked out of a converted garage in San Francisco's Mission district with the exception of Adam, who continued to do most of his work at his stepmother's house in West Oakland. Adam's job was to create the engine, the guts of the game, and because much of what they were trying to pull off had never been done before, he had to write all of the code from the ground up.

Fueled on Mountain Dew and pizza, Adam worked night and day, rarely leaving his computer. Things got even more "balls-to-the-wall" when Blake announced that he wanted to preview the game at that year's Game Developers Conference (GDC). To pull off the nearly impossible task of having the demo ready in time, Adam pushed himself to physical and mental limits he had not approached since the days of *Lucid Larry*. Creating something truly original required a kind of personal sacrifice beyond his ordinary efforts. To bring something new into the world required leaving the world. And so, like *Lucid Larry*, Adam needed to pass through a secret doorway in his mind and float untethered into unknown realms.

Blake previewed the game at GDC, and *Lust 4 Blood* instantly became the talk of the gaming world. It was unlike anything anyone had seen before. The vampire concept got mixed reviews, but the 3-D graphics and the dreamlike game play were considered by all to be sheer magic. Arriving back in the Bay Area after the conference, Blake knew he had a major hit on his hands. He also had a major problem—Adam had gone missing again. No one at Pixilate had heard from him in two weeks.

After hurrying down the driveway of Adam's stepmother's house to the back house where Adam lived and worked, Blake used the key under the mossy lawn gnome to unlock the door. Inside he discovered stacks of empty pizza boxes, flies, and piles of unwashed clothing, but no Adam. Braving the main house, Blake knocked on the back door. He had never actually been inside before, or even met Adam's stepmother, Gloria.

When an older man opened the door, Blake at first assumed he must be Adam's father, but then recalled Adam telling him that his father had passed away when he was a teenager. The elderly man turned out to be a caregiver, and he led Blake into the living room where Gloria lay in a hospice bed watching *Divorce Court* on TV. She glared at Blake with half her face, the other half drooping like melted wax. Once Blake explained that Adam had gone missing, Gloria picked up the small notepad at her side, wrote something on it, then pushed the pad toward Blake.

Dr. Ronald Mendelson.

Next to the name was a phone number.

Blake used the house phone. Dr. Mendelson's secretary answered and, after placing Blake on hold for five long minutes, she came back on to give Blake an address where she said Dr. Mendelson would meet him at 3:00 that afternoon. It was a hospital, one Blake had never heard of before. While waiting for Dr. Mendelson to arrive, Blake inquired about Adam at the front desk, and was told they couldn't give out information without permission from the patient's doctor.

Dr. Ronald Mendelson—Dr. M., as he would later be affectionately nicknamed by Adam's wife, Jane—was a tall, scholarly man with a meticulously trimmed beard and pale gray eyes.

"Hello, Blake. I've heard a lot about you. Please, sit. We have several things to discuss."

Over coffee Dr. Mendelson explained to Blake that the police had found Adam two days ago, sleeping under a hedge in Half Moon Bay. "He doesn't remember how he got there," Dr. Mendelson said, "or where else he'd been. But he's safe now. No injuries, thankfully. It seems that stress from work, along with lack of sleep and forgetting to take his medications, triggered the episode."

"Episode? Like a nervous breakdown?" Blake asked anxiously.

"Not quite," Mendelson replied. "As you know, Adam is a very intelligent young man, but there is another side to him, a more complicated side. I've been treating Adam since he was quite young. Do you know much about his family or his upbringing?"

"No." Blake shook his head. "Nothing, really."

"I know that you're close to Adam, so I feel comfortable telling you that there is a history of mental illness on his mother's side of the family."

"I thought she just had a stroke?"

"That's his stepmother, Gloria."

"Right, yeah, of course."

"Gloria is quite sane, I can attest to that. She was, in fact, a rather celebrated psychologist in her day, and a former colleague of mine, which is how I came to be treating Adam." Dr. Mendelson sipped his coffee. "No, his biological mother was not well. She committed suicide about a year after Adam was born. A drug overdose."

Blake exhaled loudly, not knowing what to say.

Dr. Mendelson continued. "Adam's father was in no shape to raise Adam on his own, so he left him in the care of Adam's maternal grandmother. Unfortunately she was not in good psychological health either. Child services weren't what they are today, otherwise Adam would have been pulled from those ungodly conditions up in . . ." Mendelson scratched his neatly bearded chin. "Somewhere up the coast, north of San Francisco—the name of the town escapes me at the moment." He took another sip of coffee. "When Adam was six, his father remarried. Luckily for Adam, his new stepmother had the good sense to rescue him from his grandmother, but the traumas he suffered during those formative years, along with his genetic predisposition, left Adam with some significant issues."

"But he's not, like, dangerous or anything?"

"Lord, no." Dr. Mendelson gave a dismissive snort.

"He never seemed like he was in real trouble." Blake searched for the right words. "I mean, he's always been unusual, but not like *crazy* crazy."

"Well, thank you. I'll take that as a compliment." Dr. Mendelson smiled carefully. "We've come a long way with Adam, and despite this unfortunate episode, I am confident that he can live a normal, productive life. It's been more difficult since Gloria's stroke, but with the proper care in a healthy environment, and assuming he remembers to take his medication, Adam can stay on an even keel." Dr. Mendelson put out a level hand. "But if he gets too stressed, if he's pushed too hard at work, say, then he'll start to do this." Dr. Mendelson began undulating his hand up and down like a wave. "And that, we don't want."

"But you do think it's okay for him to keep working, right?" Blake asked. "I don't mean right away, but eventually? Once he's better?"

Dr. Mendelson looked at Blake pensively. Then he smiled and nodded. "Don't worry, Blake. He can keep programming for you. That is, assuming you're comfortable keeping him on."

"Of course." Blake didn't try to hide his relief. "I'm just concerned for him, that's all."

"Of course you are. We all have a shared interest in Adam's recovery," Dr. Mendelson said with a reassuring nod. "And the work he's doing, in a way it's the ideal job for someone like Adam, don't you think?"

"Totally."

"As I mentioned before, Adam is quite intelligent. He has a unique mind. Games, virtual reality, it all seems to be a perfectly safe place for Adam to focus his . . . attention."

Adam was sitting on a hard, blue couch by the window when he heard Blake enter the visiting room. As Blake came over and sat down next to him, Adam kept his gaze focused on the sunlight reflecting off the polished linoleum floor in front of him. His shoulders were slumped, the shame of his illness and his failure to keep it hidden from Blake weighed heavily. For a long while they sat in silence.

"Well, here we are . . ." Blake finally got out.

Assuming this was leading to something like "And I never want to see you again . . . You're fired . . . I can't trust someone like you," Adam continued to push all of his attention into that glaring slice of sunlight on the floor, hoping that he might dissolve into it.

"You're my best friend, Adam."

For a moment Adam didn't know if Blake had spoken or if he'd imagined it. But then Blake gently patted Adam's leg and repeated, "You're my best friend."

Adam felt a walnut-size lump in his throat. "I'm so sorry."

Blake shook his head. "Everything's cool. Everything's going to work out. I promise to look out for you from now on. I got your back, brother, and that's a promise."

From that day on, everything did seem to work out. Despite a delayed release, *Lust 4 Blood* ended up being a major success, and Blake kept his promise and did everything he could to help Adam stay even-keeled. He bought Adam new clothing and a new car (although Adam didn't even have a license), and he hired a maid who came twice a week to clean his stepmother's back house, from which Adam refused to move. When Pixilate expanded to office space in Burlingame, Adam was given his own office next door to Blake's. Like a big brother, Blake did his best to keep a watchful eye on Adam and to make sure he could work without undue pressure.

For several years everything went smoothly. But after a grueling push to deliver *Lust 4 Blood 2* to their hungry fans, Blake's ability to be there for Adam had become increasingly difficult. Fortunately, right around this time, Blake reconnected with an old high school friend named Jane Duffy. Jane, a nutritionist and yoga fanatic, had recently hit hard times. Her abusive boyfriend had left her with two babies, no child support, and no idea what she was going to do. Blake gave her the keys to an old apartment, to use until she figured things out, and on occasion treated her and her kids to a nice meal. And on one such occasion, Blake decided to bring Adam along.

Jane was immediately intrigued by Adam, with his shy demeanor, his off-kilter but well-intentioned sense of humor, and his natural way with her children. He was far from being the kind of guy she was usually attracted to, and yet, as she often said about that first encounter, "there was just something so tender about Adam."

Adam was also taken with Jane. She was tall, blonde, and athletic—far more attractive than any of the girls Blake had previously set him up with. She was smart too, aware of all the big social issues that Adam knew nothing about, like AIDS in Africa and global warming.

The two began dating. Adam was very generous with Jane and the kids, and Jane responded by making him healthy, home-cooked meals and by encouraging him to exercise, to buy decent clothes, and to take his medication. Unlike the alpha males Jane had previously dated, Adam seemed perfectly happy to let her take charge. She knew exactly how to care for him, and he willingly let her.

Within months Adam was hard to recognize. He not only was passably fit and healthy but also looked happy. And that made Jane happy. And of course, it didn't hurt that Adam was now making piles of money with no idea how to spend it. Jane, after her many years of deprivation, had lots of good, responsible ideas for how to spend it. "We fit together," Jane told Adam on the day they decided to get married.

As Blake had promised Adam that day in the hospital, every-thing worked out just fine. With a house in the suburbs, a beauti-ful wife, two kids who were learning to call him Dad, and a job making video games for the world's hippest company, Adam knew he had nothing to complain about. He was a lucky man.

CHAPTER 5

NAVIGATIONS OF THE HIDDEN DOMAIN

Adam jolted upright.

He didn't know where he was or how he had gotten there. His body was shaking. Actually, everything was shaking. Confused, he saw darkness rushing by, pulsing with streaks of neon light. In his ears was a deafening roar, accompanied by pressure, as if he was on an airplane. Packed all around him, people were swaying, bouncing, and shaking, their faces expressionless, all in their own worlds—earbuds in, faces staring into the pale blue glow of smart-phones and laptops.

BART, Adam realized. He was on a train heading home, travel-ing under the San Francisco Bay on his way to the Walnut Creek station, where Jane and the kids would be waiting to pick him up.

The panic began to dissipate as Adam reconnected to the present. The last thing he recalled clearly was sitting down early that morning to start work on the *Zombies* demo. He saw himself turning on his monitors, logging in, opening the project, and the next thing he knew, here he was on BART. In between hours had passed, the entire day had passed, without him, as if some other Adam Sheppard had taken over while he slipped off to . . . some-where else.

Looking around at his fellow commuters, Adam wondered if they had all slipped off somewhere else too. Maybe he was the only person on the train right now who was fully aware of being on it—aware of the incredible fact that they were shooting through a tube 100 feet underwater.

Adam tried to make eye contact, but no one's eyes met his. Everyone was immersed in e-mails, texts, video games, reading about who's dating who or how the world will soon end. A terrible sense of dread began to well in Adam's gut as he recognized his own itching desire to follow the crowd and slip off to somewhere else. But then he remembered what was in his shoulder bag. Not another screen to get lost in, but something that lately had given him a sense of hope, a feeling that he was not alone.

He opened his bag and carefully removed *the book*. It was faded, charcoal gray with a burgundy spine. If it had ever had a dust jacket, that was long since gone. The book's hard cover was embossed with a small, gold nautical symbol, a compass rose with a sea horse at its center.

On the spine the title read *Navigations of the Hidden Domain*.

From the time Adam was a teenager, he had developed a curious obsession with books on philosophy. Whenever he happened upon a bookstore, he would impulsively rush in, find the philosophy section, pick out the densest, most incomprehensible tome, and buy it. Plato, Kant, Hegel, Heidegger, Wittgenstein—Adam gobbled them all up. He was searching for something, answers to certain questions he wasn't even sure how to articulate. He explored other aisles in the bookstore as well—religion, science, psychology, metaphysics—and often found ideas that would temporarily scratch his itch for understanding. But nothing lasted, nothing stuck. Nothing resonated with that internal longing the way Virgil Coates's *Navigations of the Hidden Domain* did.

Almost as extraordinary as the book itself were the peculiar circumstances in which Adam came to possess it. It happened a few months after Pixilate had moved into the Virtual Skies Tower. They were having issues networking the computers in the Cave, so one afternoon while the system was down, Adam took the opportunity to go outside to eat his lunch. Instead of opting for the meticulously landscaped park out front, he sought out a concrete ledge he had noticed just outside the back entrance on Fremont Street. From his perch he had a great view of the traffic, the zombielike masses of pedestrians, and the long row of out-of-use newspaper machines across the sidewalk.

While finishing his lunch, Adam decided to see if he could pick out the Pixilate offices up on the 33rd floor. He looked up at the Tower behind him and started counting floors. *1, 2, 3, 4, 5.* He hopped off the ledge to get a better view. *16, 17, 18, 19, 20 . . .*

"You see what they got up there, don't you, brother?"

Startled, Adam turned to discover a homeless man in a wheelchair. Adam hadn't noticed the man earlier; all he had seen over there was that long row of defunct newspaper stands. But he now saw that it was actually two shorter rows with a four-foot-wide gap in the middle, which this man's wheelchair filled almost perfectly. He was African-American, in his late 60s, and maybe a little nuts. On the ground in front of him a green Army blanket had been laid out with various items for sale: a few cheap watches, some toxic-smelling incense sticks wrapped in tinfoil, old magazines, and several stacks of used books.

"Sorry. I didn't see you there."

"Wait a minute, brother, I got something special for you." After a violent neck twitch, the man leaned over and picked up a book.

"Have you read this shit?" The man gave a wide-eyed smile, and even though he was missing several teeth, it was one of the warmest smiles Adam had ever seen. "This is some serious shit, brother."

"No, thank you."

"Gonna open up your mind. I think you need to read this." As he extended the book to Adam, the countless round buttons pinned to the man's jacket made a gentle clattering sound. Adam recalled Blake once had pins like these on the lapels of his faded denim jacket when they first met at college: Duran Duran, Chewbacca, "Say *yes* to drugs!" But the homeless man's buttons weren't promoting slogans or pop idols, they all depicted butterflies. Giant ones, tiny ones, monarchs, swallowtails, green, red, pink, purple, and rainbow-colored butterflies. *Definitely nuts,* Adam thought. *A vet maybe or a hippie who took one too many hits of acid in Golden Gate Park.*

Adam changed his mind and bought the book without even looking at it. It turned out to be a Hardy Boys mystery called *The Secret Warning.*

After that first meeting, whenever Adam noticed the wheelchair-bound butterfly man in his spot between the newspaper stands, he paid him a visit. The man's name was Michael. Normally Adam avoided homeless people in San Francisco; they all seemed so angry and demanding. But Michael was different. For one thing, that smile could melt a glacier. But there was also something about the way he looked at Adam with eyes that seemed to see through the triviality of everyday life to something bigger, to something Adam longed to see.

On one occasion, more to be friendly than anything else, Adam asked Michael if he might have any philosophy books. After a confusing exchange, Adam ended up with another Hardy Boys mystery. But the next time Adam saw Michael in his spot, the homeless man beckoned him over. "Hey, brother, I got something real special for you." And this time he did. From his bag Michael produced a big gray book with a tattered burgundy spine.

The book's title, *Navigations of the Hidden Domain,* was as unfamiliar to Adam as the author, Virgil Coates. It wasn't clear when exactly the book had been written, but the copyright page showed that it was published in 1974 in Berkeley, California, by a company Adam had never heard of.

For a month the book sat untouched on Adam's desk. Then, after an intense day of coding, Adam noticed it there and decided to crack it open. The first chapter was about the celestial laws that govern the ocean. It was as intriguing as it was difficult to get through, so Adam decided to take the book home for the weekend. Jane was away on a yoga retreat, and the kids were staying with Jane's parents, so Adam had the house to himself and no obligations. He began reading Friday evening, and by the time Sunday came around, he realized he had barely eaten or slept. And yet, he wasn't tired or hungry afterward. If anything his mind felt lighter and clearer after reading the book than it had in years.

On the surface *Navigations of the Hidden Domain* was an allegory about a man lost at sea. But unlike anything he had read before, this particular book penetrated right to the very heart of Adam's big questions. Its ideas were expressed in ways that seemed to effortlessly match with all of the longings, fears, and uncertainties Adam kept locked up inside. It was as if the book had been written just for him. Or perhaps about him. Buried at different levels within the text, he found ideas that were both completely alien, yet achingly familiar.

In some places the author dropped the allegorical device, laying out his ideas in plain prose. In other sections, especially the man-at-sea's journal entries concerning his dreams, the writing was so abstract that it was virtually impenetrable. Some passages made assertions about reality as outlandish as a fantasy novel, while others were constructed with the precise logic of a scientific treatise. What Adam found most remarkable was that at no point did the book seem to give him any direct answers to his big questions, at least not in words. Rather it was how he *felt* while reading the book that he came to realize was more important than any answers. The book seemed to be questioning life's meaning right alongside him, which created a sensation, a sort of light vibration in his body that grew stronger every time he picked up the book.

The next time Adam spotted homeless Michael outside the Virtual Skies Tower, he bombarded him with questions. But all of his attempts to find out anything else about this extraordinary book or its author never yielded anything more than another Hardy Boys mystery. So Adam read *Navigations of the Hidden Domain* over and over, each time feeling something different, each time dog-earing and underlining new passages. The only negative effect of this strange book was the growing sense that something was drastically wrong with Adam's own life. He had taken a wrong turn long ago, forgotten some essential something-or-other, and now the fog of habit and conformity had grown so thick around him, he might not ever remember what it was.

As the BART train slipped from beneath the Bay and into West Oakland, Adam opened up *Navigations of the Hidden Domain*. The way the book smelled was another aspect of its charm. Musty like the old comic books Adam's dad had given him, but with a hint of incense, as if it had been sitting for a few centuries in an ashram.

Flipping through the dog-eared pages, Adam found the underlined passage he had been thinking of.

As terrifying and inescapable the trajectory of Man's mortal dilemma may appear, there does exist with proven certainty a wholly different current of life. For the man willing to stand unflinching before his own nonexistence, a fissure between worlds can appear. A doorway, revealing itself not to the "man" but to something deep within the man that for years has cried out unheard. Occasionally he will catch the whispers of this abandoned voice, in the afterglow of certain dreams with that lingering sense of a paradise lost, reminding him of another kind of life, the life he was always meant to live, but for whatever reason, he did not. [1]

1 Underlining by Adam Sheppard

CHAPTER 6

WHAT'S BEHIND THE SCHOOLHOUSE

After taking off the wrapping paper, Adam examined the new book in his hands. He glanced up at the couple sitting across the table and managed a smile.

"Okay, wow," was the best he could do. Thankfully Jane was there to rescue him. Taking the book from Adam, in her effervescent voice she read aloud the title for everyone at the table to hear.

"*Tweets from the Soul: An Inspiring Collection of Life-Affirming Tweets.*"

"It's just a fun little something we found," said Stefan, the male half of the couple. "Jane told us how much you like philosophical sorts of things—"

"And since you're part of the tech industry," Annie, the female half added, "we just thought it was perfect!"

Stefan and Annie Thompson had recently relocated to the Bay Area from San Diego to be closer to Stefan's new job, and had bought a home in Blackhawk, the private community where Adam and Jane lived. Having learned that the Thompsons were interested in yoga, Jane had insisted on introducing them to all her favorite studios and instructors around Contra Costa County.

This had led to the two families "doing things together," which led to Jane inviting the Thompsons to Adam's birthday dinner.

"Thank you very much. It's very thoughtful," Adam finally got out. He knew he should at least try to like the Thompsons; they meant well, after all.

"My God, *thank you*, Adam," Annie said with fierce sincerity.

"And Jane," Stefan added, "for inviting us. This restaurant is just so cool."

"And *fun*, really fun." Annie threw in. "And to know it's so close to Blackhawk."

The Silver Oak Grill and Chophouse was an upscale chain restaurant that landed somewhere between a Ruth's Chris Steak House and a Cheesecake Factory. This latest link in the Silver Oak chain had popped up between the Blackhawk Plastic Surgery Center and a Starbucks, and it was here that Adam had been feted on the date of his birth for the past five years. Adam didn't actually like the place, but everyone else seemed to love it, so he kept his thoughts to himself. It was convenient and quasi-fancy, kid friendly while also being a hit with the blue-haired set.

This reminded Adam that tonight marked the third birthday dinner without Gloria, his stepmother, anchored in a wheelchair at the end of the table. However, Jane's parents were still in attendance. Jane's mother, Cassandra, who claimed to be 59 years old and was a frequent client at the establishment next to Blackhawk's Silver Oak Grill (not the one serving coffee), was by far the best-dressed person at the table. Cassandra jumped at any excuse to sport her latest Dolce & Gabbana ensemble.

Howard, Cassandra's husband (her fourth), was 25 years her senior, in amazing shape for his age, an avid golfer, car collector, Scotch drinker, and die-hard Republican. He was also in the later stages of dementia, and so was accompanied tonight by Malee, his caregiver. Malee was from Thailand, which irritated Howard, who had served during World War II and the Korean War and did not much like Asians of any variety. Luckily Howard had recently stopped expressing his embarrassingly racist convictions out loud, but the old man was still a ticking time bomb, especially in public.

Also present were Jane's kids, Chandler and Madison, now Adam's formally adopted children. At 9 and 10 respectively, they were behaving very well tonight, at least in the sense of not posing a problem. Chandler was fixated on his Game Boy, and Madison remained glued to her laptop, catching up on her favorite Nickelodeon shows. Jane had given them permission to use electronics at Adam's birthday dinner, Jane told him earlier, so they wouldn't be bored by all the adult talk. Adam wished he could have brought his laptop too.

This year there was one unexpected addition to the party. Christian was a programmer who had worked for Pixilate in the early days, and he and Adam had bonded over their mutual interest in esoteric history, lost civilizations, and mysteries of the occult. After six months Christian left Pixilate to travel abroad, and since he had returned, Adam rarely saw him. But the two kept in touch through e-mail. That Christian happened to be in town during Adam's birthday dinner this year was a lucky break and gave Adam hope that he would get to hear about Christian's travels. Unfortunately that didn't seem to be in the cards tonight.

When "Sheppard, party of ten" had arrived earlier that evening and was led to a large booth at the back of the restaurant, a little skirmish had taken place, the same one that had marked all of Adam's birthday dinners at the Silver Oak Grill. "I just don't see why we can't sit somewhere nicer," Cassandra had said to her daughter. "How about over there, in the center? It's Adam's birthday, for God's sake."

"If we were in the center, Mom, then we couldn't enjoy the restaurant's new centerpiece," Jane had said. "Please don't make a fuss. This way we'll have a nice view of the entire restaurant. It's fine, Mom."

"It's *not* fine. Come on Janie, we're way out in the boondocks over here."

Adam and the others had hesitated before sitting down at the table, waiting to see whether Jane or her mother would prevail.

"*Mom,*" Jane said through her clenched smile, "it's *Adam's* birthday. Not yours. You can't always have things your way, okay?"

"Jeez-Louise, bite my head off, why don't you!"

As nearby restaurant patrons had tuned in to watch the debate, the hostess calmly suggested a compromise. Halfway between the back booths and the restaurant's centerpiece, two tables were pushed together to accommodate the Sheppard party. All were satisfied. That is, except Adam, who ended up being seated as far away from Christian as possible.

After Adam opened his gifts—something Jane felt should happen between ordering and the food arriving, to fill the time—Christian called down the length of the table.

"So, you been good, man?"

"Yeah, same old, same old."

"For some reason I always thought your birthday was the tenth?" Christian said.

"That's right; it is the tenth."

Christian looked confused. "But that's Saturday."

Before Adam could respond, Jane jumped in. "We decided to do the dinner tonight since there were so many conflicts this weekend. Mom and Howie are heading up to Napa, the kids have their things going on, and Stefan and Annie, you guys are heading somewhere, right?"

"Florida, actually, it's—"

"Disney World." Annie smiled at her husband, patting his hand.

"And I've got a big yoga conference," Jane added.

As the conversation shifted to yoga, the food arrived. Adam looked wearily down at his safely overcooked chicken breast and sautéed vegetable chunks. Glancing around to see what everyone else had ordered, he happened to notice his father-in-law was staring at him. Uncomfortable, Adam tried a smile, but Howard wasn't buying it.

"Why is Jack on the cruise? Who invited him?" Howard's voice was loud and aggressive, his glare firmly fixed on Adam.

Cassandra rolled her eyes. "That's not Jack, honey, that's Adam."

Even before Howard's memory had started to go, he had confused Adam for Jane's previous boyfriend Jack, Chandler and Madison's biological father.

"Why is that freeloading jackass here? I want an answer."

"Honey, Jane is married to Adam now. You know Adam. He's very kind and very successful, and today's his birthday. Now let Malee help you with your dinner." Malee tried maneuvering a piece of broccoli into Howard's mouth, which caused him to lose interest in Adam.

While the rest of the table was busy eating, Christian made a second attempt at conversing with Adam. "Hey, did you ever get that article I sent you about the Sphinx?"

Adam came to life. "I don't think so. Did you e-mail it?"

"Snail mail. I clipped it from an airplane magazine."

Adam searched his memory. "Huh. I'm not sure I ever got it."

"Yes, you did, honey," Jane broke in. "I filed it for you under ancient history. Adam has so many interests; I try to help him keep it all organized."

Adam looked back at Christian. "So what was it about?"

"A new way of dating the Sphinx. Cool stuff. I thought you might enjoy it. You know, I'm always game if you ever want to take a trip together. Go see the Luxor temple, the Temple of Man. Just say the word, and I'll book the flights."

While working together Christian and Adam had become obsessed with alternative theories about Egyptian history. "I still have that file on my laptop with all our research," Adam said excitedly. "All the sites where—"

Jane broke in again. "But Egypt's not safe anymore, is it? For traveling?" Then she gave Adam a warm smile. "Besides, we all love Hawaii so much, and it's hard enough dragging you away from work for the family vacation."

Adam liked Hawaii about as much as he liked the Silver Oak Grill. But just as Christian was about to say something else, Cassandra, already on her third glass of Chardonnay, yelled over to Jane, "Where's Blake? Is he bringing that Russian bimbo again?"

"He flaked." Jane rolled her eyes. "Typical. Flakey Blakey."

"Now this Blake . . . ?" Stefan began.

"He's the guy who introduced the two of you, right?" Annie finished.

"Adam's partner over at Pixilate—or Virtual Skies, or whatever you're calling it now." Jane gave Adam's leg a playful rub as she looked over at him. Adam understood that this was her way of trying to gauge his emotional state; was he okay or was he going to get moody and disappear into himself?

"Yep, we're part of Virtual Skies now." Adam smiled, doing his best to reassure Jane that he was fine.

"And where do you know Blake from?" Annie asked Jane.

"We're just old friends."

There was a slight awkward silence before Annie turned to Adam and said, "Well, making video games, that's just—"

"The coolest job ever!" Stefan looked from Chandler to Madison. "You two must think your dad's a total rock star, huh?"

The kids didn't look up from their devices.

"They totally love it," Jane asserted. "They brag to all their friends, and . . ." As Jane launched into a monologue about how lucky her kids were, Adam started to feel the world slowly slipping into that dull fuzziness he'd been experiencing more and more lately. Like a fog creeping in, putting an additional buffer between him and this life he was supposed to be engaging in. Everyone at the table, even Christian, was now immersed in the thick haze.

Adam knew this was likely to be the last time he would ever see his old friend, which was probably for the best. Having Christian here just made Adam feel worse about his own life. Jane and her family were not the problem; deep down, Adam knew this. He was the problem, the source of the haze that separated him from the reality everyone else seemed to be enjoying. Adam would just have to do his best to suppress his anxiety and make it through the rest of the evening. Even if this did feel like a bad dream, it would eventually end. *It's not like you're stuck here forever,* Adam assured himself.

As if in response to his thought, Adam felt something pull his attention toward the center of the restaurant, to the giant, new centerpiece. Less than a year ago, large art installations had been set up in all the Silver Oak locations as part of a new branding effort. Dramatically lit atop a faux Grecian pedestal sat a giant glass vase filled with thousands of black-and-white marbles. Emerging from the vase's mouth was a bundled mass of 15-foot-high branches, once living, now dead and painted white. From the branches hung feathery, silver tinsel meant to look like moss.

As he stared at the monstrous centerpiece, Adam felt its massive weight pushing down on him, crushing him with its sheer meaninglessness. The taste of dread rose like bile from his gut as a klaxon of panic sounded in his ear. Everything around him—like that awful, awful fake tree—was all so terribly wrong.

❖

Later that evening, Adam encountered a very different kind of tree. It appeared to him in a dream. An enormous oak with gray-green moss hanging from its branches like a tattered silk shawl. Adam was pretty certain that he'd met this particular tree before, that it was the same tree that had helped him out in the past. Like when he was struggling for a breakthrough with the *Lucid Larry* game, or the first *Lust 4 Flesh* engine, or even recently with the new *Zombie* project. The colossal tree with all the answers lived at the center of an overgrown garden filled with eccentric flowers, in a distant realm Adam could find only in his dreams, when he could remember the secret of flying.

Landing in the garden, Adam stood beneath the great oak and looked up into its branches, spreading out wide from its formidable trunk, twisting and tangling into the air. Noticing Adam, the tree explained to him that its job was to hold sky and earth together.

"That sounds difficult," Adam said.

"It is," wheezed the giant tree, straining with effort. "But someone's got to do it."

Adam felt bad and asked if he could help in some way, but the tree informed him that because Adam's branches and roots were inverted, he could do nothing at present.

"It's really too bad," the tree wheezed again. "If you humans could only get yourselves turned right side up, you'd feel so much better. And you'd probably even be able to reach up higher than us trees."

Adam wanted to ask where exactly a human being's roots and branches were located, when, as if to answer his question, a door-frame appeared in the side of the oak's trunk. Adam understood that if he ever wanted to untangle himself, he would first need to go through the doorway. Stepping through, he felt himself falling into darkness. Down, down, down he went with a roller-coaster rush, scary yet safe, down toward a flickering, yellow light.

When he landed, Adam saw concrete below his feet. Cracks in the concrete branched out in all directions from the base of a nearby tetherball pole. Beyond the cracks were lines, thick and yellow, followed by rubbery black mats beneath the rings and monkey bars. At the far end of the playground, around the corner of the school building, something was waiting for Adam; if he could just hold on to the dream long enough, this time he might finally see it. Cautiously moving through the yard, eyes downcast to the cement in front of him, Adam saw more lines, more cracks, then an orange peel came into view (*Was this a new detail?* Adam wondered), then the old water fountain, green mold clinging to its pipes below. He had reached the edge of the building; he was turning the corner—

Instantly everything was veiled in thick fog, and in that same instant, Adam could sense he was no longer at the edge of the schoolhouse; he was now *inside* of what he was trying to see. He was part of it. And he was moving. Round and round, as if the playground was spinning around him. He felt sunlight glaring off metal, flickering against the backs of his eyelids, making it even more impossible to see. Intuitively he knew that if he strained too hard to open his eyes in the dream, he would wake up.

What he needed to know was so close, yet impossible to look at directly. Then he felt it. He was not alone. He tried to turn, to see who it was without waking up. Through the fogginess and glare, he could just make out eyes staring at him. *Bright green eyes.* He heard a girl's voice softly but urgently whisper a question.

"What lies beyond the stars, Adam?"

Adam wanted to respond, but he had no voice. He wanted to move, but his body refused to obey him. Most of all he wanted to open his eyes and see this forgotten place and not the ceiling of his bedroom in Blackhawk. *There must be a secret to opening one's eyes in a dream,* Adam thought, *in just the right way. Of choosing which reality you wake up in.*

Adam heard a faint sound, like a deep metallic rumble—*grug-grug-grug-grug-grug*—rising in the distance. He felt the green eyes turn from him, toward that approaching noise. A few moments later, he realized that he was now alone and terribly vulnerable. He couldn't move, he couldn't escape, as the sound grew louder and louder. He needed to open his eyes before it reached him; he needed to wake up before it was too late. But the terrifying rumble was already there; he could feel it slipping over his body, enveloping him like a glove. Then, one after another, he felt *the pricks*—needles piercing his skin, burrowing down into him, infecting his body with some hungry parasite, swelling inside him, taking him over, the maddening pressure slowly building from within . . .

Jane opened an eye. The digital clock read 4:25. Rolling over, she saw the empty space next to her on the bed.

She sat up, and at first she didn't see him there. He was so still that he might have been a shadow. He was standing by the window, looking out at the night sky.

"Adam? What are you doing?"

"The stars," he muttered. "You can't see any stars here."

Jane let out a sigh. "Do we need to call Dr. M., sweetie?"

"No. I'm fine. Sorry to wake you."

"Come to bed, honey. You need your sleep."

Obediently Adam went back to bed. But he didn't sleep. The terrifying rumbling from his dream was still reverberating inside; the sound of approaching disaster still echoing in his ears.

CHAPTER 7

THE MIDDLE OF THE EARTH

Anxious whining via the neighbor's yard had accompanied Adam's breakfast for the past two weeks. Four months earlier the family next door had bought a purebred Alaskan malamute puppy, which had quickly lost its appeal as it chewed its way through the family's possessions, until it was banished to their backyard. After a brief period of hole digging, door scratching, and garden trampling, the dog was moved to a long, narrow, paved space between the side of the house and the chain-link fence that bordered the Sheppards' property.

Adam drank his morning health shake and watched the young malamute through the window as it tirelessly ran back and forth. The whining and barking only intensified as the dog, its nose now pressed against the front gate, watched a man pass by with two big Labradors. Doggy torture in its purest form.

Jane, already on her cell, entered the kitchen. Like Adam, she had developed the habit of leaving her earbuds in whether using them or not. This morning she was in fact talking with her mother; Adam could tell even by the tone of her pauses. As Jane moved around the kitchen, Adam watched her carefully, waiting to see if there would be any repercussions for his middle of the night weirdness. Would she notice the cauldron of panic still boiling beneath the surface of his easy morning veneer? Jane poured a glass of filtered water, collected several tablets out of the color-coded pill container on the counter, and brought them over to the table where Adam sat. Then she left the room.

◈

The first Friday of each month, Rene Adiklein invited heads of select companies from within Virtual Skies to the 78th floor of the Tower for a private gathering known as the "Cross-Pollination Brunch." The idea had originated back when Adiklein was still an independent consultant. Originally these informal meetings took place at a private location in Marin County, and the coveted guest list included CEOs, venture capitalists, politicians, media moguls, and other powerful friends. Adiklein also invited a smattering of young entrepreneurs to present their ideas for discussion. According to a report by TechCrunch, over 30 percent of the most successful start-ups between 2001 and 2004 could be traced back to one of Adiklein's little gatherings.

Still moderated by Adiklein, the new get-togethers were held exclusively for those employed or soon to arrive in the Tower. Blake had first been invited to a Cross-Pollination Brunch while Adiklein was courting Pixilate, and on two occasions since then, he was asked to present (his first attempt was a minor hit, his second—an epic bomb). Today's brunch started out with two bland presentations that Adiklein quickly ripped to shreds. Third up was a young Indian-American hacker whose file-sharing technology had recently been acquired by Virtual Skies. As he finished up his presentation, it was not immediately clear which way things were going to go.

"So it would essentially function as a web-based application," the young programmer concluded. "We'd do a desktop version as well, but either way, the idea is to provide a client with quick and convenient transfers, as well as providing advanced analytics to our search engine."

There was a short round of applause as Adiklein leaned forward in his chair and took a sip of water. Despite the bounteous platters of food provided by The Commissary, Adiklein never ate during these brunches. Blake also noticed that he rarely took a bite of food at the handful of business dinners they had attended together.

"Revenue?" Adiklein finally asked.

"Ad based," the young programmer shot back.

Adiklein nodded, but still seemed less than thrilled. For a while he stroked the bridge of his aquiline nose while everyone waited in silence.

"What about mobile? Smartphone?"

"Mobile?" The young programmer was clearly thrown by the question. "Well, we didn't think it was worth exploring that, at least not yet. Mobile is still such a limited platform. We were just thinking—"

Adiklein put up his hand, signaling the young programmer to shut up.

"That's right; you were *just* thinking."

Adiklein pulled out his own smartphone and set it down on the massive conference table. "By the end of this year, as many as two hundred million people around the world will own one of these little devices." Adiklein stood up. "By 2010 this will be easily outselling the PC. Why? Well, for one thing, it's so easy, *convenient*, and as a consumer, there are few things I like as much as that word." Adiklein picked up the phone and began to play with it. "But even more important, this readily available device is going to become everyone's new best friend. Yes, soon we will all feel lost without it. No more wasted moments: standing in line at the grocery store, sitting on the bus, walking the dog, eating my dinner, or even making love to my wife."

This got a respectful laugh.

"Now I can fill all the wasted spaces in my life, all of that useless silence, when I can't get to my laptop, when I'm not in front of my television." Adiklein turned back to the young programmer. "Very soon, young man, every person on the planet will have a new best friend in their pocket, a little screen always at the ready to accept an offering of attention. When Mommy can't get little

Max to stop screaming in the backseat of the car, guess what she'll reach for?" Adiklein tapped his smartphone. "So I think it's time we stop calling this a *limited platform*."

As the young programmer fumbled for a response, Adiklein continued.

"What you've shown us today is not bad. But it's safe. And it bores me. And safe and boring are not what these little gatherings are for. Our salon is about what's new, what's startling, what's disruptive." Despite the fact that the programmer's face was reddening, Adiklein was going easy on the guy, and everyone knew it.

Turning around, Adiklein addressed the room. "I'm not singling out young Ali here. Let me ask the rest of you: Why have I not seen today even one idea aimed at that smartphone market? Why?"

Chairs creaked uneasily in the silence.

"Well, I've been playing around a little with an idea for a mobile game application," Blake blurted out. Everyone turned to look at him. With a slight hesitation he added, "I don't know if now is the time—"

Adiklein smiled. "Yes, Blake. Tell us more."

"I mean, it's just something that I thought could go along with our launch of our *Lust 4 Blood Expansion*. Just a promotional tool in its present form, but it might also serve as a way for us to test the mobile app market."

"*This* is what I'm talking about. This is what I'm looking for." Adiklein turned back to Blake. "Do you have something you could show us?"

Seizing the moment, Blake pulled out his laptop and did a quick search for the mock-up Adam had sent him. Blake had looked it over just out of curiosity, and right now he was very thankful that he had.

"Well, I wasn't planning on presenting anything today, so please keep that in mind."

Adiklein winked. "I promise I'll go easy on you this time."

Blake strolled up to the front of the room and plugged his laptop into the projector cable. With casual confidence, he began.

"This is just a little mock-up I threw together with some basic functionality. The design elements are only placeholders, but as you'll see, what I'm doing here is . . ."

❖

Once again surrounded by a school of commuter-fish, Adam surfaced from the Embarcadero BART station. Since leaving the house, he had not been able to shake the reverberations of his dream. On BART, the movement of the train helped mask the anxiety, but every time the train stopped at a station, he was faced with a swell of panic that, like the rushing sensation of falling in a dream, caused his body to violently jolt to attention. The first time this happened, the businesswoman next to him let out a yelp and quickly moved away. After that, Adam nervously bounced a leg up and down to keep from touching that terrible stillness again.

Outside now, moving along Fremont Street, the crisp San Francisco air helped soothe his jagged nerves. But as the looming tower came into view, he began to hear that deep, metallic rumble from his dream. That *grug-grug-grug* felt as if it were wrapping itself around his body, like the steel-gray latticework of the Virtual Skies Tower. And the closer he got, the louder it became, and the more he felt himself being pulled magnetically toward the Tower.

Adam knew his imagination was getting the better of him, so he forced himself to focus his eyes on the sidewalk in front of him: his feet; other people's feet; lines in the cement; pigeons; a shiny, laminated, pizza restaurant flier; an orange peel; a green Army blanket; books . . . tinfoil-wrapped incense.

When he looked up, he saw Michael and his wheelchair. Adam hadn't intended to stop, he wasn't even thinking about Michael, but now that he was here, he felt a momentary calm. The countless butterfly pins on Michael's jacket danced with light. In his lap a polystyrene to-go container displayed the remains of a half-eaten burrito and some refried beans. Setting his breakfast down next to his wheelchair, Michael gave Adam his soul-piercing smile and nodded for him to come a little closer.

"My brother. Listen, I got something special for you. Real special." He picked up one of the cheap paperbacks. "Have you read this shit?" This was how all of their conversations began.

Adam took the proffered book. *The Sinister Signpost.* Another Hardy Boys mystery. "I think I've already read this one," Adam said.

With a shrug Michael took back the book. His perpetual neck twitch was now growing into a violent spasm; his open smile became a tense grimace. Adam waited patiently for it to end. *While I'm here,* he thought, *maybe I can get a little more information about the Virgil Coates book.* Adam had tried searching online for information about the book, but had come up with only a few, mostly unflattering references to Virgil Coates. His name appeared on some UC Berkeley faculty lists from the late 1960s, but most search results directed Adam to the same *San Francisco Examiner* newspaper article. In it were two references to Virgil Coates. The first referred to him as a disgraced professor whose "abusive experimentation with students resulted in advancing the cause of paranoia." The second mention concluded with the words, "Thankfully the likes of men like Coates, a victim of his own delusions, have slipped into the ocean of obscurity where they belong."

A second less informative article did include a photograph of Virgil Coates, which Adam printed out and taped inside his book. Coates looked rather ordinary, professorial and serious, with a full beard and thick, messy hair. The most unusual aspect of the photo was his eyes, which were intently focused on whoever was behind the camera.

"How about some incense, brother?"

"No, thanks. I've got plenty of that too." Adam glanced around at the other items on the blanket. "You wouldn't happen to have any more books by that sixties philosopher? What was his name? Coates? Something Coates, right?"

Michael picked up his burrito and started eating. "Nah, man. I told you. No more Coates."

"Right." In the past, whenever Adam had asked about Coates or the book, Michael would stop speaking altogether. But this time

Michael went a step further. "Coates told the truth, brother. He told the truth and paid the price. You got to be careful when you start talkin' truth. Specially round here."

"Why is that?"

"Not everyone is ready for that kinda shit. And the people who run the show don't want you to know about folks like Coates. They don't want you to know what's really goin' on." Having finished his burrito, Michael looked off into the distance.

"What do you mean, 'What's really going on'?" Adam asked.

Michael shrugged. "They all lyin' to you, brother. You should know that by now. They be tryin' to trick yo' ass. Keep you trapped right where you are." Michael became very serious, but still didn't look directly at Adam. Under his breath he whispered, *"Remember what I'm sayin', brother. This all's just a big lie to keep you trapped up inside dis shit."* Then, glancing up at the Tower, he added, *"You see what they got up there, don't you?"*

Adam looked up at the Virtual Skies Tower, the distant glass pyramid, and the gray blanket of fog just beyond. Adam squinted. The Tower seemed to be pulsating again, but that was just a trick of the light. *Or was it?*

"Oh, yeah, brother. I knew you'd see it. I could tell you is someone who can see things the way they *really* are. They been weavin' that evil-ass blanket round the whole planet, puttin' y'all to sleep, and pretty soon, brother, ain't none of us gonna wake up."

Adam felt the blood draining from his face. He was wondering whether Michael was crazier than he thought or not so crazy at all.

The homeless man suddenly turned and looked right at Adam. "That's right, brother, they settin' their hooks in you. So you better do something 'bout it 'fore you can't fly no more." Then with a conspiratorial nod, Michael beckoned Adam closer. "There's only one way out."

"'One way out'?" Adam whispered.

Michael beckoned Adam even closer. *"The only way outta this shit"*—Michael moved right up to Adam's ear—*"is you gotta dig."*

"'Dig'?" Adam repeated to himself.

"That's right, brother. Find a spot far away, somewhere you know that's safe. Then you start diggin'. You go down and down and down and down, 'til you reach the center of the mothafuckin' earth! That's where the switch happens!"

Adam stared blankly at Michael.

A big smile spread across Michael's face. "See, instead of going down, now you going up! Makes sense, right? But you never gonna go up 'til first you go down." Michael's stare became ferocious. "And I mean all the fuckin' way down."

Adam held Michael's gaze. Whatever this man's words meant, they were having the unfortunate effect of adding exponentially to Adam's anxiety.

"Time's runnin' out, brother," Michael pressed. "Best to start digging before—" He was about to say something else when his mouth twisted, and again he was overtaken by a violent spasm.

Adam waited.

Finally Michael looked up at Adam, and with that warm smile back, said, "Hey, brother, I got something special for you." Michael picked up *The Sinister Signpost* again and held it out to Adam. "Have you read this shit?"

◈

Half aware of what he was doing, Adam paid for *The Sinister Signpost,* thanked Michael, and walked off. It was not until he heard the elevator ding for the 33rd floor that he realized he was inside the Tower, heading toward the Cave. Stepping off the elevator and into the Pixilate lobby, Adam tried to stop walking but found that he couldn't. Like a hooked fish, he felt his body being reeled in.

With great effort Adam finally forced himself to stop and stand still. Immediately everything around him appeared to warp slightly, becoming eerily unfamiliar. The modern gray couches in the waiting area, the frosted glass behind the reception desk, the giant *Lust 4 Blood* cardboard displays—it was as if Adam had never seen any of it before. And the panicky feeling from his dream was back, tightening around his chest. He started moving toward the

Cave again, and almost immediately, the panic lessened. In that moment a terrifying thought occurred to Adam, and to verify his suspicion, he forced himself to stop once more. Again his anxiety welled up.

Adam understood with every fiber of his being that he needed to get the hell out of this place as quickly as possible. Approaching Blake's office he scrambled to come up with the right excuse—*stomachache, Jane needs me, maybe something with the kids?* Whatever it was, Adam knew it was best to tell Blake directly, as opposed to texting him or just taking off. *With the Expansion due next week, Blake would be extra sensitive about my whereabouts,* Adam thought. *Better to be preemptive.*

Cory, Blake's secretary, who today was dressed like a 1950s housewife, informed Adam that Blake was upstairs at a meeting. "Once he's back down, sweetie, I can tell him you came by. Or you're more than welcome to wait here with me, if you'd like."

"No, that's okay. Thank you, though."

Adam had no interest in hanging with Mrs. Cleaver, but he also knew that if he continued on into the Cave and sat down at his desk, all would be lost. He needed to escape now, while he still had some momentum. He didn't know where he would go yet, just somewhere he could be alone and try to make sense of things. *Someplace where you can see the stars,* Adam found himself thinking.

The elevator doors opened, and this time Adam stepped out onto the 78th floor. It was the first time he'd ever been up this high in the Tower. From the lobby, he could see through the glass doors into the vast banquet hall where the Cross-Pollination Brunch was being held. It appeared to have just ended. Several groups of people were scattered around tables, chatting casually, while staff from The Commissary cleaned up.

Adam spotted Blake at one of the tables. Adiklein was next to him, speaking enthusiastically, while others nodded in agreement. *The brunch must have gone well for Blake,* Adam thought. He could always tell when Blake was happy by the way he shifted around in his chair.

The glass doors opened, and some executives from the brunch drifted into the lobby. Adam stepped aside to let them pass. He didn't want to go in while Blake was still with Adiklein, so he decided to wait. Adam took a few steps back toward the elevator bank and leaned against the wall. Despite himself, he closed his eyes. *If only I could make myself invisible . . .*

Buried in Adam's mind, deep in the rusty filing cabinet of lost childhood memories, was some event connected to trying to make himself invisible. *Was it a game?* Adam wondered. *Did it have something to do with the school yard in my dream?* Adam knew better than to try to figure it out now. Memories from those early years when he lived with his grandmother were too inaccessible. He could barely even remember where that was. *Someplace in the country, with big redwood trees, near some town on the coast, Mendo . . . Mendo-something?*

"Pardon."

Adam opened his eyes to find Rene Adiklein staring at him.

Adam blinked several times to make sure he wasn't hallucinating. There was no doubt about it. Rene Adiklein, lord and ruler of Virtual Skies, was standing right in front of Adam and looking directly at him, *expectantly*. But why? What could Adiklein possibly want from him? They had never met before; Adiklein didn't know Adam from—

"You're blocking the button."

Adiklein pointed to the wall behind Adam.

"Oh, I'm s-sorry," Adam stuttered. "My apologies."

Adam stepped away, and Adiklein pushed the Up button. Wishing more keenly than ever for a cloak of invisibility, Adam watched Adiklein and a few other important-looking men step into the elevator. As the doors closed, something even more unusual took place. Adiklein made eye contact with Adam again. At first Adam assumed he was just conveying his annoyance, but it wasn't that. It was a look of recognition.

The elevator doors slid closed, and Adam began to breathe again. He turned back to the banquet hall. With Adiklein gone, it would be easier to speak to Blake.

He spotted Blake alone, working on his laptop at one of the massive conference tables. Adam approached and tried to sound casual. "Um, Blake?"

Blake's head snapped up. He seemed astonished to see Adam. "Hey, Buddy!" Blake quickly shut his laptop and stood, glancing around the room. "What the heck are you doing up here?"

"I, uh . . ." Adam's throat was locking up. Luckily Blake didn't seem to notice. "I was thinking . . ." Adam cleared his throat. "I want you to know that I'm ready to hand off the final patch for the Hallowing Hollows level of the Expansion, so—"

"Wow, you're already done with it? That's great. Awesome!"

"Yeah. It's already posted."

"Okay, well, I'll make sure the guys in Testing know. They'll appreciate the extra time. They're in for a helluva long weekend."

"So I was thinking," Adam continued, "I might head home early today. I was going to work on *Zombies* at home over the weekend anyway, so I thought maybe I could just start working on it now. Is that okay?"

"Sure, sure." Blake finally seemed to notice Adam's unease. "You doing okay?"

"Fighting a stomach bug." Adam couldn't tell if Blake was buying this or not. If he didn't, Blake might call Jane, who would call Dr. M., and that would be a problem.

"Blake, *dude!*" A guy from the MyStar team walked over. "Bravo, man. You just keep rackin' up those brownie points." Blake gave a loud laugh as he reached out to give the guy a fancy, four-part handshake. It was just the distraction Adam needed.

"So see you Monday then." Adam quickly turned to go.

"Yeah, yeah, totally. Get outta here; go take care of yourself."

Adam kept walking. He reached the lobby, hit the Call button, and anxiously stepped into the first elevator to arrive. And as the elevator began its swift descent, Adam heard Michael's voice whispering in his ear again. *"You go down and down and down and down, 'til you reach the center of the mothafuckin' earth!"* Continuing to fall, the increase in air pressure caused something to shift slightly inside Adam's brain, and suddenly the name of the town he had lived near as a little boy appeared—*Mendocino.*

Adam left through the Tower's front entrance. He had to make a couple of stops in the Transit Center mall before heading home. First was the Wells Fargo ATM, where he withdrew $500, his limit. Next up was the Bank of America ATM, where he withdrew another $500. Then a third ATM, where he was able to get an additional $1,000 cash advance using his Chase Manhattan card. His final stop was a stationery store.

$$\diamondsuit$$

The images on Adam's laptop showed a small seaside town. One might assume this quaint village, with its Victorian architecture and coastal view, was located somewhere in New England, but its nearby cliffs opened up to the Pacific Ocean, not the Atlantic. Adam's search bar read *Mendocino CA.*

Adam opened a new browser page and, after a quick search, landed on a website for The Mendocino Hotel & Garden Suites.

The Only Historic Full-Service Hotel in the Heart of Mendocino Village Overlooking the Pacific Ocean and the Mendocino Headlands

He clicked the link for online reservations and started filling out the form. He had almost reached the end but stopped. They wanted a credit card number. Adam walked over to the door, and peeking down the hallway, he could see the kids watching TV in the family room and could hear Jane talking on her cell in the kitchen. He went back to his desk and dialed the hotel's reservation number.

"Mendocino Hotel. May I help you?" The woman's voice was extremely chipper.

Adam did his best to speak quietly without sounding like a stalker. "Hello. Is it possible to make a reservation online without using a credit card number? I'd like to pay for my room with cash. Is that possible?"

The woman took a moment to reply. It sounded to Adam like she was chewing on something crunchy. "To secure your reservation, sir, I'm afraid we do need a credit card."

Adam gave a frustrated sigh.

"When are you thinking about staying with us?" the woman asked.

"This weekend. Tomorrow. December tenth."

"Oh, I see." The woman's voice sounded apologetic. "Unfortunately, sir, we have a big wedding here this weekend, and so we are completely . . . Oh, wait just a sec." The woman was silent for a moment, then she came back on, her voice brightening. "Well, it looks like your lucky day. I'm seeing a last-minute cancellation . . . Hope it's not the groom." The woman snorted a few times, and then cleared her throat. "Sorry, couldn't resist. Um, so, how many people would this be for?"

Adam was about to reply when he noticed Jane's voice growing louder. He quickly hung up, grabbed a book, walk-ran to his armchair, dove in, and pretended to read.

Jane entered, earbuds in, phone in one hand and a magazine in the other. "It doesn't matter if it's a good carb or a bad carb, Mom. A carb is a carb. That's the point. And that's what they should be telling you."

Adam looked up from his book, his momentary relief turning to panic as he saw his laptop still open to the partially filled out Mendocino Hotel reservation page.

"Well, you can't believe every single thing you see on those stupid programs; they're just trying to sell you something. You need the facts, Mom. *Facts.*"

Adam crossed the room and pushed the lid of his laptop closed. Jane didn't notice a thing.

Adam went back to his armchair and picked up the book again, only just now noticing it was *Navigations of the Hidden Domain.* For several minutes he tried to read, but was too distracted. *I'm terrified of my own wife,* he thought. *The funny thing is, she's completely oblivious. As long as I'm not a problem, I'm invisible.*

As if to underscore the point, Jane walked out of the room just as unceremoniously as she had entered it.

Adam sat silently for a moment, allowing the anxiety to well back up inside, supplying him with the energy needed to again cross the room and fill out the rest of the online reservation form.

CHAPTER 8

EXODUS

His hands hovered just above the hot- and cold-water faucets. He had been standing in the shower like that for close to five minutes, no longer thinking about anything, only trying to remember the incredibly important thing he had just forgotten. The shower was a relatively safe space for an Adam moment, and he had often gotten stuck in them here. Warm water pounded down on his face and chest as his mind did endless laps, trying to catch up to whatever it was he'd forgotten. But this morning there was an additional complication. Throughout the previous day, Adam had been carried along by a current of manic energy ignited by his dream of the playground, and although it had yet to lift him off the mechanical rails of habitual life, it had been preparing him for the jump. But now, after a sleepless night, Adam was finally beginning to tire. The fire in his blood had cooled, and the impulse to forget his plans and allow the fog of oblivion to smother him out for good was creeping in.

What Adam did next, he was not fully conscious of. His hands moved down to rest on the hot- and cold-water faucets. Then, as if someone else inside him had taken charge, his left hand began to twist, very slowly shutting off the hot water. The shock of the ice-cold water just about knocked Adam off his feet.

Some toiletries, a few random articles of clothing, several packets of protein shake mix, and his medication. Along with his laptop, these were items Jane would expect him to take. But he also picked out a cleanly pressed button-down shirt and a pair of dress slacks, packing them beneath everything else. Then Adam put on his jacket, picked up the travel bag, and turned to leave the room. On his way out, he stopped by Jane's dresser and placed a small rose-colored envelope on it.

Moving down the hallway, Adam made a quick stop at the kids' rooms. He peeked in on Madison first. She was asleep in her Barbie sports-car bed. After a moment Adam realized she wasn't really asleep, but was texting under the covers. He wanted to say something, but couldn't think of anything appropriate. Finally he turned to go.

"Shut the door," called a muffled voice.

Adam turned back. "Hey, Maddie. Sorry, what was that?"

"*Shut the door, Adam,*" Madison repeated slowly as if Adam was deaf.

"Oh, okay. Sorry."

Chandler was awake in his room, lying on the floor with the Xbox remote in his hands. His eyes flicked momentarily to Adam at the door, but his deadpan expression didn't change. This time Adam dutifully shut the door.

"No, it's not just wheat gluten." Jane was at her desk in the study, staring at her laptop, talking to her earbuds. She had on her lime-green Lululemon yoga outfit. "Mom, it's *anything* that's been processed in or around the same facilities as wheat gluten."

Adam poked his head in far enough to be noticed. He was clearly in her line of vision, so he waited. And waited.

"Like nuts. You know how many people are allergic to nuts?"

Jane finally mouthed, *What?*

Adam whispered, "I'm going in to the office. Blake called. There's some work I have to finish."

Jane shrugged, as if to say, *Okay . . . and?*

Adam continued. "So I'll probably have to work some all-nighters on the Expansion. You should probably plan on me staying there until Monday."

Jane pressed Mute on her iPhone screen. "I can't drive you to BART, honey. I've got that yoga conference."

"No, I know. I called a cab."

Jane thought for a moment. "Take your medication and some packets of protein shake."

"Got 'em both." Adam patted his bag.

"And don't forget your appointment with Dr. M. on Monday. It's at nine A.M. Do you need me to text you?"

"No. I'll remember." He held up his iPhone. "You set that alert, so I'll be okay."

"Don't miss your appointment, okay, sweetie?"

"Okay, I—" But Jane had already turned back to her laptop. "Sorry, Mom, just dealing with Adam."

Adam stood at the door for a moment longer looking at his wife, and then turned to go.

$$\diamondsuit$$

The economy rental car Adam picked was beige and still had that new-car smell. Thankfully it was an automatic; they probably all were. This was a good thing because Adam hadn't been behind a wheel in over five years. A few months after Adam and Jane had bought their house in Blackhawk, they bought a BMW SUV for Jane and the kids, and a Mercedes SL55 AMG for Adam to commute to San Francisco in. Then one night, after a big push at Pixilate, Adam drove home at four in the morning and parked the car in the neighbor's family room. After that, Jane decided it made more sense for Adam to take BART to work.

Adam pulled out his iPhone to double-check the directions. So far he'd never really used the map app on the phone, so it took him a while to figure it out. With his finger he traced the purple line, like a vein in a forearm of a body builder, up the coast of California from the Bay Area to the small coastal town of Mendocino. Adam turned the key in the ignition and put the car in drive.

PING! The sharp sound came not from the car but from the cup holder where Adam had set his iPhone. Text message: **Blake Dorsey Cell—P1**. P1 meant Priority 1, which meant drop everything. Adam considered turning off his phone, then realized he needed the map. It pinged a second time. Adam decided he would ignore it.

Crossing the Richmond Bridge, Adam glanced out at the Bay. There was a small island just to the left of the bridge, and Adam found himself wondering if it had a name. He knew it wasn't one of the important islands, like Alcatraz or Treasure Island. It was just a small mound of rock protruding from the water with some trees and grass on it. *Maybe someone owns it,* he thought. *Some rich guy who built a hidden fortress inside the island accessible only by underwater passageways, like in a James Bond movie.*

PING! Text message: **Blake Dorsey Cell—P1!**

Or maybe the island contains a portal that transports you to another island exactly like it but in some far off place, in some different dimension of . . .

Oooo-Weeee-Ooooo. Now Blake was calling. When Adam first got his new iPhone, he had set it to play the sci-fi ringtone for Blake's incoming calls. For a while he had thought it was cool, but that was a year ago. He had been meaning to change it, but like so many things in his life, Adam had simply never gotten around to doing it.

Oooo-Weeee-Ooooo.

Adam continued up the 101 Freeway, past farms and cows and open meadows where giant oak trees were busy holding up the sky. The iPhone kept ringing and pinging, and Adam kept on driving. He scanned the landscape for distractions. He tried counting cows. By the time he reached Cloverdale, the phone had stopped ringing, and he'd begun to unwind a bit. He reached the point where the iPhone map indicated he should get off the 101 and get onto Highway 128, a two-lane highway. The first road sign he passed read: Booneville—28 miles, Philo—36 miles, Mendocino—45 miles.

PING!

Text message: **Blake Dorsey Cell—P1!!!**

The rental car seemed to float through the yellow, rolling hills as Adam made his way toward the coast. Moss-covered trees, dilapidated barns, and more cows; he'd counted 37 so far. *I'm 37 years old today,* he realized. *Do other people who are almost 40 count cows?*

Oooo-Weeee-Ooooo.

No. Real human beings who are almost 40 are busy counting important things like stock options and tax deductions and travel reward miles . . .

Oooo-Weeee-Ooooo.

Grown-up things that I should care about counting . . .

Oooo-Weeee-Ooooo.

ENOUGH OF THAT GODDAMN SOUND! Adam hit the brakes and pulled off to the side of the road, flung open the door, and climbed out. He took some deep breaths and exhaled with a slight humming sound. It was a trick he had developed as a child to calm himself during nighttime asthma attacks—before he had access to inhalers, when his only defense against sleep was to walk in circles or rock back and forth in bed, one deep breath after another, until morning came and he was safe.

The phone stopped ringing. Adam's pulse started to ease. Calmer now, he walked back to the car and got in. After another cleansing breath, he looked at the phone. 7 missed calls and 11 text messages—all from Blake Dorsey. Then, like the dead killer in a scary movie, the phone jolted back to life.

Oooo-Weeee-Ooooo.

This time Adam didn't put it down. He hit the green Talk symbol.

"Hello?"

"What the fuck is wrong with you? I've called you eight thousand times!"

"I-I-I-I'm sorry. My phone was off—"

"It doesn't ring if your phone is off! When your phone is off, it goes straight to voice mail! Why didn't you pick up?"

Adam had never heard Blake like this before. "I didn't see it was you. I'm sorry. I was—"

Blake interrupted. "Hallowing Hollows still has a bug."

"But I fixed all the bugs before I left."

"Ron and Sharlena in Testing are telling me that the blood splatter still goes through the tree trunks."

"The blood doesn't spatter through the tree trunks; that's one of the things I fixed." Adam moved the phone to his other ear. "What build are they looking at?"

"The one you left, and it's not working, and none of these douche bags in Testing understands your goddamn code, so you need to get back in here and fix it."

"Are they on version forty-two? They're probably not looking at the latest build."

From around the bend, a massive logging truck appeared and barreled past Adam's car.

"Adam?" Blake's voice sounded suspicious. "Where are you?"

"I'm at a thing."

"A thing?"

"I'm going to a . . . It's a thing that—"

"SPIT IT OUT!" Adam felt his chest tightening; Blake had never yelled at him before. *"Goddamn it! Adam, where the fuck are you? Because I need you in front of a computer screen, where you belong, so you can fix whatever it is you fucked up!"*

"Blake, I'm—I'm sorry. It's the weekend, and I just—"

"This is P1! Got that? Priority 1!"

"I'm sorry, I'm sorry, I'm sorry." Adam started rocking back and forth.

There was a long pause. "Ah, fuck . . ." Blake's tone had changed, now less aggressive and more anxious. "Are you having one of your things . . . an episode? Is that what's going on here?"

"No, Blake. I'm fine. I'm sorry, I just—"

"Is Jane with you? Are you alone? Do I need to call Dr. M.?"

"No! I'm fine! I don't need any help, okay?"

"Yes, you do need help; you have always needed my help. And Jane's. FUCK! Now is not the time, Adam; it's just not the time!"

"I know. I'm sorry, but I can't come in. I'm sorry, Blake."

"Do you realize all the times I've come through for you? The countless times I've saved your ass?"

"Yes, Blake, I know. And I appreciate it." Adam was mumbling now. "You're right. I'm not arguing with you." The muscles in Adam's chest were so tight they began to hurt. "I'm just sorry, I'm sorry, okay? I'm SORRY! I'M FUCKING SORRY ABOUT EVERYTHING! SO FUCK OFF! OKAY? JUST FUCK OFF!"

Adam kicked open the car door, jumped out again, and threw his iPhone as hard as he could. It floated off toward the ravine on the opposite side of the highway, then down, down, down it went, until it was out of sight.

Adam got back in the rental car and shut the door. The sun visor had been knocked out of place, so he attempted to straighten it, but he couldn't seem to get it back in the latch. Then he noticed how badly his hands were shaking. And then he heard a loud gasping sound, and in a moment, realized it was coming from him.

Adam broke into uncontrollable sobs. Instinctively he glanced around outside just to make sure no one was watching. The only witnesses were a few sheep on a nearby hillside. When a minivan came around the bend in the road, he leaned over, pretending to get something from the glove box as it passed by.

Slowly Adam began to settle down, until he was just sitting there in his economy rental, staring out through the windshield.

Here I am, he thought to himself. *I am here. Here.* No other thoughts followed for a long while. Then something outside caught his eye. *Is that tree real?*

The tall oak on the side of the highway 20 yards in front of his car had majestic wisps of gray-green moss hanging from its branches. Adam got out. He wanted to touch the tree to make sure it was real, make sure pixelated blood couldn't splatter through its trunk. Sure enough, the bark was cold and rough under his hand, like uneven stone. Reaching up above his head, Adam pulled down a large piece of Spanish moss, and with it came a fragile memory.

Bright, hot sun shining. Insects buzzing. Mud-stained knees, pushing aside tall, ocher grass. Standing atop a tall stump, triumphant, wielding a stick like a sword. Twisting moss in his hand, fashioning it into a fake moustache, attempting to hold it between his nose and upper lip. He was laughing. Somewhere close by, someone was laughing with him, someone whose love for him filled him with confidence and courage.

CHAPTER 9

ESCAPING WILD THINGS

Emerging from beneath the dense canopy of redwoods, Adam turned the car north up Highway 1, and after a few miles, rounded a bend and caught his first glimpse of the town of Mendocino. It was perched on the cliffs just like the pictures he'd seen online. The steeple of the century-old Presbyterian Church reached into the sky, snagging threads of thin, gray fog. The town's other buildings and houses, many of Victorian architecture, appeared comfortably married to the land in the way that only time can achieve. Most interesting to Adam were the old, elevated water towers scattered about. They had the aesthetic effect of securing the town down to the earth, like giant pushpins.

Adam turned down Main Street, which instead of going through the middle of town, ran along the side of Mendocino that faced the ocean. All the buildings were on the right side of the street. On the left a long white fence separated the Mendocino Headlands where footpaths could be seen weaving through blackberry patches, tall grass, and coastal vegetation. Adam parked in front of the Mendocino Hotel, but before going in, he took a moment to look out at the bluff. Tourists were scattered about, couples mostly, and a few families. The wind off the ocean was crisp.

The lobby of the Mendocino Hotel was even more inviting than it had looked online—charming Victorian-era decor,
antiques, a snug fireplace, on the walls old photos of Mendocino at
the turn of the century. As Adam approached the reception desk,
he noticed the bar and dining areas were set up for an event. A
freestanding wooden sign had a white sheet of paper taped over it
that read: Hendricks Wedding Reception.

"Welcome to the Mendocino Hotel. Are you checking in, sir?"
The woman behind the reception desk had an angled bob and
large, dangling earrings made of iridescent abalone shell. She
was in her midthirties and had a round, somewhat flat face that
reminded Adam of his stepmother Gloria's beloved pug. Her name
tag read *Dorothy*, and Adam recognized her chipper voice from his
phone call the night before.

"Yes, I made a reservation online."

"Okeydoke." Dorothy turned to her computer screen, "And
your name is . . . ?"

"Adam Smith."

"Adam Smith. Adam Smith." Dorothy clicked her mouse a few
times. "Gotcha right here. Let's see, we have you in one of our Victorian suites." Dorothy stopped to read something about Adam's
reservation. "And there's a note here about your credit card?"

"Yes. My company made the reservation for me, but I'd like
to pay for it myself. I just want to make sure that nothing will be
charged to that particular card."

Dorothy smiled reassuringly. "Okay. So don't put anything on
the card with the name Adam Sheppard?"

"Yes. No. Don't use that card. Right."

"Okeydoke. Do you have another card you'd like to use?"

"I'd like to pay with cash."

"Cash works." Dorothy smiled. "Oh, but we still need to run a
card for any room charges."

"You do?" Adam frowned.

Dorothy leaned forward, her tone playfully conspiratorial.
"Don't you worry. Nothing actually appears on the card unless
I charge it. So even if you go crazy and raid the minibar, I just

keep track for you. We've got those little sensors inside the bars, so when you take something—*bing*—it pops up on my computer. *But* I don't actually charge anything until you leave, so when you check out, we can settle up with cash!"

Adam relaxed a bit. "Okay, that's great. Thanks."

"You're very welcome. So, this your first time in Mendocino?"

"Well, no, actually, I lived around here as a kid."

"Awesome. Whereabouts?"

"Down the coast a bit. I think it was called Little Creek?"

"*Little River*! Oh, wow, that's cool. So it's like a homecoming for you, then?"

Adam nodded, then looked around the room for a way to politely disengage.

"All right, then. You're in room 25b, just up those stairs and to the right. Last door on the left. Everything should be set, but if you need anything—extra towels, things like that—don't hesitate to ask. I'm Dorothy."

Dorothy handed Adam two key-cards.

"One is fine."

"Oh, all right. I just thought—" Dorothy bobbled her head as if to say, *What was I thinking?* One of her dangly earrings got tangled in the longer half of her bob. "Okeydokey. So, my name is Dorothy." She laughed. "But I already told you that, didn't I? So if you need anything, just let me know."

Like the hotel's lobby, Adam's room was furnished with antiques. There was a balcony, from which Adam could look out at the bluff and the Pacific Ocean beyond. *The perfect place to be alone and sort out one's life,* Adam thought. *That's why I came here. Isn't it?* Adam stepped onto the balcony and put his hand on the railing. It felt cold and slightly damp beneath his fingers. A lone seagull floated motionless out on the wind, and as Adam watched it, he thought about the envelope he had left on Jane's dresser, imagining her reaction when she read what he had written.

There is something in me that knows of a different kind of life. The life I was meant to live, but for whatever reason, I did not.

He wondered if she would understand. Jane wasn't dumb, far from it. But she often accused Adam of being frustratingly convoluted. She had once told him that there were crucial links missing between what he was trying to express and what he actually said—the much-needed context required for others to understand him. Adam knew *Jane was right about this.* And so in the rest of the note, he had tried his best to be as direct as possible, making it absolutely clear she shouldn't try to find him.

With night came mist off the ocean, drifting in low across the bluff. Beneath the streetlights on Main Street, glowing yellow cones formed out of the thick sea air. Toward the bottom of Main, a stray cat slipped through a fence and darted under a parked car. From the opposite end of the street came sounds of laughter as a handful of wedding guests hurried down from the Presbyterian Church toward the Mendocino Hotel.

Up in room 25b, Adam Sheppard was looking himself over in the mirror. He had showered and done his best to neaten the shirt and pants he'd stuffed into the bottom of his bag. He tried combing his hair, but it looked strange, like a toupee. He tried mussing it up, but that only made him look 15 years old. Giving up on his appearance, Adam stared into his own eyes, which very quickly became unnerving. *Is this really me?* he thought. *This sad-looking man. Wasn't I just a kid not that long ago? How did I end up here, alone in this strange hotel room on my birthday?* The sad man in the mirror looked back with such despair that it scared Adam.

The Hendrickses' wedding reception had kicked into high gear, and the restaurant and bar area were filled with guests. Adam was actually happy for this unexpectedly cheerful addition to what would have otherwise been a quiet birthday dinner alone. He stood in the bar area while Dorothy checked to see if it was all right for him to eat there since the wedding party had reserved the entire downstairs. As he waited Adam did his best to dodge the gesticulations of the three well-lubricated groomsmen between him and the bar. They were reenacting some adventure that apparently involved having one's arms outstretched for balance. The men found it hysterical, and one even turned to Adam as if to include him. Adam attempted a smile, but the man must have realized Adam was only pretending to be a human being, and so he quickly pivoted back to his true brethren.

Dorothy returned, handed Adam a menu with a winning smile, and informed him that it was fine if he wanted to dine at one of the small tables by the front windows.

"Okeydokey. Enjoy yourself." Dorothy gave a flirtatious wink and started to leave but then turned back. "I'm Dorothy, by the way. Did I . . . ?"

"Yes, you did," Adam said patiently.

She laughed cautiously, as if finally latching on to the idea that Adam wasn't living in the same carefree universe she enjoyed.

Adam looked over the menu. He wasn't hungry yet he was determined to order things he wasn't allowed to eat at home: red meat, French fries, gluten, and wine. After ordering, Adam got up and wandered around the lobby, looking at the old photographs on the walls. One showed a cluster of ragged lumberjacks dwarfed by a recently timbered redwood. Another captured Main Street at a time when there were buildings on both sides of the street. The townspeople looked busy to Adam, too caught up in their lives to care about having their picture taken. Near the fireplace and half-hidden by a Tiffany lamp was a photo with the caption, *Pomo Indians.* The Pomo didn't look as busy as the white people, and even less interested in being photographed. In another picture a Native American boy stood awkwardly posed next to some rocks with carvings on them. The caption read, *Petroglyphs found on the Mendocino Coastline. Markings so old, even Indians have forgotten their meaning.*

As the wedding reception continued, the lone bartender, who had introduced himself to Adam as Pete, struggled to keep up with the tide of drink orders. From his table by the window, Adam watched Pete mix cocktails, recommend local wines, chat up guests. Pete was young, probably in his midtwenties, tall and slim with a well-groomed mustache and dark, pomaded hair meticulously slicked back. Observing Pete, Adam was impressed by how much he appeared to enjoy everything he was doing. He seemed optimistic about life in a way Adam had never been, which automatically made Adam want to hate the guy. Of course, Adam knew he was just envious.

"How is everything, sir?" Pete called over. Adam's dinner had arrived, but he had barely touched it. Not that it wasn't good, it was beyond good. Adam just didn't have an appetite. That heavy current of dread was back, making him suddenly unsure about what the hell he was doing there.

"It's great, thank you." Adam picked up his fork and took a bite of steak.

"Cool." Pete eyed Adam's empty wine glass. "Ready for another Cab-Franc?"

Adam knew he must have looked pathetic sitting there alone while the wedding party surged around him. "Sure, why not? Thank you."

Pete came over with a bottle of wine wrapped in a cloth napkin. "Forgive me if I'm stepping out of line here, but in my opinion, she's not worth it."

Adam looked confused. "Sorry?"

"You got stood up. Right?"

"No. Actually, I'm here by myself."

"Oh, sorry. My bad. My bartender-Spidey senses must be off—maybe it's the big crowd here and all. Usually I'm spot-on. My nickname's Peter Parker."

Adam nodded, obviously not getting it.

"As in Spider-Man," Pete added. "Anyway, if there's anything else you need, don't hesitate to ask." Pete and his perfect hair headed back to the bar, leaving Adam and his shitty hair to drink his second glass of Cab-Franc.

Adam turned to look at the darkness beyond the window. *The unknown,* he thought. Much of the fog had cleared, and even from inside the hotel he could see stars dusting the sky. *You wanted to see stars; well, they're out there.* But Adam didn't move. The quickening sensation of panic was beginning to coil up in his chest like a spring.

"Seriously, people. Danny and I have been friends since the fourth grade." In the formal dining room nearby, the wedding party had settled down to listen to the best man's speech. The disembodied voice coming through the bass-heavy speakers sounded like Sean Penn in *Fast Times at Ridgemont High.*

"And, you know, he was like always so goddamn *good* at everything." The crowd laughed. "This son-of-a-gun used to beat me at basketball, one-on-one, every weekend. And not just hoops, I mean, any sport we played, any game that required fine-motor skills. Darts, Nintendo, you name it, and I guarantee Danny will beat you! *Danny always wins!*"

The crowd roared its approval. Adam took a gulp of wine.

"What else can I say?" continued the best man. "Danny's a winner. He's a great guy, and he's got a totally awesome bride, and my only hope is to see a Danny *Junior* come along soon; that's right, *a Danny Junior,* so he can beat his old man for me!"

An explosion of laughs and cheers was loud enough for Adam to press an annoyed finger to his ear. When he finally removed it, the ringing of his tinnitus lingered on.

"Seriously, folks, this is what life is all about! These two people. This is what it's all about, right here!"

Adam could no longer hear anything except for the buzzing in his ear, a warning that his panic levels were about to reach a critical threshold. This place, this reception, these people—it was all horribly wrong. Adam didn't belong here, and it was time to leave.

Adam stood up, downed the rest of his wine, and walked over to Pete.

"Another glass?" Pete asked.

"Actually, I'd like a bottle."

Pete looked to be caught off guard. "Okay. The same one you've been drinking, or would you like something different?"

"If you could drink any bottle of wine tonight, what would it be?"

Pete appeared blindsided by the question. Just then a DJ started up in the other room, '80s rock, for Christ's sake. Adam had to get out of this place, and quick.

"Look, I'm sorry. I know this sounds weird, but it's my birthday today, and I'd just like to treat myself to something. A nice bottle that I can take back up to my room."

"Say no more." Pete finally seemed to get it. "Let's take a look at the reserve list." Pete pulled out a leather-bound book from under the counter and set it down between them. "Let's see if we can find you something magical."

As they looked over the list, Pete went on to explain his personal theory about wine. For most people a bottle of wine, regardless of vintage or price, fell into one of three categories: drinkable, noticeably better than drinkable, or noticeably worse. Forget the bouquet and the notes of cherry, chocolate, and acorns; in the real world, wine is that simple. "However," Pete explained, "every once in a long while, a wine drinker will happen upon what I call a 'magic bottle.'" For Pete this had happened once at a restaurant in Sonoma. It was a bottle of 2004 Flowers Pinot Noir Grand Bouquet he shared with a friend. It didn't just pair nicely with their lobster bisque and coq au vin, it paired with the hint of jasmine in the summer breeze and with the strains of music from a nearby Blues festival. It went with their discussion about why Roger Moore was, in fact, the quintessential Bond. It even paired nicely with the charms of their waitress (whose phone number Pete magically obtained before leaving).

Up in his room, Adam sat on the edge of his bed with an open bottle of 2003 Ridge Independence School Zinfandel on the night table. After asking Adam dozens of questions, Pete had settled on this particular bottle, which was certainly delicious. Magical? Adam wasn't so sure. The music from downstairs—Bon Jovi—could be heard thumping dully through the floorboards. Nothing like a drunken crowd chanting along to "Livin' on a Prayer" to pair with your wine. For some reason the thought of killing himself crossed Adam's mind. Not that he was serious about it. *But what if I did? What if the reason I came up here was to end my life? Even if it's not true, it would make a kind of poetic sense. It's my birthday, so I came back to the last place I can remember being happy to complete the circle of my pathetic attempt at being a functional human being.*

There was something exhilarating about these thoughts, dark though they were. *Killing myself is something I have control over; it's something I could actually do. I've been stuck on a merry-go-round of inescapable patterns, habits, repeated actions, day in, day out, going round and round. So, in a way, I'm already dead. In a way, killing myself would be an act of life.*

Adam took a long pull of wine.

Downstairs Bon Jovi had thankfully left the building. There was a sustained whoop, followed by a brief lull before the next song started. In that blissful moment of silence, Adam could hear the distant crash of an ocean wave through the open balcony doors. It seemed to be calling to him, inviting him to step out of the comfort of this hotel and into the unsheltered night. Outside was something real, something honest. Out there he would face ocean, night sky, and an endless expanse of stars. Out there he couldn't hide. The more Adam thought about it, the more it scared the shit out of him. Staying in his room might be pathetic, but at least it was safe. At least in here he still knew who he was. Out there he might lose himself.

"Wild Thing" by Tone Lōc began to play downstairs. Adam grabbed his jacket and the bottle of wine and headed for the door.

CHAPTER 10

BEYOND THE STARS

Making it out of the hotel was not easy. A mob of wedding guests had taken over the lobby, creating a formidable barricade between Adam and the front door. Tucking the wine bottle under an arm like a football, he forced his way inch by inch through the drunken crowd, through the sweaty, psychotic faces bobbing out of sync, chanting in unison to the music, "Bah, bah, bah, bah . . . Wild Thang!"

Out on Main Street, the cold air was a welcome slap to the face. He moved briskly toward the bluff, the sound of drunken laughter and disposable pop music dissolving in the distance. Once through the opening in the white fence, he struggled to stay on the footpath. Stepping carefully in the moonless night, avoiding large shadowy masses that he assumed were blackberry patches, he made his way toward the cliffs ahead. The sound of waves slamming against the rocks grew louder with each step, pulling him closer, closer, until at last he was there.

The world's end.

Above him endless stars bore silent witness, bending from horizon to horizon, from ear to ear, in their bowl of infinite space. Below the ocean surged from its unimaginable depths, roaring and rumbling its chaotic song. Standing between these two vast domains, Adam struggled to make sense of it all. *No need to panic.*

That's just the ocean. And that up there, that's just space and stars. Don't lose yourself in it. Don't forget who you are. Then came voices crying up from a deeper place within. *Who am I, really? Who am I and why am I here? Why do I feel like I've been running away from something my whole adult life? What is it? And why can't I remember?*

Adam pulled at the bottle of wine as if attempting to drown his thoughts. The noise inside his head was becoming unbearable, a cacophony of ringing and buzzing and voices uttering random words and fragments of sentences over and over again. Then an eerily calm voice broke through the gibberish. *Perhaps you are here to kill yourself.*

Adam didn't want to start thinking about suicide again, especially out here. But looking at the edge of the cliff in front of him triggered a sudden jolt of adrenaline. It was not a long drop from where he was now, but there were higher points not too far away. *Just go take a look,* the calm voice coaxed. *That's all. It can't hurt to just look.* He took another swig from the bottle and started to climb.

It took all his concentration not to trip and spill his wine, but eventually Adam made it to a high point on the cliff. His heart was pounding so loud he could hear it in his ears. Getting down on his hands and knees, Adam inched to the edge of the precipice. Down below the waves thundered against the rocks. *That would definitely do the trick.*

Crawling a little closer, Adam set the wine bottle down and slowly stood up. He extended his arms for balance while keeping his eyes on his feet, which were now less than six inches from the edge. Slowly he lowered his arms and then looked up. In a space between waves, everything fell silent. All the noise in his head, all the tension in his body, drained away. He suddenly felt relaxed, his body light as a bird's. Adam shut his eyes.

"Are you lost?" a voice called out.

Adam's eyes popped open, and he stumbled backward, landing on his ass.

Who said that? Adam squinted into the darkness behind him. At first he couldn't see anything, but then a small orange light flared brightly. *A cigarette?* He started to make out a silhouette, but if that was a person, their head was freakishly large. Then Adam realized he was looking at someone wearing an oversize, hooded parka. Before he could make out any more details, a flashlight popped on, blinding him.

"You know this is a restricted area." It was a woman's voice, but authoritative, like a cop or park ranger.

"A what?"

"You see that rock over there?" The beam of the flashlight swung away and pointed ambiguously down the cliffs to Adam's left. "From that rock there, to the rock over here"—the light swung around in the other direction—"this area is off-limits to the public." The light swung back into Adam's face. "No one is allowed out here at night without a permit. Do you have a permit?"

"No, I don't. Sorry, but I didn't know—"

"Well, now you know." The flashlight clicked off.

Adam caught the glow of the cigarette again as his eyes readjusted to the darkness. In a slightly less aggressive tone, the woman added, "If you really want to walk around out here, you can go down thataway." She aimed the flashlight where the cliffs were much lower. "Past those rocks you're fine. You just can't be in this area. Like I said, it's restricted." With that, the light clicked off again.

Adam made his way down toward the unrestricted area. The terrain shifted from bedrock to sandstone with wind-carved alcoves here and there. Adam stepped into one and sat down. He took another swig of wine and looked up at the stars. They were spinning slightly now. His faculties clouded by alcohol, Adam struggled to review what had just happened. *Did I almost die back there?* For the first time, he became aware of just how chilly it was. He considered heading back to the hotel, back to the world of people like Danny and his perfect bride and their gang of Tone Lōc–chanting cohorts. Adam took another pull at the wine bottle.

"You wouldn't happen to have a pen, would you?" The voice was unnervingly close. It was the woman in the giant parka, standing at the entrance to the alcove.

"Jesus!" Adam spilled wine down the front of his jacket.

"Sorry. Didn't mean to scare you. It's just my pen ran out of ink." Her voice, now that she wasn't reprimanding Adam, was soft and throatier, and there was the trace of an accent Adam was too drunk to place.

"No. I don't have a pen."

The woman stepped closer, her face still hidden in the shadows of her hood. "A pencil maybe? You look like a pencil guy."

"I don't have a pencil either."

"Maybe you could check your pockets? It's important."

Adam was too tired and drunk to be polite. "Look, lady, I don't have pencils or pens, okay? I'm not an Office Depot."

The woman seemed like she might say something else. Instead she abruptly turned to go. Then just as suddenly she turned back, sat down, and pulled out a cigarette. "Well, I have to ask . . ." Her tone was casual. "Were you going to jump off the cliff back there?"

Unprepared for the directness of the question, Adam fumbled for a response. "No. No, I—"

"I'm just curious. Because from where I was sitting, it sure looked like you were."

Adam rubbed his eyes. "I was just looking at . . . the water," he said feebly.

The woman stared at Adam. "You don't like being alive anymore?"

Adam wanted to lighten the moment with humor, but nothing came to mind. "No, I guess I don't."

The woman lit her cigarette. "That's sad."

Adam hung his head. "Really, I wasn't going to jump. I just wish I had a . . . a Reset button. You wouldn't happen to have one?"

"I've got cigarettes. Want one?"

"Smoking is bad for you."

"So is jumping off cliffs."

Adam blinked a few times and then nodded. He was feeling more relaxed and more sociable. Perhaps it was the anonymity of the situation. Or maybe just the wine.

The woman handed Adam a cigarette.

"There're too many people on the planet anyway," Adam slurred. "One less wouldn't be such a big deal. I mean, come on, what's the point of all of us anyway?"

The woman considered this. "That's a rather weighty question. I assume you're not religious?"

"Do you consider the Internet a religion?"

"Your cigarette is backward."

Adam turned his cigarette around and the woman did her best to light it in the erratic wind. In the strobe-light flashes from her lighter, Adam caught three glimpses of her face. The first was a porcelain mask with clean, exotic features, like an Egyptian statue. The second gave away full, sensual lips, stained red from the cold. The last flash caught her emerald-green eyes, now looking directly at him.

The lighter succeeded on the fourth try, and Adam lit his cigarette. "I wish I was religious," he said. "Boy, that would make life easier, having all those questions answered for you. But, come on, how is that even possible today, when you've got science and technology and 24-hour news?" Adam laughed and then started to cough.

The woman waited for him to settle down. "So you have a more scientific worldview then?"

"How can't I?" Adam wiped his mouth. "Science is . . . science. It's got all the facts."

"Facts are overrated."

Adam gave a drunken snort. "But it's all we've got. It's the truth, like it or not."

"What is?"

"Science." Adam leaned back and looked up at the great expanse of stars above. "And science tells us that life is just a freak accident, right? So here we are, two random blips of life accidently stuck on an insignificant planet in a run-of-the-mill solar system, off in some corner of an obscure galaxy, one of two hundred billion, drifting through an infinite universe—which now, by the way, they think is only one of a gazillion other universes inside the multiverse."

After a long silence the woman asked, "Ever consider becoming a motivational speaker?"

The two random blips of life sitting on their insignificant planet broke into laughter. The woman looked at Adam. She had a strange, subtle smile, a Mona Lisa smile.

Adam sighed. "I guess I just need to suck it up and go through the motions. Like Danny."

"Who's 'Danny'?"

"Some guy at the hotel who just got married."

The woman took a drag from her cigarette. "And what are 'the motions'?"

Adam shook his head. "Well, you're born, you go to school, do some job, get married, make some babies, keep working until you retire, and then you die. That's it. The motions."

"Well, maybe there's something about the world that you just haven't discovered yet. Or something you've forgotten how to see."

"Like an Easter egg!" Adam added. "Sorry, stupid video game reference." An Easter egg was a secret object or level that programmers sometimes hid in games, like the dream world in Adam's first game, *Lucid Larry*. "Well, if there is something like that out there, it's too late for me to find it." Adam stood up and wobbled a few steps. "You want some of my wine? It's magic, by the way."

"No, thank you. What color are your eyes?"

"Purple."

"Seriously."

"Brown, I think. Do you want to check my license, Officer?"

"No. Do you live around here?"

"Nope. You?"

She shook her head and looked away. "I'm just here to meet someone."

"Oh." Adam dropped his cigarette on the ground and tried to step on it. "So you're not some Coast Guard person or whatever?" He danced on top of the glowing sparks on the ground. "What was all that about needing to have a permit?"

"I was bluffing. I thought you might be a drunk tourist from the Mendocino Hotel."

"Actually, that's *exactly* what I am."

"But you were trying to kill yourself, which makes you much more interesting." The woman expertly snubbed out her own cigarette, and after putting the butt in her pocket, stood up.

"Great." Adam sighed. "The only time in my life a woman says I'm interesting, and it's because she thinks I want to kill myself."

She gave Adam another Mona Lisa smile. Adam noticed a few wisps of red hair peeking out from under her enormous hood. "Good luck finding that Reset button. Last I checked it wasn't at the bottom of a cliff." And with that, she turned to go.

Before the woman got too far away, Adam called after her, "What are *you* doing out here? Do *you* have a permit?!"

"If *you* had a pencil, I'd write myself one!"

"Seriously! What are you doing out here?"

Her voice was fainter now. "Research!"

"What kind of research!"

"Personal!"

"Oh, come on, give me more than that!"

The woman, just barely visible in the distance, turned back to Adam. She slowly raised her left arm and pointed up at the sky in a gesture that was almost ceremonial.

Adam looked up and then back over at her, confused. "The stars?"

"Beyond the stars!" the woman yelled before turning and disappearing into the distance.

Adam sat back down. *"Beyond the stars." Why is that so familiar?*—

Adam jumped to his feet.

"Hey!" Cupping his hands around his mouth, he called out again, "Hey! Wait!" Adam stumbled along the cliffs in the direction the woman had gone. A thick morning mist had begun to creep in off the water, wet and biting. Adam didn't account for the slipperiness and, after an overly ambitious leap onto a rock, he slipped and fell, hard. His head hit the ground, and everything went black.

$\diamondsuit$

From deep within Adam's mind, long-forgotten impressions slowly welled to the surface. Weighty scenes, not from his ordinary memory drawers, but from somewhere much farther down. A secret hiding place beneath the filing cabinet of his forgotten youth, under the floorboards, buried in a strongbox.

It was inside this box that unconscious Adam discovered a single card of microfiche. At first he didn't recognize the outdated recording format, but as he slipped it into the dream-convenient microfiche projector, he took a moment to appreciate its vintage authenticity.

The first image was blurry, but as the focus adjusted, he began to make out what looked to be the edge of a doorframe. Looking closely at the image, Adam realized he was in it! His six-year-old self was pressing his face against the doorframe, peering around the corner, holding a stick in his hand.

Willfully immersing himself in the impression, Adam was amazed by how much he could actually see, hear, feel, smell, taste. *This microfiche is fucking amazing!* He saw chips and cracks in the white semigloss paint on the doorframe. In the room before him, he heard water boiling. He could smell sweet onions and herbs. Someone was in there, he realized, clanking pots and gently humming.

Through the steam, an elderly woman materialized, wiping her hands on her stained, floral apron. On her head was a tall, black hat with flowers and shiny little ornaments sticking out of it randomly. This was his grandmother, Anne. *Anne is powerful,* little Adam thought. *She knows things.* In his dream state, Adam came to an odd realization: the six-year-old voice inside his head sounded exactly the same as his voice now. It wasn't younger or less intelligent. If anything, his six-year-old self possessed an awareness of the world that was remarkably astute.

Adam's grandmother turned quickly, eyes wide, seeing him at the doorframe. She raised her arms and cackled like a madwoman! *Oh my God!* Adam felt an electric thrill run through his entire body as he squealed with laughter. He raised the magic wand he was holding and zapped his grandmother. She was knocked back by its force, disappearing into the steam, as Adam turned and ran down the hallway and out of the frame of microfiche.

The next image was a high overhead shot, in which Adam saw the small figure of his younger self running, taking large, bounding leaps down a grassy slope below a small wood-frame house. Dreaming Adam knew he had lived here as a boy, but now he could actually see it. The slanted cellar door, the squeaky back porch with Anne's collection of abalone shells, the broken rocking chair, and the sea glass that was glued onto the porch's wooden railing, glowing in the sunlight, red, emerald, blue, opal. Everything was here and remarkably clear.

In the third image, Adam saw his younger self sneaking through a dense grove of massive, ancient trees, the ground underfoot a thick blanket of redwood needles. He could do a backflip here, land, and not be hurt! Ferns rimmed a noisy stream that cut through the trees. Young Adam moved beneath the arboreal canopy until he saw his destination—the biggest tree in the grove, an old-growth redwood with a trunk the size of a house. Rounding it, he reached its far side, where a huge hole in the tree gaped like the mouth of a cave. *Inside is where we meet,* young Adam thought. *She discovered it.*

She? Adam wondered.

As if in answer, a girl's laugher sounded from inside the tree. Then above a flickering candle, a face appeared. Alabaster skin. Bright green eyes. Red hair pulled back into a haphazard ponytail. The girl smiled enigmatically, a Mona Lisa smile, and then beckoned with the candle, inviting Adam in.

Facing Adam, she held the candle toward his outstretched hand. Wax dripped on his skin, and Adam felt a wince of pain. More wax dripping, and her emerald eyes locked on his. Then she slid her own hand on top of his, pressing it down into the hot wax, sealing their hands together. Suddenly the scene grew dark. Adam struggled to stay with the light, but it faded, flickered, and then winked out completely.

Adam's eyes fluttered open. He was awake. In bed. He looked down at his hands. Small, six-year-old hands. *It wasn't over yet!* There was another image on the microfiche. Adam looked around. The room was cold and dark. It was the middle of the night. A few feet away he could make out embers glowing in the mouth of a cast-iron, wood-burning stove. Adam was back inside his grandmother's house, in his small bed under the living room window that faced the field behind the house and the redwood grove beyond.

Adam looked out the warped glass of the window as a sound-less gust of wind slowly rippled through the grass, moving toward him. He looked back across the room at his grandmother's art table, which was covered with odd objects and stacks of old books. He climbed out of bed and crept across the icy-cold floor, tugging down a musty tome as big as his torso. Its pages pushed dust into swirls as Adam searched for his favorite picture, the one of a shep-herd boy on his knees, peeking under the veil of the night sky and into the machinery of the universe beyond.

"What lies beyond the stars?" he heard the girl whisper.

Her breath caressed his face like the wind rippling across the grass. *"What lies beyond the stars?"* she whispered again.

Adam lay his head down on the open book and closed his eyes, drifting off into a dream within a dream, where from the heart of a redwood grove a mysterious girl with green eyes, red hair, and a Mona Lisa smile called out to him.

Part 2

BEATRICE

CHAPTER 11

WHAT THE CHICKEN BOY SAW

It was early morning out on the bluff, and the five-year-old boy had just successfully busted out of his minivan jail cell. First he ran, then jumped, then spun ecstatically until he fell flat on his face. He lay motionless on the ground like a corpse, grass and rocky soil pressing against his left cheek.

"Bobby, come back here right now!" called his jailer.

Lying so close to the earth, the boy felt like he had fallen into his own secret universe. Closed off from everything around him, there was just the sound of his breath and the microcosmic landscape directly in front of his nose. He wondered if anyone had ever peeked inside this particular universe before, noticed these little tufts of grass or this little pear-shaped rock shining opalescent like a miniature star. The boy was friends with all the stars in the sky. *So why not be friends with this little one too?* he thought. *Just because you're so teeny-tiny doesn't mean you're not special. Has anyone ever noticed you before?* There were so many other little rocks out there, but the boy decided that this one was special because he had noticed it; he was giving it his attention.

"Bobby, don't lie in dirt!"

The five-year-old corpse jolted back to life as if he'd been hit by a defibrillator. *WHAM!* He was up! He was running, the wind whooshing through his hair, and without warning, the boy started to cluck and flap his wings. Somehow he had transformed into a chicken. "Bawk-bawk!"

"Bobby, don't make me come down there and get you!"

He was a chicken, an unstoppable chicken making a break for the ocean. But as the dirt trail became rock cliff, the Chicken Boy abruptly came to a halt. On the ground only a few yards away lay a man's body, curled up and half-hidden in the tall grass. Squatting down, Chicken Boy poked its cold cheek. Nothing. Again he poked, and this time the face winced slightly. *Mostly dead*, thought the boy. Gathering some small rocks and pebbles, the boy did his best to bury the body, placing one rock on its leg, a few on its arm, one on its cheek . . .

"Come on, Bobby, we're going back into town. Ice cream!"

As intended, the last two words hooked the boy's attention. Unable to resist, he turned to go, but after a few steps, he stopped to look back at his discovery.

"Goddamn it, Robert! Get over here, NOW!"

Chicken Boy scurried off.

◈

Cold hard facts was Adam's first conscious thought as he reached up and brushed the pebble off his cheek. Trying to sit up was an even colder, harder fact. His entire body pulsed with pain. He touched the welt by his temple. *Jesus!* It felt like there was another rock stuck there, one that wouldn't brush off.

Adam staggered to his feet. *Whoa! This sun is way too bright.* He sat back down precipitously and pressed the heels of his wet palms into his eye sockets. Fragmented memories from last night intermingled with delirious dreams. He opened his eyes again and looked around. He was out on the cliffs, all right. Over on the ridge to his left, a cluster of seagulls were squawking away, while behind them a young mother was leading her child firmly by the arm toward Main Street. Adam looked back toward the ocean.

"Beatrice," he said quietly to himself. The sound fit nicely between the crashing waves.

Standing in the shower, Adam let the hot water beat against the welt on his temple. Less sharp pain now, more dull. He could deal with dull. The rest of his body was slowly thawing out as he stood there staring up at the showerhead. It was surprisingly similar to the one at home. *What if I've never left that shower?* Adam thought. *What if all of the things I think happened over the past 24 hours were just part of another Adam moment? What if I'm trapped in an endless series of Adam moments?* While Adam's mind continued to swirl round and round, something else inside of him decided to take charge. Just as it had the previous morning, Adam's left hand, which was resting on the hot-water faucet, slowly twisted. The ice-cold shock hit Adam like a belly flop.

Half an hour later, Adam walked down to the lobby. He had done his best to clean up. His hair hid most of the purple lump on his temple, but he couldn't do much about the prominent bags under his eyes. Looking around, he saw faces from the previous night's wedding that looked only marginally better than his.

"Do you have a guest at the hotel named Beatrice?" Adam asked Dorothy, who also seemed a diminished version of her perky self behind the check-in desk. "I don't know her last name, but—"

"I'm sorry, but I can't just give out guest information," Dorothy said flatly. She wasn't offering Adam any smiles today. She was either worn out from dealing with the wedding party or more likely annoyed with Adam for not being more responsive to her various attempts at flirtation.

"She's an old friend of mine. I mean, I *think* it was her. We grew up together. She's from this area; I know that." Adam tried to stay calm as he spoke, but for some reason, he was amazingly energized. His body still ached, but it was also buzzing in a pleasant way. He could feel himself standing there talking to Dorothy with a vibrancy he hadn't experienced in a long time. "I'm sorry. I know this is weird, but could you just tell me if anyone with red hair is staying here at the hotel?"

"If she's from around here, why would she be staying in a hotel?"

"Good point. But I'd still be very grateful for any help you could give me."

Dorothy reluctantly looked at her computer screen. After a moment she turned back to Adam. "Is she with the wedding party?"

Adam shook his head.

"Then she's not staying here. You're our only guest that's not with the wedding."

◈

Adam spent the next few hours walking around town, checking with the other inns and B and Bs. No luck. He walked slowly past several nearby cafés and gift shops, but acknowledged to himself how unlikely it would be to find someone like Beatrice buying an *I Heart Mendocino* tee shirt. He went back out onto the bluff and looked around. Not many people out there today. Eventually he returned to town, and after wandering aimlessly for a while, he found himself facing a sign that read Closed to the Public, hanging from a chain across the bottom rung of the ladder beneath an old water tower.

Without thinking, Adam climbed over the chain and started hand over hand up the wood rungs. Halfway up the tower, he realized that he was doing something illegal. Normally the thought would have stopped him (in fact, he never would have come this far), but today his body was moving faster and more purposefully than his self-defeating mind.

From atop the water tower, Adam could see most of Main Street, the ocean bluff beyond, as well as many of the other streets around town. Patiently he scanned for a glimpse of Beatrice.

Observing the world from his perch, Adam again noticed the subtle buzzing sensation in his body and the unusual sense of well-being. His thoughts felt clear and light, as if up on the water tower, in this place he wasn't supposed to be, his mental circuitry had been elevated above its everyday, pedestrian pathways.

Watching people strolling through town reminded Adam of the old black-and-white photographs of Main Street in the lobby of the Mendocino Hotel. *They were probably taken from this exact spot,* Adam thought. *Of course the cars were different, and the way people dressed, but everything else is pretty much the same. Different generation running around doing all the same things, following the same script, and thinking it's all unwritten.*

Virgil Coates, the man whose words had been the only thing to keep Adam going lately, had explored the idea of being trapped in cycles of repetition in *Navigations of the Hidden Domain*. In the chapter called "Currents," Coates's Everyman, now lost at sea, realizes the helplessness of his situation. As he tries to direct his small boat across the vast ocean, all his efforts prove futile. He realizes that it is not he who determines his course, but the fathomless force of the water's currents. He is a slave to their influence, not only physically but emotionally as well. Even his thoughts, which the Everyman had always cherished as uniquely his own, seem to be just echoes of thinking done by other men whose ships had plied these waters before him.

Bleak, Adam thought. *What sane person wants to believe life is predetermined, that he's nothing more than a puppet denying the truth of his strings?* Ordinarily Adam would avoid contemplating a depressing subject like this any further, but today, up here on top of the water tower, he felt brave enough to keep going.

Was that Coates's point? Unless I face the full truth of the human condition, both the good and the bad of it, then nothing else is possible. Is that what he meant?

Adam watched a group of young girls sitting at the picnic benches across from Main Street. They were all talking at once, laughing and gossiping. *Had the photographer of the pictures on the wall of the Mendocino Hotel observed the same scene, only with frocks and petticoats instead of jeans? And what about those tough guys in front of the dive bar, smoking cigarettes, acting cool? Had there been a similar group of guys in the exact same spot 50 years ago? 100? Are we all just stuck living out recycled storylines?* Unbidden, a paragraph from Coates's "Currents" chapter came to mind.

> One of the gravest mistakes made by countercul-
> ture revolutionaries of the 1960s was the belief that "Big
> Brother" was an imminent threat. Unfortunately we live
> in the world envisioned by Aldous Huxley, not George
> Orwell. In this brave new world, we are our own jailers.
> What many fail to understand is that Huxley, a skilled
> traveler through the Hidden Domains, was not predicting
> a future dystopia. In truth, his great work was an allegory
> that sought to bring to light something that happened to
> humankind a long, long time ago.

Have we all been duped? Tricked into a false sense of importance and uniqueness? Oh, and don't think for a second that being up here on top of a water tower places you above that truth, Adam told himself. *How many other Adams are out there in the world? Struggling to make sense of it all, unable to just go through the motions? Have they all been swallowed up by technology, like me? Too busy playing video games or updating their online profiles? Are any of those other Adams willing to consider looking away from their screens long enough to see if the world outside contains an Easter egg—a chance at a new level that might lead to something that has always seemed just out of reach?*

A half-hour later, Adam began to feel like he was being watched. When he looked down at the street directly below the tower, he saw that someone was. A young boy, maybe five or six years old, was staring up. He was oddly still. Then, quite suddenly, the boy folded his arms and started flapping them like stubby wings. *"Bawk-bawk! Bawk-bawk!"*

Adam pulled back a bit from the edge of the tower, concerned that other people might notice him up there. But before the boy could draw anyone's attention to Adam, an angry woman, presumably the boy's mother, ran over and latched on to him. "I told you to stop making that horrible noise! You're not a chicken!"

The frustrated woman dragged the boy and two even younger kids over to a white minivan parked on Main Street. Watching this, Adam felt an ache in his gut. The scene was somehow familiar to him. Before he could figure out why, Adam sensed something else wrong with his stomach. He was famished.

◈

Sitting at the hotel bar, Adam ordered a plate of steak *frites*, a grilled cheese sandwich, and a bowl of tomato soup. Pete cleaned glasses as he listened to Adam describe the previous night's encounter with the mysterious redhead.

"It was a magic bottle," Pete said with a profound sense of awe. "I warned you. When you get one, *anything* can happen."

Adam didn't argue. While devouring his lunch, he continued to share with Pete his efforts so far that day to track down Beatrice. "At this point I'm not really sure what else to do," he confided, dipping his grilled cheese in the tomato soup. "She said she was meeting someone, but it didn't sound like, you know, romantic. More like business or something."

"And you checked with all the other B and Bs in town?"

Adam nodded.

"Did you try across the bridge? Over at the Standford Inn?"

"No, but I called them from the room. No luck."

"And you said this redhead, she grew up around here, right?"

"Yep, I'm pretty sure. If she's who I think she is. We both did."

"Well, maybe she's still got family nearby."

"Yeah, maybe." Adam felt discouraged. "Unfortunately I can't remember where she lived back then. I don't remember a specific house—to be honest, I don't remember much of anything."

"Her last name?"

Adam shook his head. He was starting to realize how hopeless his situation was, but Pete refused to give up.

"Hey!" Pete slapped his cleaning rag on the counter. "I know who can help. Dynamic Dave."

"Dynamic Dave?"

"Yep. Works up at Shandell's Organics. Dave's lived here for what must be close to fifty years. And he knows everyone. Seriously. Everyone. The guy . . ." Pete searched for the right word. "Well, he's a bit *strange*. But I'm telling you, he has an incredible memory." Pete tapped the side of his head. "Incredible."

$$\diamondsuit$$

Shandell's Organics was located in an old wooden church that had been converted into a grocery store. Everything in the place seemed very organic—the produce, the wine, even the healthy snack bars. Up a small staircase, in what was once the choir loft, shelves were lined with hundreds of jars and bottles filled with herbs, spices, tree bark, fungi, and essential oils. This was where Adam finally found Dynamic Dave.

As Adam soon realized, Dave was anything but dynamic. The nickname was apparently more of an ironic, local joke. Simply put, Dave was about as close as you could get to the walking dead. His memory, however, did live up to Pete's billing.

"By my recollection," Dave said in his slow, monotone slur, "there have been three women named Beatrice who have lived in the Mendocino area during the past fifty years." Dave's face was directed at Adam, but his gaze seemed to be focused more on the wall behind Adam. "Beatrice McAllister lives in Comptche, approximately fifteen miles away. She is in her late sixties and owns two llamas by the names of Buck and Chuck."

"Mmmm. Probably not." Adam quickly glanced behind him to check out what Dynamic Dave might be looking at. There was nothing there.

Dynamic Dave blinked several times, and then continued as if reading carefully from a script no one else could see. "Beatrice Kelly, daughter of Bruce and Cindy Kelly. But she's dead, so it's unlikely you ran into her."

Adam looked closely for some sign that Dave was joking. His face was deadpan. "The last Beatrice I am aware of is Beatrice Duncan. Beatrice Duncan is thirty-eight years of age and lives in the town of Caspar, four and one-half miles north." Before Adam could get too excited, Dave added, "But it's probably not her either."

"Why do you say that?"

"Beatrice Duncan does not set foot outside the house anymore."

"Why not?"

"She's a very . . . large person."

"Oh."

Dynamic Dave blinked a few more times and then shifted his focus to Adam. "I don't recall your face or your name. You say you grew up in Little River?"

"I lived with my grandmother there, but only until I was six or maybe seven. Unfortunately, I don't remember much from those days."

"What was your grandmother's name?"

"Anne."

"Anne Sheppard?"

"No, she was my mother's mother. Her last name was something like . . . Bear?"

"Anne Beers?"

"That's it, Beers. Did you know her?"

"I knew Anne Beers. Lived in a little white house, one mile up Little River Airport Road, on the right." At that moment a customer came upstairs, and Dynamic Dave turned from Adam to offer his help. The customer was interested in whether black cohosh could help the circulation in her feet. Dave pedantically listed the various aliments black cohosh could be used to treat, poor circulation not being one of them, before proposing an alternative. Finally he turned back to Adam. "How old are you?"

"Thirty-seven."

Dynamic Dave blinked out some calculations and then said, "That would put you in Little River from 1971 to 1978, or then-thereabouts."

"Sure. Why?"

"Well, there were lots of hippie people around in those days. And I remember there was a group of them squatting in the woods by your grandmother's house. And one family had one of those VW campers, and the mother had a funny accent—French, I think—and the father, he was in trouble with the law, and they had a little girl. With red hair."

"Yes!" Adam half shouted. "That had to be her! That was Beatrice!"

Dynamic Dave droned cautiously, "Perhaps. Perhaps not. But sounds to me like Little River is going to be your best bet."

CHAPTER 12

ABALONE SHELLS, SEA GLASS, AND CAT STEVENS

Adam drove south down Highway 1, his economy rental car cautiously creeping around the hairpin turns. He slowed down as a sign appeared out of the fog: Little River—POP 412, ELEV 90. Just beyond the sign, Adam passed a large, picturesque inn on his left, and a gas station/post office on his right. And that was it.

He thought about turning back to stop at the inn, but first he wanted to explore another possibility. A little farther up the road, Adam slowed at an old cemetery. Before he'd left Shandell's, Dynamic Dave had given him directions to Little River, and just as Dave had described it, directly across from the cemetery there was a small road that headed inland, into the redwoods. Adam signaled and turned onto Little River Airport Road.

Five minutes later he was parking on the thin, gravel driveway of a badly neglected white house, its windows boarded up long ago. It was his grandmother's place, no doubt about it—the early childhood home that he had glimpsed in his microfiche dreams the night before. All but swallowed up by voracious blackberry vines, the house looked very different now, depressingly different.

Stepping from the car, Adam was immediately greeted by a nostalgic fragrance. As he followed the scent down into the field that stretched between the house and the redwood grove below, he recalled the image from his dream, the snapshot taken from directly overhead of a six-year-old boy running through this same field. That mental picture had been so vivid that Adam now stopped and looked up at the sky. *How could I have a memory of this place from way up there?* he wondered. *I guess dreams are just strange like that.*

The redwood grove was not much different from what Adam had recalled in his dream. But it felt different. Darker, duller, as if its magic had weakened with the passage of time. Adam continued toward the stream, trying to recall details from his memory. *Did other people live down here? Were there hippies and a VW van?* As hard as he tried, he couldn't evoke any new memories. He then spotted the giant, old-growth redwood with the burnt-out cave in its side. It was every bit as majestic as it had been in his dream. He found nothing inside. No children's fort, no Beatrice, and no further memories.

Heading back up toward the house, Adam felt a slight aching sensation behind his right eye. Perhaps it was just from his rough night, or perhaps it was that strongbox of buried memories trying to resurface again.

He stopped to look at the slanted cellar door and then climbed onto the porch, avoiding places where the wood planks had rotted. The railing was still attached, but Adam didn't find any sea glass glued to it. No abalone shells next to the door either. The front doorknob was missing, and the door was nailed shut. Adam pushed hard with his shoulder, and the rotting wood gave way. Inside a thick layer of dust caked the floor, and scraps of junk lay here and there. Adam walked over toward the kitchen and paused, positioning his face by the doorframe as he had in the dream. *It was painted white in the dream, wasn't it? Maybe the white is now buried below the other layers of paint.*

Peeking into the kitchen, he focused his eyes on the spot where he had seen his grandmother. There was nothing there now but curling, rust-stained linoleum tiles.

Adam stood, discouraged that no new memories had presented themselves. But that dull ache in his brain was getting stronger. He could feel there were secrets hidden in this house that he needed to see, if only he could find the right trigger to force open the past. He walked down the hallway into what was once the living room. The cast-iron stove was still there. Crossing over to the far window where his bed used to be, Adam looked out through the warped glass at the field outside. His hand settled instinctively on the windowsill, and there, hidden under a layer of dust, he felt something smooth.

It was a small piece of emerald-green sea glass glued to the sill. His pulse quickened as he stared at it, transfixed. There was a clicking sound in his right ear, and then a hollow pop. *The glass was now glowing.* Not reflecting light, but actually glowing from its own source, deep within. The light continued to grow brighter and brighter, filling the room, pulling Adam into a hidden dimension of time and space.

❖

The first thing Adam noticed was movement in the field outside the window. Someone was out there, looking up at him. A young girl whose white dress set off her mane of auburn tresses. She beckoned to him. *Come on. Come outside.* Her smile promising mischief.

Adam realized that he had become his six-year-old self again. This wasn't just a memory or a dream; he was actually there, reliving a moment that had been buried in the past. It was so vivid that he could even feel his young heart pounding with excitement as he gazed out the window at her. *Beatrice.*

He turned and looked back into the living room. Everything now appeared as it once was. His grandmother's art table, the old books, the lumpy couch. A log crackling in the cast-iron stove. Instinctively, Adam understood that if this lucid memory were to continue, he would not have time to linger on details; he must simply go along for the ride.

Adam hopped down off his little bed beneath the window and grabbed his jean jacket from the couch. He needed to get outside, to see Beatrice. As he slipped on his jacket, unfamiliar adult voices could be heard arguing in angry whispers somewhere in the house. Creeping down the hallway, the nonsqueaky side, Adam found his hiding spot by the kitchen door. Then, with great concentration, he made himself invisible, just like his grandmother had taught him.

Peeking past the doorframe, he saw a man standing by the stove smoking a cigarette, tipping the ashes in the sink. "What was I supposed to do, baby? I was a basket case, remember."

At the kitchen table a woman was seated with her back to Adam. Her hair was tightly pulled into a very serious-looking ponytail. Her stillness emanated power. "I can tell you right now, we are not going to leave that boy here a day longer. Not around this insanity."

Adam recalled meeting these two earlier that day when they had arrived in their noisy car. Anne had told him that the man was his father and that this woman was going to be his new mother. Adam didn't like them—they felt jittery—but Anne had seemed happy when the two showed up. After Adam's real mother had died, Anne said, his dad had become a deadbeat, the bad kind of hippie, but this woman with the serious ponytail had helped straighten him out.

"Come on, Gloria. Can we please not start again with the 'his grandmother's crazy' crap," the man in the bell-bottom jeans complained.

The woman suddenly jutted out her hand, causing the man to hand over his cigarette to her. *She has serious power,* Adam thought.

"It's not just her, Mark. There's something not right about this place, this whole area. And it's having a terrible effect on your son. Look, you have issues with responsibility; we both know that. But I can help you. I can be a real mother to Adam—"

"He's fine. That's just the way kids are."

"No, Mark, your son has serious developmental issues. I'm telling you this not just as your wife, but as a professional. He is going to end up having big problems unless we get him out of here and get him some help. Anne can't take care of him anymore, and she knows it."

Adam didn't like what he was hearing—not just the words, but the colors beneath them. He could sense something especially dangerous about this woman, just from the back of her head. Physically she was much smaller than the bell-bottom man, but in more serious ways, she was at least 10 times his size.

Feeling his invisibility starting to fade, Adam slipped back from the doorframe. Beatrice was waiting outside. He needed to get out of there. *The back door,* he thought. Creeping back down the hallway, there was another room he had to pass on his way out, but this one did not require invisibility. He stopped and peeked in.

His grandmother's bedroom. The small church organ in the corner had all sorts of colored buttons and switches that Adam liked to flip on and off, and the foot pedals were hard to push down unless he used both feet. Dark, dreamlike paintings covered the wall, many of which Adam had helped Anne with. A low table looked like the one in the living room, but this one had lots of jars on it with strange-smelling plants and things inside.

When Adam's asthma got bad, Anne could make him feel better by rubbing tingly oil on his chest and giving him a healing kiss. If his chest got really tight, like breathing through a straw, she encouraged him to inhale a nasty smoke that made him cough, but then the straw would widen and he could breathe again. Anne used to inhale that smoke as well, to help with the many bad pains in her body and her head too. Sometimes she would sit on the couch and stare at the flames in the cast-iron stove for hours without moving. That would scare Adam. He could see that she was not inside her body when that happened, that she had gone off to visit someplace else. Lately her trips had gotten longer, which was why the two jittery adults had come.

Stepping into the bedroom, Adam saw his grandmother sitting in her chair by the window. Adam walked over, reached out, and touched her hand. It was trembling slightly. She slowly turned her head to look at him. *She looks so old, so tired.*

Her lips struggled to smile. "Friends," she whispered hoarsely. "You and I, we'll always be . . . best of friends."

Adam nodded.

"Try not to forget who you are." She smiled but seemed sad. "You're the shepherd boy."

Adam nodded, understanding.

Adam's grandmother glanced out the window, and then turned back to him with a mischievous look in her eyes. "I think I spied your little friend out there." With a conspiratorial whisper she added, "Better go see her before it's too late."

Adam kissed his grandmother's hand, a healing kiss, then slipped out of the room.

Having made his escape through the back door, Adam catapulted himself down the grassy slope toward the grove. With each step he felt himself getting stronger. If he wanted he could double his leaps, then triple them, until he only needed to touch down occasionally to sustain his gliding flight. For a moment, nothing else existed but his body and running. He could see himself from high above, looking down. *Here is a picture of me running,* he thought. *Snap.*

Down among the redwoods, Adam scanned for the girl. It was never clear where he might find her; she was an expert at concealment. He looked by the stream, inside the tree-cave, behind the blackberry bushes; she was nowhere to be seen. It had taken Adam a long time to escape the house, so maybe she had given up on him, but then he saw proof that she had not. Across the stream on a rock, glistening brightly in a patch of dappled sunlight, lay an *orange peel.*

Immediately Adam knew the game. It was one of his favorites. He leaped across the stream from rock to rock (touching down only four times!) until he reached the orange peel. From there he looked around until—*There!*

He spotted the next peel on a log a few hundred feet away. He lifted off and (this time in only *three* leaps!) was on the log. From there he could see the third peel had been placed beneath a big, dusty fern at the top of the ridge. Gliding up to it, Adam looked down into the ravine to the left, where all the hippie people lived. He scanned the area quickly: a woman was hanging laundry on a line suspended between two trees, a dog was rolling in the dirt next to a group of kittens, a man leaned over the engine of a big camper van, and another man with a thick, red beard tapped the keys on a typewriter. *Click, click, clack, clack, click, click, zip.*

As he suspected, the girl wasn't down there. Adam looked the other way, toward the road. *There!* A fourth orange peel. He bounded over to pick it up, already knowing where they would lead him. Three orange peels later, Adam saw it.

The old schoolhouse. She would be waiting in the playground around back. That was where the game with orange peels had first begun.

Adam quietly made his way across the front school yard, careful not to step on any cracks or thick, yellow lines painted on the cement. Passing the tetherball pole, the rings, and the monkey bars, he reached the edge of the building. Cautiously he peeked around the corner. At the far end of the yard, he saw her, hiding her face in her hands, the remaining orange peels at her side. She was sitting on the single most important play structure at the school—*the merry-go-round.* This circular platform with six metal bars arching out from its center was like a miniature carousel that required nothing more than a tug to make it spin. It was a rocket ship, a time machine, or an ancient temple—but for this game it was the princess's fortress.

Adam heard Beatrice giggling as she peeked through her fingers; she knew he was there. In a single leap, Adam made it to his hiding place behind the leaky water fountain. He noticed his breath was getting a bit wheezy. *Probably from all that flying.* But it wasn't too bad yet. He could still play the game.

Crouching low, Adam crab-walked along the side of the schoolhouse until he reached the bushes by the sandbox. He peeked over at Beatrice, who was looking around for him through her fingers. From here, as long as he stayed quiet, he could work his way closer to the merry-go-round without being seen. One of grandmother's Indian friends had taught Adam a special technique for moving silently called "walking on the wind." That, along with his power of invisibility, might allow him to surprise her, although she was remarkably sensitive to even the slightest changes around her.

Inch by inch he crept closer. He was right behind her now. Then Adam saw something he couldn't believe. What he had thought were orange peels beside her had become *pieces of gold*. He slowly reached over and took one in his hand. It was heavy and bright—real gold.

"Ready or not, here I come," the girl sang out. "One, two, three, four . . ."

Adam tried to scoop up the other gold pieces, but she was counting faster now.

"*Five, six, seven-eight-nine-ten!*" she rattled off and then spun around. "*Caught!*" Beatrice dove at Adam, who fell backward, the stolen gold pieces falling from his hands. It was too late to get away; she was too fast. In a fit of laughter, she tackled him. Adam was laughing too, despite the wheezing in his lungs.

Helping Adam to his feet, Beatrice led her captured thief back to the merry-go-round, which now had magically transformed into an enchanted prison. Accepting his fate, Adam climbed on. Beatrice took hold of a metal bar and spun her prisoner into the great vortex of timelessness. Round and round the world went by with a rhythmic, metal squeak. Yellow sunlight pulsed hypnotically off the metal bars around him. Adam's eyelids fluttered. He was falling down, down, down, toward a place between worlds.

He could feel the girl's face close to his now. Her eyes were jade sea glass, guiding him toward another world. Into his ear she whispered the question, *"What lies beyond the stars?"*

Just as he was beginning to see the answer, he heard a distant sound—*grug-grug-grug-grug-grug*. The deep, metallic rumble grew louder, falling into rhythm with the flickering sunlight pulsing on the backs of his eyelids. Adam could hear the girl next to him, faintly pleading with him to wake up. *You can't stay here. Wake up, Adam. Run. You've got to run.* But it was already too late.

"Adam!" The voice cut through the air like a lash, the sound forcing Adam's eyes open. He looked around, confused. The merry-go-round was no longer spinning. The sky had clouded over, and the girl was nowhere to be seen. Instead Adam saw a woman standing at the edge of the schoolhouse, her expression as tight and serious as her ponytail.

"What are you doing here?" Her voice was calm, but he sensed the anger in it. "We've been looking all over for you. It's time to go."

Adam glared back.

"Adam, I want you to come over here, right now."

Adam didn't move.

"Your father and I are going to be taking care of you now, and when I ask you to do something, I expect you to do it. Now. Come. Here."

Adam said nothing.

His stepmother slowly approached the merry-go-round. "I know you can hear me, Adam, and I know you can understand what I'm saying. It is time for us to go."

Defiantly Adam stayed absolutely still. There was a lone cricket chirping nearby. Two birds were having a conversation in the tree overhead, and the wind was quietly whistling in anticipation.

In a flash his stepmother's arm shot out and grabbed Adam by the leg. She was pulling him toward her.

"No!" Adam screamed.

"Stop it!" his stepmother snapped as she struggled to get a better grip on his leg.

"No, no, no!" Adam fought back, kicking and screaming like a wild animal. Before he knew it, his stepmother ensnared his arms and yanked him to the edge of the merry-go-round.

"Stop it, Adam! Stop fighting me! This is not acceptable!" She had him by the shoulders now.

Adam continued to scream and twist and try to worm himself loose.

In a sudden fit of rage, his stepmother grabbed his face with both her hands, forcing him to look directly into her eyes. "You will *behave* yourself!" Then—CRACK—she struck Adam across the face with her open palm. It sounded like a pistol shot and was followed by a terrible silence. No birds. No crickets. Even the wind stopped to mark this moment with a void.

Gloria marched Adam by the arm to the front of the schoolhouse, where a diesel station wagon idled noisily. In the driver's seat sat Adam's father, Mark, smoking a cigarette. He reached over and pushed open the passenger door as they approached.

"Hey, little buddy. We've been looking for you."

Adam's stepmother crouched so that her face was level with Adam's. She took both of his hands in hers and in a calm voice said, "Now what do you want to say to your father, who has been very, very worried about you?"

Adam's face was stained with tears, his cheek red and puffy. "I'm sorry," he said.

"Good, Adam." She gave his hands a squeeze. "And what about your new mother, Gloria?"

"I'm sorry." There was no emotion in his voice.

Gloria opened the back door and gestured for Adam to climb in. He obeyed.

"We got you some treats, kiddo," Adam's father said over his shoulder.

"That's right. When you're a good boy, you get a reward." Gloria handed Adam a small, brown grocery bag. Inside were two Hostess CupCakes, a Dr. Pepper, and a comic book.

Adam's father stabbed out his cigarette in an overstuffed ashtray, and then gave the car some gas. *Grug-grug-grug-grug-grug.* Adam felt the rumble of the engine envelop him, vibrating up his spine from the seat beneath. Then his father turned on the radio, and the car filled with the sound of Cat Stevens singing "Wild World."

Now that I've lost everything to you,
You say you want to start something new
And it's breaking my heart you're leaving,
Baby I'm grieving.

As the car carried Adam off, he turned in his seat and looked out the back window at the school yard. There at the corner of the building, he saw the girl step from her hiding place. Tree shadows pulsed sunlight across Adam's face—on and off, on and off—as he strained to hold on to the image of Beatrice disappearing into the distance.

CHAPTER 13

BEYOND THE GRAVE

Adam looked around, confused. He was sitting inside the rental car in front of his grandmother's boarded-up house. The windshield was steamed over from his breath, and the silence in the car felt terribly lonely. Without thinking, he reached into his pocket for his iPhone, to check his e-mails, or send a text message, or search for something online—anything to distract himself from the aching in his chest. Then he remembered what he'd done. He had thrown his phone into a ravine at the side of the road, along with the immediate sense of security it had so often provided. Starting up the car, Adam knew what he would do next, and the thought filled him with self-loathing. He would drive back to the Mendocino Hotel and call his wife. He would explain to her what he had done. He would apologize, first to Jane, then to Blake, and then to Dr. Mendelson. He would go back to the safe life they all expected him to live.

Car in gear, Adam pulled out of the driveway. Turning from Little River Airport Road onto Highway 1, he headed dutifully back in the direction of the Mendocino Hotel. Passing the Little River Gas Station, he was so caught up in rehearsing what he was going to say to Jane that he almost missed the woman walking along the opposite side of the highway. It wasn't until he passed her that the information even registered.

Adam quickly slowed down and looked in the rearview mirror. *Red hair. Oversize parka. It's her! It's the woman! With a knapsack and a big loop of rope and . . . Is that a shovel? Why the hell would she—*

HOOOONK! Adam's eyes snapped across the rearview mirror to the road directly behind him. Rapidly descending on his beige economy rental car was the gleaming front grill of what must have been the largest monster truck outside of Texas. *HOOOOOOOONKKK!*

"Okay, okay!"

Adam had no choice but to hit the gas. The road was too narrow to make a U-turn, and there was no shoulder to pull over onto. He continued to accelerate, frantically scanning for a place to turn around.

"Shit!"

The bend became a curve, became a hairpin turn, twisting all the way down a hill to where Adam finally saw a turnout. He pulled over, and the monster truck drove past, its evil homunculus up in the cab letting out one last horn blast. *HOOONKKK!*

Adam swung the car around and accelerated back up through the twists and turns until he saw the gas station, but there was no sign of the parka. He continued driving until he reached the intersection of Little River Airport Road and then stopped. Straight ahead on Highway 1 he could see for almost a half of a mile. Nothing. To his left, up toward his grandmother's house, also nothing. No parka. The woman had vanished.

"Damn it!"

Adam turned and looked to his right. The Little River Cemetery. There was a small gravel opening in front of its entrance gate, just big enough for a single car. Adam pulled onto it and got out. Stepping into the cemetery, he looked around. There was no one else in sight. *But she has to be here,* he thought, *it's the only thing that makes sense.* Based on how fast she'd been walking, Adam was sure the woman couldn't have made it any farther than this cemetery. *Besides, she was carrying a shovel.*

Adam considered a number of absurd thoughts before something caught his eye. At the back of the cemetery, toward the ocean, there appeared to be a break in the fence. Adam moved closer. It was an opening, and beyond it a narrow pathway disappeared into the thick woods.

Stepping through the fence, Adam started to get a little spooked. *These woods are what the Hallowing Hallows level should have looked like,* he thought. It was picturesque in a Tim Burton sort of way, with tendrils of thick mist weaving loosely around the tree trunks. Tentatively Adam continued down the path, scanning in all directions. He was just wondering if this had been a mistake when he heard something. Or, rather, he *felt* it.

A low rumble. *What the hell was that?* Adam took a few more cautious steps forward. There was another rumble, this time louder. *Definitely time to go.* But just as he was about to turn around, he heard a voice faintly calling out, "Stop. Please, stop!"

Adam whirled back. *Was that Beatrice? Is she in trouble?* He took a few more steps, broke into a jog, and then began to run. At first he didn't see it, but luckily Adam was able to stop himself in time, as the trees, ferns, and the path itself abruptly disappeared.

A sinkhole the size of a small ice-skating rink.

Adam cautiously approached the edge and looked over. About 60 feet down, through a loose mist, he saw the bottom—sand.

Another rumble, this time much nearer, and then a loud *whoosh!* Ocean water poured into the sinkhole from a large side tunnel. With it came the woman, sloshing through the ankle-deep water. "No, no, no!" She threw her shovel down in defeat. Whatever she had been trying to do apparently had been thwarted by the tide.

Seemingly unaware of Adam, the woman trudged up to the far end of the sinkhole, where the waves didn't reach. Here her backpack, shoes, socks, and parka—which, in the daylight, Adam now saw was dark green—were arranged on top of a massive piece of driftwood. The woman reached into the backpack, pulled out a cigarette, and sat down. Up above, Adam was busy working out the best way to casually announce his presence without startling her. But before he could come up with the right plan, he saw that she had stood up. Then without warning, she started to strip off her clothes.

Adam quickly slipped behind a tree. *You've got to be kidding me. What the hell am I supposed to do now?* While working on a new plan, he did his best to show restraint and not look down into the sinkhole, but eventually he found himself stealing a peek. The woman had stripped down to her bra and underpants. Even from high up, it was more than clear that she had an achingly gorgeous figure. *Who'd have thought that hidden inside that shapeless mound of parka was this Greek goddess, all soft curves and milky-white skin?*

Beatrice, or whoever she was, impatiently tossed her mane of red hair out of her face and took another drag off her cigarette. Something about the way she did it reminded Adam of a European film star from the 1960s. Monica Vitti or Anita Ekberg, beautiful in that natural, unselfconscious way. From her backpack she removed some dry clothing. But then she stopped and suddenly looked up, directly toward Adam.

Adam pulled back behind the tree and held his breath. *Shit! Did she see me? What the hell am I doing?* He waited nervously, his heart pounding in his throat. When he didn't hear anything, he peeked back down and saw that the woman, still in her underwear, was slowly walking in the opposite direction, toward the mouth of the tunnel, where the ocean waves were rushing in. Adam's relief quickly turned to confusion. *What the hell is she doing now? Going for a swim? The water must be freezing.*

She stopped right where the surf reached her toes. *What in God's name is she doing?* Adam waited. But she did nothing. She just stood there like a statue as each new wave rumbled through the tunnel and into the sinkhole with a gust of wind that gently blew back her hair. Despite feeling like a voyeur, Adam couldn't pull himself away. It was such a strange and beautiful sight, this half-naked woman standing, as if in a trance, with the ocean breathing on her.

A few moments later, she turned and ran back to the driftwood log. As she started pulling on the dry clothes she had taken from her knapsack, Adam looked around to see how she had managed to get down there. He finally spotted one end of the rope she had brought tied to a tree only a few feet from where he was hiding.

Not wanting her to climb up and find him there like a Peeping Tom, Adam turned and quietly crept back toward the cemetery.

The redheaded woman emerged from the woods and passed through the small opening in the cemetery's back fence. When she saw that she was not alone, she stopped. Adam was standing solemnly at a gravestone, doing a rather poor job of pretending to pay his respects. As he looked up, he could tell by her smile that she recognized him.

"Hello," Adam said cordially. Then, doing his best to feign surprise, he added, "Oh, hey . . . last night . . . out on the cliffs."

She nodded. "Mr. Reset Button."

Adam smiled. "Right. Right."

She looked at Adam, and the stillness and intensity of her gaze almost forced him to divert his eyes. Still he did his best to act casual. Pointing to the shovel in her hand, he asked, "Digging graves?"

"Why, do you need one?" She gave Adam a smile and small laugh. "No, I was just looking for something I left back there . . . a long time ago. I wanted to see if I could still find it."

"Oh, cool." Adam looked toward the back fence, pretending to notice it for the first time. "So you used to live around here then?"

"You could say that," she said flatly.

"Cool." Adam cleared his throat. "Cause, you know, I grew up near here too. Kind of a coincidence, us both coming back at the same time."

"In a way." Her face turned serious. "Although I came back to find something, and you came back to put an end to something. Right?"

It took Adam a moment. "Oh, right. You mean me. Last night on the cliffs." Adam forced a laugh. "Well, I wasn't really going to—"

"You don't have to lie about it."

"No, seriously. I was just a little upset. I had no intention of—"

"Boy, you just can't stop, can you, Pinocchio?"

"Seriously, I'm not lying. I wasn't—"

"Whose grave is that?"

"Grave?"

"The one you've been pretending to visit?"

"It's my . . . grandmother's," Adam said before he could stop himself.

She walked closer and looked down at the gravestone. "So your grandmother's name is Cleveland Bertram Oppenlander? Born in 1798, died in 1857." She turned back to Adam, whose face was now burning. "I'm not great at math, but I think that would mean you must be in your nineties."

Adam looked down at the dirt, wishing that six feet of it might magically disappear.

"Lying is boring. Being honest, the way you were last night, is much more interesting." Slinging her shovel over her shoulder, she walked past Adam, adding quietly, "Bye-bye, Mr. Reset Button."

Adam stood helpless as she walked away. He tried to move, to speak, but felt paralyzed.

"Beatrice?" At first Adam wasn't sure if he had said the name out loud.

The woman stopped. Slowly she turned back to Adam. "Why did you call me that?" Her voice was barely audible. "How do you know that name?"

Adam swallowed hard. "Look, my name is Adam Sheppard, and I think . . . I'm pretty sure we knew each other when we were kids. Am I right? Are you Beatrice?"

The woman dropped her shovel.

CHAPTER 14

ELEPHANT GARLIC, HUNGRY VAMPIRES

Art Stout once lived in a teepee. He had lived in a wide variety of places during his lifetime, but the teepee was by far his favorite. His childhood was spent in a historic farmhouse in Northern Connecticut, followed by a college dormitory, and then a bunk bed on an aircraft carrier during the Korean War. During the late '60s, Art bought a used Airstream trailer, in which he traveled around the United States and Mexico. He tried living in a New York City apartment, which was really more of a broom closet. Then there was his apartment in Phoenix, which could have passed for an oven. Moving on to California, he purchased a small parcel of land just south of Mendocino County, where he set up his beloved teepee. He spent the next 10 years in it, by far the happiest years of his life. As Art got older, though, teepee living had begun to take its toll. So these days he and his dog, Nellie, shared a simple one-bedroom house that he had built, which was working out fine for both of them.

Most midafternoons Art went for a stroll in the field behind his house to check on his elephant garlic. Next week was the big farmers' market in Santa Rosa, and Art was looking forward to selling some garlic in the morning, having lunch at Gallina's, that Italian restaurant he loved (fresh-baked focaccia and rosemary

127

olive oil at every table), and then heading over to his appointment with the cardiologist at Santa Rosa Memorial Hospital. At 73 years old Art was pretty healthy, but after a scare with his blood pressure, he had agreed to checkups every three months.

Nellie was running ahead of Art, down the gentle slope, when a strange sound seemed to catch her attention. Nellie froze. There it was again. She barked loudly in its direction. Art, whose hearing was a bit challenged these days, hadn't heard the sound, but Nellie had succeeded in bringing it to his attention. He followed his dog a little farther into the field, and this time Art did hear it.

Oooo-weeee-oooo. It sounded to Art like an alien spaceship from some 1950s B movie.

Nellie charged ahead and then stopped, barking eagerly for Art to join her at the base of the large oak that marked the far end of Art's property. Beyond it a steep incline led up to Highway 128. A logging truck was passing by, but once it was gone, Art heard the eerie sound again.

Ooooo-weeee-ooooo.

It was coming from a shiny object lying on the ground.

Art reached down and picked up the iPhone lodged in the soft dirt at the base of the oak. When it made the alien sound again, Art instinctually touched the word Answer on the cracked screen, and then held it out in front of his mouth the way he'd seen done on *Star Trek.* "Hello?"

On the other end of the line, he heard muffled sounds before a woman's voice came on. "Holy Mother of God! Hold, please! *Please, hold!*"

Blake's secretary, Cory, put Art on hold and then pushed the intercom button. "Blake! He picked up! He picked up his phone!"

Blake flew out from his office. "Give it to me!"

Cory handed him the receiver.

"Dude! I've been worried sick! Where the hell are you?" Blake's voice was equal parts anger, exasperation, and concern.

"I'm under an oak tree," Art answered, a bit confused. When there was no immediate response, Art threw in, "Where the hell are you?"

Blake gave Cory a furious look, then barked into the phone, "Who is this?"

"No need to get stirred up," came the calm voice on the line. "This is Art Stout. Is this your cellular device I found?"

"You found the phone?" Blake forced himself to sound calm. "Um, okay. Where? Where did you find the phone, sir?"

"I just told you, under an oak tree. Down at the bottom of my property."

"Where is that property located, sir? What town, what city, what state?"

"Well, let's see. I'm here in California, but the nearest town isn't real close by."

Blake flailed at Cory. She just stared back, uncomprehending.

Give me a fucking pen! Blake screamed soundlessly.

Art continued. "I'm here in Me__oci_o Cou__y."

"Wait, what?" Blake panicked as the connection broke up. "What did you just say? What county?"

"And I guess the __osest town w__ld be . . ." Art continued on, unable to hear Blake.

"Art! What county? Art, can you hear me?"

"Take Hi__w_y 1__ till you reach Clo____ and turn _____ ____ ___ say, oh, eight or nine miles ___, right on___"

Then the phone cut out completely.

"Art? *Art?*" Blake yelled, then turned to Cory. "Get him back on the line!"

Cory stabbed the Redial button on the phone. Blake waited. It went straight to voice mail. Cory tried again. Again, straight to voice mail.

"What the fuck just happened?" Blake grabbed both sides of his head to keep it from exploding.

"Maybe his battery died?" Cory shrugged, refusing to join in her boss's hysteria.

"And that's my driveway," Art continued, unaware that the phone battery was dead. "There's no street sign, so just be on the lookout for that blackberry bush growing out of the old car frame I told you about. You see that, you know you're on the right road."

Art waited for a response. When none came he tucked the phone into his pocket and strolled back up the hill to tend to his elephant garlic.

◈

Blake stormed into the Cave. Yesterday after screaming at Adam on the phone, he had assumed Adam's guilt would motivate him to call right back. But when he didn't, Blake started calling and texting Adam once every half-hour, and then every 15 minutes. He called while on the treadmill at the gym, while buying condoms at Walgreens, right before screwing his date, and then again after.

The next morning when Blake woke and looked at his phone, he knew he had a major problem. Testing was now a full day behind, and there was no fucking way he was going to push the Expansion release, especially after being crucified by fans last time around for postponing *Lust 4 Flesh 2.*

Blake had called in Pixilate's top three programmers to try and assess the situation. All morning they had worked quietly in Adam's cubical, but now, as Blake came back in to check on their progress, he found that Mitch Silpa was also there. *Of all people,* Blake thought. *Why the fuck is Mitch here today?* Mitch Silpa, a supervising manager Blake had brought in from Virtual Skies at Adiklein's recommendation, was the last person Blake wanted to see in the Cave right now. Mitch was 10 years younger than Blake, good-looking, great at networking, dangerously ambitious, and considered by all to be one of Adiklein's rising superstars. "Keep your enemies close," was the moronic proverb Blake had followed by taking Mitch on. Not that he'd had a choice.

Blake pushed, not so gently, past Mitch to look over his programmers' shoulders at the screens. "Tell me you figured out something for the Hollows patch."

"Sorry, Blake." The young hacker at the keyboard shrugged. "There's nothing on here beyond build v41, which is what Testing already has."

"Fine. But can't you guys just rebuild the patch from there?"

"I know this isn't what you want to hear," the most senior programmer chimed in, "but Adam writes batshit-crazy code." The other two nodded in agreement.

The third programmer, who was flipping through one of Adam's Hardy Boys novels, added, "By the way, Blake, there's nothing more on his system for that mobile app thing you were talking about. He must have done it at home or on his laptop."

Mitch started to snort. "That was his too? Oh, I fucking love it, Blake!"

An uncomfortable silence followed, before the programmer at the keyboard broke in. "We did find those other project folders you were looking for. They were on his external drive."

"Yeah?" Blake said with relief.

"It's a huge frigging thing he named 'Zombie.v12.'"

"Right. Good. Just disconnect the drive, and I'll take it."

"Sure thing." The programmer complied. "But just so you know, it's encrypted."

❖

"I've texted him five times, I sent an e-mail, I left three voice messages." White earbud cords dangling from her ears, Jane walked through the house, looking for anything useful to help track down Adam. When Blake had called earlier that morning to explain what had happened, she was already in the parking lot of the Marriott where Day Two of *Yoga Bliss International* was about to begin. Annoyed, and of course concerned, Jane left the conference and returned home to help figure out where Adam might have gone.

"What about credit cards? And ATMs? Did you check with the bank?" Blake pressed.

"I already checked twice, Blake. He hasn't used any credit cards since renting that car. And he hasn't withdrawn any more cash. Why would he do this? I just don't see—"

"And you're sure he took his laptop with him?"

"Yes, Blake." Jane was sick of Blake asking the same questions over and over. "He took his laptop, he took some clothing, he took some books, his medicine, and some protein shake mix, and that's all—"

"Did you file the missing person's report?" Blake cut in.

"No. I called Dr. M., who's on his way over."

"I told you to file a missing person's report!"

"What I'm *missing* right now, Blake, is a once-in-a-lifetime hatha yoga intensive with Rick Statham!"

"File the goddamn report, Jane!"

Jane walked into the bedroom. "Can we please not overreact?" Jane sighed. "He'll turn up. He always has before. Right?"

"Did you two have an argument? Is that what happened?"

"No, we did not have an argument."

"Did you forget to give him his meds? Have you been feeding him?"

"*I'm his wife, Blake, not a fucking zookeeper!*" Jane exploded. Less than 24 hours ago, she had been chanting a sacred, heart-opening sutra in the Marriott ballroom, but the good vibes had definitely evaporated. Jane sat down on the bed and took a deep breath. "Look, you and I both know that I love Adam and I take very, very good care of him. But sometimes I need a little time for myself, okay? Being married to a man like Adam isn't easy, and—"

"Oh, really, Jane? How bad is it? Tell me how rough it is!"

"Jesus, Blake, why am I even listening to you?" Jane pulled her earbuds out and dropped the phone onto the bed next to her.

"*Because without me, Jane, you would be fucked right now!*" the earbuds squealed. "*You came to me when Jack left you, and you had nothing. Nothing! You would still be living in your car with two kids if I hadn't introduced you to Adam . . .*"

Jane rubbed her eyes. Then for the first time she noticed the note on the dresser. Jane picked up one of the earbuds and stuck it back in her ear. "He left a note."

"Wait, what?"

Jane slowly walked over to the dresser. "He left a note, Blake."

"A note? Well, what does it say?"

Jane picked it up and was immediately taken by the quality of the stationery—the rosy hue of the envelope, the texture and weight of the paper inside. It seemed inconceivable to Jane that Adam would have picked out anything so tasteful. That he had taken the time to do so, Jane knew, was only added cause for concern.

After reading the Virgil Coates quote about "the life I was meant to live, but for whatever reason I did not," Jane exhaled and shook her head. *Why did Adam always have to be so convoluted about everything?* But reading on, Jane found lines that were much more direct. "I can't live like this anymore . . . It's not your fault. It's me . . ." *This was starting to sound like a Dear John letter,* Jane thought. *Not good.* But as she kept reading, the letter began to imply something even graver. "You and the kids will be better off without me . . . Please don't try to find me. I need to be alone. To find my peace . . ."

"Oh God."

"Oh God? What do you mean, 'Oh God'?" Blake sounded like he was trying to climb through the phone. "Jane! What does the note say?"

"It sounds like he's going to—"

Just then the doorbell rang. Jane looked up from the note and remembered that Dr. Mendelson was on his way over.

"I have to go, Blake. I'll call you back."

"Wait! Don't you hang up on me!"

"It's Dr. M.," Jane said. "He'll know what to do."

"*JANE!* What does the note—"

Jane hung up.

Moving down the hallway toward the front door, Jane reread the note a second time. She was shocked that her husband was actually capable of doing something like this. *If he was so unhappy, why didn't he just say something? You don't just leave. What about me? What about the kids?* The whole situation was so over the top, so dramatic, that Jane was starting to feel like she was in some kind of movie. Which was oddly exciting to her.

Jane opened the door. The severe expression on Dr. Mendelson's face said he was there to take charge. "What is it, Jane? Did you hear from Adam?"

Her hand trembling, Jane held the note out to Dr. Mendelson.

Dr. Mendelson took the note and read it. Then he looked up, his face somber. "We'll get Adam back, Jane. Trust me. I know Adam better than he knows himself."

CHAPTER 15

THE PRINCESS,
THE THIEF, AND A
BOAT NAMED PARADISO

Adam sat quietly in his rental car, parked in a vacant stretch near the bottom of Main Street. Beatrice and her oversize green parka were packed tightly into the passenger seat just to his right. The circumstances of life had kept them apart for over three decades, but now all that separated Adam from his childhood companion was the hand brake and two cup holders.

They sat there staring out at the ocean for several minutes. Neither of them knew where to begin. The drive back from the Little River Cemetery had been silent, so Adam was still unsure if she remembered anything about him beyond his name. She seemed to have fallen into a state of shock the moment he had called out her name, as if the word itself had cast a spell over her.

"So . . . Do you remember me, then?"

Adam heard the crunch and crinkle of Beatrice's parka as she turned to face him. "Of course I remember you, Adam." Her voice was a raspy whisper.

Adam returned her gaze, and she greeted him with a smile—not the mysterious Mona Lisa this time, but something more direct. It felt like looking into the sun. "I can see it's you," she said. "But you've changed. Your eyes, I remember them as being lighter."

"A lot has changed." Adam gave a resigned shrug.

After some more uncomfortable silence, Beatrice said that she needed to make a quick phone call. To give her some privacy, Adam gallantly offered to go fetch two cups of coffee, with the idea that when he came back, they could sit somewhere along the bluff and catch up. *All very reasonable,* Adam thought. But once he was alone again, waiting in line for the coffee, he had time to think, and then to panic. What the hell did he think was going to happen next? They weren't kids anymore. She was a grown woman, one whom Adam knew nothing about, and she knew nothing about him.

When he returned with the coffee, he found Beatrice waiting at one of the picnic tables in the grass field across from Main Street. They began talking, and Adam was so nervous that, within minutes, he found himself unwittingly pulling out his wallet to show Beatrice pictures of his wife, Jane, and the kids. "This is from our honeymoon in Hawaii. That's why we have the, um, swimming noodles and all that," Adam said aloud, while another voice inside him was screaming, *Abort! Abort!*

"These aren't the best pictures," he continued, rushing to put them back in his wallet. "The best ones are on my phone, which I lost, but anyway, that's us."

"Your wife is very attractive," Beatrice said politely. "And the kids?"

"Madison and Chandler."

Beatrice looked confused. "And they're yours? I mean, they don't look—"

Adam had dealt with this before. "They're from Jane's previous relationship, but I adopted them when we got married. Yep, it's a good arrangement." Immediately Adam wished he could take back the words.

"Arrangement?"

"Wow, did I really just say that?" Adam gave a laugh. "I just meant . . . See, Blake, a guy I work with—my best friend, really—he set us up, Jane and me. And we got along great. Jane had just been through a tough separation, and with the two kids and all, she was in a bit of a spot, so I was happy to help her out too."

Adam felt like a schoolboy explaining why he didn't have his homework. "So I guess Jane, she keeps me grounded, and, you know . . . We fit together." *Really?* he thought. *Did I really just say that?*

"It sounds as if you're happy." There was a hint of a question nestled in Beatrice's words.

"I am." Adam shook his head then quickly switched to nodding. It was like at the cemetery when Beatrice called him out for lying. But this was much worse because she *wasn't* calling him out, she was trying to be nice. "Look, I'm sorry. I sound like such an idiot. You know that I'm not happy. It's just that . . . Sometimes when things get crazy at work, and when I get too run-down, I can get a little batty."

"What kind of work do you do that makes you batty?"

"It's not all that interesting," Adam warned, but when he looked up, he saw that Beatrice honestly wanted to know. "I'm an engineer. Computer programmer. I make video games."

Beatrice's face lit up. "You make games?" Beatrice broke into laughter.

"Wait, what's so funny about that?"

"It's just so perfect." Beatrice beamed. "When we were kids, you used to make up all these wonderful games." Beatrice scooted closer to Adam. "I remember so many crazy games, treasure hunts, and wild adventures, don't you?"

"Well, yeah, kind of. Just bits and pieces, really. It was so long ago—"

"Oh!" Beatrice broke in. "There was this one game we used to play with orange peels."

"I remember that one!" Adam brightened. "I was just thinking about that! You were like a princess, right?"

"And you were a thief." Beatrice smiled wistfully.

"That was a pretty elaborate game."

"One of your very first. And now look at you. Still putting your imagination to good use."

"Well, I'm not so sure about that."

Just as Adam was about to make some self-deprecating comment, Beatrice reached over and took his hand. Her touch seemed to open up an electrical current between them that made Adam's pulse quicken.

"I remember being so sad when you left Little River, Adam. You were my only friend back then."

Adam nodded and looked down at Beatrice's hand touching his. He could feel a strangely intense sensation of heat, almost like burning. Perhaps she was feeling the same thing, because she quickly removed her hand and took a sip of coffee.

At first Beatrice seemed reluctant to share much about her own life. But while walking with Adam on the footpaths along the bluff, she slowly began to open up. Her parents had separated shortly after Adam's parents took him away. "I went with my mother," Beatrice explained. "She's French, so we moved back to Paris. I grew up there, for the most part."

"I thought I detected something like an accent."

"*Oui*, monsieur. *C'est vrai*," Beatrice said with a playful smile. "Mom was an activist—environment, human rights, all of it. So we were constantly running around to demonstrations, protests, speaking out on behalf of one cause or another."

"Sounds exciting."

"It was. Of course, I turned out a lot like my mother, wanting to save the whole world as soon as possible." Beatrice stopped to pick up a discarded soda can on the side of the path. "In my twenties I got involved with an NGO doing charity work in India. It was an incredible experience. Then while I was working in Tibet, I met someone and ended up in a relationship . . . a very destructive one. I guess you could say he was the wrong kind of man."

"Like an evil monk?"

Beatrice laughed. "No, no. Like a wealthy, handsome, charismatic philanthropist who was also out to save humanity."

"Oh, right. That sounds much worse."

"Much, *much* worse, believe me. Especially if you follow him around the world, devoting yourself to his great causes only to find that behind the charity is just a selfish agenda. Behind the pseudospirituality is narcissism, drugs . . . other women."

"I'm sorry," Adam said gently.

Beatrice simply shrugged. "I was as much a part of the problem. Lying to myself mostly. Pretending to be something I wasn't. Years of useless virtue, trying to fix the world, never fixing anything."

Adam nodded. "And after that?"

"I traveled a lot, mostly on my own. Became very independent, but also quite closed off. I was looking for a Reset button, maybe." Beatrice looked at Adam again with a hint of a smile. "Sometimes you have to lose everything before you can discover the path you were always meant to follow."

"And did you? Discover that for yourself?"

"I did. And what's funny is that it was always right there," Beatrice said, a glimmer of serenity in her eyes. "I'd just been looking in the wrong direction."

Beatrice gazed out at the horizon.

Adam looked out as well. He wanted to ask Beatrice more. He remembered how the night before she had said something about doing research, but before he could ask about it, there was a loud ringing sound from Beatrice's parka.

"I'm sorry; hold on a sec." Beatrice pulled her cell phone from her pocket. It was unusually large, like one of those satellite phones Adam had seen mountain climbers use on the Discovery Channel.

Beatrice didn't take the call. She put the phone back in her pocket and then looked at Adam. She seemed to want to say something to him, something serious, but then she shook her head. Instead she sighed. "Would you mind giving me a ride somewhere?"

Adam drove Beatrice north out of Mendocino, up Highway 1. Just before reaching Fort Bragg, they passed over a bridge high above a river that emptied out into the Pacific. Once across, Beatrice directed Adam to turn down a steep, winding road that gradually led down below the bridge to Noyo Harbor. There were several restaurants, a few dive bars, but not much else. The nearest docks were for commercial fishing vessels, but up near a bend in the river was an area for private boats.

Beatrice instructed Adam to pull up to the far end of the parking lot, closest to the private moorings. As they drove past the booth by the gated entrance to the dock, she gave a quick look to see who was on duty. She had explained earlier that she wasn't technically allowed to dock there since she didn't have a current California registration. However, one of the night guards, a guy named Hank, had agreed to let her stay as long as it wasn't for too long.

Adam stopped the car.

"That's her, over there." Beatrice pointed to a large green-and-white sailboat. Written in script on the forward side of the vessel was *Paradiso 9.*

"Wow, you weren't kidding." On the drive over, she had told Adam that she lived on a boat, but he'd thought she was joking.

"And you sail it? By yourself?" he asked.

"All over the world."

"So you actually live *on* it—on the boat? Like it's your house?"

Beatrice laughed, clearly enjoying Adam's enthusiasm. "Not always, no. It depends on where I'm heading and where I'm docked. But, yes, it is 'like my house.'"

"What's your favorite place?" Adam blurted out. "The most amazing place you've ever been?" Looking at Beatrice, he realized how childish he must sound. "Sorry, I know that's a ridiculous question. I've just always wanted to travel, but have never really been able to."

Beatrice didn't seem to think Adam's question was ridiculous, taking a few long moments to consider it. "In the space between,"

Beatrice finally said. "Out on the open water, between destinations. That has always been my favorite place to be."

Adam tried to imagine that. "It sounds like freedom."

"It is . . . but sometimes," a remorseful smile flashed across Beatrice's face, "sometimes it's just running. There are all sorts of ways people can get stuck."

Adam noticed a gentle patter on the roof. It had begun to rain, just lightly enough to ease the sudden silence inside the car. Beatrice looked serious again as she picked at the sand beneath her nails.

"Adam," she said quietly. "Do you ever remember your dreams?"

Adam thought about it. The way she asked the question demanded a level of honesty that he wanted to live up to. At the same time, the mention of dreams immediately evoked discomfort. Dreams were something Dr. Mendelson encouraged him to talk about, but whenever Adam did, it always left him feeling empty afterward, as if putting dreams into words had somehow defiled them. He had learned to keep his dreams, those important ones, at least, to himself.

"Sometimes I do. Not always. Why?"

Beatrice didn't speak for a long while. The rain was now amplifying the intimacy within the car, giving Adam the feeling of being a child again with Beatrice, huddled inside their hollowed-out tree together.

"Three nights ago," Beatrice began, "I think it was Thursday, I was sailing up the coast. I was close to San Francisco, near the Farallon Islands. I hadn't actually been planning on stopping in Mendocino, but that night I had a dream."

Adam shifted slightly in his seat. He was doing his best to listen to Beatrice the way she listened to him, however, that slight anxiety he felt the moment she had mentioned dreams was increasing.

"In this dream," she continued, "I was a kid. And it felt as if I was back in Little River. It was hard to tell, though, because I was spinning. It wasn't a bad feeling. In fact, it felt wonderful. I felt warm and free and safe all at the same time."

As Beatrice spoke Adam could feel the blood drain from his face. Thursday night was his birthday dinner, the same night he had dreamt of lying on the school yard merry-go-round, spinning round and round. *Could it be possible that Beatrice had had the same dream?*

"Then I felt something touching my hand," Beatrice went on. "And when I looked down, I saw this little butterfly. It was beautiful, and I understood that it needed help to fly; it wanted *me* to help it fly. But then," Beatrice's expression darkened, "I'm not sure what happened, dreams can get so crazy, but it felt like something had gotten hold of it and was pulling the butterfly down into the dirt. I started digging for it, deeper and deeper into the earth, and when I finally found it again, it was filthy, and one of its wings was crumpled. But it was alive, so I tried to pick it up, but then—" Beatrice covered her mouth. "I saw *something* in the ground, holding on to it, attached to it, like . . . like some kind of parasite. And the more I tried to lift the butterfly, the more this thing pulled back, ripping it apart as I pulled and . . ."

While Beatrice had been speaking, the buzzing tinnitus in Adam's ear had grown louder and louder, as if provoked by her words. As discreetly as possible, he stuck a finger in his ear and wiggled it around, but Beatrice noticed. "Oh God, I'm sorry. Is this too much information?"

"No, no. *I'm* sorry. Please, go on," Adam said, doing his best to look relaxed. The last thing he wanted right now was a damn panic attack.

"Well, when I woke up the next morning, all I could think was, there must be something here in Mendocino from my past that I had to come back for. And the whole digging thing—" Beatrice shook her head and gave a small laugh. "I know it sounds silly, but as a kid I put some things together, you know, after you left. Keepsakes. And I put them in a box, an old, metal lockbox that I buried in this special place I used to go to—"

"The sinkhole behind the cemetery," Adam said and immediately wished he hadn't.

"You knew about the—" Seeing Adam's face, Beatrice quickly put it together. "You saw me down there."

To his surprise Adam heard nothing accusatory in her voice. "I truly didn't mean to spy on you. I was just trying to find you and I—"

"It's all right, Adam." Beatrice brushed her hair back out of her face. "Just don't tell anyone about that sinkhole, okay? There aren't many places like that left. Places with that kind of . . . energy, I guess. You know this whole area used to be considered sacred land. The Pomo, the Native Americans who once lived here, believed this was the edge of the world."

Adam remembered the photographs in the lobby of the Mendocino Hotel.

"They had a wonderful phrase to describe this area," Beatrice continued. "I'm pretty sure it was your grandmother, Anne, who told me about it. Did she mention it to you? The Pomo called this 'the land where skies grow thin.'"

"Where skies grow thin,'" Adam repeated the words. "I like that. 'Where skies grow thin.' Between what and what, do you think?"

Beatrice didn't respond right away. "The Pomo called it 'Ike Papakolu.' The Dream World." Beatrice looked at Adam with her penetrating green eyes. "Well, I couldn't find that old lockbox, but I did find an old friend."

Adam smiled at this. The tinnitus buzz in his ear had died down a bit.

Beatrice's eyes looked like they were searching his for something. "It's all very curious, don't you think? The two of us running into each other like this."

"It is." Adam nodded, not knowing what else to say. He considered sharing his own dream, the one that may have drawn him back here as well, but thinking about it only amplified the anxiety he was trying to suppress.

The patter of rain on the roof of the car grew gentler. Silently Beatrice continued to look at Adam, who did his best to relax and hold her gaze. He started to get the distinct feeling that she was trying to communicate something to him without words. Perhaps it was just his imagination, but it was as if she was tugging at something deep inside him with her eyes.

Beatrice's phone rang. The moment was broken. She pulled out the phone and looked at it, but didn't answer. "I'm so sorry, Adam, but I need to take care of this. I should really get going."

"Sure, of course." Adam felt as if he had just been snapped out of a trance. "So, what are you doing later on? Would you maybe like to . . . ?" Adam's voice trailed off as he saw the pained expression on Beatrice's face.

"Oh, Adam. I should have told you this earlier, but I have to leave."

"When?"

"As soon as possible. I was supposed to have sailed farther north by now to help with all the packing and preparations, so now I'm really pushing it."

"Oh, okay." Adam was unable to hide his disappointment. "Preparations for what?"

Beatrice took a moment, as if to find just the right words. "A trip I'm helping my father get ready for."

"Oh, that's great. So your father is still . . . "

"He and I lost touch for a long time, then we reconnected about ten years ago."

"Well, maybe after you're done helping him—"

"It's more complicated than that. It's a long trip, and it involves a lot of other people. I'm one of the organizers and, you see . . . I'm going as well . . . to help my father with the work he does—it's not easy to explain."

"That's cool. I was just thinking we could . . . How long will you be gone?"

"A long time."

Adam understood she was not going to give him any more details. Fighting disappointment, he shrugged. "Maybe we can keep in touch. Are you on Facebook?"

Beatrice stared blankly at Adam.

"You don't know about Facebook?" Adam was stunned.

"I guess I'm a bit behind the times."

"E-mail? Can I reach you on e-mail?"

"Listen, Adam . . ." Beatrice took a deep breath. "The truth is, you and I are from very different worlds, and . . . Maybe it's better, for both of us, to just leave our chance meeting as one of life's poetic little moments. Don't you think?"

It was not what Adam wanted to hear, but he nodded. She was right, he told himself. He was married, and she was about to take off on some long trip, so what was the point of trying to prolong the inevitable? "You're probably right," Adam said quietly. "Just one of those crazy coincidences, I guess."

Beatrice opened the door to get out.

"Don't forget your shovel," Adam added as Beatrice slung her knapsack over her shoulder.

As she opened the back door to take the shovel, she spoke matter-of-factly. "So, you've got to promise me you won't try to jump off another cliff."

Adam sighed as if he were at the end of a botched date. "Don't worry. Whatever I end up doing, killing myself is not high on the list."

"Why do you say that?"

The first words that came to mind were ones that he had underlined and read over and over again. They belonged to Virgil Coates, at least originally, but recently they'd become part of Adam too. "I don't want to die without at least trying to understand why I've lived."

Beatrice stood with the door open, looking stunned. Adam was still feeling too disappointed to make much of it.

"Well, I'm sorry if I delayed you," he said, starting the engine. "Best of luck on your big trip."

"Yes, thank you." Beatrice sounded as if she was still in shock.

"So, uh, good-bye." Adam looked at Beatrice, who had not moved.

"Yes. Sorry." Regaining her composure with a deep breath, Beatrice said, "Good-bye, Adam," and shut the car door.

Adam sat in the car for a few moments, watching Beatrice walk away in the rain. Halfway to the entrance of the docks, she stopped and looked back at him. Then she pulled out her clunky satellite phone to make a call.

Adam put the car in gear and drove away.

CHAPTER 16

ADAM'S IMPENETRABLE
SUIT OF ARMOR

Pete was busy restocking the well after an unexpected happy hour rush, when he noticed Adam walk through the lobby. Pete was just about to ask if he'd had any luck finding that mysterious redhead, but Adam's slumped shoulders communicated everything Pete needed to know. He'd either had no success, or he had found her but she'd changed so much in the past 30 years he wished he'd hadn't. Either way the news was not good, Pete thought to himself as he opened a fresh jar of Maraschinos.

Upstairs Adam kicked off his shoes and flopped down on the bed. Finding Beatrice had turned out to be worse than he could have possibly imagined. The incredible connection they had felt as children was still there, but as suddenly as she'd dropped back into his life, she was gone again, and this time for good.

After a half-hour of sulking, Adam found himself staring at the phone on the bedside table. Was it time to surrender? He could already feel the prison walls of his dependent past rising back up around him. Back inside, he would need Jane again. He would need Blake. He would need his medication, his work, and even Dr. M. Adam reached over and moved the phone onto the bed next to him. "I'm sorry, Jane," Adam mumbled in practice. "I'm okay. I just needed to . . . I'm fine and I'm sorry. I just . . ." Adam placed a hand on the receiver but didn't pick it up. *What if Beatrice was right?* Adam thought. *What if I really did come up here to kill myself? Maybe I should just go back out there and finish the job. Everyone would be better off if I just —*

The phone rang.

Adam jumped to his feet. *Who the hell could be calling me?* Adam's mind raced for an answer. *The front desk?*

The phone rang a second time. Adam decided the best thing to do was just answer it. He let it ring a third time, then picked up.

"Hello?"

There was static on the line before a female voice said, "Adam?"

His heart started to race. "Beatrice? Is that you?"

More static. "Yes. It's me, Adam." She sounded excited but distant.

The static got even worse. *She must be calling from that crazy sat phone,* he thought. Then the line cleared a little, and he heard her say, "Can you hear me?"

"Yes, I can hear you! Can you hear me? The connection isn't great."

"Listen, Adam, I was able to rearrange things so I can stay a little longer. Just another day, but I want to see you. Do you have plans for dinner tonight?"

Adam tried to contain his excitement. Unable to come up with anything clever, he simply said, "I would love more than anything to see you."

"Come to the harbor, then. Eight o'clock?"

"I'll be there."

"Adam?"

"Yes?"

"There's a reason we met. It wasn't just coincidence." With that, she hung up.

Adam bounded down the stairs and toward the bar. Pete was busy mixing a Sazerac for one of the leftover wedding guests, but Adam was too excited to wait for him to finish up.

"Hey, Pete, I need a favor." Adam said, a little out of breath.

Pete turned to Adam with a bewildered look on his face. "Boy, my Spidey senses must be totally out of whack. When you came in a little while ago you looked awful. You doing all right?"

"I'm doing great. In fact, I need another bottle of wine. A magic one, if possible."

Pete broke out into a huge grin. "Coming right up."

◈

Adam drove down the steep road leading to Noyo Harbor with a bottle of 2005 Goldeneye Pinot Noir seat-belted in the passenger seat. Pete had only one bottle left, but he was more than happy to contribute to Adam's cause.

When he pulled into the parking lot, Adam noticed a light was on in the guard's booth by the private docks. The muffled sounds of a television could be heard as Adam approached the window. Inside he saw a large man—Hank, he presumed—leaning back in a battered office chair, facing the small TV on the desk. A rerun of *Touched by an Angel* was on, a bit strange considering Hank looked like a former Hells Angel himself. Then Adam realized the man was sound asleep. A clipboard for signing in hung from a nail by the window, but Adam didn't want to accidentally get Beatrice in trouble, so he decided to keep walking.

The docks swayed slightly as Adam reached the last aisle, where *Paradiso 9* waited in the next-to-last slip. Beatrice was smoking a cigarette on deck. She was wearing a long, white dress, her red hair down around her shoulders, and on her feet were a pair of giant, black Kevlar sailing boots. Despite the boots and cigarette, Beatrice looked like an angel. *Not some cheese-ball TV angel,* Adam thought, *but a classic angel.* And the way the boat gently rose and fell gave the illusion that she was floating.

"Hank give you any trouble?" Beatrice asked as Adam reached the edge of the boat.

"Nope. You look beautiful . . . like an angel," Adam added awkwardly.

"Okay, thank you." Beatrice smiled, putting Adam at ease. She dotted her cigarette out in an ashtray as Adam cautiously stepped onto the boat. At first he felt a bit unsteady, but it wasn't too bad.

"I brought some wine. Pete, the bartender at the hotel, recommended it. Said it might even be magic."

"Thank you, Pete—and of course you too." Beatrice examined the bottle.

"And this," Adam pulled from his jacket a long rectangular box wrapped in a plastic bag. "Just a little something I got for you."

Beatrice accepted it, but her look was wary. "I have to warn you, Adam, I'm not very gracious when it comes to gifts from men. That evil philanthropist I told you about once tried to win me back with a rather expensive bracelet, which I not-so-accidentally tossed overboard."

"Phew! Thank God I didn't get you that expensive bracelet I was looking at." Adam smiled. "Go ahead. If you don't like it, you can throw it overboard too."

Beatrice reached into the bag and pulled out a box of new number-two pencils.

"Just in case you have to do some more late-night research. You won't have to go bothering any drunk tourists."

Beatrice was unable to suppress a smile. "Thank you. Now, Mr. Sheppard, if you would follow me, please." Pencils in hand, she turned to lead Adam down into the cabin.

"Holy cow," was the best Adam could muster. The interior of Beatrice's boat was a wonder in itself. Judging from the outside—a neat, trim, no-nonsense green sailboat with white trim—Adam never would have suspected the plush, Bohemian world within. Velvet drapes, Persian carpets, and amber lamp shades lent everything a warm glow. The built-in bookcases were crammed with assorted volumes, seashells, lanterns, and other knickknacks. Throughout the cabin hung framed photographs, maps, and unusual pieces of art from all over the world. *Her own clutter*, Adam thought, *in a boat-shaped cubicle.* He was most amazed by how everything fit inside the modest space.

On top of one of the bookcases, Adam noticed what looked like a statue of an Egyptian cat. Then it sprang down onto a railing and walked over to him. "This is Anush," Beatrice said. Adam reached out to pet her. "Careful, she bites." Adam pulled his hand away just in time. "She's an Abyssinian," Beatrice said, kicking off her boots. "Take your shoes off and make yourself comfortable. I'm just finishing up with dinner."

Beatrice took the bottle of wine from Adam and slipped into the galley.

Careful to avoid Anush, Adam removed his shoes before looking around. He recognized the temples of Angkor Wat in the background of one photograph. Beatrice was sitting inside a giant tree root that wrapped around her like a snake. "You've been to some amazing places," Adam said as he continued to look at the pictures.

In the more recent ones, Beatrice appeared to be with the same group of people. One older man, probably in his 70s, looked familiar to Adam, although he couldn't quite place him. Before he could ask, he spotted a photo of Beatrice sitting with her friends in front of the Great Sphinx.

"Wow, you've been to Egypt." Another picture showed Beatrice smoking a hookah in a crowded café. "I've always wanted to go to Egypt." Adam sighed. "I keep planning to go there, but for some reason, I always end up in Hawaii instead."

"If you look on the wall behind you," Beatrice called from the galley where she was chopping vegetables, "just above that abalone shell there's a little keepsake from my last trip there. You might find it interesting."

It was a small, copper medallion the size of a silver dollar, hung from a black leather string. On its face was a worn symbol that looked like a backward S with a curlicue at the bottom. *Not a hieroglyph,* Adam thought. *It doesn't even look Egyptian really. More like those Native American petroglyphs I saw back at the hotel. Obviously old, and . . . vaguely familiar.*

"How old is it?" Adam finally asked.

"About 3500 B.C. My father gave it to me. I think he found it in Alexandria."

Travels with her father, Adam thought. *Probably the old guy in the pictures.* "The symbol, what is it?" Adam asked.

"A hippocampus," Beatrice said as her knife glided from fennel to parsley in her vegetable-chopping sonata.

"Hippocampus? Like the part of the brain?"

"Yes, but it's also the proper name for something else."

"What?"

"A sea horse."

"Okay, right." Adam touched the *S* with his finger. "I thought it looked familiar."

There was a rest in Beatrice's chopping recital. "Familiar?"

"Just reminded me of this book I have. It has a little sea horse on the cover."

"What book?"

"It's pretty obscure. Called *Navigations of the Hidden Domain.* Sort of a philosophy book, written in the '60s by a guy named Virgil Coates. Brilliant, but a bit of a crackpot, by all accounts."

Adam thought he heard a stifled laugh come from Beatrice. When he glanced over, though, her back was to him and she was chopping again.

"Sounds interesting."

"Well, I've always had a thing for philosophy. I mean, I'm no scholar or anything, and even though I don't always understand it, there's something about *Navigations* that really—I don't know—speaks to me."

Adam noticed that the chopping had stopped again. When he glanced over, he saw that Beatrice had turned and was looking at him directly now.

"And where did you find this obscure book?"

"Where?" Adam shrugged. "I bought it from a homeless guy who sells stuff outside the building where I work in San Francisco. That, and a nearly complete library of Hardy Boys mysteries."

There was a pause. "I'll be right back," Beatrice finally said. "I need to fetch a corkscrew." She turned and disappeared through a beaded curtain that softly clattered when she passed.

Alone, Adam continued to explore the cabin. At the front of the boat was a set of heavy drapes, behind which he found a much smaller room with a low ceiling. On the floor were tatami cushions and a black, lacquered Japanese table with candles on either side of an elaborately carved incense bowl.

Half-hidden beneath the table, Adam saw some open shoe boxes that seemed to have been hastily stowed. Quickly crouching down he saw they contained cassette tapes—*my God, she still has cassettes*—some half-burnt candles, assorted papers, and glass jars filled with herbs and dried plants. Adam stood up and was about to close the drapes when he noticed the painting hanging just above the table. It was of Beatrice. Nude.

Her body floated in the night sky above the ocean, and her face was almost completely obscured by her mane of red hair. It had a dreamlike, surreal quality, but still it made Adam flush. Top among the conflicting emotions it aroused in Adam was jealousy of whoever had painted it.

"A friend of mine from Paris painted it." Adam turned to see that Beatrice had returned to the main cabin and was pouring wine into two glasses. "He was in art school at the time. A bit of a Magritte rip-off, but I've always loved it." She came over with the two glasses of wine and, handing one to Adam, she smiled and said, "Here's to reunions." She raised her glass. "And to my old friend, Mr. Reset Button—no, wait, I've got a better name for you. To my old friend, the Thief."

Adam raised his glass in response. "It's wonderful seeing you again, Beatrice."

They both sipped their wine. Adam thought it was good, perhaps even magical, at least to his uneducated palate. Beatrice seemed to like it too, which made it magical enough.

"Did you know," Beatrice's eyes twinkled, "that Beatrice is not my real name?"

"Wait. What?"

"It's a nickname. Your grandmother Anne gave it to me. It's from Dante's *Divine Comedy*—at least I think that's where she got it. Beatrice is the angel who leads Dante up out of Purgatory."

"So what's your real name?"

"Are you sure you want to know?" Before Adam had a chance to respond, Beatrice added, "I love the name Beatrice, and I love that you're the only person in the whole world who calls me that."

"Well, okay, cheers to Dante then." Adam smiled and raised his glass.

They sat at the small built-in dining table, Beatrice sipping her wine, Adam devouring his food. Pasta in a red vodka sauce with garlic and black olives, lightly steamed broccoli with lemon juice and olive oil, crusty French bread, and a butter lettuce salad with fennel and orange—it was, Beatrice said, simple fare, but for Adam it was a feast fit for the gods.

"This is delicious. Is this spaghetti?" Adam said between mouthfuls.

"Pappardelle," Beatrice corrected.

"I love pappardelle." Adam inhaled another bite, completely unaware of the sauce that had splashed onto his nose. "I can't tell you how tired I am of health shakes and protein bars and tofu and kale."

"Why eat those things if you hate them so much?"

"To stay healthy. Since I sit at a desk all the time. I've got a lot of stomach issues too. My wife, Jane, is really into nutrition."

"It's nice she takes care of you like that," Beatrice said, buttering a piece of baguette.

"Yeah. But every week some new study comes out saying that what used to be good is now bad for you and whatever used to kill you will now make you live forever. Drives me nuts."

"Maybe those studies are looking too much in one direction."

"What do you mean?"

"Well, maybe they should take into account how a person feels while they're eating the food, not just the food itself."

Adam, puzzled, looked at Beatrice. "What do my feelings have to do with a food's nutritional value?"

"You're half the equation, aren't you?"

"Sure, to a certain extent. But, I mean, a carrot is still a carrot and a pepperoni pizza is still a pepperoni pizza, no matter how I feel about it."

"Does that mean that a protein bar made by some computer program, tossed down while you're racing to work, is better for you than pasta, salad, and a slice of buttered French bread eaten while relaxing on a sailboat in a scenic harbor with an attractive woman?" Beatrice batted her eyelids comically.

Adam conceded the point with a smile as he bit into his bread.

Beatrice served the salad. Adam wasn't sure why the salad came last, but he was enjoying himself too much to ask any questions. Before he could dig in, Beatrice disappeared momentarily and returned with a small, dried purple flower, crumbled it in her hands and then sprinkled it over Adam's salad.

"What's that?"

"You mentioned that your stomach was bothering you, and this will help." Beatrice held out her hand. "Smell."

Adam did. Instantaneously the scent transported him back to his grandmother's house, to racing down the field to meet Beatrice.

"That smell—" Adam couldn't finish his sentence.

"It's called horsemint. It grows wild around here."

Adam didn't have words to describe how it made him feel. *Was it simply nostalgia? Or something much deeper?*

"Horsemint?"

Beatrice nodded. She was looking at Adam in that strange way again, the way she had done back in his car in the rain, as if trying to reach him on a frequency that he did not yet know how to tune into.

What Adam did next was so impulsive and unlike him that he was as shocked by it as Beatrice. Without thinking, Adam sniffed Beatrice's hand again and then let out a remarkably accurate sounding horse whinny. The brief silence that followed was broken when Beatrice burst into laughter. Relieved, Adam laughed as well.

Outside, a thick mist crept in off the ocean, blanketing Noyo Harbor. Off in the distance, a foghorn sounded. Frogs along the riverbank croaked, boats creaked at their moorings, and from a green-and-white sailboat in the next-to-last slip, faint laughter could be heard.

Adam took another sip of wine and then readjusted the throw pillow he was leaning against. Beatrice was lounging comfortably on the cushion next to him. After dinner they had slipped into an easy banter: sharing stories, teasing each other, arguing points back and forth, but with no need to win. Perhaps it was the gentle rocking of the boat on the water, or maybe just the effects of the wine, but Adam felt relaxed in a way that he had not known in years. He was, at last, "engaging with the present moment." *Dr. M. would be proud*, Adam thought with a smile.

During a lull in the conversation, Adam noticed his hand was resting on the floor only a few inches away from Beatrice's. He began to imagine how easy it would be to just reach over and take her hand in his. *Would that be too forward? She touched your hand back at the picnic table on the bluff.* Building his nerve, Adam's pinkie gave a little twitch; it was enough to cause his heart to jump up into his throat.

He glanced up to see if Beatrice was aware of the epic struggle taking place inside him. She seemed lost in thought. But then, out of nowhere, and as casually as reaching for her wine glass, she reached over and touched Adam's hand. Adam's pounding heart slammed back down from his throat into his chest like a falling piano. "Is this all right, Adam? That I hold your hand?" she asked.

"Of course." Adam's voice was unaccountably hoarse.

Beatrice scooted closer to Adam and took his hand in both of hers.

"Adam." Her voice was low and intimate.

"Yes?"

"This has all been so wonderful." Beatrice's smile was a touch flirtatious, but there was also a serious note to it. "I want to talk to you about something important."

"Something important?" Adam was trying to keep focused.

Beatrice took a moment and then asked, "What do you remember about Anne?"

"Anne . . . " Adam's mind went completely blank. "Who the heck is Anne?"

"Your grandmother, silly." Beatrice gave Adam's hand a reassuring squeeze. "You know, Anne. Do you have fond memories of her?"

"Right. Sure. I liked her a lot, even though she was a little . . ." Adam finished his sentence by rolling his eyes.

Beatrice didn't seem to understand. "A little what?"

"Off her rocker."

"Who told you that?"

"Well, Gloria—my stepmother—she said Anne had serious mental health issues, just like my biological mother. Things with Anne got worse as she got older, so Gloria and my dad had to put her in a facility up in Fort Bragg."

Beatrice was very quiet. Adam could tell she was upset.

"I loved your grandmother," Beatrice said softly. "I used to visit her even after you left, before my mother moved us away. Anne taught me many things."

"Like what?" Adam asked.

"Adam, try your best to hear what I'm about to tell you." Beatrice took a deep breath. "Anne was not crazy." She watched Adam's reaction to this and then slowly continued. "She was just open to things that other people don't normally access. That was how she described it, anyway. *Open.*"

The boat lurched unexpectedly as Adam tried to follow what Beatrice was saying. But this wasn't exactly the conversation he expected to be having, and now his hand was sweating. It was that strange burning sensation he'd felt the first time she had touched his hand.

"Your grandmother had a very strong connection to . . ." Beatrice searched for the right words. "Someplace else. A place beyond the world of appearances. Does that make sense?"

"Beatrice," Adam broke in. "I'm sorry, but my grandmother really did have a medical condition, a chemical imbalance.

In her blood, her genes or whatever. Trust me. Of all people, I should know—"

Beatrice's voice was even. "It's very easy to mistake people like Anne for being mentally ill or irrational or . . . 'batty.'"

"Why are we talking about my grandmother, anyway?" Adam laughed, hoping to lighten the mood.

"Because it has to do with *you*, Adam, with the man I saw standing on a cliff last night." Her voice grew even more solemn. "I think you're in serious danger. More than you realize."

Again the boat rocked hard in a sudden swell. Adam started to become aware of his tinnitus ringing in his ears. His vision had grown blurry, and the shadows were dancing wildly around the small room. *How had things moved so quickly from romantic to surreal?* he wondered. Beatrice seemed aware of his rising panic but she forged ahead. "What I'm trying to say is that for people like your grandmother, people more naturally *open*, the world can become a very unbearable place. It can force a person to bury that other, more vulnerable side of himself. And that can evolve into something very dangerous."

"It's hot in here; my hand is really hot," Adam stammered.

"Why did you really come back here, Adam?"

"To get away, that's all."

"To kill yourself?"

"No. I told you . . . Okay, maybe the thought crossed my mind when I got here, but I wasn't going to—"

"Did something happen recently? Something you're afraid to talk about?"

Suddenly Adam had had enough. He sat up, wrenching his hand free from Beatrice. This was not the romantic conversation they were supposed to be having. Then it dawned on him. "You just feel bad for me. Is that what this is all about?" he said incredulously. "Why did you say there was a reason we met? You want to try and save me or something? Is that it?"

"No, Adam, that is not what I meant."

"Am I a quick charity case before you set off on your next big adventure? Is that what I am to you?"

"No. I care about you."

"You care about me, or you *feel sorry* for me?" The pause that followed was enough to convince Adam that he had nailed it.

"Adam, look at me." Beatrice calmly reached for his hand again, but he wouldn't give it to her. "I am just trying to talk to you, that's all."

"Okay. Fine." He shrugged. "So I don't really know what to say then. I'm sorry. Okay? I'm just—sorry."

"Why are you apologizing, Adam? You haven't done anything wrong."

"Obviously I did, and now I am sorry. Okay?"

"Why do you keep saying you're sorry?"

"I'm sorry for . . . I don't know . . . for everything! So yes, you're right; I haven't done anything—and that's the point, I haven't *done anything*. I haven't lived. Everything, my whole life since I last saw you thirty-whatever years ago, it has all been one gigantic *lie*."

Beatrice said nothing.

"I mean, that's what you want to hear, right? You said I was a liar, and guess what? You were right. While you've been out there sailing around the world, I've been wasting my life staring at computer screens all day long. *I make video games!* I make fake fucking worlds for a world that's already fake! The whole point of my job is to trick other idiots into becoming just as stuck and isolated and detached and lonely as I am!

"I have lived my entire life through a *screen*. I work on a screen, I communicate with other people through a screen, I look at all the places I'd like to visit on a screen, I even watch other people having sex on a screen."

Adam was sure this would trigger a reaction, but Beatrice's face remained composed, her eyes fully focused on him. "There is an endless army of *me's* out there—all chained to our screens, and I just can't accept that this is my life, that this is who I am, that this is what I was born for. To just . . . to just—what? To . . . to what?" Adam bowed his head and fell silent.

"Adam?" Beatrice's voice was soft and without judgment. "It's all right—"

But Adam had nothing more to say. He felt like he might get physically sick. Beatrice reached over and touched his arm, but Adam was already staggering to his feet.

Adam stood alone at the boat's railing, looking down at the water. He wasn't sure if he might throw up or not. His hands were shaking, and he could hear his teeth chattering, even though he wasn't cold. Just empty. There was a hollow silence in the misty harbor.

"I came very close to dying once."

Adam glanced over his shoulder and saw Beatrice seated in her deck chair behind him, wrapped in a giant comforter. Adam wasn't sure how long she had been there; he hadn't heard her come up from below deck. She lit a cigarette, and the smell of burning tobacco was strangely comforting.

"About ten years ago," she went on, her voice soft and intimate. "I was sailing off the coast of Chile. Things had gotten pretty bad; I had been on my own for a while—drifting. Just as I was hitting bottom, I decided to open this packet of mail that had been forwarded to my last port of call by a friend in France. And it contained a postcard from my father. I hadn't seen or heard from him since I was a child. I didn't even know he was alive, but he was, and he had found me, and we reconnected. And from that point, everything in my life shifted."

She paused for a moment. "But it was that first postcard, postmarked a full year before I had received it, that somehow came to me exactly when I needed it. And I'll always remember this quote he'd written on it. *'If you bring forth what is within you, what is within you will save you. If you do not bring forth what is within you, what is within you will destroy you.'*"

Somewhere in the distance a foghorn cried out. "Whatever's in me is already dead," Adam said quietly.

"No. You wouldn't have come back to Mendocino if that were true." Beatrice snubbed out her cigarette, and a brief shower of sparks flew past Adam's shoulder. "You've just grown a very thick suit of armor."

Beatrice stood and moved toward Adam and slowly opened the blanket, wrapping it, as well as herself, around him. Like a giant cocoon floating in the sea mist, inside the blanket, the warmth of Beatrice's body slowly melted into Adam. What took place after that, Adam would only later recall in broken dreamlike fragments. At some point he must have turned to face her, to hold her in his own arms. He remembered her lips pressed against his cheek, inches from his ear. She had whispered something to him, the words themselves forgotten. For what felt like forever, they stood there, their bodies entwined, their faces, moist from the sea air, slowly, gently pressed into one another. Adam remembered saying at some point that he should probably go, or perhaps he just thought the words. When exactly they began to kiss was lost to him, but the next thing he knew, Beatrice was leading him by the hand below deck.

◈

A gust of wind rippled across the tall, yellow grass on the bluff. The air was crisp, and the morning sun was already crackling over the dew-drenched land. Adam sat on an unusually high section of curb on Main Street, soaking in the morning. It was breathtakingly clear out, as if someone had Photoshopped Adam's view. *A touch of Sharpen,* Adam thought, *with some Dust & Scratch removal, bump Luminance, bump Gamma, +10 on Brightness, +6 Contrast.* Adam realized that he was destroying the world with his thoughts, turning it into 1s and 0s. He closed his eyes to reset himself. Now all he saw was the orange-pink of the inside of his eyelids, all he felt was a warm sensation in his body, and the tiny ant that was dancing across his pinky on the sidewalk. When he opened his eyes, the picture returned to its original brilliance, with one additional component—Beatrice walking up Main Street. She was a little late, but she had come, and that was all that mattered.

They had made love several times the night before, in the dimly lit front berth of *Paradiso 9.* It had started slow and cautious, physical desire almost secondary to the raw emotional need they both had to hold on to one another and never let go again. Adam remembered feeling the tears on Beatrice's cheeks at times, as she kneaded her face into his neck like a cat. Then he had drifted off to sleep for a time, only to wake and find they were making love again, this time more forcefully. Eventually he fell into a heavy, dreamless sleep.

He woke just after dawn. Beatrice was already up and out on deck, talking on her sat phone. It sounded as if she was negotiating a further delay before departure. Sensing her need for privacy to talk, Adam quickly suggested he'd head back to the hotel to shower and clean up. Beatrice had given him a quick kiss and had said she'd come meet him once she'd sorted through her various arrangements. Her parting words were, "At the very least, we can spend the morning together."

On his way back to the hotel, thoughts of Jane and his life in the Bay Area briefly drifted across his awareness like a thin layer of stratocumulus clouds high in the sky. Surprisingly he felt no anxiety or guilt for what he had done. If anything, the thought of Jane brought up feelings of fondness, as if she were a fictional character in some novel he had gotten caught up in. A story that he had briefly mistaken for his life. *This may change,* Adam thought, *but for now there's no reason to find conflict between my current reality and the one where Jane exists. They're simply different worlds.*

Adam jumped up from the curb, grabbing the two coffees and the bag of pastries he had brought for them, and walked down to meet Beatrice. When he reached her, she offered a cautionary smile.

"I have until four, possibly a little longer."

Adam nodded. Less than six hours, but more than he had expected.

"There are things we should talk about." Beatrice looked at the ground. "Important things I feel like . . . well, that I'd like to explain to you."

"Yes, of course," Adam said. He had the sense that she wasn't just referring to what had taken place between them in the boat last night.

As if to confirm his suspicions, Beatrice looked at Adam, and again he felt that uncanny sensation that she was trying to speak to him without words. Then she said, "But first, let's just play. Nothing serious. Just fun. Okay?"

The innocence in Beatrice's expression was an invitation, as if she had once again become the girl standing outside Adam's grandmother's window, beckoning him outside.

"Nothing serious," Adam replied as he held out one of the coffees.

Beatrice was about to take a sip when she looked more closely at Adam's jacket and started to laugh.

"What?"

"*Tu as attaché lundi avec mardi.*"

Adam was totally confused. "You don't like my jacket?"

"No, silly, it's a French expression that means you buttoned it one button off." Beatrice helped him fix his jacket before they strolled out onto the bluff.

CHAPTER 17

THE BUTTERFLY EFFECT

Rene Adiklein's earthly existence began in the small town of Saint-Maurice in the Swiss canton of Valais, where French is the dominant language. His parents were unremarkable apart from being fluent in English, which they had learned in school. They met, fell in love, married, and both worked as tour guides at the *Grotte aux Fées* (Cave of the Fairies), prehistoric caves in the cliffs above the town that had drawn tourists since the mid-1800s. The Adikleins never intended on having children, but both miracles and mistakes do happen, and Rene Adiklein was both of them.

From an early age, it was clear Rene was no ordinary child. At school he rarely played with the other children, but rather stood off to one side observing them, almost as if they were some exotic species. He attentively studied his parents as well, eventually going so far as to take detailed notes on their provincial habits. Perhaps as an outgrowth of this unusual degree of attention, young Rene possessed an astonishing ability to predict what people were going to do next. At breakfast he could tell if his mother was going to come home drunk from work that night. At school he could anticipate whether a child who rarely cheated was planning to sit next to Rene and peek at his answers on an upcoming test. Once, when a classmate attempted to bully Rene, he threatened to reveal that the boy was being sexually abused at home—something that had never been intimated by anyone. After that, Rene was never subjected to bullying again.

Finishing at the top of his class at Collège de l'Abbaye Saint-Maurice, one of Switzerland's most famous secondary schools, Rene headed off to Paris to study at the Sorbonne. While there, he devoured everything he could find on human behavior, including cultural anthropology, sociology, and psychology. Digging his way tirelessly through any existing knowledge of the human psyche, Rene sought not only to understand the roots of human motivation and desire, but to discover nutrient-rich soil beneath those roots that caused them to take the shapes they did. He earned three degrees: a master's in psychology, a master's in social behaviorism, and a doctorate in medical anthropology.

Yet his studies in Paris were not enough. In order for Dr. Rene Adiklein to begin the great work that he had clearly been placed on earth to perform, he needed knowledge unavailable through traditional pedagogical means. New research was required at a level that could transform theory into practical tools. While outlining a proposal for his first research experiment, Adiklein realized he faced several major stumbling blocks. He would need grant money, of course, along with a college willing to support his rather unorthodox approach. More importantly, he would need to find the right subjects. He needed a wide range of psychological types, a difficult task even in Europe's largest cities. Harder still would be finding men and women willing and able to psychologically open themselves up in ways that were not commonly acceptable in modern society.

Then everything changed. Adiklein arrived in Berkeley, California, during the summer of 1966, just in time for the counterculture revolution. His move could not have been timed more perfectly. Amid the progressive upheaval of protests and sit-ins, of tie-dyed flower children and psychedelic experimentation, Rene found everything he needed, including funding.

Soon after arriving in the Bay Area, Adiklein forged what would eventually become a lifelong relationship with an investment firm named Blanchefort and Rhodes. From its head offices in Europe, B&R became increasingly active in America in the late 1960s. They provided funds for the construction of San Francisco's Transamerica Pyramid, which became the site of their West Coast offices, and expanded their profile to include increasingly more U.S. investments, particularly in pharmaceuticals, technology, and media.

Learning through various channels about Adiklein's proposed research, U.S. representatives of B&R contacted him for a meeting. Shortly thereafter, backed by the deep pockets of B&R, Adiklein conducted a full array of psychological trials, both at SRI International (Stanford Research Institute) and UC Berkeley, culminating in his most successful and secretive project, the Extended Dimensional Attention Study at Berkeley between 1968 and 1972.

Not long after Stanley Milgram was getting research subjects to zap their neighbor, and just before Philip Zimbardo was turning his students into sadistic prison guards, Rene Adiklein was quietly digging his way deeper and deeper into the collective subconscious, past the neocortex, through the limbic system, all the way down to the reptilian brain, where he finally discovered what he was after: the philosopher's stone of marketing, capable of turning dross into gold.

◈

Blake Dorsey hooked a left onto Pine off Kearny. On his way through Chinatown he tried again to calm his nerves. *Breathe deeply. Just relax.* At the next red light, he started digging in the glove box for those Focusing Your Intentions CDs Jane had lent him. But when he saw an ad on the side of a passing bus for L4B Expansion Worlds—Prepare to Bleed—December 14, he slammed the glove box shut. Deep breaths. Everything would be all right as long as he could tell Adiklein what was going on before the boss heard it from Mitch or some other V-Skies toady. If Blake played it right, he might even be able to impress Adiklein with his willingness to solicit guidance. Blake hit the gas.

Reaching the top of Nob Hill, he quickly checked a new text from Jane.

Text message: **Dr. M got cops to correct bad rental car descrip from idiots at Enterprise. Now correct on MissPersReprt. No other news.**

Blake typed frantically while swerving around two old ladies in the crosswalk with matching hats and poodles. **Hospitals? Credit Cards?**

Jane immediately texted back: **No other news!**

Left on Jones, left on Post, left on Taylor. Blake couldn't stand the hills and one-way streets in this part of the city. He had been invited to Adiklein's private men's club only once before. He had, of course, driven past it a thousand times. The inconspicuous brick building, half-covered in ivy and with no visible sign, sat on the corner of Taylor and Sutter. Shoppers, tourists, and junkies wandered past on the sidewalks outside, completely oblivious as to what and who lay just beyond those weathered brick walls.

Since he was a guest and not a member, Blake used the main entrance. Heading up the steps, he quickly glanced down at his phone in hopes of news about Adam that might allow him to cancel this meeting. No such luck. Inside the massive double doors and behind the security desk loomed an enormous statue of an owl, the symbol of the private men's club.

"Hello, I'm Blake Dorsey, here for a meeting with Rene Adiklein." Blake was already pulling out his identification for the security guard, who looked like a Muppet beneath the giant owl.

"Welcome, Mr. Dorsey. Have you been a guest with us before?"

"Yeah, yeah. I've already done the background check. I'm in the system."

Positioned at the heart of the club was a grand lounge with an open ceiling extending up six stories to the massive, stained-glass skylight floating high above. Tropical plants and a variety of armchairs, couches, and love seats were scattered about. The room centered around a fountain, an exact replica of the Pyramid Fountain of Versailles, only smaller. The club's fountain also differed from the original in that it had been engineered to be virtually silent. Almost as remarkable, to Blake at least, was how the hundred or so club members in the room were equally quiet. They read, sipped tea, napped, and looked at electronic devices. But no one spoke.

Blake walked around the room several times searching for Adiklein. Wandering past various nooks and small meeting rooms, Blake finally approached a friendly enough looking gentleman reading *The Wall Street Journal*. "Excuse me, sir," Blake said quietly. The man looked blankly up at him. "Is this the Redwood Room? I'm looking for Rene Adiklein."

The gentleman turned back to his newspaper without a word.

"Okay . . . I'm sorry, I'm just trying to find—" Blake felt a large hand firmly grip his left elbow. Turning, he looked up to see a man almost as tall as the owl statue dressed in a charcoal suit with a discreet bronze name tag.

"Oh, hey. I'm looking for—" The man placed a long finger to his lips. Then turning, the man silently guided Blake toward a massive staircase.

The Redwood Room was a second-floor banquet hall, which seemed improbably long, and when Blake was ushered in, it was completely empty but for one person. Rene Adiklein sat at a small table at the far side of the room, having lunch while watching the giant flat-screen TV that hung behind the bar. Crossing the room Blake realized that for the first time he was about to witness Adiklein actually ingest food. Perhaps some great dietary secret of sprightly tech moguls was about to be revealed. Or perhaps the rumors that he ate only phosphorescent algae imported from the Philippines were about to be borne out.

Adiklein's lunch turned out to be quite simple, albeit odd: a sandwich of thinly sliced radish with sweet butter and sea salt on a baguette, which he was washing down with two small, red bottles of Sanbittèr. More interesting than his lunch was what he was watching on television. It was the new reality show *America's Most Popular*. Blake knew it not only because it was an enormous ratings success but also because one of the digital advertising firms at Virtual Skies handled the show's online media promotions.

The premise of *America's Most Popular* was straightforward. Each season people across America who had been voted most popular in high school were tracked down to see how they had fared in their adult lives. Like *American Idol*, judges spent the first half of the season whittling down contestants who had remained popular, while eliminating those who had fallen from grace. In the second half of the season, those who had made the cut earned lockers at the fictitious "High School USA," where they engaged in a variety of nostalgic competitions—bake sales, dance-a-thons, spirit week skits—while viewers voted people off the show each week. For the season finale, on "prom night," the two final contestants were crowned "Most Popular Man" and "Most Popular Woman."

As Blake reached the table, Adiklein continued to watch for a few long moments before turning to his guest with a playful grin. "I tell you, reality TV is among the most brilliant inventions of the past century. *Anyone* can be famous. *Anyone* can become the star of their own show." Adiklein took a small bite of his radish sandwich. "And why not? Why do we need actors and scripts when we can watch the real thing unfold right before our eyes?"

Adiklein had once written an op-ed for *Wired* magazine titled "Fame—The New World Religion." In it he had argued that the more science and technology dominated our worldview, the more we would see an increase in the desire for personal fame. *"Without religious assurances of an afterlife to contend with the inevitability of one's death,"* he wrote, *"the psyche of the modern, scientifically bound mind will have but one direction to turn. Fame—our only hope for the eternal."* The study of fame was, of course, a small facet of Adiklein's work on attention. But with it he had rightly predicted the rise of the ubiquitous importance of fame within society, from something only politicians and movie stars dealt with, to become as common a need as toilet paper.

"Rene, thank you for making time to see me," Blake said. He cleared his throat. "I could use your help resolving an issue. Just a little thing, but I wanted to get your guidance on how best to—"

"You know what my favorite thing is about the reality show?" Adiklein continued as if Blake hadn't spoken. "This feeling, this . . . There is a word in German, I don't think you have this word in English—*Schadenfreude*. Do you know this word, Blake?"

"No, I don't," Blake replied.

"It means to take pleasure from the misfortune of others." Adiklein chuckled. "Leave it to the Germans to come up with such a word."

Blake realized this conversation was not going to be as easy as he had hoped.

"Yes, that is my favorite aspect of this reality television. That is the brilliance of it," Adiklein continued. "I cannot stop watching because these people make me feel so much better about my own miserable life. I get to revel in their stupidity. *Schadenfreude*. It is a very addictive emotion, located in the limbic system, in the ventral striatum, the reward center." Adiklein ate the final bite of his sandwich and then carefully wiped his fingers on a linen napkin.

Blake tried again. "One of my key engineers has . . . gone missing."

Adiklein reluctantly pressed the Mute button on the remote control before turning to look at Blake. After a pause he said, "Let me guess," and pressed a single finger to his temple and closed his eyes. "Sheppard, right? Alan Sheppard?"

Blake was momentarily stunned. "Yes . . . Well, actually, it's *Adam* Sheppard."

Adiklein snapped his fingers. "Alan, Adam—close enough."

"How did you know about Adam Sheppard?"

Adiklein gave Blake a small, conspiratorial smile. "I know who he is, Blake."

"Right. Of course you do," Blake stammered. "He's one of the original Pixilate partners. And a good friend of mine—"

"No, no, Blake. I know *who* he is"—Adiklein leaned in—"and *what* he is, for you."

Blake felt the blood rushing into his face. "I'm not sure I know what you mean."

"Oh, I think you do, Blake." Adiklein raised his eyebrows. "Let us see . . . There was that idea you presented at a Cross-Pollination Brunch, a very clever new way to interface Ruby and Flash. And there was that unorthodox but brilliant redesign concept you casually suggested to Justin Whitney—right in front of me, of course—which helped save his Virtual Skies Photo Booth from looking like a Segway. Then, there is the mobile app idea you presented at the last meeting. And I imagine Adam has more than a little to do with this new *Zombie* concept you keep telling me about, the one with all the new social media integration. All of your best ideas, Blake, they all have a very particular *fragrance* to them. And I"— Adiklein tapped his nose—"am a connoisseur."

Blake's feet and hands were tingling now. It had happened to him once before, in high school when he played Kenickie in *Grease*. That was the last time Blake ever did a play.

"I assure you that every single one of my ideas, every single move I've made—"

"Blaaaake, please. Relax." Adiklein smiled reassuringly. "I'm not accusing you of any wrongdoing. On the contrary, my friend, I'm complimenting you. All on your own, you have discovered one of the greatest secrets of success in business." Adiklein stood up and beckoned Blake to follow him. "Come."

Adiklein led Blake out to the second-floor balcony overlooking the grand lounge. They sat down side by side on a bench and gazed over the railing at the men below, as if looking into a giant terrarium.

"That man there, with the large head and tiny spectacles," Adiklein whispered and pointed to one of the men near the center of the room. "Do you know who he is?"

Blake shook his head.

"Head of an asset management fund with a personal worth of, oh, five or six hundred million."

Adiklein pointed to another table, where two men sat reading different parts of the same paper. "Over there, those two VCs are worth roughly two billion. A piece.

"There." Adiklein pointed to a man on a couch who had a book on his lap but was obviously asleep. "There we have the former CEO of Baldwin Shane Equity Management, a man worth somewhere between three and four billion. And on the other side of the couch there"—Adiklein gestured toward a man silently talking to himself—"the current CEO of Open Channel Broadcast, also worth several billion."

Adiklein turned and looked at Blake. "As you may or may not know, Blake, there are really only two classes of people in the world. These men you're looking at belong to the first one. They are the job creators, the policy makers, the landowners, the bankers, the men who direct and maintain the world as we know it."

"Like, B&R kind of money?"

"Yes, Blake, we can most definitely include our good friends at Blanchefort and Rhodes in this first group," Adiklein agreed. "Now, the other class of people is where everyone else belongs. That's right, the entire rest of the planet. All 99.9 percent. It doesn't really matter how these people see themselves; in truth, they are all the same. They are the worker bees."

"Okay."

Adiklein continued. "Now you might be asking yourself, 'How does a worker bee become a Blanchefort or a Rhodes?'"

Blake nodded. In fact, that was exactly what he was asking himself.

"For, as you know, it is every worker bee's dream to gather enough honey so that one day he can be allowed to sit down there in this very special room. No?"

Blake looked down at the room full of silent men and nodded again.

"All the worker bees are told, 'If you work hard all your life, blah, blah, blah.' Or 'You just need to be in the right place at the right time, blah, blah, blah.' He or she is told that everyone has the chance to make it, that there are many paths leading to this room. But, of course, this is a lie. All those paths lead nowhere."

Adiklein stroked the bridge of his nose a few times before continuing. "There is no way into that room because the Blancheforts and Rhodeses of this world don't like to share. They don't want noisy bees buzzing around. They like it nice and quiet, as you can see."

Blake smiled his agreement.

"So they have put a system in place to keep all the bees out. We could call it an 'economic system,' if you like, but in truth it is much deeper than that. It is a system of control based on the understanding that human beings, like bees, are easily *trapped by their own mechanical nature.* Once hooked into certain patterns of behavior, they will forever replicate those behaviors. Imprisoned, all by themselves. And so as long as the worker bees are trapped going round and round in circles, the walls of this room remain inviolable.

"This is the way it has always been, and the way it will always be." Adiklein leaned closer to Blake. "*But.* There is, of course, a secret way into this room."

Adiklein stood, and for one terrifying moment, Blake thought the conversation was over. Thankfully Adiklein gestured for him to follow. The second floor balcony was a loop around the circumference of the grand lounge below; they were apparently going for a stroll.

"When we study this two-class system closely," Adiklein continued, "as with all things in nature, we find a third force, in this case, a third class, so to speak."

"Like a different kind of worker bee?" Blake interjected.

"In a way, this person looks like a worker bee, but something about him is not quite right. This bee flies a little erratically. This bee is unpredictable. Let's call him *le papillon,* the butterfly."

Adiklein ran his finger along the smooth marble railing. "Now this papillon, he doesn't fit in with all the other bees. 'No, no, no,' they say. 'We don't like this guy. He's weird; he is not like us.' This is because this papillon can see things that worker bees cannot. Le papillon does not see the world as it is. He sees the world, but he also sees . . . a . . . someplace else."

"What's the someplace else?"

Adiklein smiled broadly. "How would I know, Blake? I am no papillon."

As if working out a riddle, Blake began verbalizing his thoughts. "Maybe it's like where the mind goes when you get a great idea. Like when I'm at the gym and I just—"

"Blake, please," Adiklein said while suppressing a laugh. "Don't embarrass yourself. I am not talking about you. You are most definitely *not* a papillon. For you this someplace else will always be unknown."

Blake was too confused now to conceal his disappointment. "But aren't you saying that in order to join those guys down there, you have to become a butterfly first?"

"No, Blake. The men you see down there were never le papillon. Le papillon is too fragile, too easily crushed. But more importantly le papillon has no interest in sitting in a boring room filled with ugly old men. He would rather flutter about and dream. Those men down there don't give a shit about fluttering and dreaming; they don't even have wings. And they don't need them; if they want to go somewhere, they just get in their private jets and go."

"So what's the deal with this papillon, then?" Blake said a little too loud. "I don't get it."

Adiklein put a finger to his lips. "I beg to differ. You *do* get it, Blake." His voice intensified but remained soft. "You see, sometimes a worker bee who is a little more *clever* than the others meets one of these papillons but doesn't go along with the popular belief that he is crazy or worthless. *Mais non*, this clever bee is intrigued by the butterfly and decides to follow him. And every so often, this clever bee is rewarded, as his papillon leads him to someplace else, a *special garden*, let's say, where many exotic flowers grow.

"The butterfly, well, what does he care about the value of these flowers? He wants only to dance in the glow of their beauty. But the clever bee knows exactly the value of these new flowers, and he knows exactly how to harvest their precious and exotic pollen. This is the real secret of how the clever worker bee can one day join the Blancheforts and Rhodeses of this world."

Adiklein looked down again. "These men, Blake, they understand the art of collecting butterflies. You have caught your first one. Good for you. But unfortunately he has flown away." With a casual shrug, Adiklein added, "Too bad."

"I'll get him back," Blake said. "I promise."

Adiklein smiled gently. "I have confidence in you, my friend. And when you do get him back, may I suggest something?"

Blake nodded.

"Pin him to a display case." Adiklein pressed his thumb down hard on the marble railing as if pushing in a thumbtack. "Where he can produce without flying away. Because without your butterfly, to me, Blake, you are just one more worker bee among many. And there is nothing like stepping on an obsolete bee to give one a quick taste of Schadenfreude."

CHAPTER 18

This Is Not an Orange

A pair of orange butterflies floated along the edge of the bluff, dancing around the rocks and shrubs that stood guard over the otherwise unprotected 100-foot drop. Below lay a crescent-shaped beach cluttered with driftwood and tangles of reddish-brown seaweed. In a few places, the wood had been piled into barricades against the wind and the remains of a beach fire could be seen.

"Hey!" Adam called down.

Beatrice looked up from the spot where she had just dragged a surfboard-shaped piece of driftwood.

Adam help up a large, white paper bag. "Ham and Swiss! Macaroni salad! Root beer! Sound good?"

Beatrice gave a thumbs-up. "And here we have our picnic table!"

"I like it! How do I get down there?"

"Jump!" Beatrice said, deadpan.

Adam shook his head, smiling. "Funny!"

"Over there!" She pointed to a spot where precarious wooden steps zigzagged down to the beach.

They had spent the morning out on the bluffs, walking the paths and exploring the cliffs. Searching through tide pools for sea anemones, Adam proudly identified most all of them. As Beatrice had suggested, there was no serious talk, and no mention of the night before. It felt awkward at first, pretending like nothing had

176

taken place between them, and Adam even wondered if he had made more of their sexual encounter than he should have. But then he caught Beatrice looking at him with a glint of longing in her eyes and he understood, she was protecting them both against the moment, very soon, when they would be saying good-bye.

As the minutes and hours slipped by, they slowly found their way back to that friendly banter they had forged on the boat the night before—teasing each other, joking, arguing playfully—and by lunchtime all awkwardness had dissolved.

"I can't believe you went to the Galápagos Islands and didn't go on a single nature tour." Adam wiped away bits of sand and macaroni salad from the corner of his mouth; it was by far the best macaroni salad he had ever eaten, sand or no sand. "Did you even go to any of the nature reserves?"

"Afraid not." Across the surfboard table, Beatrice struggled to keep from eating her hair along with her ham-and-cheese sandwich. The wind on the beach had picked up.

"Did you see any blue-footed boobies?"

"Sorry, missed the boobies."

"What the hell did you do there? Don't you remember anything? Come on, you've got to give me something."

"Well, let's see." Beatrice closed her eyes. "What I remember most about the Galápagos Islands . . . the aquamarine-colored toilets at the Barranco Bar on San Cristóbal Island."

Adam stopped chewing his sandwich. "Toilets?"

"I got smashed on some cheap rum with this wannabe pirate named Guillermo—he had a parrot and everything. I ended up getting horribly sick." Beatrice shrugged and took a sip of root beer.

"You don't understand how much I *love* those islands. For months I was obsessed. I watched every National Geographic special, every documentary, every YouTube video. Oh, and there's even this great virtual tour thing where you can scan around each island. Seriously, I know everything there is to know about the Galápagos Islands."

"You don't know *everything*," Beatrice countered.

"There are seventy-three different species of lava lizards; would you like me to name them?" Adam gave a cocky raise of his eyebrows.

"You've never even been there," Beatrice shot back. "For all you know, the Galápagos don't even exist!"

"Of course they exist—"

"Prove it," Beatrice challenged.

"Wait, don't tell me you're one of those crazy creationist people?"

"I'm much worse." Beatrice gave Adam an evil scowl. "Seriously, what empirical proof of its existence do you have, besides what you've seen on your computer screen?"

"Well, for one thing, I've seen a map!"

"Paper and ink. Or with you, probably just glowing pixels or whatever."

"You just told me you were there!" Adam pointed at her. "You're my proof!"

"I was lying." Beatrice's Mona Lisa smile was on full display. "I used to be a phenomenal liar, you know."

"It is a scientific fact that the Galápagos Islands exist! It is an established fact!"

"What's the difference between blind faith and blind facts?"

Adam paused for a moment, distracted by how much fun it was arguing with Beatrice like this. "'What's the difference between blind faith and blind facts?'" Adam repeated the question, buying himself a little time. "Facts can be proven."

"But *you* haven't proved them. You just sit there accepting them, one blind fact after another." Beatrice pushed harder. "And the more you stuff your head with information that you yourself have not experienced, or discovered, or pondered, or even questioned, the more you confuse *information* with *knowledge*. Therefore, Mr. Scienceman, until you've seen the aquamarine-colored toilets at the Barranco Bar, the Galápagos Islands do not exist for you." She finished her root beer.

Adam had no rebuttal, just a strong urge to push Beatrice down in the sand and make love to her right there on the beach.

As if sensing this, Beatrice leaned across the driftwood table and mock-whispered, *"Facts are dead."*

Adam laughed. "'What do you mean, 'facts are dead'? Like as in, 'God is dead'?"

"Yep, that's right." Beatrice's face lingered close to Adam's as she continued to playfully push to win the debate. "You've got all these militant atheists out there, so happy to denounce religion, without the balls to even consider the assumptions of their own materialistic belief system. Sorry, but science does not have *all* the answers. Facts are dead. The brain is just as unreliable as the heart."

"Oh, I see," Adam said with mocking smugness. He was aching to kiss her but not yet ready to concede her point. "So basically what you're saying is that knowledge is evil? Education is evil?"

"Of course not," she rebuffed. "It's *lopsided*. Like you. Your head is so packed full of answers that you've forgotten what it's like to be in a state of *question*. To be open." Beatrice pushed the macaroni salad out of the way so she could lean closer. "That was the Adam I fell in love with. The boy who knew how to create worlds. And I don't mean digital ones."

As Beatrice continued to stare into Adam's eyes, the sounds of the world around him were slowly fading away. Again she seemed to be posing a question without words, trying to reach something inside of him that was aching to respond. But the intensity of her look was too much, and Adam started to fidget. Seeing this, Beatrice quickly broke the moment with a smile and a quick kiss on his cheek.

Seagull cries and the sound of pounding surf returned to Adam's ears. Beatrice stood up and looked out at the water for a moment before turning back to Adam. "Last night you told me you thought this other part of you was already dead."

Adam nodded.

"How about I prove to you that it's not?"

An hour later Adam sat at one of the picnic tables on the bluff facing Beatrice. They had just spent 20 minutes at a grocery store, meticulously picking out two oranges from the produce section. Beatrice insisted that they be as similar as possible—in size, color, and ripeness. Now she set both of them down in front of Adam.

"Pick one."

After Adam randomly pointed at one, Beatrice picked up the orange and started peeling it. "This is a version of a game I learned from some kids in Lhasa." Beatrice handed the peeled orange to Adam. "Now since we bought these both at the same market, they should taste pretty much the same, right?"

"Right."

"First taste this one."

Adam pulled off a section of orange and ate it.

"How is it?"

Adam shrugged. "Pretty good."

"What does it taste like?"

"Like an orange."

"Okay," Beatrice instructed. "Now with this orange"—she pointed to the second orange—"we're going to feed your other half—the part of you that you think is already dead."

"This is silly."

"It isn't silly. Now pick it up."

Adam took the orange and started to peel it. Beatrice reached over and stopped him.

"Wait! Don't peel it. Not yet. First just look at it. Look at what you're holding in your hands."

Adam looked at the orange for a moment then back to Beatrice. "Okay. I looked at it."

"Don't look at me." Beatrice sounded like a schoolteacher. "Keep looking at the orange." Adam did as he was told.

"Now just tell me what you see. What are you holding?"

Was this a riddle of some sort? Adam shrugged. "I'm looking at . . . an orange."

"No, it's not," Beatrice asserted. "What is it?"

"It looks pretty much like an orange to me."

"No. That's just a word. That's not what you're holding in your hand," Beatrice said. "Just listen to the question I'm asking, and don't try to answer it with your mind." Beatrice's voice became quieter. "Pretend for a moment that you've never seen one of these before, and just look at it. Consider it. Stay with the question, 'What is this thing I'm holding?'"

Adam stared at the orange-colored ball in his hand. The skin had a shine to it but it was also porous. Adam noticed how uniform the pores were, like his own skin but more so. The color itself wasn't uniform. Within the orange was a range of colors, lighter and darker.

Beatrice had slipped over to sit next to Adam. Her mouth was close to his ear, her voice breathy. "Now close your eyes." Adam did. "Just feel it in your hands," she continued. "How heavy is it? Is the skin cool to the touch?" Beatrice slipped her hand onto one of Adam's hands, guiding him. "Now with your fingernail, just scratch the skin."

Adam did, and Beatrice slowly brought the orange up under his nose. Adam took in its scent as Beatrice continued. "Smell is a language. Try to hear what it's saying."

Beatrice guided Adam's hand to puncture the skin with a fingernail. He inhaled again.

"Imagine what could be inside something that smells like that. Let your mouth imagine what it's going to taste like. Is it sour? Sweet?"

Adam was salivating so much he had to swallow.

"Now let's peel the skin away. Slowly. And as we do, I'm going to tell you a secret." Beatrice helped Adam slowly peel the orange. "Inside this protective skin, beneath the outer wall of this miraculous object, there is a treasure made of pure light. Light that has traveled millions of miles from the nearest star just for you. Just to be tasted by you, to be consumed by you. And now it's here, in your hands, a sweet golden ball of pure light, right in front of you."

Beatrice brought the peeled orange up to Adam's lips.

"Now bite."

Like an animal Adam bit into it, his eyes still closed. Juice spilled down his face. He opened his eyes and looked over at Beatrice, blinking at the brightness of daylight and the beauty of her face.

It was by far the best fucking orange Adam had ever tasted.

Beatrice smiled. "Why hello . . . There's the Adam I remember. Still here, and despite reports to the contrary, *very* much alive."

CHAPTER 19

CHICKEN BOY RETURNS

Adam leaned against the white fence that separated the bluff from Main Street. Behind him were the public restrooms where he washed up following the transcendent orange experience. Splashing cold water on his face had only emphasized what he was already feeling: physically and mentally refreshed. Open, the way he had felt sitting up on the water tower the day before.

Adam's sense of contentment, however, was short lived. There was a white minivan parked directly across Main Street, and until now the sun's reflection had made it impossible to see into the van's back window. But when a delivery truck slowed to a stop just beyond the van, casting a shadow over it, Adam became aware that someone inside was watching him. It took a moment, but Adam eventually recognized the face; it was the boy who had seen him up on the water tower, the boy who had made those crazy chicken sounds, and now, for whatever strange reason, that same boy was staring at him. What's more, it appeared to Adam that the boy's face was stained with tears.

Adam then witnessed something that absolutely terrified him. The boy in the van began to shake his head back and forth, violently, before *slamming* it repeatedly down into the headrest in front of him.

The delivery truck moved on, and the boy disappeared into the sun's glare. But the line of cars that had backed up behind the truck now flowed freely past, creating a flip-book of shaded images: adult arms reaching back to contain the boy, the boy flailing, the boy being flipped around in his seat, the boy being strapped in. After a moment, the brake lights went on, the minivan pulled out, and as it accelerated away, a final blast of direct sunlight off the back windshield shot Adam in the face.

"Are you still checking out today?"

It took Adam several moments to realize there was someone standing on the sidewalk next to him. Blinking away the sunburn his irises had just received, Adam finally made out Dorothy, the woman from the front desk at the Mendocino Hotel, standing there, looking at him expectantly.

"Because you've already missed checkout," Dorothy said with a somewhat exacerbated smile, "and we, like, need to get into your room and clean it."

"Oh, right. Sorry about that. I'd actually love to stay another night. Is that—would that be possible?"

Dorothy sighed. "Weeelll, if you want to stay in the same room, we might need to move some other people around . . ."

Adam realized he was being cued to grovel. "It would be really wonderful if you could do that for me. I would really appreciate it . . ."

"All right." Dorothy broke into the more flirtatious smile she seemed to have been saving. "I'm heading in to work now, so let me see what I can do."

"Thank you." Adam hoped that would be the end of it.

"You seem awful chipper today. Do you need any touristy recommendations? I know some totally awesome places for sightseeing."

"Thank you. I appreciate it. But I'm fine. I'm spending the day with a friend."

"Okeydoke." Dorothy held firmly onto her smile. "So I guess you found her, then? The, um, redhead you were looking for?"

"I did."

Dorothy looked around with wide-eyed mock curiosity. "So where is she?"

"She's in the bathroom. Freshening up—"

"Sure you're not just trying to—oh, I don't know—get rid of me?"

"*No.* Honest—"

"Cause I can take a hint, folks," Dorothy said to her imaginary audience.

"Seriously," Adam pleaded. "I'm really not trying to—"

"No, that's fine. I was just trying to be helpful, so just . . . Have a great day!"

Dorothy turned and walked toward the hotel. Between her and the head-banging kid in the minivan, Adam felt like his blissful day with Beatrice was somehow under attack.

A few moments later, Adam felt something touch his ear. A bug? Again—this time on his cheek. Adam swatted at it and heard a giggle behind him. Turning, he saw Beatrice had snuck up on the other side of the fence and was tickling him with a long reed of oat grass.

"Hey!" Adam said, relieved to see her.

Beatrice laughed and took off running.

Adam jumped the fence and chased after her. The dirt path wove down toward the Presbyterian Church then eventually curved off into a small grove of cypress trees at the edge of the bluff. Beatrice disappeared into the grove, well ahead of Adam. The stand of trees was thick, and as he entered it, Adam's eyes took a moment to adjust to the unexpected darkness in the cool sanctuary. "Beatrice?" She was nowhere to be seen. Adam walked farther into the grove.

Something about the moment reminded him of an Alfred Hitchcock film. The one with Kim Novak. *Didn't something like this happen to Jimmy Stewart in that movie?* After a few twists and turns, the trail made its way through the cypresses and back out into the open right at the edge of the bluff. Adam slowly approached the edge and looked down, thinking perhaps there might be another set of stairs leading to the beach. There was nothing, no possible way for Beatrice to have gone any farther. A hundred feet below he could see the rocky base of the cliff, and out beyond it, the beach. To fall from here would be a direct splat. If Adam really wanted to end it all, this would be the spot to do it. *Vertigo—that was it!* Adam suddenly remembered the title of the Hitchcock film.

"*Wanna jump?*" Beatrice whispered in his ear.

Adam just about jumped out of his skin and over the edge of the bluff. Beatrice quickly grabbed on to him to keep him from going over.

"Oh my God! Oh my God!" Adam's heart was close to bursting.

"I'm sorry! I couldn't help it!" Beatrice said, gasping with laughter. She was hugging him from behind now, pulling him back into the grove.

"Where?" Adam sputtered. "Where were you?!"

"I was just hiding, silly. Behind a tree."

"You almost . . . killed me!" Adam's voice was colored slightly with anger.

"I'm sorry. Please don't be mad!" Still laughing, Beatrice flipped Adam around and buried her head against his chest. Adam's heart continued to thump, but the panic was dissipating. He looked down, wrapping his arms around her. Beatrice looked up, her eyes glowing, like emerald sea glass. For a long while, they simply stood there, holding each other.

There was a raw vulnerability in Beatrice's face that Adam had not seen before. Since meeting out on the cliffs, she had always seemed checked behind a wall of self-control. Even while making love the night before, there had been something safely anonymous about it. But now that wall was down. She was revealing herself to him, like a marble statue turning to flesh. Adam could feel the entire landscape disappearing around them. He was falling, deeper and deeper into her gaze, following her down, until falling became ascending, ascending toward something beyond this world—

It ended. Just as effortlessly, Beatrice closed off the circuit she had opened between them; the marble sheen returned to her skin, covering back over her delicate inner world. Releasing Adam, she turned to look at the ocean. *Her big trip,* Adam thought. *She's leaving and she may not be coming back.* He didn't need words from her to understand. After a few moments, she looked back to Adam with a bright, unexpected smile. "The wind is perfect!" Turning, she ran up the path toward town. "Come on!"

$$\diamondsuit$$

Paradiso 9 flew across the open water with Beatrice at the helm. At her side Adam carefully watched her every move. She trimmed the sails and adjusted the lines, then shouted, "Now you do it!" It was harder than it looked. Given the strong wind and choppy water, just keeping the boat on course required constant attention, leaving no time to get lost in anxiety or self-judgment. He simply did his best. At one point while they were trying to tack into the wind, the boat came around so hard that Adam almost lost his footing on the slick deck. Still, for a first-time sailor, Adam wasn't doing that bad.

A few hours later, the water was calm enough for Adam to sit up near the bow of the boat with his feet dangling over the side. Before him the ocean extended all the way to the horizon. It looked different from this perspective. From a boat on the water, the distant line that signified the edge of the world looked closer and sort of two-dimensional, like a painting on the wall. *A wall that doesn't seem so far away,* Adam thought. *I might even be able to touch it if I just reach hard enough.*

Adam heard the sound of Beatrice's sat phone ringing. Glancing back toward middeck, he saw her answer. He tried not to eavesdrop, but he still caught small bits of conversation. She was needed . . . weather conditions . . . how long it would take . . .

When the clock strikes midnight, Adam thought. *Maybe the boat is going to turn into a pumpkin.*

Beatrice was giving nautical coordinates to someone. Her voice had that tone of authority Adam had heard when they had first met out on the cliffs, and he had mistaken her for a park ranger. Now she was asking to speak with someone else, and her voice grew quieter. Adam wasn't able to make out much more after that, but he thought he heard his own name mentioned several times.

Beatrice hung up.

"No more hooky, I guess?" Adam called back toward the helm.

Beatrice shook her head, frustrated. "We don't launch until the day after tomorrow, but I have supplies on board that are needed up there tonight."

"If you really need to go, then you should go. I don't want to hold you up any longer . . . well, actually, I do." Adam shrugged. "Trying to not lie so much."

Beatrice flashed a sad smile.

"Sounds like quite a trip," Adam said casually, hoping Beatrice would share more information about it. She set the auto-helm to keep the boat on course, and then headed up the side of the boat toward Adam. For a while they both sat quietly looking at the horizon.

"I came across a place once," Beatrice finally said, her chin slightly nodding toward the distance. "Out there. An island. Unlike anywhere I've ever been. Like a completely different world. Pristine." She seemed to be choosing her words carefully. "It's extremely remote, this place. So difficult to get to that very few people have ever made the journey. I know it's hard to believe—that there is still somewhere out there that's remained relatively hidden from the globalized world. But it really exists. I've seen it."

Adam did think that was hard to believe but chose not to say anything.

"My father," Beatrice continued, "the kind of research he does requires conditions that, for many reasons, have become nearly impossible to create in the world today. That's one of the reasons we've organized this trip."

"Sounds like a lot of people are involved."

"We're one group of several coming from different countries. The others are involved in similar work, some first-rate minds, all of whom have been preparing for this for years now." Beatrice looked down at her hands. "And for me—I've always wanted to be a part of something that could make a real difference, that could truly serve a greater cause. Everything I was doing before, all the protests and activism and charity work, was always just . . . like rearranging deck chairs on the Titanic. Nothing changes when you try to fight directly."

"The currents are too strong," Adam threw in, thinking of *Navigations of the Hidden Domain.*

Beatrice glanced at Adam when he said this but then turned her gaze back to the horizon without saying anything.

"So what will you be doing there?" Adam asked. "I'm not sure I understand."

"Actually you do." Beatrice took a deep breath. "Remember when I told you there was a reason we met? That it wasn't just a coincidence? What I meant was—there is more to us meeting than just . . . you and me."

"Okay. Now I'm really confused."

As the afternoon sun filtered through her hair, amplifying it into an amber brilliance, Beatrice again searched for words.

"Sometimes things happen in life, and on the surface, they seem random or meaningless, but in truth they're part of something much bigger. It's like there's this invisible layer to the world, folded into this one, connecting everything in a very deep and sacred way. And even though we've been conditioned not to see it anymore, conditioned not to give our attention to it . . . Certain people can still make contact."

Adam felt her words tugging at that hidden place inside him that was longing to breathe again. "I think I understand, but . . . What does that have to do with me?"

Beatrice weaved her fingers into Adam's. Again that sting, the slight burning sensation tickling his skin. "Would you come with me to where the boat is loading? It would be for just one night. I'll bring you back in the morning. There's someone I'd like you to meet."

CHAPTER 20

BLEEDING THROUGH GLASS

Blake sat alone in the glass aquariumlike conference room of the abandoned offices on the 34th floor. The rumors turned out to be true when the floor's former occupants, Ad-Detailer, got the axe last week. Already an apocalyptic wasteland of a tech company gone bust, strewn with empty cubicles, tangled piles of Ethernet cable, random keyboards, and power strips.

When the end comes, it comes quick, Blake thought.

Almost as bad as the fear that this unthinkable fate might one day befall his own company was the knowledge that this office space would not remain empty for long. If Blake was going to take advantage of the misfortunes of Ad-Detailer and expand Pixilate to an additional floor, he needed to move quickly. He needed to show Adiklein an idea so exciting that he would have no choice but to green-light it. He needed *Zombies*. Specifically the ones that were locked up inside of Adam's b-drive in an encrypted project labeled Zombie.v12.

USER NAME: SheppardA@PixalateGH.Vskies.com

PASSWORD: _____

Blake stared at the password prompt. He had snuck up here to have room to think and hopefully to hack his way into Adam's drive. If humanly possible, he wanted to do this on his own. Blake was familiar with cracking passwords using a brute-force attack, a method of traversing the password window with every possible key combination, but that would take an incredibly long time. It made more sense to try some good old-fashioned guesswork first.

So far he had tried all of Adam's personal information: birthday, address, family names, and family birthdays. No luck. He had then moved on to the zombie theme, but the hundred or so variations he'd come up with had all been declined. After a few other fruitless approaches, Blake decided to go with free association, but that quickly deteriorated into pure frustration.

IHATEBLAKE; password declined. IHATEBLAKEDORSEY; password declined. IDONTAPPRECIATEBLAKEASMUCHASISHOULD; password declined.

IHATEMYLIFE, I'MAFUCKINGNUTCASE, I'MAFUCKINGNUTJOB. Declined, declined, declined.

Blake stood up. Of course he didn't really think Adam was a fucking nut job. *I'm just pissed off right now, that's all,* Blake told himself. *And I have every right to be. If he was feeling so overworked, why didn't he say something? Or maybe choose a better time to snap? Like after we showed the Zombie idea to Adiklein. Or at least after the Expansion launch.*

Blake had never been a big drinker, but he sure felt like a shot or two of whiskey right now. After all that talk about butterflies and bees with Adiklein, Blake wondered if his boss was the one with the mental health issue. *One thing's for sure—Adam's no butterfly, and I'm not about to pin him to some fucking case. All I've ever wanted was to help him. Adiklein just doesn't know the complexities of our relationship. Our history.*

Blake sat back down in front of the laptop. He needed to crack this password, but he kept hearing Adiklein's voice in his head, whispering in that sneaky accent. "I know who he is, Blake . . . I know *what* he is, for you."

I have always had Adam's best interest in mind, Blake argued back in his head. *Even those few times I wasn't completely honest, that was only to protect him.* Blake was now thinking about Softools, where he'd gotten Adam his first job. *It was absolutely true that no one at the company liked Adam. I had only suggested they fire him because I knew it would be better for him to be near his stepmother and work out of his garage. And it did work out better. For everyone—especially Adam.*

Blake went on to assure himself that he had always given Adam credit for his work, and he'd always seen to it that Adam got paid generously. *So Adiklein insinuating that I'm somehow stealing Adam's ideas—that's complete bullshit. They're Pixilate's ideas. Adam contributes to the company just like everybody else.*

The plain and simple fact was that Adam would be nowhere without Blake, and Blake had nothing whatsoever to feel guilty about. There was no need for Adam to know about Blake's history with Jane. It wasn't like they had ever officially dated. *Just the occasional hookup in high school . . . and a few times after that,* Blake admitted to himself. But that had all changed once Adam entered the picture. *Once Jane and Adam became an item, the whole fuckbuddies thing ended. Okay, there was that one time we slipped. But that was 100 percent Jane's doing.* Jane had come over to Blake's place one night when the kids were at their grandparents' and Adam was pulling all-nighters at work. *She was just lonely and horny, and Adam wasn't paying her any attention, so whose fault was that? Certainly not mine,* Blake told himself.

He began to type again. BLAKEUSESME, BLAKELIES, BLAKECHEATS, BLAKESOLDHISSOUL, BLAKEISNOTHINGWITHOUTME.

Blake slammed the laptop shut.

Back down in his own office, Blake leaned his forehead against the glass wall that faced the Bay. It was late enough now that no one would interrupt him. On his desktop he'd started up the brute-force attack on Adam's drive. As the software cycled through possible combinations of characters, the time estimator gave Blake a projection of 6,065 hours—not a number he wanted to dwell on.

Leaning with his forehead against the windows was oddly comforting. Ever since moving into this new office, this was the position Blake took whenever things got stressful. In the weeks after he bombed at that Cross-Pollination Brunch, he had stood here for hours. What no one else knew about that epic failure was that the concept Blake had presented that day was 100 percent his own; Adam Sheppard had had nothing to do with it. At the time Blake hadn't been completely aware of why this idea was so important to him, but now he saw it clearly. He'd wanted to prove to himself that he didn't depend on Adam, that his own ideas were valuable.

And here he was again. Back up against the glass, this thin layer of crystalline matter holding him in place, keeping him suspended in air. Without it he would plummet down into oblivion. *The glass is Adam,* Blake thought, despite himself. *The glass is Adam.*

On one of the smaller buildings across the street, a new billboard was going up. Blake watched as two men used their push brooms to glue up a section of a woman's cheek. It was an advertisement for Hawaii travel and pictured a family of four laughing on the beach. The copy read: **Live the dream. Be the dream. Be Hawaii.**

Blake wondered how the fuck someone could *be* Hawaii. Why wasn't it enough just to *go* to Hawaii? Blake had listened to Adiklein speak many times about the innovative marketing he'd done early in his career, about "identity culture," and "pulling the invisible strings in the collective subconscious." Blake honestly couldn't give a shit about any of that. All he knew was that if he didn't get Adam back, Adiklein would make Pixilate disappear. *Like he did to the company that used to occupy the floor above us.*

Looking down at the street below, Blake imagined where his body would go *splat.* Right there on the sidewalk, maybe. Right between the building's back entrance and that row of old newspaper stands.

At that exact moment, 33 stories below, Michael looked up from his wheelchair and, despite his cloudy, damaged vision, saw not only Blake but Blake's *thoughts* as well. Plain as day, Michael watched them bleeding through the window at the spot where Blake's forehead touched the glass, precipitating on the opposite side of the pane in a milky, gray mist. Collecting together like drops of rain on a windshield, the mist formed into small rivulets sliding up the side of the Tower, growing into capillaries, then veins, merging with larger and larger vessels. This pulsing, gray latticework that Michael saw covering the Virtual Skies Tower was no less than the collective mental chatter of every distracted, overstimulated mind in the city. A constant flow of attention, in the highly potent form of low-level anxiety, collected here against the walls of the Tower, the city's magnetic center. Up the sides of the Tower, gray tentacles continued to merge, again and again, swelling in girth until they reached the Tower's foggy crown and disappeared into the glass pyramid.

Of course Michael knew that the Virtual Skies pyramid was not *really* empty. Michael knew all about pyramids, how potentates had used them for thousands of years to project their influence. Michael had even witnessed San Francisco's other "empty" pyramid being constructed back in the '60s. They had put that one up to stop the cracks that were starting to form in society back then, and it had worked. After the Transamerica Pyramid went up, everyone fell back in line. And that was nothing compared to the new one.

There was something special about this Virtual Skies pyramid, how it linked to the emanation of other towers in other cities, slowly blanketing the earth. Michael had been keeping watch from his post between newspaper stands since the day the new tower opened, studying the technology it employed to access people's minds and entangle them in its web of digital distractions. Most disturbing of all to Michael was that there was something about the quality of this tower's vibrations that he recognized. His suspicions were verified the day he caught a glimpse of the Tower's high priest slipping into the garage in his black limousine.

It had happened late one night when another homeless man, new to the block, had set down cardboard in front of the Tower's garage entrance. When the limo pulled up, its driver jumped out to shoo him off. That was when Michael saw the rear window lower and a face appear—first yelling at the driver and then looking in Michael's direction. For a split second, their eyes met, but it was enough. It was *him*. The same man who 30 years before had destroyed Michael's life—had betrayed him along with the rest of their group, stolen their work, and then set in motion the terrible accident that left Michael in a wheelchair for life, his brain all twisted and tangled, his wings forever broken.

The man didn't seem to recognize Michael before the window slid up, and the limo eased away. But Michael knew without a doubt. Hidden beneath the seat cushion of his wheelchair, he kept a large manila envelope with a few important things inside, including an old photograph. It was Michael's only evidence of past events that he could now barely remember. Everything else had been destroyed in the psychedelic blur that was the aftermath of the '60s. But this photograph was proof that what he was able to see looking up at the Tower tonight was not just his imagination.

Michael reached down and slipped the photograph out of the envelope. As painful as it was to look at, he needed to see it from time to time. In the light of the Tower, he used a finger to scan the rows of faces, friends—all lost. At the center of the group was a tall black man with an Afro as proud as his smile. It was hard for Michael to look at who he had once been, so he quickly moved on. Trembling now, his finger drifted up toward the back of the group, where he found the man's face. Younger but definitely the same face he had seen in the limousine.

Before the accident, when Michael had his wings and could fly between worlds as freely as most men walk the streets, he had known the potential of a thunder-perfect mind. But tonight all Michael knew was how tired he felt. Just as the doctors had warned him, his seizures had been getting worse. The bright explosions in his temples had gone from occasional firecrackers to full-on Fourth of July extravaganzas. There were medications that could help, and hospitals willing to treat him, but meds blunted what was left of Michael's ability to see, to *really see*, and now he couldn't afford to look away. Right now his job was to keep watch on the Tower.

CHAPTER 21

MAN IN THE WOODS

Beatrice and Adam sailed north for about three hours until they reached an area of California called the Lost Coast. If someone wanted to get lost, this was definitely the place to do it. Due to the steepness of the coastal mountains, no state highways or even county roads had ever made it into this stretch of the state. The only means of access was either a network of logging roads that had fallen into disuse when the old-growth redwoods became protected by environmental regulations, or by boat.

The inlet where the pier was supposed to be located was not visible from the open water, and as they sailed closer to land, Beatrice had to motor the boat through a series of dangerous rocks and small islands. Finally the entrance to the cove revealed itself— a narrow break between high cliff walls rimmed with twisted cypress trees hanging on for dear life. As they approached, Adam saw that the inlet widened, and the cliff walls sloped back and down to the far side, where a small riverbed emerged from the forest. Next to the river, an old, wooden pier extended out into the bay. Beatrice explained that this place had once been used by a lumber company to gather and ship their dressed trees.

Several local fishing boats were anchored in the natural harbor. Dwarfing them all was the boat docked alongside the pier, a rugged, 100-foot-long expedition vessel built to face off against icebergs and sea monsters. Adam saw men hauling supplies up a gangplank onto the broad deck.

Once *Paradiso 9* had been tied up, Adam waited as Beatrice made her way over to the massive ship. He could see her talking to several members of the crew. A few minutes later, she came back on board.

"He's still up at his house. It's not far. Give me a couple of minutes. I need to grab a few things, check in with Anush, and then we can drive up."

"Anush?"

"The cat."

"Oh, right. Is it okay to leave her here?"

"She never leaves the boat. Why don't you go down to the parking lot and get the Jeep he leaves down here. It should have a card in the window that says Camp Nineteen."

Beatrice went below deck as Adam headed off to look for the car. It was already getting dark, but he found the Camp 19 card in the window of a vehicle that had the unmistakable shape of a Jeep, although it was so caked with dried mud that it may very well have been a giant turnip. Ten minutes later he and Beatrice were bouncing up a winding, rutted dirt track as the vehicle's headlights carved a narrow tunnel of light through the dark canopy of redwoods. With each turn the track grew rougher.

"What's Camp Nineteen?"

"The lumber companies left a lot of abandoned structures up in the hills, old camps that people later converted into homes or whatever. After my parents split, my father wanted to stay off the grid, so he ended up here. His version of Walden Pond, I suppose, but without the publicity."

"Who else lives up here besides your dad?"

"Mostly folks who knew my dad and wanted to stay involved with his work, or who discovered him through—oh, watch out right here."

Adam slowed as they approached a large mound of rock taking up the entire right side of the road.

"Go slowly, and if you stay left and keep one tire on the side of the rock, you'll have just enough room to squeeze by," Beatrice said.

Adam did as she instructed, and as the vehicle tilted, Beatrice fell into Adam, laughing. At the top of the next ridge, they came to a wooden gate encrusted with the same sepia-brown dirt that covered the Jeep and everything close to the road. Beatrice jumped out, and Adam watched in the headlights as she pushed open the old gate. Before returning to the car, she bent down and picked something growing on the roadside. Back in the passenger's seat, she placed it under Adam's nose. Horsemint.

After a couple of hundred yards, the silhouette of a large cabin came into view. Light from inside leaked out through shaded windows onto the lush surrounding greenery. Several old pickup trucks were parked out front, one of which was full of bulging cardboard boxes. Beatrice led Adam toward the front porch via a footpath that was lined on either side with a collection of rusty metal objects—gears, saw blades, engine parts, and other odd lumber camp relics. The front door led straight into a large, open living space that, despite everything being packed in boxes, felt warm and inviting. There was a pleasant musky odor, a mix of wood fires, oil lamps, wet wool, and another scent—powerfully familiar to Adam but too elusive to name. Beatrice was now leading him down a dark hallway, toward the glow of a back room, and as he stepped in, Adam was immediately awestruck by what he saw.

The room, almost as big as the one they had just passed through, was filled floor to ceiling with books. Packed bookshelves against all four walls. Desks, tables, and chairs covered with books. Moving boxes crammed with books, surrounded by towering stacks of books, teetering precariously high. Tucked away here and there Adam saw other objects—a lamp, a reading chair, a side table with a collection of bird feathers in a large Mason jar, an old Chinese diagram of the human body, and prints and paintings of various sacred places from around the world. It reminded Adam of his own cluttered cubicle back at Virtual Skies—only this was the supersize version. And just as in his old work space, Adam sensed a hidden order to this labyrinth that only its creator could navigate.

"Glad to see I'm not the only one holding things up," Beatrice said to the room, which so far had shown no signs of life.

"They're telling me I can't take any more books," came a gravelly voice with a hint of childish concern. A moment later Adam noticed a large head poke out from behind a distant literary mountain range. The man was in his late 70s, with deep-set eyes completely shadowed in the dim light, and white hair sticking up all over the place as if he had just woken from a nap.

"You can take a few of your books, Dad. You just can't take them all," said Beatrice.

"These *are* just a few of my books," he replied with a wry smile.

Beatrice's father made his way toward them through the obstacle course of books and boxes. He wore a plain, beige Windbreaker that reminded Adam of the one Dustin Hoffman wore in the movie *Rain Man*. His slow movements gave an initial impression of infirmity, and for a moment, Adam wondered if they might need to dive into the book maze and help him out. But as Beatrice's father drew closer, Adam saw that he was more than capable of managing on his own. He had a pleasant scholarly face with weathered lines to match the volumes around him. And he emanated a sort of clumsy yet good-natured serenity, Adam thought, like an adorable grandfather on some TV sitcom.

Except for his eyes.

With enough light now to pull them from their hollows, his eyes were revealed as large, black opals, coiled and intense, like a panther lying in wait. Adam immediately sensed that he had seen these eyes before.

"Hey, pumpkin," Beatrice's father said as he embraced her. "Nice of you to finally show up." The family connection between Beatrice and her father was more than clear, yet they acted more like old comrades than father and daughter. As they separated from their hug, Beatrice's father turned to look at Adam. "And this must be the troublemaker you told me about. The grandson of the remarkable Anne Beers, isn't that right?" His dark eyes lit up with astonishing warmth.

"Yes, that's right. Adam. Adam Sheppard."

Adam was still trying to piece together where he had seen this man's face before. *The pictures on Beatrice's boat,* he thought. *The old guy in the photos. But it feels like I must have seen him before that. As a kid maybe?*

"Ah, yes," said Beatrice's father, examining Adam's face. "I see it now. You were quite the force of nature. You probably don't remember me, though. You were just a boy, and I looked rather different back then."

"Sorry, but I don't remember much from those days."

"Quite an extraordinary thing, the two of you running into each other again." Beatrice's father glanced at his daughter then looked back to Adam. "And it sounds as if you and I have already reconnected too, at least in a way."

Adam looked to Beatrice for help, but all he got back was her enigmatic smile.

"She tells me that you've happened on a copy of a particular book I wrote?"

"Book?" Then it hit him. "Wait—you're—"

At once, and from two completely different quadrants of Adam's brain, came the answer to the identity of these fathomless eyes now looking at him. This was the man he had seen as a child down in the hippie grove, the man with thick, red hair and a bushy beard, typing endlessly on his typewriter—*click, click, clack, click, click, ziipppp.* The man to whom Adam could put any question, knowing it would be treated seriously. The man who had warned him about evils he would one day face out in the world, things like "domestication," and "the system." These were the eyes of the outlawed professor squatting in the woods below his grandmother's house, the man who had told Adam that he was writing a book that one day might help him—*"a book just for you."* Adam also recognized these same eyes as belonging to the man whose black-and-white photo he taped into the back of an obscure book he'd bought from a homeless man in San Francisco. They were the eyes of the "crackpot genius" who had written *Navigations of the Hidden Domain*, the disgraced professor who had slipped off into the ocean of obscurity.

◈

"Would you *please* stop unpacking everything—"

"Your friend might want some coffee. You want me to be rude to a houseguest? Don't have many of those out here."

"Don't use Adam as an excuse just because *you* want a cup of coffee."

Still in a mild state of shock, Adam sat at the kitchen counter, watching Beatrice and her father, Virgil Coates, bickering like an old married couple.

"You like kimchi, Adam?" Coates held up a rather disgusting-looking Mason jar he had pulled from somewhere or other.

"Dad, stop it!"

Just then a man came through the front door. "Got the truck filled up, so I'll take a load down now. You still want to ride down to the dock with me?" he asked Beatrice.

"Yeah, thanks. Be right out." Beatrice grabbed her parka and went over to Adam. "I just need to help sort out a few things, but I'll be back up here later on. Give the two of you a chance to talk."

Adam nodded.

Beatrice gave him a quick kiss and then whispered, "Don't mention the cigarettes. He thinks I quit." Moments later Adam heard the truck outside rumble away, leaving him alone in the house with Virgil Coates.

Coates had unpacked two coffee mugs, a kettle, and an old French press, but was still rooting around for some coffee. Just beneath the rummaging sounds Coates was making, Adam noticed for the first time the thick silence that comes with being out in the woods. Hoping to fill it, Adam searched for something to say. He was still trying to accept the fact that he was in the same room with the man who had written *Navigations of the Hidden Domain*. *I should say something about the book*, Adam thought. *I had so many questions reading it, all those times I was like, "If only I could talk to the man who wrote this . . ."* Well, here's your chance. Of course now Adam could not think of a single question.

"In a way," Virgil Coates said, breaking the silence, "I wrote that book for you." He filled the kettle with water and went over to the stove, struck a match, and lit the gas burner. "For people like you. I'm curious to know how you came across it."

"I . . . um . . . I know this sounds strange, but I bought it from a homeless person."

Coates smiled. "I've heard stranger." He then seemed to consider Adam's words more seriously. "Where did you meet him? This homeless person?"

"Just outside the building where I work. In San Francisco. He's always at the same spot by these newspaper stands, with his blanket and books and incense. His name is Michael. He's got pins all over his jacket. Butterflies."

Coates said nothing at first but then gave a very slight nod. He turned to the French press and started scooping ground coffee into it. "Black okay? There's no milk, and I can't find the damn sugar anywhere."

"Black is fine, thanks."

Coates heaped a few extra scoops of coffee into the French press. For a moment it seemed as if the conversation might be over, but then Beatrice's father said, "And this building, where you work, would it happen to be that new tower downtown?"

"The Virtual Skies Tower, yes."

Again Coates nodded. "Rene Adiklein?"

"Yep, he's my boss. Actually, more my boss's boss."

"I know Rene," Coates said.

Adam was unsure he had heard him correctly. "Did you say you know Rene Adiklein? As in personally?"

"It's been a long while, but yes. And in the interest of full disclosure, I once tried to shoot the man."

The water on the stove started to boil. Coates turned off the burner, took the kettle over to the French press, and began to slowly pour the hot water into it.

Adam was blinking rapidly like Dynamic Dave, trying to grasp what he had just heard. "Shoot?" he finally asked. "You mean, like, with a gun 'shoot'?"

"Not a moment I'm terribly proud of. But those were very different times, and I was a different man back then."

Adam tried to picture Coates holding a gun and pointing it at someone—not an easy image to construct. "If you don't mind me asking, why did you want to shoot Rene Adiklein?"

Coates was carefully stirring the water and grounds with a large, wooden spoon. "We were involved in some research together. I was at Berkeley, teaching philosophy and religious studies. A group of my students and I had become interested in certain ideas. Extremely old teachings, forgotten, you might say. Inner disciplines that we began to experiment with." Coates placed the top onto the French press but waited to push down the plunger. "When Rene found out about us and got involved, he was already a big deal on campus—the social psychology hotshot from the Sorbonne. Very intelligent, obviously, and ambitious. He was able to help expand our work and bring in some much-needed funding."

"So what happened?"

"We started to make some rather important discoveries about the unconscious mind. I felt we needed more time to investigate our findings so they could be used responsibly. Unfortunately Rene had a very different agenda."

Coates turned back to the French press and checked the color of the coffee. Apparently it wasn't ready yet.

"Is that why you tried to shoot him?"

Coates shrugged. "Like I said, not something I'm particularly proud of. But things happen for a reason. Sometimes things need to go down before they can come up." Coates pushed down the plunger. He then poured a cup of the coffee for Adam and brought it over.

Adam took a sip. It was the strongest, most bitter coffee he'd ever tasted.

CHAPTER 22

THE CONVERSATION

Adam sat down on the wooden bench facing the fire pit behind the cabin. The fire, which must have been well underway when he and Beatrice had arrived, was mostly glowing embers now. With a few pokes with a stick and a couple of well-placed logs, Coates expertly brought it back to life.

"Are you warm enough?" he asked.

"Yeah, I'm fine, thanks." Adam actually wasn't fine. Even with Coates nearby, he found the woods unnerving. *It's so damn quiet out here*, Adam thought. Lurking just beneath the little noises—his breath, the creaks of the wooden bench, the crunching sound his shoes made on the frosty earth—was a weighty silence that felt almost like a living thing. *Why does silence frighten me so much?*

"So." Coates settled into a nearby camping chair and was looking at Adam. His face was relaxed and open, with an avuncular look that seemed to say that everything was going to be okay. *But everything isn't okay*, Adam thought. That awful silence was really goading him now, inviting a sticky dread to well in his gut. Adam racked his brain for appropriate things to say, just to fill the void, but then, to his surprise, Coates set his cup on the ground next to him, took a deep breath, bowed his head slightly, and closed his eyes.

Okay . . . Adam waited. *Am I supposed to say something? Or do something?* He readjusted his hands on his lap—making scratchy fabric sounds. His hands felt awkward now, so he shifted them again—more scratchy sounds. His breathing was halting, and his thoughts were racing like a swarm of wasps. *Is he taking a nap? Did he have a heart attack? I thought we came out here to talk.*

After a time Adam found himself imitating Coates. He closed his eyes and tried to sit still and quiet. But before long his body began to rebel, itching and twitching in every conceivable manner. *Why is this so damn difficult?* He suddenly had an overwhelming urge to check his cell phone, which was in a gully somewhere on the road to Mendocino. Adam's eyes popped open, and he saw that Coates still had not moved.

The fire made a loud hiss, and then, to Adam's horror, another sound began to fill his head. It was the maddening ring of his tinnitus, rising up as if to fill that unbearable silence. Fearing a panic attack, Adam quickly pressed a finger to his ear.

"That."

Adam looked across the fire. Coates was still sitting with his eyes closed. *Did he say something?* Adam wasn't sure. But then Coates continued to speak in a low voice. "That . . . is not your enemy. Don't pull away from it. Welcome it, like you would an old friend."

As Coates spoke Adam felt something inside him slowly relax, creating a small space detached enough for him to step into. The dread was still there, rising from his gut to his chest, the tinnitus was still there ringing violently in his head, but a small part of Adam seemed to separate from it all.

"Focus on the fire." Coates's voice was soft.

Adam did as he was told. There was a spot low in the coals that Adam found himself drawn to, a small cave deep within the logs, glowing orange and white. As Adam kept his eyes focused on this one spot, he felt himself falling in toward it. The crackling of the fire grew louder, displacing the ringing sound; the warmth was now filling his chest, burning away the dread. Adam heard a hollow pop, possibly from a log, and then everything fell silent.

It was like being inside a bubble. The stillness of the woods, which had seemed so threatening, had given way to something altogether different. This new silence seemed to accept Adam, to invite him into it. And he began to feel a subtle vibration fill his body, replacing the panic that had been about to overwhelm him. Blinking several times, he looked around. He was sitting in front of the same fire pit in the same woods behind Virgil Coates's cabin. But something had changed. Everything he looked at seemed clearer, more vibrant. The towering redwoods around them weren't just trees anymore. They seemed to have come to life—shifting, breathing, reaching proudly into the night sky.

The stars also appeared brighter. Closer. Adam had the uncanny feeling of no longer being outside, but of somehow being *inside* the world around him. He was part of it all, and it was part of him.

Across the fire Virgil Coates was watching Adam intently. Panther eyes, yes, but they also conveyed a sense of infinite compassion. Adam suddenly understood he was no longer sitting with a sitcom grandpa in a *Rain Man* jacket. He was in the presence of a truly remarkable human being. Not just a charismatic personality like Adiklein, but a man of an immense *inner* strength. *If an asteroid were to hit the earth right now,* Adam thought, *and blow everything to smithereens, the man in front of me would not be shaken by it. Not in the least.*

"Here you can speak from your heart," Coates finally said. "You know how to do that. It's not something you ever forget."

Adam wasn't sure he was capable of speaking at all. His entire body had begun to feel heavy and sedated.

"I'm not sure . . . I can." It took a moment before Adam realized the voice was his own. It didn't sound like his voice, even though he had felt it resonate in his chest.

Coates didn't respond. He seemed to be listening to what came after Adam's words. Then he said, "What is it that you want to know?"

What came next from Adam spilled out unbidden. "I want to know who I am. I want to know why I'm here. I want to know . . . what I'm supposed to do, *really* supposed to do." Adam's head began to flood with judgments railing against the clumsy things coming out of his mouth. There were so many intelligent questions he had dreamed of putting to Coates, but here he was babbling on like a five-year-old.

Coates's eyes held Adam's, giving his full attention to every word. After a long silence he asked gently, "Are you afraid of death?"

The question cut right through Adam's mental clamor, hitting on an underlying truth he had not seen was there. "Yes." Adam took a deep breath, and tears appeared in his eyes. There was no emotion with them; it was simply a release. "Yes, I am . . . I can remember now, as a boy back in Little River, there was this kitten. And I remember watching it play . . . in a dirt driveway, next to this old truck. It had some fishing wire and it was all tangled up in it, wriggling around. Then someone started up the truck and was backing up, and the kitten wasn't able to move in time and . . . and I watched as the tire slowly backed over it." Adam looked down at his open palms. "I heard it mew for a few seconds, and then it was over. The kitten's little body was crushed and limp, when just moments before it had been so . . . full of life.

"That night I remember for the first time understanding that one day I'd be dead too. And I wondered what that would feel like. What does it feel like not to *be* anymore? The thought terrified me so much that I couldn't sleep. I had asthma pretty bad as a kid, so I already worried that if I fell asleep I might not wake up again. And so I promised myself that I wouldn't go to sleep ever again. It sounds silly now, but I remember being so serious about it. I just didn't want to let go of the urgency I felt to . . . *be*. As if giving in to sleep was somehow accepting the prospect of someday *not* being. Like the kitten."

Adam smiled. "I think I lasted a day, maybe two, struggling to keep my eyes open." Adam looked at Coates. "Since then, I guess you could say I've slept quite a lot. And lately it feels like I've been sleeping through most of my adult life."

"Would you say that the fear you experienced as a child might be related to the panic you struggle with now?"

Adam nodded. Years of psychotherapy with Dr. M. hadn't taken him as far as Virgil Coates had gone in just a few minutes.

Coates picked up a stick and poked the fire. A swirl of sparks burst into the air, and Adam watched them float up into the night sky.

"What if I told you that what you're after is not necessarily answers to your questions, although they are important. What if what you're looking for is, in truth, that intimate connection to the world you once had as a child . . . that sense of everything being woven together, and you were not separate from all this, but part of it."

Coates looked at Adam to make sure he was following. Adam nodded. "But as you grew older," Coates continued, "the part of you that could see that aspect of the world fell asleep, and the world as it truly is disappeared from you. The pain you feel of loss is your growing awareness that this other world still exists— another life you're meant to be living."

"Yes, like the man in your book, searching for the Hidden Domain . . . but I thought that was just a metaphor? Some unobtainable utopia, something not real."

"I assure you, it's quite real. You've just been taught to no longer see it." Coates took a moment before continuing. "And now you are too busy, like everyone, not just in our culture, but throughout the modern world. We are all too busy in the pursuit of what we've been brought up believing we need to focus on."

Coates picked up his coffee mug and took a sip.

"We need to get things to give us comfort, we need achievements to give us a sense of self-respect, we need money to give us a sense of value, we need to appear a certain way—in other words, happiness has become synonymous with the satisfaction of desire. And so, to satisfy desires, systems have been put in place, not only to satisfy our desires but also to create new ones in order to keep it all moving. More and more products must be invented, more and more things must be bought. Part of the very nature of desire is that it can't be satisfied for long, so once we're *hooked* by something, breaking free becomes a terrifying prospect.

"But there is another part of who we are, a side that, you could say, we have lost touch with almost entirely. Sometimes we experience it in moments of great crisis, or in the presence of extraordinary beauty or great love. Maybe there is an earthquake, or maybe it's the moment your child is born, or sometimes for no apparent reason at all—you simply step off a plane in a new country and look around and realize—'I'm here . . . I'm me . . .' And in that moment, it's as if this other self appears. For a moment you are alive in a completely different way . . . and then it's gone."

Adam knew the feeling, at least he had since returning to Mendocino. "But why can't I feel like that all the time? Why does that 'me' have to go away?"

"Because it hasn't been fully born yet; it's been covered over. The thing we call ourselves is largely cultural conditioning. We take the product of our outside influences to be who we are. I am my name, my career, my complicated past, my ambitious future, my social security number, my credit card debt. And if I ever have doubts about who I am, I've got plenty of relatives and friends with endless pictures to prove it." Coates gave a hint of a smile.

"This patina of information covers this other self like a cocoon until this other, true self becomes too weak to appear on its own. And so, a kind of inner struggle is needed to help that self to break free. That small voice inside you is longing to be heard, but first we need to learn how to nurture it."

"Nurture it how? With what?"

Coates leaned forward in his chair, the light from the fire catching in his pupils.

"With *attention*."

The word hung in the air between them. *Attention*. The same word at the heart of Adiklein's TED Talk. But the way Virgil Coates invoked it was as if intoning the name of an ancient god. "Your own *attention*, that is what you are starved for. Your attention, which today serves the dreams of other men."

Coates's eyes glowed. "This thing we call attention is the most uniquely human characteristic we have. Your attention is the one thing you can truly call your own. Everything else belongs to those outside currents existing through you, regardless of you, pulling you this way and that. But what you choose to give your attention to is truly unique. Your attention is who you really are." Coates allowed Adam a moment to consider this.

"And yet, almost every moment of every hour of every day, it is taken away from you—stolen by the endless distractions of our busy outer world: getting, doing, needing, buying, worrying, craving, and a hundred thousand other attachments that have hooked into your being and are quite literally *feeding* on you."

Adam couldn't help but think of *Lust 4 Blood*.

"Constantly bleeding attention, we are too weakened to make any meaningful contact with our inner world. We never come to know that what we call *attention* has the capacity to develop in ways quite unknown to the ordinary mind.

"And yet, to become aware of this hidden domain is not only our birthright, it's our duty. If humankind doesn't begin to evolve inwardly, soon I'm afraid we'll see life on the planet change in other, less fortunate ways."

This last sentence gave Adam a chill. "You mean we'll self-destruct?"

"Our existence is not the only thing at stake. Human beings are part of a much larger system, and like the other life forms that came before us, we arose on this planet to serve a very definite purpose. One we've lost touch with.

"And now, unfortunately," Coates continued gravely, "there are powerful forces out there working to keep humanity the way it is, holding us on our current course. Certain kinds of men, some of whom you and I both know, who feed on the sleep of others."

Adam nodded, understanding whom Coates must be referring to.

"Like parasites. It has worked this way throughout history," Coates went on. "Charismatic individuals come to possess an incomplete understanding of this inner domain, and then use it to manipulate the masses. An invisible slavery, woven so deftly into our cultural fabric that we don't even notice it's there."

Coates took a deep breath before setting his mug back down beside him. His fierce eyes focused back on Adam. "Despite what appear to be impossible odds, Adam, there is still *hope*. I've seen proof. It doesn't take many people, working together in the right way, to make a crack in our prison walls."

Coates looked into the fire, as if looking into the past. "There's a phrase that an old student of mine always liked to say. 'In times of change, a single, conscious man can equal a million sleeping.'"

Adam quietly repeated the words to himself. The embers of the fire had dimmed considerably, and Coates made no move to add more wood. Adam felt a sense of relief. There was still so much he wanted to know, but he realized that he had been given more than enough to digest in one night.

As if sensing this, Coates once again bowed his head and closed his eyes; the conversation was apparently over. Adam became aware of the deep silence all around them, and for the second time, it gave him a profound sense of well-being. He relaxed into it and noticed the return of those subtle vibrations, warm and tingly inside his body. A stronger sensation centered in his solar plexus seemed to rise and fall like his breath, but in its own rhythm. Relaxing further, Adam felt his eyes begin to flutter.

He heard a voice. Someone or something was speaking to him. And it was coming from inside his own chest. He had to be imagining this, he thought, or inventing it. But the voice felt so real, so familiar. It seemed to be speaking a language that was not English, not even words really. Adam was able to understand only fragments; it was trying to tell him something about the earth, about the deeper nature of things. *The earth is not what you think it is.*

Adam began to wonder if Virgil Coates was somehow doing this. It wasn't his voice, but at the same time, Adam sensed he might in some way be facilitating the experience. Adam tried to relax into his chest again, allow his thoughts to recede. The voice was still there, and this time Adam had a vague memory of having come in contact with it before. In dreams, in some distant garden. A strained, wheezing voice telling him something about his roots and branches being inverted. And now it was communicating with him again, trying to tell him something about humanity and a requirement that Adam himself must fulfill, an unmet personal obligation of some kind. But what could Adam possibly do to help? He was just one person among billions crawling on the planet's surface, a speck of stardust in an infinite cosmos.

Adam had drifted into his head again. But then as if to overcome his doubts, the voice pulled him back with unmistakable force and clarity. *"One human is capable of making all the difference. One life may be all it takes to tip the balance."*

When Adam came back to his surroundings, the redwoods had returned to the shadows, the stars had receded into an inky sky, and the man in the chair by the fire was once again a grandfatherly figure, preoccupied with picking something out of his coffee mug.

"My daughter should be back soon," Coates said. After a beat he looked up at Adam seriously. "She's smoking again, isn't she?" Before Adam could respond, Coates added, "No, no, that's all right, you don't have to answer that." Coates smiled. "She's her own woman. I think meeting you has made her happy. I thank you for that."

Adam shrugged. "I only wish I had met her sooner. You as well."

"Ships in the night, as they say." Coates stretched his legs and stood up. "Well, my ship apparently isn't big enough for my damn books, so I'd better go sort that out." He looked over at Adam. "Coming?"

"I think I'll stay out here a bit longer."

Coates gave a nod then walked toward the cabin. When he got to the porch, he stopped and looked back. "Have you ever read Dante? *The Divine Comedy?*"

"Just the comic book version," Adam said apologetically. "And to be honest, I just skimmed it for a video game I was working on."

"I see." Coates smiled before his face became serious. "To drastically alter the course of one's life midway through the journey, that is no small feat. It's one thing to get lost in a dark wood, but in order to descend like Dante, to go all the way down, a great deal is required. A sacrifice that you may or may not survive."

"What kind of sacrifice?" Adam asked warily.

Coates held Adam's gaze. "You're like a fish. You want to evolve, to climb onto the land, but the ocean won't let go of you so easily. The currents of your past would sooner destroy you than let you go free." Coates smiled again to soften the ominous warning. "Sooner or later, you'll have to face them. Please accept my gift of the powerful wish that you survive. Carry that with you, along with your own."

CHAPTER 23

BURIED IN YOUR HEART

Adam woke in an unfamiliar bed. Disoriented, he looked around. The room was not much bigger than a walk-in closet, with nothing in it but the bed, a bedside table, and a chair by a window. Something about the chair disturbed Adam. It was an ordinary old chair with a woven wicker seat and a high, straight back, but set by the window all alone it looked sad to Adam. A steaming mug had been set on the bedside table. When Adam took a sip, he was immediately reminded of where he was. *Beatrice, sailing up the coast, the cabin in the woods, meeting Virgil Coates, our conversation by the campfire.*

Adam dressed and, after a quick visit to a bathroom at the end of the hallway, made his way downstairs.

The main room looked emptier. Most of the boxes and furniture had been moved out. All that remained was that elusively familiar smell. Adam heard talking from the back porch where the night before he had followed the older man out to the fire. Moving closer to the screen door, Adam recognized Beatrice's voice.

Beatrice and her father were sitting in lawn chairs, drinking coffee, facing away from Adam toward a breathtaking mountain view. Just beyond the charred remains of last night's fire, the redwoods descended down the near hillside into a massive valley beyond. Fog filled the lower part of the valley like a milky lake.

"Yes, you were right . . . He is," Coates was saying in a low voice. "But there's only so much you can do for him. True under- standing is never given; it must be earned. We all abide by the same rules."

"I know. But to meet him again after all this time and then just walk away doesn't seem right."

"It's a tough one, sweetie. Just don't forget how hard you've worked for this trip."

"I know . . . If it were anyone but him, it would be so much easier to let go."

Coates reached over and placed his hand on Beatrice's fore- arm. "Do what you need to. If it's more time, I can always stall for you. Worse comes to worse, I can insist that they take more of my books."

Beatrice laughed, which gave Adam the opportunity to noisily open the screen door.

"Good morning."

Coates and Beatrice both turned. Coates returned the greet- ing, and Beatrice gave him a sunny smile.

"Hope I didn't oversleep. I'm guessing we probably need to head back soon."

Beatrice nodded. "Yes, we do."

Sailing back down the coast toward Mendocino, the waters were much rougher than the previous day. As *Paradiso 9* cut through the waves, Adam tried assisting Beatrice as best he could, but she seemed to prefer handling the boat on her own today, no longer the enthusiastic instructor. Adam also noticed that today she had a bit more of the cold park ranger in her voice. Perhaps she was preparing for the inevitable good-bye that awaited them back at Noyo Harbor.

Ordinarily Adam could imagine himself reacting to her remoteness by distancing himself in return. But not now, not with Beatrice. *I respect her too much to play games like that*, Adam thought. He watched her at the helm, moving like an extension of her boat. Even buried in her ridiculously oversize parka, she was a vision from heaven.

"Thank you for bringing me up to meet your dad," Adam finally said. "It means a great deal to me."

Beatrice looked over as if only just remembering that Adam was there. She gave him a quick smile. "Want to take over?"

"Uh, sure." Adam jumped up to the helm and took hold of the wheel. He felt more confident today, but Beatrice stayed next to him just in case.

"Keep to this course, directly into the waves. Don't let them get alongside you."

Adam did as he was told.

"How much do you know about your dad's research back in the sixties?"

Beatrice considered the question for a few moments. "He poured his whole life into it. Spent close to ten years setting it up and gathering the right group of subjects. Different types of people, but with one important similarity. He called them butterflies. People less bounded by their identity, more naturally inclined to be—as your grandmother put it—open."

The boat hit a big wave, and Beatrice reached out to help Adam, but he had already recovered on his own.

"So what happened? Your dad said they made discoveries of some kind?"

"They were experimenting with a variety of disciplines that involved very intense focusing of attention, looking at the link between the subconscious mind and physical reality. They were trying to map out ways to tap into what you might call 'the subconscious world.'"

"The Hidden Domain?"

"Right, dad's term for it. Apparently he had this one student in particular that came along, who was able to do some pretty unbelievable things. And then everyone else in the group started advancing exponentially. One of the most important discoveries they made turned out to be purely accidental."

"What was that?"

Beatrice brushed the hair from her eyes. "They began seeing effects in the environment on campus. Small things at first. Changes in how plants grew in the building they were working out of. A separate lab in the same building saw sudden changes in the behavior of the mice they were studying. The more intense their work got, the more the whole atmosphere on campus started to shift. Of course there were big cultural changes taking place at the time, but this was something else. It was as if the sky above Dad's building had cracked open, and for a brief window in time, reality itself seemed to be in question. Open and alive . . . but then Adiklein got involved."

Another large wave hit the boat, shaking it violently. Beatrice quickly adjusted the mainsail, slowing the boat, which gave Adam time to recover control.

"All right?" Beatrice asked.

"Fine." Adam gripped the wheel firmly. "So what did Adiklein do?"

"He saw a very different purpose for their work. Real world applications. New forms of marketing, subconscious methods of persuasion, the dramatic potential to influence people and control their attention."

"Like looking at E equals MC-squared and seeing the atom bomb?"

"Good analogy. My dad, of course, wanted nothing to do with it. So Adiklein turned on him and claimed his research—stole it, really. To cover that up, he did some pretty unthinkable things. Corrupting the study by introducing drugs, which led to paranoia and to accusations of abuse against my father. A bunch of the students involved, people who had trusted my dad explicitly, ended up psychologically damaged. Some even—" Beatrice stopped herself. Adam got the feeling that she was being careful about how much to say.

"It got really bad," she went on. "And it broke my father's heart, but there wasn't anything he could do. Adiklein had powerful friends inside and outside the university. They bought people off, manipulated the press, and ended up pinning everything on Dad by making him look like a monster."

I once tried to shoot him, Coates had said to Adam. Now it didn't seem so difficult to picture.

"That's how we ended up on that land below your grandmother's house all those years ago," Beatrice said with a smile. "Dad had a connection to Anne, I don't remember what exactly, but she was one of the few people who didn't believe all the lies about him. She also understood his work on a level that not many people did. She had a natural connection with the side of the world he was trying to reach. So my parents and a few of their friends, the ones they still had, came up to Little River to try to start over. It wasn't easy. Especially for Dad. He started writing as a way to cope, and *Navigations of the Hidden Domain* was the eventual result. But my mother and I left before he finished it."

"Why did your mother leave him?"

"She hated hiding in the woods. She was angry and she wanted to fight back. I think most of all she couldn't forgive my father for trusting Adiklein. The more powerful and famous Adiklein got, the more she blamed Dad."

Beatrice quickly adjusted the luffing mainsail that Adam had been too engrossed in the conversation to notice.

"Thanks." Adam took a moment to check that everything else was okay before continuing. "But then you reconnected with him, right? He sent you that postcard?"

"Right. We exchanged letters for a while. I was twenty-five when I first went to visit him. I had expected to find a bitter old man, but as you see, he's anything but."

"What had he been doing all those years?"

"Continued his work in private with small groups of people. Over time his book found its way out into the world, although Adiklein tried to suppress it. It attracted a community of people from different backgrounds, different disciplines, quietly working together. Scientists, psychologists, doctors, people from various spiritual traditions, all interested in solving the same problem."

"And what is that?"

"How to break through again, on a global level. How to unlock mankind's dormant potential, before we self-destruct."

Turning the tiller toward the entrance to Noyo Harbor, Adam felt his heart sink. Waiting for them at the docks was the inevitable good-bye, after which Adam would have to pick up the pieces of his other life, the one he had been avoiding thinking about.

When they pulled into the slip, Beatrice tied up the boat and began taking down the sails. A bit confused, Adam helped her as she started folding up and storing the mainsail.

"I've got this, Adam. You do the jib."

"So, then . . ." Adam started toward the front of the boat. "You're heading back up there today, right?"

"Not right away. I'll have to check the tide tables, and it's late enough so that I may wait to head out until the morning." Beatrice shot a glance at Adam, sensing his apprehension. "Unless you need to—"

"No. I'd be happy if you stayed."

"I didn't mean to assume that you—" Beatrice started to turn away. Impulsively, Adam went straight over and kissed her. Since the night they spent together, Adam had longed to be close to her again, to hold her. And although she had been affectionate, she had kept her distance. Now, though, she clung to him and buried her head in his chest so he couldn't see her face.

Adam spoke softly into her cold, damp hair. "I want to spend every last second I can with you, but I also know that you have to go. You belong out there with your father. What you're doing is important, and I don't want to keep you from that."

After a moment Beatrice pulled back and looked up at him. Her serious expression slowly gave way to a smile. "I'm staying until morning, whether you like it or not."

Adam gave her another kiss. "Then until morning I am yours to command."

"Good," Beatrice said. Her smile became sinister. "In that case, I've got an idea."

She turned and went below deck, heading all the way down into a storage area in the hull to grab a few supplies she said they would need. While waiting for her in the cabin, Adam briefly considered trying to pet Anush, who was stretched out in front of one of the bookcases, but wisely decided against it. Through the glass doors behind the cat, Adam noticed a new item had been added to Beatrice's collectables. Squeezed tightly between a bust of Isis and a conch shell was the box of number-two pencils he had given her.

Beatrice emerged from the storage area with a kerosene lantern and a crate of Virgin Mary jar candles. From the harbor they drove to a hardware store in Fort Bragg, where they bought a large shovel and a cheap metal detector. Next they hit a grocery store for picnic supplies: French bread, cheese, jam, olives, wine, and chocolate— and no protein bars. After that they drove down to Mendocino and stopped by the hotel. Up in room 25b, Adam grabbed some towels out of the bathroom and the comforter off the bed. He was on his way out when he realized that they didn't have any drinking water, so he emptied the minibar fridge.

Adam found a back stairwell and slipped out a side entrance to the hotel. Running over to the car where Beatrice was waiting, he got a few odd looks from tourists as he shoved the stolen contraband into the backseat. "If I get arrested for stealing hotel bedding, I'm going to tell the police you made me do it," Adam said as he slid into the driver's seat and quickly started the engine.

Heading down Highway 1, Adam got stuck behind an elderly woman driving an ancient Ford Pinto.

"Pass her, Adam!"

"I can't go! It's a double yellow line!"

"Low tide was at three thirty-five P.M. We're going to miss our chance. Go around her!"

Adam punched the gas and passed the old lady as Beatrice rolled down her window and waved.

Lugging their supplies through the cemetery and the hole in the back fence, they approached the sinkhole. It was low tide, so there was no scary rumbling from below and no waves washing in. After some deliberation they ended up bundling everything into the comforter, like a giant Santa Claus sack, and then using the rope to slowly lower it down into the hole. Once the sack landed, they tied the rope to a tree, and after Beatrice used it to climb down, Adam followed. By the time they both reached the sand, it was almost five o'clock.

Adam quickly downed a bottle of water while Beatrice organized the rest of their supplies. The tunnel that led out to the ocean was still relatively quiet. "Come on, Indiana Jones. Let's see if we can find it."

Beatrice grabbed the kerosene lantern and the metal detector and walked into the tunnel. Adam followed with the shovel. About halfway in, Beatrice stopped. She held the light up to the ceiling. "Here! See that!" She was pointing to a white, star-shaped rock.

"Some kind of calcium deposit!" Adam said. "Or maybe quartz with some—"

"It's my marker, silly!" Beatrice punched Adam in the arm before moving toward one of the walls. As she got closer, the lantern light revealed an alcove some four feet deep. "It's back in here! This is where we have to dig!"

Adam looked skeptical. "You seriously think it's still here?"

"Should be. It's surrounded by bedrock."

Before Adam could say anything, a large wave crashed into the far end of the tunnel. They both watched as the water rushed toward them, then slowed down and eventually stopped about 15 feet away. Beatrice shouted, "Come on! We've got to try!"

Adam dug. Even with the shovel, it was backbreaking work. He piled the wet sand on the side of the alcove that faced the ocean, attempting to create a barrier against the water, which was creeping closer with each break. Taking a short rest to catch his breath, Adam leaned against the slippery rock wall. Beatrice stepped into the hole and slowly waved the metal detector over the wet sand.

"Anything?"

"No."

"How do you know it's still here? Maybe it got washed out to sea."

"It's here!" Beatrice yelled over an approaching wave. "I can feel it!" She picked up the shovel and dug furiously as Adam watched the wave travel down the tunnel toward them. It stopped just a few feet away. Beatrice grabbed the metal detector again and did another sweep. Nothing. But then a faint *beep*. "Over here! On this side!" Beatrice shouted.

Adam grabbed the shovel, jumped back into the hole, and started digging where Beatrice had pointed. It was hard for him to tell how much progress he was making, since the farther down he dug, the wetter the sand was and the more it caved in on itself. Beatrice did another quick sweep. The beep was louder now.

"Keep going! We're close!"

Just then a huge wave came barreling into the tunnel with enough force to reach the sand barrier Adam had built at the lip of the hole. Adam started digging like a maniac as Beatrice used her hands to reinforce the sand wall. Just as the next wave started to crash into the tunnel, Adam heard a loud clink of metal against metal.

"I hit it! I hit it!"

Adam dropped to his knees and dug with his hands. Beatrice watched anxiously as a new wave came roaring toward them.

"Stop! Stop!" she yelled at the water. But this time the wave had enough force to rush up and over the sand wall and into the hole, partially flooding it.

"Damn it! We're so close!" Beatrice yelled. She was holding up the metal detector and the lantern to keep them out of the water. Adam, still on his knees, clawed at the sand with numb fingers. "No way! I'm not giving up!"

"Adam! The waves are only going to get bigger!"

"No! I can feel it! I can feel the top of the—" Adam's voice was drowned out by the thundering crash of the next wave.

"Adam! We have to get out of here!"

Adam wrapped his fingers around what felt like a metal handle. He pulled, and it snapped off.

"Shit!"

"Adam!" Beatrice was trying to pull him out of the hole by his jacket when the water reached them, completely flooding the hole and soaking Adam. But he had both hands around the metal box now, and with the water in the hole, it was starting to loosen the sand around it. He tugged with all his strength.

Out of the watery hole he pulled a rusty metal lockbox.

"You got it! Oh my God!" Beatrice screamed as Adam handed her the box. "Quick! Come on!" she yelled, running back toward the sinkhole.

Adam struggled to his feet, grabbed the shovel, and slogged down the tunnel as the biggest wave yet came rushing in. Already back in the sinkhole, Beatrice was jumping up and down, rooting Adam on like a cheerleader. "C'mon, run!"

Adam emerged from the tunnel with water at his heels and fell exhausted into Beatrice's arms.

Protected on all sides by flickering Ladies of Guadalupe candles, Adam and Beatrice sat, wrapped in towels, on the hotel comforter. The rusty lockbox, unopened, sat across from them like a third guest. "Are you afraid to see what's inside?" Adam asked.

"No." Beatrice said. But then she bit her lip. "But I think you should open it."

With a shrug Adam reached over and grabbed the box.

Opening it was tricky, but with some manly banging, Adam eventually popped off the rusty lid. Inside were the remains of what looked like an old, polyester raincoat. Adam gently unraveled it, revealing an odd assortment of childhood memorabilia: a hand-carved magic wand, several toy horses, some tinfoil stars, and metal pieces of an ERECTOR Set. Beatrice found a plastic butterfly with a missing wing, and smiled.

"Hey, just like your dream," Adam said. He picked up a strange-looking object. "I think it's a piece of wax," he said, examining it. "Any idea what this is?"

Beatrice looked at it. "I have no idea. Maybe—" Before she could finish her sentence, Adam saw tears welling up in her eyes as she placed the piece of wax flat on his palm. Now he noticed the impressions of little fingers. He flipped it over. More grooves, more fingers. The shape of a palm, another small hand pressed into the wax.

Suddenly Adam recalled the bizarre microfiche dream he'd had after meeting Beatrice on the cliffs. One of the images he'd seen had been a memory of Beatrice as a child, leaning over a lit candle, her green eyes sparkling, her matted, red hair pulled back in a ponytail. He saw her again now, slowly tilting a candle, allowing wax to drip onto his left hand. He could still feel the sharp sting of it hitting his skin.

"We made it the day your parents showed up to take you away," Beatrice said.

Adam was still inside their tree-cave in his mind, watching young Beatrice as she pressed her own hand into his, allowing the hot wax to slowly encase their hands, making them into one. "My magic spell," Beatrice whispered. "To bind us together forever."

The distant blare of a foghorn brought Adam back to the present. He blinked at the gnarled piece of wax in his hand and then looked up to Beatrice.

"Maybe this is the real reason you came back," Beatrice said. "Maybe it's why I came back."

Adam set the wax back down and reached for Beatrice's hand, the same hand that had been melted into his over 30 years ago. She was leaning in toward him, her lips trembling slightly, tinted blue from the cold. Adam touched her face, and she responded by rubbing her cheek into his hand. Their lips slowly met. "I don't want to lose you again . . ." Beatrice whispered between kisses.

"What if—" Adam stopped himself.

"What if what?"

Adam shook his head. It was something he'd been thinking about all day but hadn't found the courage to express. Besides, there were those things Coates had warned him about—trying to change too quickly, the currents of his past, some kind of sacrifice.

"Say it, Adam. What?" Beatrice pressed herself against him.

"What if . . . I came with you?"

Beatrice stared at Adam.

"I know, maybe that's impossible . . . Maybe I'm not even welcome, but my life here means nothing to me anymore, and—"

Beatrice silenced Adam by covering his mouth with hers. *"Yes,"* she whispered as she pushed him down into the comforter. *"Yes."*

❖

Dorothy had a special method for eating potato chips while working at Reception. By placing the open bag on the shelf beneath the desk next to her left knee, she never had to touch the chips with her right hand, which was needed for the computer mouse and the phone receiver. And next to the chips she kept a cloth napkin that she occasionally squeezed to remove grease from her fingertips before handling any paperwork.

Just as Dorothy bit into her first chip of her second bag of LAY'S Garden Tomato & Basil, the phone rang. She quickly finished her chip before picking up.

"Mendocino Hotel, may I help you?" Occasionally Dorothy risked eating during a phone conversation, but the tone of the person on the other end of the line made her forget about her chips entirely.

"Yes, I charged his credit card," Dorothy responded defensively, her face reddening. "My computer shows that the guest took items from his minibar, and so it's, like, my job to charge him for it. Just because he didn't want anything to appear on his company card, that is not my problem, okay? And he has been very unclear with me, so—" The person on the other end of the line cut Dorothy off. It took her a moment to understand that she wasn't the one in trouble.

"Yes. Adam Smith . . . or Sheppard or whatever." Her voice was now calmer. "Yes, of course, he's staying here. For three days. In the same room, thanks to me."

The voice on the line was talking again, telling Dorothy things that at first didn't sound possible. She almost thought that this might be a practical joke, as the voice described what was sounding like the plot to one of her favorite mystery shows. Unconsciously, Dorothy slipped a potato chip into her mouth as she listened.

"Oh my God!" she suddenly blurted out, bits of Garden Tomato & Basil flavored saliva showering the once-clean phone receiver. The voice on the phone warned her to stay calm. "Right, yes. Sorry," Dorothy said in hushed, secretive tones. "Of course, I want to help. Just tell me what to do."

$$\diamondsuit$$

The kerosene lamp had run out of fuel, but a scattered few Virgin Mary candles were still holding vigil. Adam and Beatrice lay snuggled in the comforter together, looking up at the circle of night sky visible from the bottom of the sinkhole.

It was no longer high tide, but Adam still felt the soft breaths of ocean air being pushed into the sinkhole from the waves inside the tunnel. He remembered the first time he had seen this strange place, spying down on Beatrice as she stood half-naked not far from where they were now lying. That was before she knew he was her childhood friend, her thief. It was before their dinner on *Paradiso 9* and the surreal night of lovemaking that followed. Before their carefree morning on the cliffs the next day, their picnic, the sailing lessons, and their journey north. Before Adam knew that Beatrice's father was Virgil Coates, the man who wrote *Navigations of the Hidden Domain*. It all seemed so fantastical, and yet it was real, so much more so than the past few decades of his life.

Adam felt Beatrice's breath against his ear as she nuzzled into his neck. "The first leg of the trip will take about two weeks," she whispered. "We'll travel as an ocean-going caravan, meeting up with boats from other countries along the way. Once we arrive, you'll see, it's like another world—"

"Where skies grow thin?" Adam whispered back.

Beatrice touched Adam's cheek with her pinkie, brushing away specks of sand. "Where skies grow thin," she repeated.

Adam felt himself drifting toward sleep. There was so much he needed to think about, to figure out before leaving. Jane, the kids, Blake, Pixilate. Could he really just walk away from his life completely? He'd already taken the first steps, that was for sure. But he knew he should at least e-mail someone. Blake, maybe. Jane would of course think it was heartless of him to abandon the kids. But would they even notice? There was just too much to think about . . .

Adam pushed his head down into the comforter, arching his neck slightly so he could look up over his forehead toward the tunnel behind them. He could see one last jar candle still flickering in the sand between him and the mouth of the cave. As his eyes strained to stay focused on the small flame, he felt as if he was falling. His eyes fluttered shut, and then he strained to open them again. Then shut . . . then open . . .

"Sometimes when I'm out on the open water," Beatrice was saying softly in his ear, "I'll lay on the deck of my boat like this. And I look up at the night sky . . . until it feels as if I'm floating in a sea of infinite space."

Adam's breath had fallen in rhythm with the breath of the ocean echoing up through the mouth of the tunnel. The flickering candlelight now seemed to be inside his forehead, the flame growing, filling his body with a heavy vibration. Overtones of subtler vibrations began to appear, and Adam imagined them lifting him up, out of his body. He imagined himself drifting down toward the ocean tunnel, gliding into it. Looking around inside, he saw everything with incredible clarity: the wet rock walls, the white mark on the ceiling, the alcove off to one side where they had dug. He continued moving toward the ocean, faster now, the opposite mouth of the cave approaching quickly. Then suddenly he emerged on the opposite side, gliding along the surface of the ocean. Slowly he turned his attention upward, toward the endless stars that arched around him on all sides.

"The sky out there," Beatrice whispered, "is like an enormous fishbowl. Inside it are all the things people give their attention to, all the things we believe in, all the things we know. And I like to imagine that all those twinkling lights up there aren't really stars, but actually tiny holes. Pores. And the light coming through them is the light from an unknown world . . . just waiting to be revealed, waiting for us to reach it."

The candle had flickered out, and Adam was suddenly aware that he was back in the sinkhole, back in the container of his physical body, lying completely still in the darkness. His eyes were open but he could see nothing, not even Beatrice beside him. He still heard her voice, though, as if she were inside his head now.

"Once you've learned to see beyond the stars," she whispered. "You begin to understand that anything we give our attention to, anything we dream, can become real."

❖

When Adam pulled up in front of the Mendocino Hotel, the sun wasn't quite visible yet, but the sky had begun to glow gray-blue. A thin layer of dew sparkled everywhere. Beneath the water towers, massive spiderwebs glistened like crystalline chandeliers. Adam barreled through the front door of the hotel, his hair matted, his face dirty, the stained, sandy comforter wrapped around his shoulders.

Dorothy stared wide-eyed as Adam approached with a huge grin.

"Morning, Dorothy!"

"Good morning, Mr. Smith," Dorothy said with a forced smile.

"I'm sorry to have to leave you, but I'll be checking out today."

"Okeydokey." Dorothy looked over to her computer screen.

"I just need to clean up, send a few e-mails, and then . . . Let's see, what time is it?"

"Almost six thirty." Dorothy's smile was fixed firmly in place.

"You know, I might want to rest for just a bit, a little nap maybe, but I need to make sure I'm out of here by nine at the latest. Do you think—"

"Would you like a wake-up call?"

"Perfect. Can we make it for eight fifteen?"

"No problem." Dorothy pretended to make a note on a piece of paper. "Are you heading home today?"

"Nope. Taking a trip." Adam smiled. "Going sailing."

Reaching the door to his room, Adam fumbled for his key-card, finally finding it in his back pocket. As he brushed sand off it, he noticed something odd. The room door wasn't completely shut. And the Do-Not-Disturb sign was no longer hanging on the door where he was sure he had hung it when he left with the bedding and towels.

Adam pushed open the door and stepped inside. In his room stood a man Adam had never seen before. He was in his late 50s, muscular build but with a potbelly, military-style cropped hair, and wearing a Mendocino County sheriff's uniform. The sheriff was not alone. On the couch sat Dr. Mendelson, flipping through Adam's copy of *Navigations of the Hidden Domain*. Looking up at Adam, he gently set the book aside.

"Adam." Dr. Mendelson's voice conveyed gravity and concern.

"Dr. M.," was all Adam could respond with. The incongruity of seeing Dr. M. sitting in this room was like running into a high school teacher at the mall.

"Come in, Adam. And shut the door, if you don't mind."

Adam didn't move. The sheriff took a step forward. The movement wasn't threatening, but it was enough to convince Adam to reach behind him and close the door.

"A lot of people are very worried about you," Dr. Mendelson said.

This was not the scene that was meant to take place right now. Adam was supposed to be sprawled out on the bed, falling like an anvil into a hard, dreamless sleep.

"I'm sorry to . . . hear that," Adam replied. "However, I can't really stay and talk with you about it right now—"

"No, Adam. I'm afraid right now is the moment when we must talk about it."

CHAPTER 24

Caught in a Substation

Blake Dorsey was so focused on negotiating Highway 128's twists and turns that he didn't even notice as his BMW sped past the nondescript dirt road on his left. Had he noticed the turnoff and been inclined to take it, he would have driven up a hill, around a bend, past an old car frame with blackberry bushes growing out of it, and eventually arrived at the front door of Art Stout's one-bedroom house. Art had kept Adam's iPhone on top of his refrigerator next to Nellie's chew toys, just in case that upset man he had spoken to showed up.

Today would not be that day. Today Blake and Jane were en route to Mendocino, where according to the police, Adam had used a credit card to buy six bottles of water from a hotel minibar. Jane sat quietly in the passenger seat, earbuds in, staring at her phone. As they rounded a bend, she saw the reception bars suddenly fill in and she quickly hit Dr. Mendelson's contact number.

The phone rang several times before someone picked up.

"Hello? Hello, Dr. M., can you hear me?" Jane held the phone out toward the windshield in an attempt to improve reception. "What's going on? Did you find him?"

Blake waited anxiously through the long pause that followed.

"Oh, thank God! Thank God you found him!"

"Yes! I knew it!" Blake slapped the steering wheel. "Adam, you fucking crazy bastard!"

"Yes, I think we're getting pretty close. The last sign said twenty-seven miles."

"Does he have his laptop with him?" Blake half whispered at Jane.

Jane shushed Blake with her free hand and then reached for her purse in the backseat. "The sheriff's station? Okay." Jane dug out a pen, but there was no paper.

Blake popped open the glove box and pulled out a flyer for an after-hours club. It was laminated, but Jane did her best etching on it.

"One-five-two Seacliff, right behind the post office. Dr. M.? I'm losing you, Dr. Mendelson . . ." The bars on her phone were dropping. "IF YOU CAN HEAR ME—WE'LL MEET YOU THERE. TELL ADAM WE'RE ON OUR WAY."

❖

Dr. Mendelson hung up the phone. He didn't catch the last bit, but Jane had repeated the address, and that was all that mattered. They had taken Adam to a sheriff's station only a half-dozen blocks from the hotel, which was convenient, but it was also small. "A substation," the sheriff had warned. "And it's a bit of a mess. We don't really see much action up here." When they arrived, the receptionist, the sheriff's aunt, was clearing her jars of canned pears out of the holding room Adam was to be placed in.

Dr. Mendelson peered in through the window of the door at Adam sitting quietly at a metal table. He had just been searched over by the sheriff, who was now heading for the door, holding a plastic tray.

"Keys, some papers, lot of sand," the sheriff said as he exited the room. He shook the tray like a skillet. "No sharps, no drugs."

As Dr. Mendelson examined the contents of the tray, the sheriff added sympathetically, "You know, he seemed pretty passive to me, but if you think you might need them, we do have a set of restraints somewhere around here."

"No, no," Dr. Mendelson said. "At least, not yet."

The few pieces of paper in the tray were all badly water-stained and mostly illegible, except for a receipt from a hardware store that showed the purchase of a shovel for $40 and something listed as a "Bounty Hunter VLF MD" for $79.95. Dr. Mendelson frowned, scribbled something on his notepad, and then stepped into the holding room.

Adam was staring at his shoes. The sheriff had taken his shoelaces, explaining that California State Law required him to remove any object that Adam could conceivably harm himself with. Adam couldn't imagine how the hell he could hurt himself with shoelaces. Regardless, they were now gone, a fact he was not thrilled about.

Dr. Mendelson sat in the chair opposite Adam, positioning his notepad and pen on the table just to his right. Then, as Adam had seen him do thousands of times before, Dr. M. steepled his hands, brought them to his lips, and began to lightly tap. He inhaled through his nose, his eyes locked on Adam's. All that was missing was the chessboard, Adam thought, and they could reenact Bobby Fischer versus Boris Spassky, game one.

Dr. Mendelson made the first move. "How many days have you been off your meds, Adam?"

Adam glanced at the clock—7:55 A.M. Another fact he was contending with.

"This has nothing to do with my medications," was Adam's response.

"I think that's for me to judge. When did you stop taking them?"

"A few days ago, I guess . . . but they weren't helping me. In fact, I feel better now than I've felt in years. I feel great, I . . . Look, Dr. M., I know what you think, but—"

"Adam, slow down."

Adam knew he was playing sloppily, giving away too much material too quickly, but he couldn't stop himself. "No, listen. Everything that's happened this time, it's different from before. I just needed to get away. To be able to hear myself think, and—"

"Adam." Dr. Mendelson lowered his hands, exposing his thin, pursed lips. "Slow down and talk *to* me, not *at* me. We're on the same team. And, as I hope you know by now, I am here to help you."

"Fine. You want to help me? Then help me get out of here."

Dr. Mendelson pressed his fingers back to his lips.

"You can't just keep me against my will. I haven't done anything wrong—"

"Actually, Adam, I can. You've shown intent to harm yourself."

"To what? What are you talking about?"

Dr. Mendelson reached into the breast pocket of his jacket, slowly produced a small, rose-colored envelope. Adam watched speechless as his therapist began to read aloud the private letter he had written to his wife. "I'm sorry, I can no longer go on living like this . . . You and the kids are better off without me . . . Please don't try to find me. I need to be alone now. To find my peace . . ." Dr. Mendelson set the letter down and calmly looked back at Adam. "I think your intent is pretty clear."

"But that's not what I meant! I was just trying to tell her how I felt. I wasn't going to DO anything! I didn't—"

"Calm down, Adam." Dr. Mendelson raised his eyebrows in warning. "Getting overly excited does nothing to help your case."

"Okay, fine. I'm calm." Adam took a deep breath before continuing. "I'm calm. And I'm telling you, calmly, that I had no intention of killing myself. I didn't come up here to jump off a cliff or whatever. I was—"

"What cliff?"

Adam stopped himself. He had lost the first match. Time to throw it and start a new one. Spassky 1–Fischer 0. Hanging his head, Adam searched for a new opening, a new approach that could get him out of this mess. "Look," he finally said, his voice flat, "I don't want to play games with you, Dr. Mendelson."

"Then stop playing them."

Adam knew his only chance to beat Dr. Mendelson was to draw him in, give him the impression that he'd already won.

"Dr. M., something incredible has happened to me. Something—" Adam sighed and shook his head. "I don't know if I can explain it, really—"

"Talk *to* me, Adam."

Adam looked up at Dr. M. and considered the dangers of the honest approach. It was potentially disastrous, but Adam couldn't think quickly enough to come up with an alternative.

"Adam, please," Dr. Mendelson coaxed. "How long have we worked together? Since you were seven years old, I have seen you through every single bump in the road. So, like it or not, I have a vested interest in your well-being. You need to trust me."

Adam took a deep breath and dove in. "I've met someone."

Dr. Mendelson nodded encouragingly.

"Someone special. Someone who has helped me see that these issues I've struggled with my whole life, maybe they're not what they seem to be."

Dr. Mendelson frowned slightly. "So you've met a woman?"

"Yes. And she's helped me figure out what's been missing in my life—"

"Who?" Dr. Mendelson interrupted. "Who did you meet?"

"Beatrice. Her name is Beatrice."

"Beatrice?" Hearing the way Dr. Mendelson pronounced her name made Adam regret having told it to him. "Beatrice. What's her last name?"

"Well, I'm not totally sure. Coates, I think. But then, Beatrice isn't her actual name. I know it sounds weird, but I don't actually know her real name."

Dr. Mendelson's hands returned to his lips.

"That's just what I've always called her," Adam stumbled on. "A kind of nickname from childhood. See, we were friends when I was a kid growing up here. Before Gloria and my dad took me away."

Dr. Mendelson pulled out his pen and began taking notes. "So Beatrice is a childhood friend that you came up here to meet?"

"Yes—I mean, no. I didn't plan on meeting her, she just happened to be visiting at the same time. It was a total coincidence. Or maybe not."

"What do you mean by that?"

"Nothing, I just . . . See, she was on her way to meet with her father, and it turns out that I know who he is. I mean, I knew him as a kid, sort of, but I also knew him from this book he wrote. My God, I can't believe I actually met him—"

"Adam, slow down. One thing at a time." Dr. Mendelson frowned. "First, who is Beatrice's father? Second, what book?"

The clock now read 8:48 A.M., and Adam was starting to panic. He had told Dr. Mendelson almost everything in the hopes that he would at least allow Adam to get a message to Beatrice at the docks. Adam hadn't said anything about where they were heading, only that she had invited him to go sailing for the day and that she was expecting him between 9:00 and 9:30.

Adam had also avoided saying too much about Virgil Coates after sensing Dr. Mendelson's disdain once he learned that Coates was the author of the book in Adam's hotel room. Instead Adam focused on Beatrice and what she meant to him. Dr. M. seemed to appreciate all this and said he had to make some calls to see what could be done, "considering the circumstances." He assured Adam that everything would work out, and to just be patient.

That was 20 minutes ago.

"Come on!" Adam yelled, banging on the window in the door to get the sheriff's attention. Adam could see him sitting at his desk in the other room. "I have to be somewhere! Can you please get Dr. Mendelson?"

The sheriff shrugged, pantomimed talking on the phone, and then pointed to the side of the room beyond Adam's line of vision.

At the desk that Adam couldn't see, Dr. Mendelson was on the phone. "No, these aren't the right ones," he said impatiently. Using one of the station's prehistoric computers, he was searching through medical records that his secretary had sent to him. "Look, just e-mail me all his transcripts, and I'll go through them myself. Yes, all the session notes from his early childhood; there's a specific name I'm looking for."

Another phone rang, and the sheriff answered it. After a moment he called over to Dr. Mendelson, "I have Dorothy Conway on the line; she's the woman from the hotel. Line two. You want to take it?"

"Yes, thank you," Dr. Mendelson told the sheriff. Then, to his secretary on the phone, "Ellen, I've got to take another call, but stay on hold until I get the files." He pushed a button on the phone. "Hello, Dorothy. Dr. Mendelson here. Thank you so much for calling—"

"*Come on!*" Adam was now hammering on the door with both fists.

Dr. Mendelson tried to shield the receiver from the noise. "Yes, you've been a great help, Dorothy," Dr. Mendelson said. "I just have one question for you regarding Adam's behavior that could help us out quite a bit. Adam told us that while he was in town here, he reconnected with an old friend of his, a woman named Beatrice. Did he ever say anything about running into someone he knew?"

The computer showed that transcripts of Adam's early childhood sessions had just arrived via e-mail. Dr. Mendelson opened them and did a document search for the word *Beatrice* while Dorothy rambled on about Adam's rudeness. Dr. Mendelson finally broke in. "Dorothy, hold on a second. Did you ever actually see the two of them together?" As Dorothy replied, the computer indicated 139 matches for the name Beatrice.

Jane and Blake sat side by side on the red Naugahyde couch in the front waiting room until Dr. Mendelson emerged from the back.

Jane rushed to meet him. "Oh my God, Dr. M. How is he?"

"Is Adam all right?" Blake followed.

"Yes, but the situation is delicate." Dr. Mendelson gestured for the two to sit back down, and then he leaned against the reception desk, careful not to knock over any of the receptionist's canning jars. "The most important thing is that Adam is safe. He hasn't hurt himself, which is very good news." Dr. Mendelson's tone was grave. "However, the law requires that he be seen at the county hospital, where he'll be placed on a seventy-two-hour watch."

"What?" Jane covered her mouth in disbelief.

"I may be able to waive the hold if we can get him admitted to a hospital in the Bay Area."

"I want to see him, Dr. M. He's my husband, and I want to see him."

"Yes. I do think that would be a good idea, Jane." Dr. Mendelson walked over to the couch and put his hand over hers, comfortingly. "However, there are a few things I want to go over with you first."

The clock now read 9:25. Adam had been pacing back and forth like a dog in the narrow space between the table and the wall when he heard sounds coming from the other room. A door opened and closed. People were moving around. Adam pressed his face against the small window in the door and tried to see what was going on.

Suddenly the sheriff appeared. He went straight to his desk without looking at Adam.

"What the hell is going on here? Where's Dr. M.? When am I going to be released? Hey! Look at me! Please, just look at me!"

Adam watched as the sheriff took an outdated, ball-shaped webcam out of a drawer in his desk. He then positioned it on top of a filing cabinet so it was facing toward the window in the holding room door.

"What the fuck is that? Please, just let me talk to—"

Dr. Mendelson came into view. He spoke to the sheriff briefly before they, together, approached the holding room. Adam stepped back as he heard the door unlock.

The door opened halfway, revealing only Dr. Mendelson; the sheriff had already stepped away. Adam considered rushing Dr. M., trying to make a run for it. However, when the door opened a little farther, Adam felt like he'd been punched in the gut. "No, no, no. How could you—" Adam turned away, looking for somewhere to hide.

"Let me know if you need anything," Dr. Mendelson said as he put a reassuring hand on Jane's shoulder. "We'll be right outside."

Jane nodded and walked into the room. She appeared calm, yet her eyes were wide, as if she was approaching a wounded animal.

"Adam?" she began softly, "Oh dear God, Adam. You can't imagine what we've been through, what the kids and I have been through."

"No, I'm sorry—I can't do this . . . I'm sorry." Adam refused to look at her. He had pushed himself into the far corner of the room, not wanting to face the humiliating fact that his wife was here.

"Adam, honey, everything is going to be all right. I promise." Jane crossed over to the table and slowly sat down. "I know you, Adam. I do. I know that this is your way of crying out for help. You've been overworked, and Blake even said he felt awful for pushing you so hard lately. He's going to make some changes at work. Adam, would you just look at me, please? . . . Adam, look at me."

Adam slowly looked up from the floor to meet Jane's gaze.

She was smiling at him, her lips trembling. "My God, sweetie, I love you so much. We just need a damn vacation." Jane let out a laugh. "That's all this is. You just need a break. You need Hawaii."

In the other room, Blake was trying to peek over the sheriff's shoulder at the computer screen that he and Dr. Mendelson were watching. The sheriff had explained that, due to budget cuts, the station had not been equipped with proper monitoring for the holding room, so this was their work-around.

On the screen Jane could be seen sitting at the table, her hands folded. Adam was across the room, in a corner. The image wasn't bad. The problem was the lack of sound.

"Did we find all of Adam's belongings?" Blake quietly asked the sheriff. "If they're still at the hotel, I could—"

"His laptop is safe, Blake," Dr. Mendelson cut in.

"I'm just trying to be helpful—"

Dr. Mendelson raised a hand, making it clear that Blake needed to keep quiet. He and the sheriff were listening intently, trying to hear Jane's muffled words from the other room. She seemed to be pleading with Adam. Adam was still pressed against the far wall, his body now rocking slightly.

Jane stood up. "I never told you this, Adam, but I made a promise to your stepmother just before she died. I promised Gloria that I would take care of you, sweetie, the way she had done before her stroke." Jane approached Adam, tentatively. His gaze remained firmly fixed on the floor. "I promised her I would help you stay balanced and grounded." Tears were beginning to well in Jane's eyes. "So you see, Adam, I failed. *Me*, not you. I'm the one to blame for all this."

"No. You didn't—you don't—" Adam's jaw clamped down tight. Various parts of his brain were beginning to short-circuit.

"You need support, honey. That is a fact," Jane said as she cautiously approached Adam. "That's a big reason we got married; remember our deal? We fit together. And I have not been living up to my end of the bargain. I've been neglecting you, Adam."

Jane's face was streaked with tears. She continued to move closer. "I won't let it happen again. Your medication, your diet, your work schedule, your exercise—we're going to get things back on an even keel."

"But, I—I—" Adam felt a surge of panic and quickly pressed his fingers to his ears, trying to contain the tinnitus that was spilling out.

"Everything is going back to the way it was—only better—so that you can do what you're so good at . . . what you *love doing.*"

Jane was directly in front of Adam now. She reached up to touch his hands, gently at first, trying to pry them away from his ears.

"No, I don't—I just—" Adam sputtered.

"You don't what, honey?"

"I'm not—I'm—"

Jane pulled her hands away in frustration. "Christ, Adam, just say it already!"

At that moment, Adam felt the pressure inside his head suddenly ease as if a valve had been opened. Everything in the room became very still. Time slowed. It was that uncanny feeling of being inside a bubble, his senses oddly enhanced. And beneath the small sounds in the room—the tick of the wall clock, a low rumble of water pipes, a car horn far away—Adam began to notice the *silence*. That same silence that he had heard beyond the campfire with Virgil Coates. It was here in the room with him, that original vibration from which all other vibrations arise. Silence was presenting itself to Adam, making itself available as a source of strength.

"I don't love you."

The clock ticked out several long seconds.

Jane said nothing at first. When she finally spoke, her face betrayed no emotion. "Right now you're exhausted, Adam. So what we're going to do—"

"Jane, I don't love you."

Now it was Jane who was forced to divert her gaze.

Adam continued. "I haven't been happy for such a long, long time now. I'm not saying our marriage was always this way, but over the years it has become a lie."

Jane nodded. "Okay, sweetie, that's okay. There are definitely some things we can work on and—"

"No, you're not hearing me, Jane." Adam's voice grew more resolute. "I don't want to be in this relationship anymore. I've met someone else."

Adam waited, but he didn't get the reaction he was expecting. Instead of anger or tears, to Adam's utter disbelief, Jane reacted with a smile.

"It's all right, sweetie. I promise. It's all going to be all right."

"Did you hear what I just said? I've met someone else."

"Once we get back home—"

"I've fallen in love with someone else. I've *slept* with someone else."

"It's okay, Adam." Jane took a step back. There was a flash of
panic in her eyes, but she was still smiling. "We can figure everything out as long as we just—"

"No!" Adam started after her. "Listen to me!"

Jane shot a quick look at the window, at the small webcam, her
eyes pleading for help.

At the computer monitor in the other room, the sheriff turned
to Dr. Mendelson. "Should we—"

Dr. Mendelson raised a hand. "Not yet. This needs to play out."
His eyes were glued to the screen where Adam was now standing
directly in front of his wife.

"I don't *love* you. Do you understand that?" Adam's tone wasn't
aggressive. It sounded more like he was trying to get through to
someone with a broken hearing aid. "I don't love you, Jane. I don't
even like you. We have absolutely nothing in common. I hate
yoga, I hate health shakes, I hate Blackhawk, and I fucking hate
Hawaii. Look at me, Jane. This time, you need to look at me!"

Jane looked at Adam; her jaw was clinched tight, the muscles
in her neck strained as if holding a difficult yoga pose.

"I am leaving you." Adam waited for a reply. Nothing. *"Do
you hear me?"*

Jane took a deep breath in, followed by a long exhalation. All
of the tension in her face fell away. "I hear you, Adam."

It was a voice Adam didn't recognize. The sweet, wheedling
notes were gone. The change was so unnerving that Adam had
to take a small step back. "So what exactly do you think you're
doing?" Jane continued flatly. "Leaving me for someone else?"

"It's not what I think; it's what's happening."

"I see." Jane's voice remained eerily cool. "And this person
you've met, what's her name, Adam?"

Adam became aware that the nurturing silence inside himself had evaporated. "Her name is Beatrice. She's a friend—well, more than that now. We grew up together—"

"How sweet," Jane said softly. She took a step toward Adam so they were face to face again. "And where is she now? Where is this Beatrice right now?"

"She's waiting for me," Adam said cautiously. "I'm supposed to meet her at her boat. I was supposed to be there already." Adam looked at the clock—9:50.

"So you're going sailing with this Beatrice? How romantic. Sail off into the sunset together, is that it?" Jane's eyes glowed with a vindictive fire.

"No—I mean, yes. We are going sailing but . . ." Adam stopped himself, took a breath, and then started again. "Jane, I know this is all very difficult, but please try to understand. It's not just about Beatrice. There are people she travels with, and this work that she's doing . . . Look, it's something that I need to be part of. This isn't personal. It's just something I've got to do."

"Well, that sounds just *wonderful*." Now Jane's tone was blatantly patronizing. "Oh, and let me guess. I bet this Beatrice of yours is going to take you to some really exciting places, right? Places you've always wanted to go? Places like, oh, I don't know, Egypt?"

"Yes—well, she's already been there, but—" As Adam realized Jane was mocking him, rage began to swell in his chest. "What are you saying?"

"Nothing, Adam. She just sounds so perfect. Too good to be true; just a little too good to be true."

Just then the door opened, and Adam turned to see Dr. Mendelson.

"All right, Jane. I think that's enough. Can you and I have a word outside?"

But Jane wasn't finished. She stepped closer to Adam like a little girl tormenting another child on the playground. "You met your *dream* girl, didn't you, Adam? Isn't that's *just soooo* sweet?

Your long-lost childhood friend? Your fairy-tale fantasy? Your little pixie dream girl—"

"You think I'm making her up?" Adam looked incredulously at Dr. Mendelson. "Is that what you fucking told her?"

Dr. Mendelson held up both hands. "Let's all calm down. Adam, we need to get you back home where we can sort this all out in the right environment—"

"I didn't fucking make her up!" Adam kicked the chair next to him in frustration.

"Sheriff?" Dr. Mendelson shot into the other room.

"Beatrice is waiting for me right now!" Adam yelled. "I was supposed to be at the docks half an hour ago!"

Jane laughed. "Right! So you can sail off together? Grow up, Adam. Start taking some responsibility for your life! This isn't just one of your stupid fantasy games."

"Jane! Please step outside and get yourself some coffee. I'll be out in a minute," Dr. Mendelson said sternly.

"I don't know what the hell he told you," Adam yelled, pointing at Dr. Mendelson. "But Beatrice is real! I've spent the past three days with her! I've been on her boat. I've met her father."

"Oh, really?" Jane said. "You mean the whacko who just happened to write that dumb book you're obsessed with! How likely is that? Give me a fucking break!"

Adam looked at Dr. Mendelson, speechless.

"Okay, Jane." Dr. Mendelson moved toward her. "You've said your piece. Now it's time to back off."

"Back off?" The veins in Jane's neck were bulging. "What about me? Am I supposed to just stand here and take this crazy shit? I'm his wife, goddamn it. I'm his wife!"

"Heeey, buddy." Everyone turned. Blake was in the doorway. "Thank God you're all right. We were all so worried—"

"Fuck you, Blake!" Adam had regained the power of speech. *"Fuck you!"*

"Sheriff! Get in here, please!" Dr. Mendelson called past Blake. Then, turning back to Adam, he put his pacifying palms back up. "Okay, let's all just settle down."

"NO! You all think I'm crazy? Well, I've got news for you. I've finally figured out what's going on, and *you're* the ones who are crazy!" Adam pointed at each of them in turn. "You! And you! And you!"

"And *you're* the one who was going to commit suicide," Jane screamed back. "But I guess you didn't have the balls to go through with it!"

Just then the sheriff appeared in the doorway, fumbling with what looked to be some kind of medieval bondage device. Adam's eyes went wide in disbelief. "What the hell is that?" The sheriff started toward Adam with the restraints.

"It's going to be all right, Adam," Dr. Mendelson said.

With the table in the way, Blake found himself awkwardly stuck between the sheriff and Adam. "Out of the way, son!" the sheriff commanded. But it was too late. Adam saw his opportunity and went for it, shoving Blake into the sheriff so that both men tumbled back. In that instant Adam slid over the table, reached the door and darted out. In the next room, he spotted the plastic tray with his car keys, grabbed them, and ran.

Flying into the waiting room, Adam was greeted by a wide-eyed woman behind the reception desk with two jars of canned pears held up, ready to throw at him. Adam made a move for the front doors. The receptionist stayed frozen in place, her eyes moving from Adam to the back room, where she could hear shouting. By the time she looked back, Adam was gone.

CHAPTER 25

Noyo Harbor

Running without shoelaces is not easy, but Adam did his best while at the same time trying to orient himself. The ocean was somewhere to his right. The main part of town was down and to the left. Then he spotted the water tower he had climbed, and he knew where he was. Main Street, where his car was parked, was not terribly far off.

A quick glance over his shoulder revealed that the sheriff had just emerged, followed by Blake and Dr. Mendelson. Luckily there was no sign of the deputy or the patrol car that had driven Adam to the station. Seeing Adam, the sheriff began to give chase while fumbling with the walkie-talkie on his belt.

Adam turned onto a side street. Halfway down he decided to ditch his shoes, jump a low fence, and cut through someone's backyard, giving him a more direct path to Main Street. On the next street over, Adam found himself in the middle of a small farmers' market. He did his best to move briskly through the thin crowd without appearing too frantic. Glancing over his shoulder again, he saw no immediate signs of pursuit.

"Did you ever find your friend?" said a familiar mono-tone voice.

Adam jerked his head around. Dynamic Dave stood a few feet away, next to a stand of organic rutabaga. "Your lady friend?"

"Oh, yeah. Hi. I did. Thank you. Thanks again for your help."

"Well, that's good I was able to help you find your friend."

"David, honey, come stick with the group," said a woman directly behind Dave. She appeared to be in charge of some people, who were all wearing bright blue Windbreakers. Adam also noticed that they all seemed to be . . . challenged. As in, mentally challenged.

"That's Adam Sheppard," Dave said to the woman as they walked off. "Grandson of Anne Beers, who lived in Little River from 1956 to . . ."

Wait, is Dynamic Dave autistic or something? Adam wondered. There was something disturbing about this possibility, but before Adam could give it any more thought, he saw the sheriff, who had not followed Adam through the yard but instead ran all the way around and was now directly in front of Adam at the end of the block. Luckily the sheriff was noticeably out of breath and had yet to spot Adam.

Adam shrugged out of his jacket, stashed it behind a farmer's van, turned, and walked briskly in the opposite direction. Just past the other side of the farmers' market, he could see Shandell's Organics, the place where he had first met Dynamic Dave. There was a walkway on the far side of the building, Adam recalled, which connected directly to the back of the Mendocino Hotel. If he could just make it there without being spotted, he'd be able to reach his rental car.

Just then a patrol car pulled up at the end of the block, right where Adam was heading. The deputy was driving, and Dr. Mendelson was in the passenger's seat. Adam was boxed in.

Trying to stay cool, Adam kept walking. He had only a little ways to go before he could make a move toward the side path.

"There!" Dr. Mendelson spotted Adam. The deputy jumped out of the car and started running toward him.

Adam shot a glance over his shoulder. The sheriff had also seen him and was closing in fast. Adam made his move, quickly darting to his right between two booths, and by the time the deputy and the sheriff got there, he had already disappeared down the path.

He reached his rental car with his chest heaving, his body shaking from exertion. Fumbling with the keys, he started the ignition and threw the car into reverse. Shifting into drive, Adam caught a glimpse of the sheriff running down the walkway alongside the Mendocino Hotel, walkie-talkie in hand. Adam nailed the gas.

◈

While driving, Adam had time to acknowledge the sharp throbbing behind his eyes—a migraine headache so stupendous it seemed to obliterate everything beyond the first 50 feet of highway. It wasn't until he was approaching the bridge to Noyo Harbor that he noticed flashing lights in the distance behind him. A new dose of adrenaline kicked in. The patrol car was far enough back so that he could make it down to the harbor before they did. That was all that mattered now; it was all Adam could focus on. *Just make it to the harbor. Just make it to Beatrice's boat.*

Reaching the opposite side of the bridge, he swerved recklessly down the steep incline toward the harbor. Avoiding potholes, Adam drove straight toward the entrance to the private docks, wanting to get as close as possible before skidding to a halt. He could hear the approaching siren as he jumped from the car. Out of the corner of his eye, he saw the patrol car was already speeding down the hill from the bridge.

Just make it to the boat, Adam kept telling himself.

Two men were inside the guard booth talking. One he recognized as Hank, the guard Beatrice had made a deal with to moor her boat. The other man was wearing a dark blue uniform, not a cop, but some kind of official. They both turned and looked out the windows when they heard the approaching siren, just as Adam hobbled toward them.

Hank picked up a clipboard and slid open the help window. "Hi, welcome to—"

Adam didn't stop.

"Excuse me. Hey, you need to sign in. Hey, fella—!" Hank called after Adam.

Just get to the boat. Get to the boat.

Directly in front of Adam, at the main loading dock, there was a large ship that Adam hadn't seen there before. Coast Guard, maybe? A cluster of men were standing out in front of it, joking around. They wore the same uniforms as the man with Hank in the guard booth. As Adam got closer, he noticed Department of Homeland Security was printed on their jackets. With his head down, Adam made his way quickly past them toward the metal ramp that led down to the private docks.

"Hey, fella, you need to sign in!" Hank was now hurrying after him. Out of the corner of his eye, Adam saw the men in uniform turn and look at him. Adam's barefoot hobble turned into a sprint. Something sharp dug into the ball of his left foot, but he could only acknowledge the pain and keep going.

Just get to the boat, get to the boat . . .

Seagulls flew from his path as Adam rushed down the pier toward the farthest moorings. Behind him he could hear Hank's heavy footfalls. The siren beyond had reached a peak volume and then suddenly cut off. Adam turned onto the last aisle of boats and was greeted by a violent glare of sunlight reflecting off the water. The throbbing pain in his head ignited and extended down into his body. Adam kept pushing forward, through a wall of pulsating light—light that was trying to hold him back, trying to keep him from reaching the second to last slip, where . . . Adam slowed to a stop.

"What the hell is wrong with you, fella?" Hank had come to a halt at the end of the aisle. He was winded and had a hand up to block the sun's glare as he slowly approached Adam. "You need to—"

"Where's the boat!" Adam demanded. "Where did she go!"

"Stop him!"

Hank turned to see who was yelling. The sheriff, followed by his deputy and Dr. Mendelson, were hustling down the metal ramp onto the private docks. Following them was a group of curious Homeland Security agents.

Hank looked back to Adam, who was now pacing back and forth on the opposite side of the slip like a mad dog, barefoot and limping, holding his head with his hands.

"Where is Beatrice's boat?"

Hank looked confused. "Who?"

"Beatrice!"

"Adam, you have to stop right now!" Dr. Mendelson yelled.

Hank turned again. Dr. Mendelson was now leading the pack.

"Where is it, Hank?" Adam pleaded. "You had a deal with Beatrice—a deal so she could dock her boat here!"

Hank shrugged. "Hey, fella, I'm sorry but I don't know who . . ." He turned back around just as Dr. Mendelson and the other men arrived. "I don't know what this guy is talking about," Hank said.

Eyes focused on Adam, Dr. Mendelson asked Hank, "Has there been a boat here at any point in the past three days?"

"Nope. Not for the past couple weeks."

"There haven't been any boats here at all?" Dr. Mendelson asked again.

"I can show you the log, if you want." Hank turned back to Adam. "Sorry, fella, but there's been no boat. Not in that slip."

Adam's entire body began to shake uncontrollably. He reached for one of the wood pilings to keep himself upright.

Dr. Mendelson took a wary step toward Adam. "It's okay, Adam. It's okay."

"*No!*" Adam's face was pale with disbelief. "You made me late. If I'd been on time, she'd still be here . . . she'd . . ."

"She's not real, Adam," Dr. Mendelson said gently. "None of it is. You imagined it all."

Adam's mind raced, scanning for evidence that Beatrice had really existed. The cliffs at night, Pete's magic bottle of wine, the woman at the entrance of the alcove, wisps of red hair escaping her giant parka, flashes of her porcelain face above a lighter flame—yes, it was her, it was real. "Her boat, it's called *Paradiso 9.* Get the Coast Guard to check it out. She's real! I know she's real!" Adam screamed hoarsely.

"Adam, Beatrice exists only in your mind. We've checked, and no one has seen her but you." Dr. Mendelson's voice sharpened as he attempted to get through to Adam.

Adam kept running through mental snapshots. His internal display fired off picture after picture: Beatrice walking along Highway 1 with a shovel. Beatrice down in the sinkhole. They spoke in the cemetery; she remembered him; they sat in his car, only a hand brake between them. He had driven her to *this* harbor—just over there, rain on the windshield, her dream about the crushed butterfly. And that night, on the deck of her boat, she'd stood in a white dress like an angel, like Dante's Beatrice, his guide to paradise. *But Beatrice is not an angel; she's real! She's flesh and blood.* And they had made love. And Adam had met her father, and they had made an arrangement to travel together. It had all been so perfect. Like a dream.

Like a dream? . . . Or *really* a dream?

A rising panic threatened to sweep Adam away. "No, it was real, it was all real . . ."

"You have been off your medication, Adam," Dr. Mendelson pressed in his reasonable, reassuring voice. "You have been under tremendous stress. The areas of your brain responsible for creative thinking, imagination, and dreams have gone into overdrive, blurring the line between fantasy and actual memory. You think you remember events, but they never actually happened. Beatrice is like one of your video games, Adam. She feels real, but she isn't. And there's nothing wrong with that. You just have to learn to accept the difference," Dr. Mendelson continued. "No one else saw this woman, Adam. No one but you."

"I met her father. I met Virgil Coates! And I didn't make him up; Virgil Coates is a real, living person."

"Virgil Coates?" Dr. Mendelson snapped. "I did some research into that disgraced fanatic. You've been reading his delusional, pseudospiritual garbage—which has provoked in you nothing but a false hope for things that simply do not exist. You have been staring at his picture taped inside your book, and so your mind naturally incorporated him into this fantasy you desperately wanted to believe was true."

"No, I met him. I did."

Adam scrambled to re-create the image of Virgil Coates in his mind. But the memory of the old man sitting across the fire was quickly receding. Fading into the darkness around him, until all that remained were his burning, compassionate eyes, like sparks thrown up from the fire pit, like two smoldering coals beneath the logs. Now all Adam could see was himself alone in the woods, staring into a dying fire. All that was left of Coates was a voice warning him of the currents of his past. Was this the test Adam had to face? Were all these people lying to him? Trying to trick him, pull him back into *their* version of reality? Or was that voice not Coates's but Adam's own, warning of a truth so unbearable that his conscious mind refused to face it. The truth that Dr. Mendelson was right, that Beatrice lived only in his own . . .

No, no, no!

"You have a condition, Adam," Dr. Mendelson continued. "A disorder. It is genetic, it is chemical, it is in your blood, and it is not *your fault*." Dr. Mendelson's voice was gently reeling him in. "It's not your fault, Adam. What else were you to do, as a boy, living alone with a grandmother who was unable to take care of you for days on end? What else could you do but go inside yourself and create a fantasy, an imaginary friend named Beatrice who could save you from all that traumatic loneliness."

It was a lie. Adam loved his grandmother. He loved his childhood. It wasn't traumatic; it wasn't abusive.

Adam pushed over the rickety filing cabinet of unreliable memories in his mind and went for that secret hiding place in the floor, to those deep childhood impressions, the ones that had so recently revealed themselves. They were his salvation, his last hope. He had to see his grandmother's house again. The living room. The cast-iron stove. His grandmother in her chair, himself as a boy again at his window, looking down at a yellow grass field that led to the redwood grove. And there she was! Beatrice. There she was, *absolutely real.*

But then the image began to shift, blur, and distort. Beatrice's white dress was blending in with the milky warps of the old glass window. And now her hair was starting to flicker, to become flashes of sunlight filtered through the red hummingbird feeder. And her eyes, her emerald-green eyes, becoming nothing more than sunlight refracted through a piece of jade sea glass on a windowsill, feeding the lonely heart of an abandoned six-year-old boy.

"NO!" Adam's chest heaved with wrenching sobs as his body sank against the dock's wooden piling. "*Why? Why are you doing this to me? I'm not crazy. I'm not.*" The sunlight dancing on the water in the empty slip was now so blinding that Adam was unable to keep his eyes open any longer.

"You're going to be all right, Adam. I promise."

Eyes shut now, Adam saw himself lying at the bottom of the sinkhole, wrapped in a white comforter, looking up at the stars. He could no longer see Beatrice next to him. All that remained of her was a voice whispering inside his head. *Anything we give our attention to, anything we dream, can become real.*

❖

By the time Blake and Jane arrived at Noyo Harbor, Adam had been escorted from the docks to the backseat of the patrol car. Prying him away from the piling by the empty slip required the sheriff, the deputy, and two large Homeland Security agents. However, once torn free, Adam's body went limp. He offered no resistance as they fit him into the sheriff's restraints and led him back to the parking lot.

Among those present, Hank seemed the most affected by Adam's meltdown. He was chain-smoking his third straight cigarette when Blake wandered over to the guard booth to bum one. "Boy, oh, boy," Hank said, offering Blake a Camel Light. "To see a grown man fall to pieces like that—Christ."

Blake cupped his hands around Hank's BIC lighter. After a long drag, Blake said, "Doesn't sound pretty."

"Hey, man, I've seen some ugly-ass shit go down, but nothing compares to that." Hank spat on the ground. "I feel awful. I didn't mean to get him in trouble, but there wasn't anything else I could do."

"Adam's had issues his whole life," Blake said. "Really, you were just calling it like you saw it."

"I guess." Hank glanced over at Adam slumped in the back of the patrol car alone. "Fuckin' Homeland Security." Hank was now looking over at the men walking through the aisles of boats, checking registration numbers against Hank's logbook. "They never used to bother coming up here, but after 9/11, when they took over the goddamn Coast Guard. Fuckin' Bush, man." Hank stabbed out his cigarette on the guard booth's railing. "Waste of taxpayer dollars."

"Well, I don't know. To me this looks to be a likely place for the next big terrorist attack," Blake said, deadpan.

Hank didn't laugh. He was looking out beyond the docks, at the bend in the river where it turned and disappeared into the redwoods. After a moment he looked back over at Adam and shook his head. "So, he's, like, a friend of yours?" Hank asked. "A good friend?"

"Best friend. Close to twenty years now. But trust me, it's never been easy."

"So you're gonna probably talk to him, then? I mean, after things calm down a bit? Maybe you could tell him I'm sorry. Pass on a message for me, once he's feeling better?"

Blake smiled. It had been awhile since he'd been around anyone like Hank, a real guy's guy. "Sure, man, no problem. And trust me, I've seen Adam through all sorts of crap. Trust me, he'll bounce back."

Down in the parking lot, Dr. Mendelson had taken Jane for a walk, explaining that it would be best if she stayed away from Adam for the time being. And after everything that had happened back at the sheriff's station, Jane could probably use some distance as well.

"You have to understand that was not your husband speaking in there," Dr. Mendelson insisted. "If you work with me, Jane, in time Adam will make a full recovery. But he needs your help."

Jane nodded and sniffled. "How did you know he was making it all up? That she wasn't real?"

"The name, Beatrice," Dr. Mendelson said. "When he first mentioned it, I kept thinking . . . Beatrice? Why does that name sound so familiar? Such an unusual name."

"Sounds like an old person's name to me," Jane said.

"Then it hit me. I dug into his early records, and there it was. Beatrice, first referenced in therapy as a childhood friend, but after further analysis, Gloria and I'd determined that this Beatrice was imaginary, a way to escape the traumatic effects of living with his grandmother. So for Adam to come back here, to this place, it must have triggered that protective mechanism and . . . brought her back to life, as it were."

A few minutes later, Dr. Mendelson went back over to the sheriff, and Jane sent Blake a text telling him to pick her up at the front gate so she could avoid going near Adam in the patrol car. She could see Blake was still over at the guard booth smoking and talking with the security guard. They were both looking out at the river beyond the docks, and the guard was pointing something out. When Blake received Jane's second text, she saw him read it and then turn and look over at her. He held up a finger, as if to say, *Hold on a second.*

"Jesus, Blake! Come on!" Jane said to herself. Finally Jane saw Blake stamp out his cigarette, say good-bye to the guard, and hurry over to his car.

As Blake pulled up, Jane barked, "What were you guys talking about?"

"Nothing. Just bullshitting. Can we stop for lunch? I'm starving."

Jane got into the BMW, and they drove off.

Adam had not moved since being placed in the back of the patrol car. Along with the restraints, he felt an enormous pressure wrapped tightly around his body, immobilizing him. It wasn't until the patrol car began to pull out of the Noyo Harbor parking lot that Adam used the last ounce of energy he had to turn and look back toward the dock. He watched it slowly receding, like a dream.

There, just beyond the boats, near the bend in the river, he could just make out the figure of a woman standing on the far bank. He was unable to see clearly at this distance, and yet he knew who she was. He had seen her from this same perspective more than 30 years ago, through a back window of a departing car, slowly fading away into the distance as he strained to hold on to her image.

Oh baby, baby it's a wild world,
It's hard to get by just upon a smile.
Oh baby, baby it's a wild world.
And I'll always remember you like a child, girl

Part 3

WHERE SKIES
GROW THIN

CHAPTER 26

206 EINSTEINS, 374 LIGHTSABERS, AND THE ONE UNFORESEEABLE TRIGGER

Today's fog was high yet dense, thick enough to contain the infinite drone of the city below—the endless subatomic clattering of 1s and 0s, the titanic reverberations of big-data analytics, the mind-numbing screech of teen trending buzz. And there at the center of it all, holding the sky's gray comforter firmly in place, was the Virtual Skies Tower, that massive tree trunk of glass and steel, with only its headpiece veiled above the noise. Eighty-one stories below the Tower's pyramid, also not visible today, was Michael the homeless man. His spot between the two rows of old newspaper stands was now as breezy as an eight-year-old's gapped teeth. No more wheelchair, no green Army blanket, no cheap incense, no Hardy Boys paperbacks, no butterfly buttons, no Michael. And no one passing on the sidewalk nearby noticed the difference.

"'With fourth quarter earnings exceeding all expectations, there appears to be no limit to the ubiquitous reach of the ever-expanding 'Virtual Sky,'" Mitch Silpa read aloud from the chair he stood upon. "The article goes on to talk about V. Skies 2010 acquisitions, blah,

blah, blah." Mitch scrolled down on his new tablet to the part he wanted the room to hear. "Okay, okay, here's the good bit." Mitch adjusted his big, white Albert Einstein wig, which had been included in the swag bag everyone had received. *"'Virtual Skies' increasing market dominance is thanks in no small part to the inspired social gaming services provided by Blake Dorsey and his fellow Pixilate geniuses.'"*

The 206 Einsteins gathered in the room broke out in a whooping cheer.

This was the first Pixilate Employee Appreciation Luncheon held on the 78th floor, in the same sacred banquet hall used for Adiklein's Cross-Pollination Brunches. And for many of the Pixilate employees present today, this was their first time this high up in the Tower, looking down at the city a quarter of a mile below, dining on The Commissary's specially prepared buffet culled from a database that tracked the taste preferences of every employee within the Tower.

Mitch shouted over the cheers as he continued. *"'Their new hit—'* Calm down, bitches, calm down! *'Their new hit, Lust 4 Flesh, with its addictive social-networking features, has quickly grown into an international phenomenon. The U.S., Europe, China, the entire world is hooked on a nonstop feeding frenzy that's devouring friends, neighbors, and co-workers alike.'"*

The room erupted in applause.

"'More impressive still,'" Mitch continued, *"'is the game's new spin-off,* Zombie Babies, *aimed at the growing kiddie/pretween market. Not only has the game quickly become the go-to parental godsend for keeping little ones distracted in the car, it has also given Virtual Skies' floundering social network, MyStar, a much-needed injection of young profiles hungry for new product.'"*

More applause. Some whistles and whoops.

"You guys put your hearts and souls into this shit!" Mitch shouted. *"Lust 4 Flesh, Zombie Babies*—these are milestones you will all look back on and be proud of for the rest of your lives."

Einsteins throughout the room continued to applaud, and some even rose to their feet.

Mitch raised a hand to let everyone know he wasn't done. "All right, all right. There are a few people I want to single out today. Of course, none of this would've been possible without our fearless leader, Bad Boy Blake!"

Blake stood and gave a casual wave.

"All I can say to you, brother," Mitch continued, "is that you are *killin' it!*" Everyone laughed at hearing Blake's favorite catchphrase.

Blake flashed a smile, anxious to sit back down. It was then that he noticed someone watching the event from the lobby just beyond the glass doors. Rene Adiklein, smiling proudly like a father at a graduation ceremony. He gave Blake a thumbs-up.

Blake returned the smile, a bit forced.

"And . . ." Mitch went on, "there's someone who doesn't always get the recognition he deserves, someone whose genius has kept us from going totally crazy down in the trenches. That's right, I'm talkin' about the guy who wrote the damn code that started it all—our one and only Engine Master!" Mitch started to clap as he looked around the room full of Einstein wigs. "Adam? Where the hell are you, buddy?'"

Blake waved, drawing Mitch's attention to the person seated right next to him.

"Oh, shit, didn't even notice you there. You look just like everyone else with the damn wig and all." Mitch laughed. "Stand up, buddy. Stand up."

Adam didn't move. He was staring blankly at the table in front of him, the white puffball wig dutifully on his head, unaware of Mitch's request.

Blake gave Adam an encouraging pat on the back. "Hey, buddy, Mitch wants you to stand up."

"Right, sorry." Adam stood.

The room cheered, politely at first, then more enthusiastically after Blake's familiar whistle of encouragement rang out.

Even Adiklein back behind the glass doors was clapping. In the lobby behind him, a gaggle of assistants were waiting meekly, and as the applause for Adam ended, one of them politely cleared his throat. "Excuse me, sir," he said, "the blimp people are waiting."

Adiklein turned and gave the young man a quizzical look.

"Project Bloom. The Wi-Fi expansion program?"

"Yes, yes, of course." Adiklein nodded. Project Bloom was the new Virtual Skies initiative to use high-altitude blimps to provide Internet access to remote areas of the earth. "Send them up to B&R. I'll join the group in a few minutes." Adiklein turned back to the banquet hall to catch one more glimpse of Blake's butterfly.

Adiklein had been more than pleasantly surprised when Blake retrieved Adam from wherever it was he'd disappeared to a couple of years ago. Without Adam, Adiklein was sure Blake Dorsey and his Pixilate team wouldn't have lasted out the year before being tossed in the proverbial tech company trash bin. Instead Blake's little *papillon* had brought back something more valuable than even Blake was aware of yet. Adiklein recognized it though. The raw potential of Adam's new code had a very particular fragrance to it, and Adiklein was, of course, a connoisseur.

$$\diamondsuit$$

Due to the luncheon, Adam was allowed to leave the Tower early that day. He walked straight to the Embarcadero BART station, making it in time to catch a train that would get him to the Walnut Creek station approximately an hour and a half earlier than he would normally arrive. Before boarding the train, he sent Jane a text to let her know. Jane immediately returned the text, thanking him for remembering to inform her of the change in his routine, but that Blake had already forewarned her about the luncheon so she could be prepared to be in Walnut Creek in time to pick him up.

As always Adam boarded the first car of the train and quickly moved as close to the front as physically possible. Earbuds in, he kept his eyes locked on the nearest window. Even with the new medications, riding the train was tough, especially during the three and a half minutes required to travel beneath the San

Francisco Bay. The feeling of being packed inside a communal coffin, along with the train's deafening roar and the slight change in pressure, sometimes triggered a wave of panic. So Adam kept his attention on the darkness outside the window, counting the fluorescent tunnel lights as they zipped by like horizontal lightsabers. Of the half-million people commuting on BART each week, Adam Sheppard was perhaps the only one to know the exact number of lights in the tunnels beneath the Bay. There were 374 lights in the eastbound tunnel (347 white and 27 yellow) and 393 in the westbound tunnel (349 white and 44 yellow), each one flying past the train almost as quickly as each day of the past two years.

"Om shanti, shanti Om . . ." a female voice chanted softly.

Adam opened his eyes. Jane was at the end of the bed. Dangling from one hand was her Tibetan Tingsha, while in her right hand she held the small mallet she used to gently strike the chime.

Ting . . . ting . . . ting . . .

"Cock-a-doodle-doo, Adam Sheppard. Tuesday, November 11th greets you with a smile."

Adam's life now ran on a schedule as precise as the German rail system. Each day of the week had a meticulously designed routine. Tuesday mornings started at 5:45 A.M. with the same gentle *ting, ting, ting*. After a trip to the bathroom and two eight-ounce glasses of water, Adam spent 20 minutes on the elliptical. At 6:20 Jane joined him in their home gym and led him in a series of personally designed stretches to help his posture and counteract the effects of sitting at a computer all day.

At 6:45 Adam showered, shaved, dressed, and drank two more glasses of water. By 7:10 he was in the kitchen, where a protein shake, vitamins, and medication awaited him. Madison and Chandler would also be there, ready to spend a few minutes of quality time with their dad (they both called him "Dad" now). At 7:30 the Sheppard family left the house together. Jane dropped off the kids at school and then took Adam to the Willow Terrace Office Park in Walnut Creek for his biweekly therapy session with Dr. Mendelson. At 9:00 Jane returned for Adam and drove him to

BART. And at 9:14 Adam—earbuds in—stepped aboard the first car of the San Francisco/Daly City–bound train and prepared to count subterranean lightsabers.

Adam's evenings were just as methodically planned after work, from the moment Jane retrieved him from BART, up to the moment he lay his head down to sleep. Weekend routines had slightly more variety: swim days, family-friendly movie nights, dinners with friends and relatives, marriage counseling, couples yoga, trips to museums, and occasional trips out of town.

"Routine is the cornerstone of mental stability," Dr. Mendelson had advised Jane and Blake early on in Adam's recovery. After the events of 2008, Adam had spent several months in a private facility that had a long-standing affiliation with Dr. Mendelson. After enough therapy, marriage counseling, and various adjustments to his medications, Adam was eventually reintroduced to the real world.

Dr. Mendelson was right. Routines and rules marked clearly with solid, yellow lines were essential in keeping Adam level. Structure and consistency were his new companions, and with the love and support of those around him, it became easier with each passing day. Not to mention all of the remarkable technological innovations that were appearing left and right—new devices, programs, and apps that could help keep Adam's life more organized and more efficient, help remind him of his appointments and medication, and keep all his lists updated. It was as if technology itself was conspiring to help Adam stay comfortably in sync with life as it zipped by.

Of course there were still bumps along the road. Dangerous "triggers," as Dr. M. called them, were bound to appear, regardless of how routine Adam's days became. Associations with the delusional events of 2008 were unavoidable: passing a red-haired woman on the street, seeing an online article on sailing, hearing a distant seagull cry, or just walking through the produce section of the supermarket and noticing the stack of bright navel oranges. "These triggers are not to be underestimated," Dr. M. warned. "But they are manageable so long as we don't try to suppress them. We need to talk them through, defuse them with words."

Occasionally Dr. Mendelson tested Adam's commitment by purposefully placing small triggers in his path to see if he chose to bring them up in his sessions. Like the *National Geographic* magazine strategically positioned on the coffee table in the waiting room; on the cover was a dramatic photograph of a man standing on a cliff, looking out past crashing waves, under the title "Beyond the Blue Horizon." Adam resisted the first few times he saw it, but eventually he picked it up. He then noticed the date of the issue, which was 10 years earlier than the issue date of any other magazine on the table. During his session that day, Adam admitted to looking at the magazine.

"Which is absolutely okay, Adam," Dr. Mendelson said. "You are only human. How you feel is not the problem. Hiding how you feel, *that* is the problem. Like coming to grips with your thoughts of suicide." Adam had eventually admitted to those dark emotions at the root of his previous breakdown.

Adam's life remained on an "even keel" for a good long stretch. However, Dr. Mendelson ended up being right about the dangers of these small triggers. And unfortunately, the one that would eventually set off the time bomb ticking away inside of Adam was something no one could have foreseen. No amount of openness with Dr. M. or regimented routines with Jane or pampering from Blake could have kept it from cracking right through all the protective layers around Adam and piercing what was left of his broken heart.

It happened on December 8, 2010, just a couple of days before Adam's birthday, two years to the date of his last episode.

The trigger was a dog.

CHAPTER 27

SOME CRACKS
DON'T MEND

"The word was *parachute* or *salamander*. It was tricky, wasn't it, Maddy?" Jane set Adam's pills next to his murky, green protein shake. The Sheppards had reached the sixth stage of Adam's Thursday-morning routine. Across the breakfast table, Madison and Chandler were providing Adam with quality time, while Jane recounted Madison's triumphant spelling-bee win.

"What was the word, baby?" Jane prompted.

"*Porcupine*," Madison said without looking up from the phone she held just under the table. Next to her, Chandler ate cereal while simultaneously flicking angry birds at militant pigs on his phone.

"Right, *porcupine!*" Jane tossed bags of baby carrots into the kids' lunch bags. "Madison got it right, and the snotty girl from Diablo was *eliminated*."

As Jane continued narrating juicy details, Adam did his best to appear interested. However, an acute awareness that something was different about the breakfast nook had been nagging him all morning. It was nicer somehow, more pleasant, and he couldn't figure out why. Had Jane repainted the room back when he was away recovering and he was only now noticing it? Or had she changed the drapes? No, everything was exactly the same, yet Adam still sensed a change, something . . . missing.

"And then that boy with too much hair product totally blanked on . . . oh God, what was that word . . . ?" Jane searched for it. "A total softball, something like—" She shouted over to Madison. "What was the word, Maddy? Some breed of dog, right?"

"*Malamute*," Madison said flatly, eyes on the text she was composing.

"*Malamute*, right! And so, Mr. 'NSync just froze up, which allowed Madison to move on to the final round."

The neighbor's dog, Adam realized. That was what was different. There was no more whining and yelping coming from next door. In fact, Adam couldn't even recall the last time he had heard the dog out there.

Maybe they got rid of it while I was away, he thought.

Without appearing to have lost interest in Jane's retelling of Madison's spelling-bee exploits, Adam casually glanced out the window toward the fence separating their property from the neighbor's. To his surprise, the dog was still there—still confined to the same long, narrow space between the neighbor's house and the fence. The same crazed dog Adam used to watch running tirelessly back and forth along the side of their house every morning, whining and crying. That same pain-in-the-ass dog was still out there. But it had changed.

The dog that Adam saw now was lying on the ground near the front gate with its nose pressed firmly into the cyclone fencing. Quiet, motionless, yet alert, it sniffed at the air on the other side, at the occasional fragments of life passing by. Adam felt a knot the size of a monkey's fist forming in his throat. Recognizing the hazard in the situation, he quickly drew a hand over his eyes to cover the inappropriate tears welling up.

"Did you show Dad the trophy, Maddy? Go get it from your room. It's a huge trophy."

Adam tried focusing on his breathing. He needed to think of something other than that dog out there. Despite himself, Adam looked out the window again. The neighbor's dog let out a long huff and then lowered its head onto the cold cement between its front paws.

That night Adam lowered his own head down onto the cool comfort of his pillow. Throughout the day he had remained in control of his emotions with the aid of additional medication, regulated breathing, and routine distractions—the same tools that had allowed him to survive thus far. But the wound delivered by the neighbor's dog refused to scab over and was now threatening to bleed into the unprotected underworld of his dreams.

Sensing the approach of a nocturnal storm, Adam tried a delay tactic: reading before bed. Plato's *Republic* was one of the few books sanctioned by Dr. M. to have in the house.

> Behold! human beings living in a underground cave, which has a mouth open towards the light and reaching all along the cave; here they have been from their childhood, and have their legs and necks chained so that they cannot move, and can only see before them, being prevented by the chains from turning round their heads . . .

After 20 minutes of staring at the same paragraph, Adam gave up and turned off his bedside light. *Click.*

Eyes shut, Adam spent the next hour watching the grainy dance of capillaries pulsating behind his eyelids. At last he began to slip into the darkness. Down, down, down toward the first subconscious musical strains to catch his untethered attention. They appeared in the form of old song lyrics, repeated over and over, like a stuck CD.

Now that I've lost everything to you . . .
  Now that I've lost everything to you . . .
    Now that I've lost everything to you . . .
      Now that I've lost everything to you . . .

The first visual impressions joined the song, rippling toward Adam in gentle waves. *Lines on the ground, cracked and yellow, marking boundaries. Weathered gray cement leading to crumbling, rubbery black mats, there to cushion his fall.*

Down, down, down . . .

You say you want to start something new . . .
　You say you want to start something new . . .
　　You say you want to start something new . . .
　　　You say you want to start something new . . .

He was back in front of the country schoolhouse, just as he had been in so many dreams before. He was moving quickly toward the playground out back where *it* was waiting. As he approached the corner, the turning point that would reveal what he needed to see, the old feeling began to creep in, the dread of having left something essential behind.

Adam turned the corner. This time the yard was no longer cloaked in its usual dreamy vagueness. This time he saw everything as if he was wide awake. Down to his left was the water fountain, with its neon-green mold, the engraved button on the head of the spout that read *PUSH,* the *U* and *S* worn beyond recognition. The metal basin, painted white, chipped in places to reveal the black cast iron beneath. Below the fountain the eternal puddle was shaped like the continent of Australia. Every detail was as clear and crisp as a Mendocino morning.

On the opposite side of the yard, the merry-go-round spun slowly. Lying on it was the body of a young boy. Motionless. Alone. Seeing himself as a six-year-old boy made Adam's heart pound faster (he could actually feel it racing in the dream). And he knew what was about to take place.

First he heard it, the high metallic sound of the approaching diesel engine—*grug-grug-grug.* Then the car door slamming, followed by the *crunch-crunch* of footsteps on cement coming around the schoolhouse. Gloria, his stepmother, appeared and walked past him in the dream. She stopped when she saw the boy on the merry-go-round and called out to him.

The boy sat up, face confused and then alarmed as he looked around for someone other than his stepmother, someone he expected would be there. Gloria was now demanding that the boy come with her, just as Adam had recalled before, but it was slightly different this time. Something about her voice.

"*I know you can understand me,*" she said. Her words were a little too punchy. A little too well pronounced. "*It is time to go, Adam.*" There was something unnerving about it, as if there were a second voice coming from her, an incomprehensible language hissing between the words. Adam wished he could see her face, but from where he stood in the dream, he couldn't. She was all ponytail, tight and serious.

She was now moving toward the frightened boy. When she reached the edge of the merry-go-round, she stood there for a moment, and then without warning latched on to the boy's legs. The boy began to scream hysterically, "*No, no, no!*" as she pulled him toward her. Like a trapped animal, he fought back, kicking and screaming, holding on to the metal bars, his life depending on it. She continued to reel him in closer with her arms. *Or was something else happening down there?* From where Adam was witnessing the scene, he couldn't quite see over his stepmother's shoulder. He needed to move closer.

Adam willed himself forward to where his stepmother was grappling with the young boy's legs. Then what he saw sent a thunderbolt of terror into his dreaming body. Reaching out from his stepmother were not arms but tentacles of milky-gray mist, slithering over the screaming boy's body, winding their way around his legs, and moving up his torso like snakes. At the end of one of these dark tendrils, a barbed hook was working its way through the boy's clothes, into his skin, and burrowing down into his body.

With a sudden jolt, the boy was torn off the merry-go-round. Screaming in terror he stood face to face with *something that was not his stepmother.* Shrouded in gray mist was a festering, parasitic void, a black hole sucking in everything within its event horizon, feeding off the never-ending cycles of pain and suffering that had crept into the hearts of men and women since time began. Then it screamed out the incantation that would enslave its new host.

"YOU WILL BEHAVE YOURSELF!"

A tendril became a hand that reached out and struck the boy's face. *SMACK!* And then it was over. No more tentacles, no hooks, no terrifying, endless void. Just a little boy and a frustrated woman who had momentarily lost her temper.

Adam's stepmother reached down and took the young boy by the hand. Obediently he followed her.

As she led him away, something barely perceptible took place. Like a cell undergoing mitosis, Adam watched as his younger self *split in two*—one boy following his stepmother toward the waiting car out front, while the other boy turned away and defiantly climbed back onto the merry-go-round.

Adam sensed the dream beginning to slip away. As he felt himself slowly rise up into the air above the playground, he tried to resist but was unable to stop his ascent. Floating above the schoolhouse, he saw one younger self being driven off toward a future life he was not meant to lead, while the other remained in the school yard, locked in a dream state on the slowly spinning merry-go-round.

Again the dream was shifting. Adam could still see the boy spinning on the merry-go-round below him, but the sight no longer had a visceral element. He was now watching it like a scene in a movie shot from above. He began to sense that he was elsewhere. He felt something beneath him, his own weight pressing down on a chair. *Where am I?* All he could see was the boy in the school yard, slowly spinning round and round on the rusty, metal pinwheel, but now the scene appeared flat and two-dimensional.

He was looking at a screen. A computer monitor. But where the hell was he? When he tried to turn and look around, to his horror he found that his body was paralyzed. Even his eyes were unable to shift away from the screen in front of him.

Adam's panic increased as an even more terrifying realization struck him. Although he was lucid enough to know he was dreaming, he was starting to sense that *he might not be able to wake up.* Then came the even more dreadful thought. *Perhaps this dark place was where he really was, where he had been all along. Perhaps what he thought of as his life was just a series of images on the screen before him.*

As if provoked by his panic, the screen began to twitch like a video presentation run amok. Violent flashes of light—*BART tunnel lightsabers*—pulsed over the boy on the wheel. Moving faster and faster, until it erupted into a maddening stream of endless content, an explosion of scenes from Adam's memory files. Scenes from his life mixed with lines of computer code and video-game landscapes. Jane, Blake, zombies, a whining malamute, redwood trees with pixilated blood splattering through their trunks, pills the size of oranges, men in Einstein wigs striking Tibetan chimes. Adam struggled to get free of the rush of images, but he could not look away.

In flashes rapid as machine-gun fire, Adam saw his stepmother slapping him in the school yard over and over again, followed by images of unspeakable horror, as if the entire history of human violence were spilling out in a horrific mosaic of war, murder, rape, torture, and piles of festering bodies—a pornographic orgy of sex and death that played out in an endless cycle.

Helpless, paralyzed, and unable to look away, there was no way for Adam to escape the utter madness pouring out of the screen, forcing him to consume it.

Then he realized that there was something he could do. There was one small yet vital aspect of himself that he could still control. His *attention.* Although he could not avert his gaze from the screen, he could focus on the screen itself, on its flat, two-dimensional form. Instead of getting lost in what was going on inside of it, he could hold on to an awareness of this place he was in.

As he did, he began to see more of it. The screen had edges. And now something else—a slight reflection. In the screen a reflection of the space behind him, and the more he concentrated on it, the clearer it became. He could start to make out things around him. Now he could even see where he was!

He was *inside the Cave.*

He was in the Virtual Skies Tower, at his desk in his cubicle, and he was not alone; behind him he could just barely make out other people, all staring blankly into their own glowing screens. The Cave was much bigger than he ever realized, extending as far as he could see in all directions. A cold, dead universe filled with countless glowing faces—small, pale moons glowing in the reflected light of their screens.

Adam was not sure what was worse, the assault of images on his screen or what he saw now. Either way, it felt like he was seeing too much, witnessing a dark truth about humanity that was never meant to be seen. All he wanted was to wake up, or go back to sleep, or whatever would take him away from this utterly hopeless place.

"What lies beyond the stars?" It was only a whisper, coming from another dimension altogether.

"What lies beyond the stars, Adam Sheppard?"

He felt the voice echoing in his chest now. And then, from the infinite ocean of tiny dead moons, he saw a soft, warm glow moving toward him. He was unable to turn and look directly at it—his eyes were still locked on the screen—but he could see it in the screen's reflection, approaching him from behind. He could just make out the figure of a woman, naked, floating in infinite space, the flames of her red hair a sun among moons.

Adam began to weep. Not since Mendocino had he allowed himself to even consider her. He had banished every thought, every image from his mind, erased file after file, wiping his internal hard drive clear of all references to her. Yet despite his efforts, he knew that, like an addict, he could never truly recover. She was in his cellular material, and if he allowed himself to believe in her again, there would be no turning back. He had chosen instead to accept that she was a fantasy, the first game he had ever created as a child. He had accepted that, in the real world, a hope like Beatrice was not allowed to exist.

"Do you exist?" asked the voice within Adam's chest.

"I'm a dead fact," his mind responded. *"Just one more pale moon."*

Being in her presence, in the mere reflection of it, was too much to bear. He almost wished for the lesser pain of nonexistence. With all of his will, Adam focused on trying to turn around, to actually see her, to make her real.

On the screen in front of him there was now only a single image, the original overhead shot of a boy on the merry-go-round, spinning round and round, sleeping as if for all eternity.

"AHHHH!" Adam felt his insides tearing apart as he struggled to free himself and turn. Blood began to pour from his eyes and ears. On the screen before him, the boy began to toss and turn, eyelids fluttering, struggling to wake up.

"AHHHH!" Like a lightning bolt, a single crack appeared across the screen.

Adam opened his eyes.

His pillow was soaked with perspiration. It was still dark in the room. Adam's vision was too blurry to read the clock on the bedside table. Holding his breath, he slowly turned his head toward Jane. She lay turned away from him, snoring softly.

CHAPTER 28

THE DOORWAY REVEALED

Wrapping paper in his lap, Adam examined the book in his hands. *More Tweets from the Soul: An Inspiring Collection of Life-Affirming Tweets, Volume III.*

"Oh," Jane sang out, peeking over Adam's shoulder. "This is just so funny. What do you think, Adam?"

Adam could feel himself nodding and smiling. He no longer needed Jane's cues for moments like this. The practiced grooves of appropriate social behavior were carrying him along safely this evening. He had ridden through the day on these auto-response rails without a single person, including Jane, noticing anything was amiss.

"We have the first two volumes. This must have just come out," Jane said as she flipped through the book. "We don't have this one yet, do we, sweetie?"

"Nope. Not yet." Adam's performance tonight had been supported by several key factors. First was the familiar environment of the Silver Oak Grill—safe and reliable, with its festive decor and eager-to-please waitstaff, its dependably large portions, and its clean, cinnamon-scented bathrooms.

Also keeping Adam on an even keel tonight was the dependable cast of characters around the birthday table. There was Jane's mother, Cassandra, hidden behind her designer sunglasses, checking out other women's outfits. Howie with his new caregiver, Don, a large African-American man. Chandler and Madison were also present, along with their electronic devices. And there was the extra setting for Blake, just in case he showed up.

One small variation tonight was the new set of neighbors, Zach and Brittany Lynch, who were now living across the cul-de-sac in the faux Italian villa that Stefan and Annie Thompson had lost to foreclosure. From Adam's perspective their new neighbors were not discernibly different from the old ones.

"This book is so right on for Adam." Jane smiled. "It's like you're psychic or something."

"No, no, we're not psychic—" Zach shrugged as Brittany finished his sentence.

"We just thought since Adam likes philosophy and he's a tech guy, this would be perfect." She smiled enthusiastically.

"Ha. Right," Adam said while experiencing an almost imperceptible twinge of panic. *Hasn't this moment happened before?* Adam thought. *Maybe Zach and Brittany actually are Stefan and Annie, just hiding under different skin. They finish each other's sentences, just like Stefan and Annie . . . But, no. Stefan and Annie were from Southern California and automatically agree with whatever you say, whereas Zach and Brittany are from New York and automatically disagree with whatever you say.*

"Well, thank you for the book," Adam heard himself say.

Adam was beginning to suspect that the restaurant's overhead lights had been set dimmer than usual. The room looked fuzzy, as if a layer of television static had been superimposed over everything. Glancing up at the three pathetic birthday balloons floating above his head, he struggled to make out their colors. *Three shades of beige.* And then there was the grating buzzing noise. *Also coming from the light fixtures?* Or maybe it was just his tinnitus acting up.

Adam gave his head an Etch A Sketch shake to try to clear his mind. If he were to survive the evening, he would need to "stay in the moment," as Dr. M. liked to say. *Just stay at the table and focus on the conversation. Just stay in the room.*

The conversation currently going on at the table had veered toward home security systems. Zach worked for a company called IDCS, "Iron Dome Community Security," he explained. "And I'm excited to be able to share the news that IDCS is being acquired by none other than—drumroll, please—Virtual Skies! That's right, buddy, we'll all be under the same umbrella." Zach laughed. "Crazy, isn't it? Video games and home security? But hey, man, everything's integrated these days. We're all connected."

"That's right." Adam nodded.

"So, now what kind of setup do you currently have?" Zach asked.

"Well, let's see . . ." Adam wasn't sure what Zach meant by *setup*. He looked to Jane for help.

"We have a house alarm," Jane answered. "I don't remember the brand name—"

Zach cut her off. "No, no, no. That's not what I meant."

"Yeah, no, that's not what he meant," Brittany added with a smile.

"What other preventive measures do you have in place?" Zach looked at Adam, who still didn't know how to answer. He blinked a few times to try and wash away the noisy static that was making it hard to focus on Zach's face.

"We have an emergency kit somewhere," Jane jumped in. "The kids both have their cell phones. And of course Blackhawk security is always driving around the neighborhood. We let them know when we take trips out of town, right, Adam?"

"Yes, we do." Adam nodded agreeably.

"Okay, well, that's good as far as it goes," Zach said.

"But what IDCS does," Brittney picked up, "is offer a completely revolutionary way of looking at home and family security."

"*Integrated* security, *holistic* security," Zach went on. "Taking in all the variables, considering all the hazardous elements—"

"And let's face it, nowadays there are a lot of *hazardous elements* out there," Brittany tacked on with a laugh.

Adam noticed the buzzing sound in his ear jump up a few decibels.

Zach laid a muscular forearm on the table and leaned in. "Adam, let me ask you a personal question. Do you keep a firearm in the house?"

Adam stared blankly at Zach. *A gun?* Adam thought. *Wait, why is this guy asking if I have a gun? Does he know I tried to kill myself once? Is this some kind of test?*

Jane gave Adam a little poke. "Sweetie, Zach asked you a question."

No, of course it's not a test, Adam realized. *He's just asking you because of his fucking job. I'm seeing meanings that aren't really there, just like Dr. Mendelson warned me about.*

Jane nudged him more forcefully. "Adam, honey, are you there?"

"Yes; sorry. I'm sorry. What was the . . . What was the question?"

Jane laughed. "That's our Adam. Game programmers are always lost in their heads, dreaming up new worlds for the rest of us to enjoy." Jane was smiling, but the side-glance she gave Adam contained the subtext of worry.

Adam smiled and bobbed his head to reassure her. "Sorry. She's right. Sometimes I do drift a bit."

"No, no, no—" said Brittany.

"No, no, no," Zack continued. "My bad. I'm always talking about my work. It's your birthday; we should be talking about *your* work." Zach smiled. "Making video games, I mean, that is really friggin' cool. That's just—"

"Just the coolest thing *ever*," Brittany sang out. "And your kids, my God, they must love it. Huh? Don't you?" Brittany, her eyes Japanese-anime wide, looked over at Madison and Chandler.

Both kids offered perfunctory nods before returning to their devices.

Adam sipped his water in an attempt to dampen the dread that was slowly clawing up from his gut to his lightly buzzing head. Reality seemed to be flip-flopping tonight, swapping roots for branches as if the external world was becoming more surreal just as the phantoms of Adam's inner world seemed to be preparing to step boldly into the light. Last night's dream seemed more real than anything he could see as he looked around the Silver Oak Grill. *Did I somehow end up on the wrong side of reality?* Adam wondered. *Just stop thinking about it and breathe. This is just a tough night. Just be in the room. Focus on the conversation.*

"Oh, I refuse to watch *X Factor*, or that new one, *The Voice*," Brittany was sharing with Jane. "I am totally loyal to *Idol*."

When the food arrived, Adam tried to concentrate on eating; however, everything in the restaurant seemed to be making an effort to distract him. The drone of banal conversation. The flickering imitation candles on the table. The grotesquely enlarged chicken breast on his plate. And towering above it all, the navel of absurdity itself, the Silver Oak centerpiece with its painted branches rooted in the enormous crystal bowl filled with thousands of black-and-white marbles. Adam could not stop looking at the fucking thing. And the longer he stared, the more it appeared to be *growing*, reaching up toward the ceiling as well as spreading down over the tables below it. It reminded him of something else, some other towering monstrosity. A building . . . reaching up into the fog.

"What the hell are we doing here?"

Adam froze. *Did I really just say that out loud?*

"I hate this place. The food is disgusting."

Adam exhaled, relieved to find that the voice belonged to Howie, Jane's dementia-laden stepfather at the opposite end of the table.

"This is your favorite restaurant, Howie. You love it here," Cassandra asserted.

"No. This place is a fucking joke," Howie continued. This was the most vocal Adam could remember Howie being in years.

Cassandra put down her fork and with both hands tried to soothe her husband. "We've been here a million times, darling. We practically live here, for God's sake—"

"No, no, no. You're wrong. Why would I ever come to a place like this? I hate it here." Howie suddenly locked eyes with Adam, and in that moment, Adam saw something he couldn't believe. Howie was completely cognizant. Behind his panic-stricken eyes, he had woken up! Physically depleted, yes, but mentally he was right there, fully aware of everything that was going on. Everything.

"Oh dear God. This is hell. This place, it's a living hell! Get me out of here. *Please get me out . . .*" His weak voice cracking, Howie sounded like a pitiful, helpless child. *"Please . . . please . . ."*

It was as if Howie, the end of his life nearing, had just discovered that he'd been sleeping through it all. On the very last step up to the gallows, he'd been given one last look at his life before the hood went on.

Don, Howie's caregiver, stepped in like an executioner to control the situation.

"Okay, big fella. Let's try to focus on that cauliflower. Let's get a piece of that cauliflower on your fork. Okay, here we go . . ."

As Don placed the cauliflower into Howie's mouth, the old man gave Adam one final, desperate look. And then, just like that, it was over. Howie was gone—the vacant stare returned, the momentary spark blinked out.

The implications of the moment weren't lost on Adam. *Yes, Dr. M. warned me about reading too much into things,* Adam thought. *But you know what? Fuck Dr. M. Fuck pretending like I don't see what's going on here. No matter what drugs they put me on, no matter how strict they make my routine, there's no hiding that something is going on beneath the surface of what we're all supposed to just accept as normal life. Something is seriously wrong with this place, and Howie saw it, and maybe it's too late for him, but I've got to get the hell out of here.*

"I do think there's a lot to be said for a safe environment," Jane was saying. Zach had maneuvered the conversation back to home security.

"No, absolutely." Zach nodded. "And allowing us to help maintain *control* of the environment, that is really the key—"

"Keeping the unknown out," Brittany chipped in. Then, with a forced smile, she turned to Adam. "How's that chicken, Adam?"

Adam gave the best nod-shrug he could muster. But his auto-response system was breaking down. Jane was already sensing something was up with him, but worse was this damn Lynch couple. Adam could feel them both eyeing him suspiciously. He knew he needed to extract himself from this situation as quickly as possible. He needed to find the right exit, not just out of the restaurant but out of everything it stood for. There had to be a way out, a doorway or portal hidden somewhere.

"At IDCS we call it *perimeter control*," Zach said loudly, his eyes locked on Adam now. "Like, if you imagine an enormous fishbowl, maybe. You can picture that, can't you, Adam?" Zach made a big circle with his hands. "And inside are all the things we know and love. It's safe here, right? But outside the bowl, this stuff out here"—Zach waved his hands around—"this is the unknown, all the things that we want to keep out. You follow me, right, Adam?"

Holy Christ! Adam was following all right. *This guy's not talking about home security, he's talking about something much, much bigger. Something hinted at in that picture of the shepherd boy looking under the veil of the stars. Something Beatrice—yes, Dr. M., I fucking said her name!—something Beatrice said about the fishbowl of stars that aren't really stars but holes that allow the light to come through. But why is Zach, or whoever this is who's posing as Zach, why is he saying this?*

Then Adam saw it. Something so terrifying flashed across Zach's blurry face that it made Adam's heart jump into his throat. Through the white noise of Zach's sales pitch, Adam caught a glimpse of something ancient and dark—that same parasitic force that had acted through his stepmother, Gloria, in his dream, and had turned humanity into a sea of computer-obsessed zombies. *It* was now speaking to Adam, no longer veiled in dreams, but right here, in Blackhawk, California, sitting across the table from him smiling, here in the fucking Silver Oak Grill.

"So what we do, Adam, is we focus our attention on the bowl itself, the barrier between worlds. To keep all the unknown elements out while keeping all the known ones inside. And it's important to keep that barrier strong, or God knows what might get in. But when we're vigilant, and do our job . . . well, then we can all sleep safe and sound, can't we?"

Adam stood up. The tumblers had suddenly fallen into place. He had discovered the way out. The hidden doorway.

"I have to go," Adam said matter-of-factly.

"You what?" Jane was confused.

"Excuse me," Adam said to no one in particular and then left the table.

"Are you going to the bathroom?" Panic rose in Jane's voice. "Adam?"

Adam kept walking, not toward the bathrooms but toward the center of the restaurant.

"Adam?" Jane stood up. "What are you doing? Adam!"

Without slowing down Adam took hold of an empty chair from one of the tables he passed and dragged it toward the center of the restaurant. The young couple seated at the two-top had just received their entrees, and they were so distracted taking pictures of their food with their phones that they hardly noticed Adam setting the empty chair down next to their table. They did, however, react when Adam stepped up on the chair and then onto their table. Then with considerable effort, he pushed over the massive Silver Oak centerpiece.

$$\diamondsuit$$

The sleeping boy on the merry-go-round shuddered and then opened his eyes. The sound that woke him came from far away. It sounded like a giant glass object had shattered. Squinting, the boy looked around, shielding his eyes from the glare of the afternoon sun. His eyes, which had been closed for so long, needed time to adjust. As the abandoned school yard around him came into focus, so did the sounds—the buzz of cicadas, the gentle wind sighing through the redwoods, and the *drip-drip-drip* of the water fountain.

A blue-and-white dragonfly landed next to the boy on one of the warm metal bars of the merry-go-round. "How long have I been asleep?" the boy asked.

"My goodness, what a silly question," the dragonfly responded. "That would, of course, depend on: one, who is asking; two, what you consider to be long; and three, what your definition of sleep is."

"I see," the boy said. "But do you at least know the time?"

"Time, time, time. It's such a boring concept."

Boring or not, the boy felt the day was getting on. It would be dark soon, and now that he was awake, he needed to go somewhere. Didn't he?

The boy began to climb down off the merry-go-round, but then he stopped. He realized that he didn't really know where he was meant to go or what he was meant to do. Even though the merry-go-round had been a prison, at least it was a familiar one.

After some consideration the boy decided to wait where he was. Perhaps someone would come to help. His grandmother Anne had told him that if he ever got lost in the woods, he shouldn't panic, but should simply sit still, stay calm, and wait patiently.

"Eventually, Adam, someone will come for you."

CHAPTER 29

FORGETTING ADAM

Adam sat in his straight-backed chair by the window and watched the fog bleed through the distant row of cypress trees. A sharp tug, and the chair jerked a foot to the left and then twisted with a squeak. He was now facing the coastline beyond the hospital property.

"Is that better, handsome? Does that feel better to you?"

Miss Ferguson searched Adam's eyes.

She had recently discovered her patient's tendency to turn and face the ocean while at his window. Even when his chair had been set to face another direction, Adam Sheppard leaned forward or contorted his neck to face the coast. Miss Ferguson tried to convince him, verbally, that he could move the chair himself. "Set it wherever you want, dear. This is your room now, your chair." But nothing seemed to get through to the silent newcomer. So Miss Ferguson took it upon herself to check in with Adam's chair situation every morning. He was a recent arrival at the Presidio House, but she already knew there was something special about him.

Three months earlier, Adam had done his best to completely destroy the Silver Oak restaurant. After tipping over the false tree, he proceeded through the room like a wrecking ball, methodically breaking everything he could get his hands on. Most patrons fled, stumbling through a sea of bouncing black-and-white marbles toward the exits. Adam's new neighbor Zach, along with Howie's caregiver, Don, were the first to try to talk Adam down from his rampage. After dodging plates, silverware, and a flying chair, they wisely backed off.

Several of the younger members of the waitstaff were next to give it a go. One, fresh out of high school, tried to rush Adam and actually managed a decent tackle before attempting to get him into a headlock. But two years of high school wrestling is no match for mental insanity. Adam wormed free and, with bloody hands, dug through broken glass and ceramic until he got ahold of a large, wood-handled steak knife. Wielding the blade like Spartacus, he quickly convinced the young waiter to abandon his attempt at heroism.

By the time the police arrived, Adam was behind the bar, smashing through vodka, tequila, and Scotch, working his way up to top-shelf Cognacs. Luckily no steak knives were within reach, or he might have been shot. Instead he was Tasered, followed by enough kicks and baton strikes to fracture four ribs and a collarbone.

Dr. Mendelson pulled up to the Silver Oak Grill 20 minutes after receiving Jane's call. He was greeted by a parking lot full of police cars, confused patrons, and several ambulances treating minor injuries. Eventually he found Jane.

"I tried, Dr. M., I really tried," Jane sobbed as she collapsed into Dr. Mendelson's arms.

Dr. M. did his best to console her as he scanned for Adam. He finally caught sight of him in the back of an unmarked Crown Vic. It wasn't easy, but Dr. Mendelson was eventually able to convince the police to bring Adam to a hospital for treatment before taking him in to be booked. Once they arrived at St. Joseph's emergency room, Dr. Mendelson swiftly arranged for a psychiatric evaluation, which got Adam admitted to the hospital's closed psychiatric unit, thus avoiding a trip to jail.

In the days that followed, lawyers set to work untangling Adam's various legal messes while he remained at St. Joseph's sedated and in restraints. His body, however, continued to strain against the physical and chemical bonds with unbelievable strength. There were nightly flare-ups, violent storms that once brought a 250-pound male nurse to tears. But with each day, Adam's waves of rage receded a little further, until at last he submerged into a completely nonresponsive state.

A decision was made to transfer Adam to San Francisco General's psychiatric ward. For several weeks, doctors there poked and prodded, trying without success to bring him back from wherever it was he had gone. Psychiatrists weighed in, suggesting a wider range of treatments and medications. Electroconvulsive therapy, which had shown great results for many bipolar and clinically depressed patients, had no effect whatsoever on Adam. So as his physical health waxed and the hope of mental recovery waned, arrangements were made for long-term care. Options were limited in California, thanks to the Reagan budget cuts of the 1970s that had shut down nearly all long-term mental health facilities in the state. But a private endowment had helped keep the Presidio House open, and on January 27, 2011, Adam Sheppard moved in.

On that particular morning, two doctors sat in the staff lunchroom at a Formica table. Dr. Agopian was looking over Adam's records, while Dr. Mendelson looked tentatively over the poor excuse for coffee he had been offered.

"You've been treating Adam for a long time, I see," Dr. Agopian remarked.

Dr. Mendelson simply nodded. Against his better judgment, he had agreed to take some time out of his busy schedule to stop by the Presidio House and sit down with Dr. David Agopian, the young psychiatrist taking over Adam's case.

Dr. Agopian looked back down at Adam's paperwork. "I'm sure you're already aware of this, but we'd be more than happy to include you in Adam's treatment if you'd like to remain involved.

We welcome the participation of family and professionals invested in a patient's well-being, especially a private practitioner like you, who—"

"Yes, yes. I am aware of it."

Dr. Agopian paused, waiting for the older man to say more. When he didn't, Dr. Agopian opened his laptop and turned it to the side—an invitation for Dr. Mendelson to look on with him. "Well, his insurance coverage is excellent, which is to say that there are plenty of funds available to pay for your—"

Dr. Mendelson again cut off Dr. Agopian. "Money is not the issue here, Dr. Agopa."

"That's Agopian. It's an Armenian name."

"Yes, well." Dr. Mendelson cleared his throat before continuing. "The point is, I've done all I can for Adam. From here on I think it would be best to allow others, like yourself, who can bring a fresh perspective to the case, to manage Adam's care."

"Right . . . Well, perhaps we can consult with you as needed?"

"Of course." Dr. Mendelson stood. "I'll have the rest of his files, including all of his earlier records, sent over to you next week. All you need to know about Adam Sheppard will be in there." With that, Dr. Mendelson stood and headed for the hallway.

Dr. Agopian quickly got up to follow him. "And his wife? Do you know if she will be involved?"

"To be honest, I wouldn't count on that," Dr. Mendelson said as they reached the lobby. He stopped and turned to Dr. Agopian. "In fact, I would anticipate a change in conservatorship in the very near future. I expect the State will soon be in charge of Adam's affairs." He extended his hand for an obligatory handshake.

"Best of luck, Doctor." And with that, Dr. Ronald Mendelson turned and walked away.

◈

Clouds heavy with rain pressed in on the 18th floor windows, causing the office to be unnaturally dark for 2 P.M. Nevertheless Jane Sheppard kept her sunglasses on. They had become a useful accessory these days, a handy prop in the many dramatic scenes she had found herself in since Adam's meltdown.

"There are, of course, certain things we cannot touch," the lawyer was saying from across the desk. "His pension, certain assets accumulated prior to marriage, things of that nature."

Jane liked her new lawyer. He looked like a lawyer. Approachable yet at the same time formidable. Not quite the leading man, but great hair, and he certainly knew how to put on a good show. She liked the way he straightened and squared the stacks of documents on his desk while he was talking, a habit he'd probably picked up from someone playing a lawyer on TV.

"Those particular assets aside," he continued, "in this type of situation, it's really up to the spouse to determine what to go after."

Jane turned her veiled gaze toward the windows, toward the slate-gray misery outside, and let out a long, deep sigh to convey just how distressing the entire situation was for her.

The lawyer looked sympathetic to her plight.

Since that night at the Silver Oak Grill, Jane felt as if she had been cast as the lead actress in her own series, Blackhawk's new number-one-rated reality show, *Dark Secrets of the Sheppard Family Revealed*. She could feel the cameras dollying behind her and the attention of others flowing magnetically toward her wherever she went. She had become a local celebrity, which was terribly exhausting and, of course, exhilarating beyond belief.

"How about we start with me asking a few simple questions?" Jane's lawyer said, leaning forward across the gleaming oaken expanse of his desk. "With all you've done for Adam, and all you've been through, what do you *feel* you deserve?"

Jane looked down at the floor and gave a slight shrug. Then she took a deep breath, lifted her head, and slowly removed her sunglasses. "Well, Bill, I think I deserve as much as possible."

The law office scene lasted another 20 minutes, and Jane felt that it had gone well.

"We'll get everything in the works," Bill said. "My secretary will set up a time for you to come back early next week, if that's convenient."

"I should be able to fit that in," said Jane.

"Oh, and I'd appreciate anything you can do to help get Blake Dorsey and his attorneys in here for a meeting. The transfer of Adam's conservatorship and healthcare directive really needs to be taken care of as soon as possible. I know Mr. Dorsey is a busy man these days; I see his name in the papers all the time. But this needs to happen as soon as possible."

"Oh God." Behind her Gucci shades, Jane rolled her eyes. "I'm so sorry about that. Blake's been acting weird lately. I'll call him right away."

At the elevators the lawyer put a gentle hand on Jane's shoulder. "You know, Jane, we all miss your energy at Rayana's morning class." Jane had met her new lawyer at a yoga studio in Lafayette.

"I'll be back soon," Jane said. "It's just still a little hard being around everyone. This whole situation has been devastating."

"Of course, of course. But you should know that everyone's rooting for you." The lawyer pushed the Down button for Jane.

"I've been hitting this restorative class over at Core Power in Alamo," Jane added casually.

"Oh, that's Vendra's class, isn't it? I hear she's good. Is she good?"

"She's all right." Jane shrugged. The elevator gave a ding. "I'll see you next week. And, thank you."

"Of course." The lawyer smiled and gave Jane a big, supportive hug.

Jane stepped in the elevator. As the doors were closing, her lawyer put his hands together and bowed. *"Namaste."*

Jane bowed back. *"Namaste."*

As Jane reached her car, the rain started to come down in torrents. Safely inside with the seat-warmer on, she watched as fat globs of water exploded against her windshield. Before leaving the parking lot, Jane popped her earbuds in and tried Blake's cell. Things had gotten strange with him lately. Jane half wished her call would just go straight to voice mail, but after the third ring, he answered.

"Yeah . . . Hi, Jane." Blake's voice was rough and slightly muffled.

Jane looked at the clock on her dashboard. "It's three o'clock. Don't tell me you're just getting up?"

"Earnings report was through the roof . . . big party last night." Blake began to violently clear his throat.

"You need to go to Bill Waverly's office and sign the goddamn papers."

"I signed those papers already."

"No, Blake, you haven't. I just left his office, and he said you and your attorneys haven't even responded to his calls."

"Bill Waverly . . . the guy handling the restaurant damages?" Blake sounded as if he was struggling to get out of bed.

"No. Bill is *my* attorney, the one handling the divorce settlement, the attorney who can't proceed until *you* get your ass in there and take over Adam's conservatorship and healthcare directive like you said you wanted to do, because you *care* so goddamn much."

"Jesus, Jane, don't fucking start with me, okay? Just because you and Dr. Douchebag are giving up on him—"

"Here we go again."

"He's going to be all right, Jane. You'll see. He's done this before."

"No, Blake. This is different. Adam's not going to be all right. In fact, if you care so much, why don't you go visit him and see for yourself?"

"I can't right now, okay?" Blake snapped, before getting suddenly quiet. "Things are crazy at work . . . and I just . . . I just can't see him right now."

"Why, Blake?"

"Because . . . Look, I'm not blaming you, Jane. You didn't do anything wrong. I mean, maybe if you had reminded me about his birthday dinner like you said you would, I would have been there, and maybe I could have—"

"What? What could you have done? Save Adam from himself? I don't think so. It's time to accept that there is nothing you, me, or anyone else could have done."

"I should have at least been there for him," Blake mumbled.

"Blake, stop it. Stop blaming yourself and go sign those papers—"

"I'm not blaming myself! I didn't do anything wrong."

"I'm not saying you did. Christ." Jane checked the rearview mirror for lipstick on her front teeth.

"I have *always* done what was best for Adam," Blake went on. "I covered for him. I tried to help him. I never thought . . . this would happen."

Jane could hear the sound of Blake filling a glass with crushed ice from his refrigerator. "Blake, listen to me," she said. "Are you listening?"

"Yes, Jane, I'm fucking listening!"

"It's time to let go. Both of us have to move on. Just let the State take over everything like Dr. M. suggested."

"Just forget about Adam? Just abandon him?"

"Yes, Blake. Forget about Adam and move on."

Jane had already planned her next step in that process, complete with beaches and yoga, sunsets and Mai Tais, and a brand-new reality show set on the lovely island of Maui.

CHAPTER 30

CONTROLLING
THE NARRATIVE

Blake stood watching as maintenance workers finally removed the clutter from Adam's cubicle. He had kept everything exactly as it was in the hopes that its former occupant would eventually return. But six months had passed, and according to Adam's new doctor, there had been no change in his condition.

Blake had followed Jane and Dr. Mendelson's advice and decided against becoming Adam's conservator. Instead he let the State take over after Jane and Adam's divorce had been finalized. But Blake had continued to call the Presidio House several times a week to check in on Adam's progress. He'd spoken directly with Dr. Agopian, who had sounded optimistic, though he'd also cautioned taking the long view. After several months of patience, Blake had started to lose hope. These days he only checked in with Dr. Agopian once every other week.

Twice Blake had attempted an actual visit. The first time was in early spring, but after booking the appointment, things had gotten conveniently busy at work. The second time Blake had made it all the way out to the Presidio House parking lot, where he sat in his car, trying to work out why he was so terrified to face Adam. *You're Adam's best friend, for God's sake,* Blake assured himself. *You've done so much for him; even now, after everyone else has abandoned him, you're still here.*

Blake had pulled his key halfway out of the ignition, but that was as far as he got before the key got sucked back in. *You are in no way responsible for what happened to Adam. He did this to himself.* By the time Blake had finally gotten the key back out of the ignition, he was no longer in the Presidio House parking lot. Without being fully aware of it, he had driven all the way across San Francisco to the Financial District, and had parked in front of The Whisky Shop, where a special order of Laphroaig 25-year-old Scotch was waiting for him inside.

"What do you want done with stuff like this?"

Blake blinked several times before he realized that one of the maintenance workers clearing out Adam's cubicle was talking to him. He was holding up a large framed photograph of a Hawaiian sunset, something Jane had given Adam to brighten up his work space.

"That? I don't fucking care," Blake mumbled. "Throw it out. Or keep it if you want."

"Okay, and what about the rest of this?" The maintenance man pointed to the dozen or so large plastic moving crates filled with photos, pill bottles, health shake mix, and books, lots of books. "Should we toss all this crap out too?"

"That's not *crap!*" Blake snapped. Then he added, "Sorry. No, I'll keep that."

Later that afternoon Blake stood in his office, facing the floor-to-ceiling windows, watching the heavy mist outside silently dance in violent swirls. Blake took a couple of steps closer until he could just begin to make out his own reflection in the glass. It was the closest thing to a mirror he had dared look at in recent weeks. He had been gaining weight; how much exactly, he couldn't say. Fifteen, twenty pounds maybe, hidden for the most part beneath looser-fit clothing.

What Blake now saw was what couldn't be hidden, what had caused noticeable reactions from friends he'd run into that hadn't seen him in a while. His face and neck had puffed out substantially, the sharpness of his chin reduced to a slope. His mouth, normally full and expressive, had been pushed into tighter quarters by two bloated cheeks. There were new lines in his skin as well, creases that hadn't been there a year ago. Worst of all were his eyes—dark and sunken. *You're just worn down, that's all,* Blake told himself. *Too much partying, too much booze. It's time to rest and reboot.*

Another step closer to the window now, Blake leaned forward until his forehead hit the glass. His old spot. The glass felt dangerously thin today. *Adam was the glass,* Blake's inner voice whispered. *He held you up all these years. And now that he's gone, there's nothing to stop you from falling, is there?*

Blake made an ironic little snort, fogging the glass under his nose. He knew nothing could really threaten his career at this point. Even with Adam gone, Pixilate had become too integral to the success of Virtual Skies, and as Pixilate's founder, Blake was close to untouchable; firing him would be a PR nightmare, not to mention that he controlled the intellectual property rights to all of their source code. In fact, he had only gotten more indispensable without Adam there.

Blake's latest achievement inside the Tower had less to do with his first love, video games, and more to do with the idiosyncratic social networking platform Pixilate had introduced in their *Lust 4 Flesh* series. Based on its popularity with younger users, Blake had suggested integrating some of the game's network functionality directly into the main MyStar network interface. As a social network, MyStar was still struggling for relevancy, so the team running it up on the 60th floor was open to Blake's idea.

The reaction was immediate: users loved the redesign. Sharing, posting, and messaging through MyStar skyrocketed, so much so that within three months it had leapfrogged the competition on its way to becoming the most popular social networking site among preteens, and the third most popular network among teens and under-thirties. Virtual Skies' stock split that month, and Blake made the cover of *Wired* magazine under the headline,

"Blake Dorsey Navigates the Stars." The issue came out the same day Adam had been transferred to the Presidio House.

The proprietary code behind Blake's MyStar coup had, of course, been written by Adam, a fact that Blake never tried to deny. *Sure, Adam created it, but I'm the one who knew how to leverage it, and that's just as important,* Blake justified in his head. However, when he heard people around the Tower referring to it as "The Adam Code," the nickname stung Blake like a poisonous dart.

Blake leaned a little harder against the window as if to test how well it could handle his extra weight. Looking down he could just make out the row of newspaper stands on the sidewalk below. *That's where my body would probably land if the glass suddenly dissolved,* Blake thought. Something seemed different about those old stands. The countless times Blake had looked down from here, he had always seen the newsstands as being one long row; but now he saw they were arranged in two shorter rows with a little gap in the middle. *How is it possible that I never noticed that before?* Blake wondered. It was a meaningless little detail, but for some reason it really bothered him. *How many other things have I missed?*

"Hello, Blake."

Startled, Blake pulled back from the window and turned around. At his door stood the man he had been unconsciously avoiding since the beginning of the year, actually since Adam's meltdown at the Silver Oak Grill.

"Hi, Rene."

Adiklein was silent for a while, taking in Blake's appearance. His face didn't register the same surprise Blake had seen from others. Instead Adiklein smiled, which somehow made Blake feel even worse.

"May I enter?" Adiklein asked, waiting politely just outside the door as if he actually needed permission to come in. Blake suddenly noticed how much his boss looked like a vampire out of *Lust 4 Blood*, with his salt-and-pepper hair slicked back and his pale skin glowing with preternatural health.

"Yes, yes. Of course. Come in. I was just thinking about some new games we're testing—*Tower Defense* stuff." Blake walked over to his desk, knowing Adiklein was aware that what he'd just said was bullshit. Blake hadn't been actively involved with any development at Pixilate for months now. Since his big triumph with MyStar, he'd been spending less time in the Tower and more time out destroying his liver with friends.

"I haven't seen you around recently," Adiklein said, drifting silently into Blake's office. "We've missed your creative input at the Cross-Pollination Brunches. There are some bright new minds up there, hungry young minds."

If this was an attempt to provoke Blake's competitive side, it wasn't going to work. He was too tired to even care. "I know. I've just been swamped."

"Oh? What's been keeping you so busy?"

Blake shook his head and rubbed his eyes. "Actually, I've been dealing with some personal issues." He hoped this would be enough to derail the conversation, but it wasn't.

"Ah, yes. I heard about your friend . . . Adam. I suppose condolences are in order," Adiklein said gravely. He was moving around the room, casually looking at things. "But as I've told you, butterflies are fragile. They are easily crushed."

Blake turned and glared at Adiklein, expecting to see a sarcastic grin, but instead the man's look conveyed absolute compassion. Blake took a deep breath. "Thank you." He was tired and irritable, but the last thing he needed was to lose his cool with Adiklein. "It's been tough, but I'll be fine. I *am* fine."

"Yes, of course you are." The compassion in Adiklein's voice had given way to something more patronizing.

Jaw clenched, Blake forced a smile. "We've been having a hell of a year already. The work I'm doing with MyStar is just the beginning—"

"Of course, Blake, of course." Adiklein was looking out the windows now, toward the abstract shapes of a city shrouded in mist. "The Adam Code is quite the talk around here." The poison dart landed squarely in Blake's chest. Adiklein continued. "Yes, you absolutely deserve to relax and *indulge* for a time. You have nothing to worry about."

There was an uncomfortable silence.

"Worry about?" Blake asked hesitantly. "What's that supposed to mean?"

"Oh *mon Dieu*, don't be so sensitive." Adiklein turned back to Blake with a light chuckle. "I only mean you're to be congratulated. Your butterfly left you with quite a little gift, one that will keep you relevant, at least for the rest of this fiscal year. Of course, sooner or later you'll need to get out your net and start hunting around for a new—"

"*Adam is not a bug.*" Blake couldn't stop himself from blurting it out. He could feel his face flush with anger. He didn't have the courage to look at Adiklein, but he maintained his defiant tone. "His name is Adam, okay, and he's my best friend. And his little gift is providing this company with a series of profit gushers, not to mention that all-important commodity—attention. And it's Adam—not me, not you. He's the one who deserves . . . who actually . . ." Blake's voice, which had begun so forcefully, trailed off.

There was a long silence as Blake looked down at the carpet, waiting for the wrath of Rene Adiklein to descend upon him. Instead he felt something far more shocking: a hand touching his shoulder, giving him a gentle pat. Looking up Blake saw Adiklein was now next to him, leaning on the desk. And for the first time since he'd met this extraordinary man, Adiklein appeared to Blake to finally be just that—a flesh-and-blood human being.

"Blake, my boy," Adiklein said softly, a hint of a smile in his eyes. "Do you know why I am here? What I am trying to do here in the Tower? Why as a researcher I moved from psychology to marketing to technology? Do you know why I do all this? What drives me?"

Blake shook his head.

"Love," Adiklein said.

"*Love?*"

Adiklein nodded. "I love people. I love the human race, Blake." Adiklein emphasized his words by drawing them out. "But the human race is . . . fragile. Civilization is fragile, far more than you might imagine. And to keep us moving in the right direction requires constant vigilance and effort, just to keep us from destroying ourselves. And I'm not only talking about what goes on out there." Adiklein gave a vague gesture toward the windows. "No, far more important is what goes on in here." He lightly tapped Blake's forehead.

"People need help knowing what to believe, what to care about, what is relevant, and what is not. More than anything, people need to know where to focus their attention. You see, Blake, to act as a shepherd of humanity, to help guide us all toward a more positive worldview, and to help purge us of our barbaric past—that is an act of love. Otherwise, what happens? We slip right back into the Dark Ages, with everyone running around with their own conflicting versions of reality." Adiklein's eyes glittered. "Warding off chaos—that is the salvation technology offers us. Unifying everyone with one vision, one inner narrative."

"Inner narrative?" Blake's eyebrows knitted together in confusion.

"The voice inside here"—Adiklein again tapped Blake's forehead—"that chatters away, narrating the story of your life as it unfolds. Put this voice together with the next person's voice and the next person's, and before you know it, we are narrating the story of the world. Which you might think would sound like a cacophony of madness. However, as we humans share more and more of the same experiences, the same information; as our inner worlds begin to run on the same operating systems, and we begin to hear the same inner narrative; the closer and closer we come to a time when, as the Lennon song goes, 'The world will live as one.'"

"But," Blake sputtered, "if everyone is following along to the same inner narrative . . . who controls the narrative?"

There was silence, long enough for Blake to realize he was holding his breath.

"That would be me, of course," Adiklein said with a wink.

Blake looked away from Adiklein, at his own ghostly reflection in the window.

"Sacrifices are required, my boy. Your friend Adam is a small price to pay for helping to keep the rest of us steady and on course."

Blake felt sick to his stomach. He didn't even look up when he heard Adiklein walking away.

When Blake finally did raise his head, he was surprised to see that Adiklein had not yet left the room. He was standing completely still, halfway between Blake's desk and the doorway, with an odd expression on his face, a look that Blake could have sworn was . . . fear.

"What is this?" Adiklein's voice was eerily restrained.

"What's what?"

"This, here."

Blake realized Adiklein was staring down at something on the floor in front of his desk. Leaning forward, Blake saw the large moving crates filled with stuff from Adam's cubicle.

"That? Nothing. Just clutter from a cubicle that was cleared out today."

"Whose cubicle?"

"It's Adam's stuff. It's just his old junk." Blake was about to ask what it was Adiklein was so concerned about, but Adiklein's expression had changed again. Now he was smiling as if nothing had happened.

"Well, if it's only junk, I suggest you throw it out." And with that, Adiklein turned and left Blake's office.

Blake had no intention of throwing out Adam's stuff. He planned to hang on to it in case Adam got better, but Adiklein didn't need to know that. Walking around the desk, Blake went to where Adiklein had been standing to see if he could determine what had spooked him so badly. Nothing looked out of the ordinary. There was one book that had fallen out of an overstuffed box, but there was nothing special about it. Just one of Adam's philosophy books, it looked like. Its jacket was gone; it had a burgundy spine, and embossed on its cover was a little, gold sea horse.

CHAPTER 31

REFLECTIONS
OF AN OLD FRIEND

Folding chair in one hand, laptop in the other, Dr. Agopian used an elbow to give a polite *thump-thump* on Adam's open door. "Good afternoon, Mr. Sheppard."

"Good afternoon, Dr. Agopian."

It was Miss Ferguson responding; she was in the room, clearing Adam's lunch tray. The doctor set down his things and went over to the chair by the window to have a look at his patient. He took Adam's pulse and used a penlight to quickly peer into both of his eyes. "How're we doing with the new meal plan, Adam?"

Adam did not respond.

"See for yourself," Miss Ferguson said, showing Dr. Agopian the tray. All of its subdivisions were relatively empty, except for some broccoli in a corner.

"Sauerkraut's a hit; that's good." Dr. Agopian gave the over-cooked broccoli a poke with the back of his penlight. "Yeah, I wouldn't touch that either. Miss Ferguson, would you mind talking to Carlos—"

"Already did. He said his hands are full tryin' to whip up these special meals on top of everyone else's food. Said if you want to come cook Adam's broccoli yourself, he'd be more than happy to show ya where the pots are kept."

Dr. Agopian looked back at Adam and gave an exasperated snort. "Can you believe that?"

Adam did not respond.

"Would you like me to close the door, Doctor?" Miss Ferguson said as she pushed the food cart out. "Drama therapy starts in the solarium at four fifteen, and it tends to get a bit raucous out there."

"Yes, thank you." Before Miss Ferguson left, he quietly asked, "So there's been no change this week? Nothing since the adjustment to his meds?"

"Sorry, Doctor." Miss Ferguson had a sympathetic smile. "But trust me, you'll be the first to know." With that she shut the door.

Dr. Agopian set the folding chair next to Adam and then removed his glasses and placed them in his breast pocket.

"All right, Adam. I'm going to remind you that I'm here for you whenever you wish to speak. If you're not ready, that's perfectly fine. No pressure. But this is your hour—well, our hour, I guess—and I actually look forward to our sessions together. Some nice quiet time away from all the crazies out there." Dr. Agopian watched Adam, hoping his humor might make it through.

Adam did not respond.

"Okay, well. I'm here when you're ready." Dr. Agopian took a deep breath and then became as quiet as Adam.

David Agopian had always wanted to be a doctor. Even as a child, he had been particularly concerned about those around him. If a classmate looked sick or got hurt on the playground, he'd be the first to escort him to the school nurse.

"You are very special boy, David-djan," his grandfather would say in his thick Armenian accent. "You are old soul, older than me! You have gift. Very *sense-sa-teeve* eyes." Then pulling David close to him, his grandfather would whisper the words he would never forget. "With your eyes, David-djan, you can heal world."

When David was a teenager, after his grandfather had passed away, he first learned about the Armenian genocide from his parents. He was told how his then-eight-year-old grandfather had barely escaped a mass execution in his village in 1915, and about the unspeakable horrors he had witnessed, including the slaughter of his entire family. Hearing this, David was struck by how his grandfather had never expressed anger or even the slightest bitterness. Instead he spoke to David only about the importance of helping others.

David Agopian's decision to go into psychiatry came when his older brother Raffi returned home from college between semesters and accidentally left behind a book titled *The Man Who Mistook His Wife for a Hat*. David read the book from cover to cover before going on to devour all of Oliver Sacks's other books. The mysterious neurological cases he learned about fascinated David so much that by college he knew without a doubt which field of medicine he wanted to practice. Of course the reality of a career in mental health was quite different from what he had imagined. Working with violent and abusive patients, with psychotics, schizophrenics, and attempted suicides day in and day out, year after year, had taken its toll on David's sensitive eyes.

And then Adam Sheppard showed up.

On the morning of Adam's arrival, Dr. Agopian happened to catch a brief glimpse of the new patient in the hallway outside registration. With his slack face, tousled hair, and vacant eyes, Adam looked every bit the Oliver Sacks mystery case that Dr. Agopian had long ago imagined he would get to treat. And in many ways, the circumstances surrounding Adam's case were ideal. He was nonviolent, there was no pressure from hovering family members to dictate the course of care, and no insurance companies pushing for a quick fix. With Adam, Dr. Agopian would have time to properly assess and treat his condition.

On the surface Adam's semicatatonic state appeared to be caused by severe depression. *"Bipolar 1 with psychotic features,"* Dr. Mendelson had written on his admittance form. But Dr. Agopian wasn't too sure about Dr. Mendelson's diagnosis, or about Dr. Mendelson himself, for that matter. There was something about Adam that didn't fit neatly into the bipolar spectrum. If anything, he seemed more like a trauma case—a raw wound that had been fussed with too much.

From the beginning Dr. Agopian decided to insulate Adam from other patients. He was given a private room, excused from group therapy, and—in response to a recommendation from S.F. General to continue with electroconvulsive therapy—Dr. Agopian decided to suspend it until he'd read through Adam's voluminous records. Just getting the transcripts ended up taking several months and a barrage of reminder calls to Dr. Mendelson's office. When the four large boxes finally did show up, they included stacks of dot-matrix computer printouts, which indicated just how old they were.

Wading through the records, a picture of Adam's past treatment slowly began to take form. His stepmother first brought Adam to Dr. Mendelson at the age of seven back in 1978 to be treated for, as stated on Adam's initial mental status exam, rapid speech, distracted attention, mood swings, inappropriate euphoria, delusions of grandeur, imaginary playmates, and emotional outbursts. Dr. Mendelson started Adam on what was a fairly new drug at the time, methylphenidate (later known as Ritalin). Back then it was given at radically higher doses, and for Adam there were immediate complications, including vomiting, headaches, and digestive issues, as well as tremors and nightly outbursts.

The transcripts showed that by age nine, Adam's condition had begun to stabilize. Still, in 1984 Dr. Mendelson advanced his diagnosis from ADHD to Bipolar 1. During Adam's teenage years and early adulthood, Mendelson had tried lithium, Depakote, Epitol, and many other well-marketed medications, and with each one came more side effects, complications, and health issues.

The records also showed periodic psychotic breaks of varying degrees. The episode recorded in December of 2008 was of particular interest to Dr. Agopian. Apparently Adam, in a delusional state, had returned to the town where he had been raised to search for an imaginary childhood friend named Beatrice. Though specifics of this event were difficult to follow in the notes, Dr. Agopian found it peculiar how extensive Adam's hallucinations were—another indication Mendelson's diagnosis was potentially off.

Out of curiosity Dr. Agopian did some online research into Dr. Mendelson's background and found he had undertaken his medical studies at a place called Devonport University. The school had a reputation for turning out pill-pushers and had eventually lost its accreditation after a congressional investigation found it had financial ties to multiple drug companies.

Not that Dr. Agopian was opposed to the use of pharmaceuticals. On the contrary, he had personally seen lives saved with a prescription, patients who literally could not function without them. Medication was an undeniably powerful weapon against mental illness, but Dr. Agopian also believed that with any great weapon there is the potential for abuse, especially when big money is involved. Kickbacks for prescribing drugs to patients who really don't need them was, in Dr. Agopian's opinion, about as immoral a crime as false imprisonment. Society, on the other hand, seemed pretty willing to accept it as one of those innocuous evils not worth fighting against. *But at what cost in the long run?* Dr. Agopian wondered. *More cases like Adam Sheppard?*

Dr. Agopian glanced over to quickly check on Adam. Same position. Same fixed stare. Same living statue.

Sitting here quietly with Adam, Dr. Agopian often considered the numerous well-known people throughout history who had struggled with mental illness in times before medication was available. People like Abraham Lincoln, Mark Twain, van Gogh, Edgar Allen Poe, Winston Churchill, Virginia Woolf, Isaac Newton, Charles Dickens, Emily Dickinson, Ralph Waldo Emerson, Plato, Beethoven, and Mozart. Would Poe have written "The Raven" if he had been on lithium? If a five-year-old Mozart had been put on Ritalin, would he have composed Andante in C Major? On the flip side of the equation, would Joseph Stalin still have murdered 20 million people had he been properly medicated? Considering both the good and the bad, one is forced to ask—to what extent should we be evening out society before it becomes flat?

This slippery question always reminded him of the film-noir classic *The Third Man*, when Orson Welles makes his case to Joseph Cotton, saying, "In Italy, for thirty years under the Borgias, they had warfare, terror, murder and bloodshed, but they produced Michelangelo, Leonardo da Vinci, and the Renaissance. In Switzerland, they had brotherly love, they had five hundred years of democracy and peace . . . and what did they produce? The cuckoo clock."

Had Adam Sheppard been turned into a cuckoo clock? Quite possibly, but at this point there was little Dr. Agopian could do but wait and see. For the foreseeable future, he would continue to spend an hour a week sitting here with Adam in the hopes of a clue that might shatter the barrier of silence that had molded itself around this broken man.

"With your eyes, David-djan, you can heal the world."

It had been almost nine months now, and still Dr. Agopian was struggling to clearly see the right course of treatment for Adam. The best he had done was to develop a theory, a rather unconventional theory, but a theory that at least contained some hope. The idea arose during one of their silent therapy sessions, when Dr. Agopian noticed a small, white butterfly fluttering outside Adam's window. With it came the thought, *What if this was not a depressed state at all, but more like a cocoon of some sort?*

As a psychiatrist Dr. Agopian had been trained to look into a patient's inner world, but what if he wasn't looking deeply enough? What if he had been considering only Adam's psychological outer layers (which were definitely battered and bruised and in need of healing)? What if there was something else taking place on a deeper level, on what could only be described as a metaphysical level? Something closer to the fundamental biological processes, like birth and death.

What if I'm looking at a chrysalis?

A memory came back to Dr. Agopian of an experiment he had once performed in a biology class as an undergrad. He and his lab partners had cut open the chrysalis of a caterpillar in the process of becoming a butterfly, and what they found inside absolutely stunned him. Instead of a caterpillar sprouting wings out of its back as he had anticipated, the chrysalis was filled with yellowish goo. They had learned that in order for a caterpillar to become a butterfly, it first had to completely dissolve; its head, its legs, its antennae, its entire body had to melt down into cellular soup, and only then could it reconstitute itself as a butterfly.

Looking at Adam motionless in his chair, it was difficult to say what exactly was taking place inside of him. Most likely the butterfly metaphor was complete nonsense. But for now it was the most optimistic way Dr. Agopian had found for looking at the situation.

"Dr. Agopian? Excuse me, Dr. Agopian?"

His eyes popped open, and for a moment, his heart raced at the thought that it had been Adam saying his name. But it was Miss Ferguson, standing at the door.

"Sorry to disturb you, but your wife called the nurses' station to find out if you're still joining her for dinner, or if you're having 'date night' with Adam Sheppard instead?"

Dr. Agopian took out his cell phone. Three missed calls. "Could you please tell her that I'm on my way?"

"Call her yourself, Romeo. I've got Adam to look after." She walked over and patted Adam on the forearm. "What do you say we move over to the solarium for a while, now that those drama therapy queens are done with all their yellin' and screamin'?"

"Do you want my help moving him?" Dr. Agopian asked.

"No, no. You go be a loving husband. I got newbie Ken to help." Ken, a new orderly at the hospital, followed Miss Ferguson into the room and together they got Adam to his feet.

Looking back from the doorway, Dr. Agopian felt an unusual twinge of doubt. Perhaps Adam really was a cuckoo clock, broken beyond repair. And perhaps Dr. Agopian had been irresponsible by choosing not to give Adam electroshock therapy, or by not increasing his course of lithium. Perhaps.

The view of the coast from the solarium looked much the same as it did from Adam's room. The only noticeable difference was the foreground: more parking lot, less lawn and wind-twisted cypress trees. But Adam had little concern with the lower portion of the view. His attention had to remain out there, beyond this hospital, beyond the fog, beyond the horizon.

Nine months had passed since he had come to realize that to struggle outwardly was useless. His countless attachments were simply too deeply rooted. His only hope was to become still, to give in to the tension of his chains, to relax into their burrowed hooks, and slowly turn inward. That was where he had discovered the doorway through which he could slip unnoticed and make his way back to the cliffs. That distant horizon was where *she* had come from, and so that was where Adam searched patiently, day in and day out, waiting for his heavenly guide to appear once more.

The compassionate Dr. Agopian had been right about Adam. He was not locked up in some immobilizing depression. He was not insane. What he was attempting to do, however, was beyond insanity. Like Sisyphus with his boulder, Adam started each day focusing on one thing and one thing only: seeing Beatrice's face again. Over and over, his efforts began anew, working to reduce the distance between their two worlds. And over these nine months, he had perhaps moved an inch closer, perhaps two. Closer to Beatrice, but also to the cliff's edge.

It was around seven that evening when the sun broke through the low sea fog, bathing the solarium in a glow of warm light. Although Ken the new orderly had done an honorable job facing Adam toward the ocean, he had failed to observe Miss Ferguson's second rule of chair placement: angling Adam to avoid seeing his own reflection in the oversize glass windows. Miss Ferguson had been right about this, as what Adam saw reflected back at him now was enough to pull his attention back into this room. He saw himself. The simple truth of what he had become. A hunched man-child, eyes lost in lunacy, dreaming that life could be something more than it had turned out to be.

Before this vision could completely consume him, though, a sudden glint of reflected light drew his attention to someone sitting in a chair a few yards behind him. Not Miss Ferguson, who Adam could hear at the nurses' station talking to Ken. Perhaps another patient? Adam strained to look more closely at the reflection and noticed that this person's jacket was covered with dozens of small circles, each reflecting sunlight that pecked annoyingly at Adam's eyes. And then the apparition began to glide toward him.

In the reflected light of the window, Adam saw a wheelchair pull to a stop at his side.

"Hey there, brother," a familiar voice greeted him. Michael was there, looking back at him through the reflection in the glass with a hint of a smile in his eyes.

Adam did not respond, but as Michael's eyes shifted their focus out to the coastline beyond the trees, Adam's did as well. And for the next 20 minutes, the two men sat quietly watching the sun go down.

"You just keep on digging, brother," Adam heard Michael say in his hoarse whisper. The wavering orange ball touched the line of the horizon and slowly began to slip from Adam's world into hers. "You got to go all the ways down 'til you reach the center of the mothafuckin' earth. That's where the shift happens. That's where *down* becomes *up*. But you ain't never gonna go up until you first go down. *All* the way down."

The two men continued to watch the sun sink below the horizon. And then it was gone, and with it Michael's reflection.

CHAPTER 32

WHERE DOWN BECOMES UP

It happened on Tuesday.

Tuesday was movie night at the Presidio House. After dinner, interested and able patients gathered with the aid of the orderlies in the solarium, where a film played on the big-screen TV. Movie selections varied from animated films to black-and-white classics, with the occasional nature documentary thrown in. On this particular Tuesday, Walt Disney's *Fantasia* was on the docket.

Early on in his stay at the Presidio House, Adam was included in movie night, but after Dr. Agopian arranged for him to take meals in his room, he no longer attended. Regardless, Miss Ferguson still checked in to tell Adam what was showing, whether she had seen it or not, whether she liked it or not, and finally she'd add, "So what do you think, handsome, shall we make it a date?" Adam never responded, and Miss Ferguson never took it personally.

As *Fantasia* began to play, Adam was just finishing up his dinner. A little while later, Sam, one of the nighttime caretakers, came by to help wash Adam up and put him in bed. Sam didn't notice anything out of the ordinary that evening; Adam seemed no different than he had on the numerous other times Sam had put him down for the night.

"Okay, my man, sweet dreams."

The lights clicked off. The door shut. And for some time, Adam lay awake, listening to the distant strains of music coming from down the hall. First there was Bach, bold and dramatic, followed by Tchaikovsky, his "Dance of the Sugar Plum Fairy" lightly plucking along. Then came "The Sorcerer's Apprentice," with Mickey Mouse, the giant book of spells, the wand, and the hat. And as a legend of enchanted broomsticks began to wreak havoc on poor Mickey and the castle, Adam at last closed his eyes.

What lies beyond the stars?

The voice woke Adam, or at least that's what he thought at first. His mind was suddenly alert, and he was aware he had been sleeping, but when Adam opened his eyes, he found he was not in his bed anymore. He was in Mendocino, out on the bluff at night. In the distance, he could make out the hazy streetlights along Main Street. A gust of wind rippled across the tall, yellow grass, and as it reached him, Adam looked down and saw his light blue hospital garments fluttering silently against his body.

Turning toward the ocean, he could see he was not far from the spot on the cliffs where, for nine months, he had imagined himself standing. Without thinking he walked a little farther and took up his designated position. He looked down the craggy coastline to his left, then to his right, and then gazed down at his bare feet, only a few inches from the edge. Taking in a deep breath of salty ocean air, he looked out toward the horizon, that delicate divide between heaven and earth. This was more than a dream. He was here. Fully present. He could feel the wind on his skin, the weight of his body, and the cold, wet rocks underfoot.

The story of Adam Sheppard flickered vaguely in the background of his mind, the tale of an average man born in the 1970s, who spent his life in front of a computer screen; a man who never quite fit in, yet never really stood out; a not so extraordinary version of a social outcast, an outsider, the kind that seemed less and less needed in the homogenized world. That life was the dream now, quickly dissolving into the endless folds of time.

Adam caught the sharp scent of horsemint in the air, and he realized he was no longer alone. *She* was standing at his side, looking out at the horizon with him. Her hand slipped naturally into his, and immediately he felt hot wax binding them together. He wanted to turn and face her, not just sense her in the corner of his eye, but see her fully. But when he tried to turn, he found he could not. Something deep within him was still locked in place.

She gently released his hand and, without warning, stepped forward off the edge of the cliff. She did not fall but kept walking out through the air toward the horizon, each step relaxed and confident. Adam watched as she moved away from him, and he knew this was it. This was the moment he had been preparing for. His final chance to break through.

He stepped right to the very edge of the cliff, and then, just as Beatrice had done, stepped off. But instead of continuing forward, Adam fell . . .

Down, down. Ten thousand fishing lines with their barbed hooks ripping from his earthly body without mercy . . .

Down past the shock of cold water and into the earth itself . . .

Down through the outer crust of history, through the rise and fall of civilizations . . .

Down past the mantle of evolution, from the dawn of humanity and back through the animal kingdom and all the way back to the embryonic stages of organic life itself . . .

Down past the roaring furnace of the earth's outer core, through the inconceivably pressurized inner core, and into the very center of the earth . . .

It was there that Adam fell, into that singularity where the laws of physics are no longer irreversible. To a place where *down* becomes *up* . . .

$$\diamondsuit$$

The sun had dipped behind the redwoods, but patches of sunlight still dappled the upper half of the schoolhouse. Here on the merry-go-round on the far side of the yard, the boy was now in complete shade. Since waking he had followed his grandmother's advice and had waited patiently for someone to come and find him. But he was getting tired again. Watching the day's last sunlight dance on the side of the school, along with the rhythmic purr of cicadas, made his eyelids heavy.

He was about to lay his head back down and go to sleep when he noticed a man standing by the corner of the schoolhouse, next to the water fountain. The boy thought that perhaps he was lost. He looked like it. And he was wearing funny blue pajamas, which didn't look nearly warm enough. The man slowly walked across the yard toward the boy.

It's a good thing I stayed on the merry-go-round, the boy thought. *If this man turns out to be a bad guy, at least it will provide me with some protection.*

But as the man moved closer, the boy could see there was nothing to be afraid of. He had the face of a good guy. He even looked familiar, though the boy wasn't sure where he could have met him before.

The man in the blue pajamas stopped a few feet in front of the merry-go-round, and for a long while, he just looked at the boy, unable to speak.

"Hello," the boy finally said, breaking the silence.

The man tried to respond, but the word caught in his throat. His eyes were wet.

"I was sleeping," the boy continued. "For a really long time."

"I know," the man in pajamas said. "I've been looking for you."

The boy considered the man's face again. It was familiar, no doubt about it. "How did you find me?"

The man took a moment to consider the question, and then he smiled, but just slightly. "You're a friend of Beatrice's. She led me here."

This made the boy smile too. There was no doubt now. This man was a good guy if he knew Beatrice.

"Do you know where she is now?" the boy asked hopefully.

"I'm not sure," said the man in pajamas. "But I think maybe together we can find her. Do you want to help me look?"

This seemed like a good idea to the boy. He knew that finding Beatrice was something he was good at.

And so the man in the blue pajamas helped the boy off the merry-go-round where he had been sleeping and waiting for so long, and together they began their journey.

Up from the center of the earth.

CHAPTER 33

Time to Start Flying

Dr. Agopian was just biting into the *non*-gluten-free brownie his blessedly devilish wife had snuck into his lunch bag when he heard a commotion out in the hall. It sounded as if someone was running toward his office. Reluctantly setting the brownie down, he got up to have a look, but as he reached the door, it violently swung open.

"Miss Ferguson! What's wrong? What is it?"

"Ad . . . Ad . . . Ad," she sputtered. The last time Miss Ferguson ran at full speed was 30 years ago to catch a bus out of Glasgow.

"Catch your breath and tell me what's happened."

Miss Ferguson leaned onto Dr. Agopian's outstretched forearms for a moment before finally she blurted out, "It's Adam. Adam Sheppard."

Less than five minutes earlier, Miss Ferguson had strolled into Adam's room, as she had done practically every morning for the past nine months. "Rise and shine, handsome." She set Adam's morning medications and breakfast tray down on the bedside table, and then went to open the curtains and let in the morning light. Turning around with a cheerful smile, she realized that *Adam was not in his bed.*

The second shock came when she saw him lying on the floor next to the bed. The third came as she began to make sense of what it was he was doing down there. He was *stretching*. But what finally sent Miss Ferguson tearing down the hallway toward Dr. Agopian's office was the moment when Adam Sheppard looked up at her and whispered in a voice hoarse from disuse, *"Good morning . . . Miss Ferguson. You look . . . bonny today."*

His own heart now pounding, Dr. Agopian reached Adam's door and looked in. At first nothing seemed out of the ordinary. There was Adam, sitting in his chair by the window, stoically gazing out at the coast, same as always. But as Dr. Agopian moved into the room, goose bumps formed along his forearms. This man by the window, who only yesterday was no more than a zombie, now exuded such an overwhelming sense of wakefulness that Dr. Agopian could feel it just looking at his back.

Cautiously approaching him, Dr. Agopian took in Adam's face. His forehead, which had once displayed a permanently furrowed brow, was now as smooth and tranquil as a pool of water. His gaze had also relaxed. His eyes, no longer painfully fixated on some distant point, had opened up, widened, and now seemed to be taking in everything around him at once.

Slowly Adam turned to face Dr. Agopian.

"Hello, Adam." The tremor in Dr. Agopian's voice betrayed his emotions. "I'm your doctor. My name is David Agopian."

Adam said nothing at first; he simply stared up at Dr. Agopian, taking him in. It was a moment the doctor would remember for the rest of his life.

"Yes," Adam finally said, his voice still rusty. "Yes."

Dr. Agopian broke into a huge smile. With that single word, Adam had conveyed everything. *Yes*, Adam was fully aware of who Dr. Agopian was; *yes*, he was conscious of all that had transpired between them in the past nine months; *yes*, everything Dr. Agopian had done for Adam had been right; and finally, *yes*, Adam was grateful for all of it.

The two men spent the rest of the day together. There was so much to talk about, so much Dr. Agopian wanted to learn, but he did his best to keep the conversation light, the questions basic. "How is your stomach doing?" "Is there anyone you want us to contact?" "Would you like anything to drink, something hot maybe? Tea?"

There were many long breaks between questions, during which they sat together in silence. However, it never felt uncomfortable, like one of those holes in a conversation most people rush to fill with words. The silences between Dr. Agopian and Adam were already full of an unspoken language they had forged together over the past months.

After lunch Adam asked to go outside. Together doctor and patient strolled the grounds of the Presidio House. Miss Ferguson, along with several other curious staff members, gaped from the windows, watching in amazement as the pair walked around the parking lot, past the admin building, and all the way down to the bottom of the hospital property, to the row of old cypress trees Adam had been looking out at for so very long.

Adam spent awhile touching the trees, feeling their thick trunks and their gnarled branches. Watching Adam, Dr. Agopian thought he appeared like both a curious child and an old sage, completely engaged in the world around him, yet utterly detached.

Before returning to the hospital, Adam sat down beneath one of the larger trees to rest. Dr. Agopian was standing up on the lawn a few yards away, not wanting to intrude on the moment, but when he saw Adam looking directly at him, Dr. Agopian understood it as an invitation to come over. Adam had something to say.

Dr. Agopian sat down next to Adam. After a moment Adam began to speak, more easily this time. "There was something my therapist used to always say to me. His name was Dr. Mendelson."

"Yes." Dr. Agopian nodded. "I met with him once. Briefly."

"Dr. M. would tell me we're all the same. People. Everyone thinks they've got big problems, but the truth is, we're never really as bad off as we imagine we are, and at the same time, things will just never be as good as we want them to be. And that's okay. We're only human."

"Sounds like Freud." Dr. Agopian smiled.

There was a long pause while Adam looked up at the great cypress above them, its branches reaching out like arms and fingers stretching for the sky.

"I think Freud might have gotten it backward," Adam finally said. "What if we're actually much worse off than we realize?" Adam turned to face Dr. Agopian, his eyes gleaming. "And at the same time, we have the potential to become far greater than we can possibly imagine."

◈

It took only two weeks for Dr. Agopian to set a date with the hospital board to review Adam Sheppard's application for release. He was particularly eager to share the details of Adam's recovery with some of the doctors from S.F. General who had been critical of Dr. Agopian's hands-off approach. Before Adam was brought into the room, Dr. Agopian summarized the case for his colleagues, starting with Adam's history of questionable treatment under Dr. Mendelson's care—the premature diagnosis and the barrage of medications.

One of the senior doctors on the board recognized Mendelson's name. "Oh, yes," she said with a nod. "He's got quite the reputation as a pill-pusher. But this is sounding more like borderline malpractice. "

"Yes," Dr. Agopian replied with measured restraint. "Despite my recommendations, however, Adam has decided not to take legal action."

Dr. Agopian went on to explain how and why his own treatment of Adam was based on the premise that he essentially *stop* treating him. "Before introducing any new medication or therapy," Dr. Agopian explained, "I felt it was best to allow Adam to be given the chance to heal on his own. To assist Adam in this process, I began by gradually reducing the dosage of his medication over a controlled period of time, eventually replacing them with placebos."

"So what medications is he currently taking?" asked a young Asian doctor from SF General who had been involved with Adam's treatment before his transfer.

"None," Dr. Agopian replied.

"Mr. Sheppard is no longer on any medication?" The young doctor's tone was incredulous. He had seen Adam at his most violent, just before he sank into his catatonic state.

"He takes a few aspirin in the morning to help with the pain in his muscles, but that's it."

"So you're saying you took him off all his meds and then left him alone in a room for nine months, and as a result, he has made a miraculous recovery?"

"I also adjusted his diet. As I'm sure you're already aware, there have been multiple studies connecting the gut to mood disorders and serotonin levels."

The young doctor started to challenge Dr. Agopian again when one of the more senior doctors interjected. "So if Adam Sheppard was misdiagnosed as bipolar, what would your diagnosis be, Dr. Agopian? What is his condition?"

"He doesn't have one," Dr. Agopian said flatly. But then he shook his head. "No, let me correct that. Adam Sheppard suffered from not being what others wanted him to be. He suffered from being overtreated, which only caused bigger problems that required bigger solutions, causing even bigger problems. Stuck in that cycle, going round and round, his fate was inevitable. Eventually he crashed. Therefore, the only solution was to let him fully shut down. Then fully reboot.

"It is my opinion that there is nothing medically wrong with Adam. He may not be what the world considers 'normal,' but he is not mentally ill, nor does he pose a danger to himself or others. But perhaps it's time to let Adam speak for himself."

As Dr. Agopian expected, any lingering doubts evaporated the moment Adam Sheppard entered the room. When he spoke he commanded attention with his sincerity and discerning insight. Several times a question turned into a discussion during which the doctors talked to Adam about his condition with the same respect and consideration they would have given a colleague. For the most part, Dr. Agopian said nothing. He simply sat back and watched, seeming to take as much pleasure as if he were watching a beloved nephew ace his oral argument before a medical review board.

Practical questions about where Adam would go when he left the Presidio House and what he would do felt trivial, but nevertheless the doctors had to ask.

And Adam had a ready answer. He told the board members, "I'm going to go live my life, the one I was always meant to live."

Adam stood motionless, allowing the water to run over his body. It was an amazing feeling. Looking straight up into the showerhead, he opened his mouth. He didn't drink the water, but simply let it fill his mouth until it spilled out. He thought about all those times he had taken a shower in the past, lost in his head, never really *in* the shower. He could still go there if he chose to, still let his mind wander out beyond the circumference of this overhead stream. He could let his thoughts take him away toward the worries of the past or the anxieties of the future, but why? Life was happening right here. And it was a life he now had very good reason to stay focused on.

Adam was no longer alone inside himself. The boy from the merry-go-round was now there. His young voice was still weak, but Adam could hear it clearly now. Unlike the voice inside his head, this new voice resided deep within his solar plexus.

Looking down at the hot- and cold-water faucets, Adam smiled. He now understood who had been covertly helping him escape his old mind loops. Adam reached out and turned off the hot water. After a few seconds, the icy shock hit him. Adam danced around the shower stall, howling like a proper madman before twisting the hot-water faucet back on.

As the warm water eased back over his skin, Adam leaned against the shower tiles, gasping for air and laughing. A few moments later, he heard a whisper inside of him say, *"Again, again!"*

With each passing day, Adam was beginning to understand that it would be his responsibility to help nurture this underdeveloped side of himself, the six-year-old boy in need of experiences in order to grow. And at the same time, he was also learning to trust that this six-year-old boy was there to guide and protect him in return.

$$\diamondsuit$$

They threw Adam a going-away party in the solarium. Dr. Agopian brought his wife, who was eager to meet Adam after everything she'd heard about him. Of course Miss Ferguson was there too, wearing her favorite SpongeBob party hat. Since Adam's health-care directive had been taken over by the State, there was no requirement to inform anyone outside the hospital of his recovery or release. Adam asked the administration office to keep it that way. Blake had stopped calling a few months ago, but if he ever did call again, Dr. Agopian would handle it for Adam. "I'm sorry, Mr. Dorsey, but Adam Sheppard is still unreachable," or something along those lines.

There was one guest who made an appearance at the party who Adam wasn't expecting to see. Adam first noticed him sitting alone by the window, facing away from everyone else. He was in his wheelchair, in pretty much the same position as the last time Adam had seen him.

It was Michael. Not a reflection, but a flesh-and-blood human being.

Carrying slices of cake on a tray, Miss Ferguson walked past Adam, over to the window, and offered one to Michael. He took three. Miss Ferguson walked away, and after a moment Michael glanced in Adam's direction. Their eyes met.

Michael looked a little different, Adam thought. A little older, a little less crazy, and a little more physically compromised. Perhaps a little more heavy-hearted as well. But as Adam moved closer, Michael gave him that same glorious smile, bright as sunshine, eyes full of wonder.

"My brother, look at you. Look. At. You," he said before taking a big bite of cake. "I knew you'd make it. Oh, yeah, I knew."

Adam pulled up a chair and sat down. Still feeling a sense of disbelief, he watched Michael eat; his movements were slow but steady, with none of the old tremors. Adam spotted a small paper cup, the kind they use to give out medication, on the food tray set across the arms of his wheelchair.

"Don't get too comfortable now," Michael went on, his voice clearer than Adam remembered. "You already done enough sitting around. Time for you to get moving, brother." Then leaning in with that conspiratorial look in his eye, he added, "*They* gonna be needin' yo' ass."

As usual, Adam wasn't quite sure what to make of Michael's words. "'They' who?"

Michael shrugged and went back to his cake. After another bite he added, "An old friend of mine used to say, 'In times of change, a single conscious man can equal a million sleeping.'" Michael looked directly at Adam. And with all affectation suddenly gone, he said, "Time you started flying, brother. For both of us."

Reaching down beneath the seat cushion of his wheelchair, Michael pulled out a manila envelope. After fiddling with the worn brass latch, he opened it and slid out an old photograph. He handed it to Adam without a word.

CHAPTER 34

THE FIRST ORANGE PEEL

Hank reached into his breast pocket for his Camel Lights. It was time for his lucky cigarette. Like many smokers, whenever Hank opened a new pack, he'd ritualistically pull out a cigarette, flip it around, and put it back in, tobacco end up. Like many smokers, Hank had no idea why he did this. He just knew it made the cigarette lucky if he smoked it last before opening a new pack. Although there were plenty of myths out there, mostly dealing with soldiers and war, this maneuver had actually originated for sanitary considerations (a flipped cigarette allowed one to offer someone a smoke with a relatively clean filter). The term "lucky" had most likely developed over time (perhaps if no one bummed from you for your whole pack, then "lucky you" got to smoke it yourself). Whatever the case, the virtuous origins of this sacred move were slowly forgotten and usurped by superstition, so that today, as far as Hank understood it, taking a lucky cigarette out of someone else's pack was not only rude but also incredibly bad luck.

Some dickwad once took my lucky cigarette, he thought. *When the hell was that?*

Hank stepped out of the guard booth to stretch his legs. It was just after nine, and the morning fog had burnt off, leaving a high cloud cover and a gentle breeze. Leaning on the railing, he looked

out on the boats. Nothing much doing today. All the local fishing boats were long gone, Don and Marty Barksdale were over on
their busted-up ketch repairing the mainsail, and there were some
seagulls fighting over something on the far shore.

There was also a man Hank didn't recognize standing alone
at the far end of the last pier. He seemed to be examining one
of the empty slips. *Strange,* Hank thought. The man was too far
away to make out his face, but there was something familiar about
him standing out there. *That slip was where all that weird shit went
down, two, three years ago,* he recalled. Taking another long drag
off his lucky cigarette, Hank headed down toward the docks to
investigate.

Adam had been in Mendocino for nearly a week. He had taken
a room at the Sea Gull Inn, a quaint bed and breakfast. From his
room he could walk a block, cross Main Street, and reach the entrance to a footpath between the gas station and the Presbyterian
Church that led out to the bluff. He took this route to avoid walking down Main Street. For the most part he wanted to keep to himself as he adjusted to the outside world. He felt a bit like a newborn
since leaving the Presidio House, hypersensitive to every nuance
of the environment around him, as if all the nerve endings in his
body had been scrubbed raw.

The few hours he'd spent in San Francisco before getting out
of town had proven almost too much to bear. The cars, the people,
the sounds—it was like someone had turned the volume up full
blast in the city. More disturbing than the sensory assault were the
faces of people he passed on the streets. The groups of kids waiting
at the bus stop, the bouncer outside a bar, the housewife pumping
gasoline into her SUV, the young couple outside the café, the busi-
nessman in his fancy suit, the taxi driver, the four-year-old girl in
her car seat. Almost every face . . . lost in the pale glow of a screen.
Even those not looking at devices seemed half-asleep, off in their
own private nowhere.

Outside the city the noise was less pervasive, the faces less
foggy. For several reasons Mendocino was the natural place for

Adam to go. Wandering the headlands alone was just about as much stimulation as he could handle at first. He'd found a big bench made from driftwood where he went to sit those first few days and just take in the coastline south of town. After that he went a little farther down the bluff where familiar, precarious wooden stairs led down to the beach below. The next day he ventured a bit farther, past the giant blowhole.

It was high tide when he first made it out to the cliffs. The waves smashing against the rocks were deafening but exhilarating. He climbed down to get as close as possible to the action. As sunset neared, Adam climbed back up to the high point on the cliffs to that same spot he had visited so many times in his mind's eye. Standing now a few feet from the edge with the rocks solidly underfoot, he watched the horizon as day turned to dusk. Endless thoughts rambled through his mind, but they no longer consumed him as they had in the past. He could now simply allow them to scud by like clouds in the background, and only when a thought was worth focusing on did he move it forward into view.

One thought Adam did allow to the fore while standing on the edge of the cliff was of *her*.

We need to find her, the young boy's voice whispered in Adam's chest.

It's not that easy, the older, more pragmatic voice in his head reasoned. *Even if she was really flesh and blood, how would I ever find her?*

Look for the orange peel, the boy whispered. *Once we find the first one, we'll be able to spot the next. That's how the game works.*

The next day Adam headed up to Noyo Harbor, not really sure what he was looking for, but trusting that this would be a good place to start.

"Hey there!"

Adam looked up from the empty slip. Hank, the big security guard, was standing at the end of the pier, taking a final drag of his cigarette before dropping it to the ground and rubbing it out with his boot.

"You're that crazy fella, right?" Hank squinted at Adam. He took a few steps closer and then stopped. "Oh, wait. Shoot, I'm sorry. Got you confused with someone else. Beg your pardon, sir."

"No, no. I'm who you think I am," Adam said plainly. "The crazy fella, that was me."

Hank continued to walk toward Adam, looking at him intently. "Oh, yeah. Okay, so I was right. You look different. I mean that in a good way." Hank stopped at the opposite end of the slip and gave Adam a big, friendly smile.

There was an awkward pause. Adam could sense that Hank wanted to ask him something. Since his recovery Adam had found it curiously simple to gauge people's thoughts just by looking at them.

"Your name is Hank, right?" Adam said to break the silence.

"Right, right." The look of concern was still there. "So . . . He told you, right?"

Adam's new mind reading skills failed at that point. "'He' who?"

"Your buddy, that slick fella with the Beamer."

"You mean Blake?"

"I guess. He never told you nothing? For me?"

"No, I don't think so."

"Boy, oh, boy." Hank stroked his beard a few times and then pulled a fresh pack of cigarettes out from his jacket pocket. "I shoulda known I couldn't trust that guy. Now that I think about it, he was the dickwad who bummed my lucky cigarette that day!" Hank took off the plastic wrap and slapped the pack of cigarettes against the heel of his left palm. "Never trust a dickwad who takes your lucky cigarette, that's for sure."

"What was he supposed to tell me?"

Hank pinched out two cigarettes. One went to his mouth, the other he dutifully flipped and stuck back in. "I'm truly sorry about what happened but"—Hank dug in his jeans and pulled out a lighter—"there just wasn't nothing else I could do, you know?"

"No, I don't. What was Blake supposed to tell me?"

Hank shook his head. "That day, with the Coast Guard and Homeland Security here, and the sheriff and all, I didn't have the chance to tell you, or I would've. But it was all just so crazy."

"Hank," Adam said a little louder. "Tell me what?"

Hank lit his cigarette and took a long drag. "Your friend? The redhead?"

"Beatrice?"

"Is that her name?" Hank shrugged. "I always just called her Red." Hank exhaled tendrils of smoke through his nose. "You see, the Coast Guard came in that morning just a few hours before you showed up. I warned her they were coming, and since she didn't have no papers and with Homeland Security in charge of things now, well, she decided to move her boat." Hank pointed up at the bend in the river. "Took it just around that bend."

Adam looked out at the river.

"Red told me you were coming to meet her. Said when you showed up, I should tell you where she was, but then, like I said, with all them cops and Homeland Security agents and everything else, there was just no way I could do that."

Near the river bend there was a spot on the opposite bank and what looked like a footpath. Adam recalled how he had seen, or thought he'd seen, the figure of a woman standing there as he was driven away in the back of the patrol car.

"That Blake fella told me he was your friend, said he'd give you my message once things calmed down. It was all I could think of to do, considering." Hank took a long drag off his cigarette.

Adam looked at Hank and gave a small nod. It was enough to allow the big guy to understand he wasn't mad at him and to encourage him to continue.

"After you left the Coast Guard stuck around for another hour, thumbs up their arses. When they finally took off, I was able to get up there to Red and tell her what happened. Boy, oh, boy." Hank exhaled loudly, shaking his head. "She was not happy. Got this look in her eyes, and her voice, man, it was like she turned into some kinda evil cop or something. Scared the shit out of me."

A slight smile flashed across Adam's face, but Hank was too busy telling his story to notice.

"Then she got on that big-ass phone of hers, talked to someone for a while, don't know who. But when she got off, she was cool again. She asked about getting a lift somewhere, but I felt so bad, I just let her borrow my truck. I thought maybe she was gonna go after you or something, but after a couple hours, she was back. Then she set sail, just barely got out before a big storm hit."

Adam gave another small nod but still didn't say anything.

Hank shook his head. "Sorry, buddy, but I guess she really had to go somewhere."

"Yes," Adam finally said. "She did."

Hank glanced up at Adam's face, surprised he was taking it so well. He dragged his smoke again before adding, "She did say, just before she left, that if you were to ever come around looking for her, you'd be able to figure out how to find her."

Just find the first orange peel, the boy softly whispered.

Back up in the harbor parking lot, a truck was pulling in with a small sailboat trailing behind it. Hank squinted at it. Recognizing the driver, he gave a wave as if to say he'd be right there. "I'm gonna need to go deal with that."

Adam nodded and smiled. "No problem. Thanks for your help, Hank."

"Sure. Best of luck to you. Hope you find her." Hank dropped his smoke and stepped on it. He started to leave, but then stopped as if something else had crossed his mind. "Oh, hey, you mind doing me a favor?"

"Sure, what?"

"Well, if you're planning on seeing Red again, she left a few things in the back of my truck. I've actually been meaning to throw them out, but if you think you'll see her, you mind taking them to her?"

"What'd she leave?"

"Just a shovel and some rope. Nothing special, but, you know, it's a nice shovel and pretty expensive-lookin' rope."

Slowly a smile spread over Adam's face. The first orange peel had come into view.

He was better prepared this time around, arriving at Little River Cemetery at 1 P.M., an hour and a half before the day's low tide. Adam had the rope and shovel from Hank, as well as an additional hand shovel, several plastic buckets, two wooden planks he thought could be useful as wall supports, towels, and a lantern with extra batteries. He hoped he wouldn't need the metal detector this time around.

The sinkhole hadn't seemed to notice the years that had passed since Adam's last visit. The place was timeless. But Adam had changed, enough to now see why Beatrice had said there were few places like this in the world. It was a natural wonder that also contained something not of the material earth—a place where the physical and allegorical sides of the worlds met, where "skies grow thin." Although Adam was ready for a physical challenge, the job turned out to be much quicker and easier than he had anticipated. Digging in the alcove below the strange white mark was still exhilarating. Like a boy running through a grass field toward a redwood grove, he felt the life force within his body so fully that he even snapped a picture of the moment from high above.

Adam hit the metal box four feet down. It was almost too easy. So for fun, before leaving the tunnel, he decided to refill the hole, even though the coming waves would have surely done the job for him.

Back in the sinkhole, Adam ate a light lunch before prying open the metal box. Inside he found several thick, waterproof plastic bags. They contained a stack of nautical charts, a copy of *Navigations of the Hidden Domain*, a note with his name on it, and a shriveled-up, petrified orange peel.

Adam unfolded the note.

Dear Thief,

I know in my heart that you will one day read this. I know because I can see you here now, down in our private grotto, sitting in the sand only a few feet from where I now write this letter. But there is something different about this Adam. This new Adam is no longer searching for a Reset button. This Adam has finally freed himself from his impenetrable suit of armor.

As much as I wanted to, I realized it was not my job to save you. "Freedom is never given, only earned," as my father is fond of reminding me.

I still believe you belong with us, that you were always meant to play a role in the work we are doing. Just like you, the world is facing a time of reckoning. Whatever the outcome, the signs of a great struggle are near. I have left charts and directions that will lead you to where I am heading. The journey will not be easy. Just know that wherever I go, I will always leave a trail of orange peels for you.

You are forever in my heart and I in yours. And as long as you keep moving forward, I will keep pulling you toward me, and eventually we will meet again, and touch again, and with our hands melted together as one, we will peek behind the celestial curtain and see the new world waiting for us, just beyond the stars.

Yours (and yours alone),

Beatrice

CHAPTER 35

LEAVING THE
SPHERE OF ATTENTION

With the tear across his mainsail mended, the Man prepared at long last to enter those uncharted waters he had sought from the outset of his journey. He had faced off against relentless headwinds, violent gales, and unexpected swells. He had spent countless lifetimes dead in the water and a greater number struggling to stay afloat. He had faced external challenges at every turn, but none compared to the inner despair inflicted by those powerful currents, those invisible strings beneath his vessel, dragging him around in endless recurrence, leading him forever back to the shallows he so longed to escape. The Man's decision to aim his bow directly into an approaching storm had at first appeared to be an act of insanity. But through this irrational embrace of his own annihilation, his vessel had at last slipped free, breaking from the enchanted circle he had been locked within. Untethered, the Man now moved forth from Purgatory and into the undiscovered domains beyond.

Chapter 27—A Break in the Circle
Navigations of the Hidden Domain

Adam gazed out at the sun dipping toward the horizon off the port side. With a poled-out Genoa sail and his mainsail well out too, Adam's boat eased west at roughly five knots. There had been no squalls in the past 48 hours, and it looked as if he was in for a relatively calm evening. There also seemed to be a possible break in the cloud cover, promising a viewing of the stars Adam had yet to see since leaving Noyo Harbor several weeks before.

He had noticed the For Sale sign before even knowing he would need a boat. On that first day Adam had returned to Noyo Harbor, on his way out to Beatrice's slip before speaking with Hank, the handsome blue-and-white sailboat caught his eye. Glancing down at the name on the back of the stern, *The Blue Sea Horse,* Adam felt a light flutter in his chest as if the boy was tickling him. Several times since leaving the hospital, he had experienced these presentiments and was learning to pay more attention to them.

"That's Al Marcotti's boat. Big Al," Hank told Adam when he came back to Noyo Harbor the following day to take another look at it. *The Blue Sea Horse* was a 37-foot Tartan built in 1987. Even Adam, who knew nothing about boats, could tell that it had been well maintained.

"Been for sale for about two years. Lots of potential buyers, but Big Al, well . . ." Hank shrugged. "I gotta warn you. He's been a bit of a dickwad in terms of who he's willing to sell her to."

"Why's that?" Adam said without a hint of concern. He could already see the boat would soon be his.

"That boat means one hell of a lot to Big Al. Calls it his 'baby-love.' He used to sail her all over the world with his wife, Maria, but then Maria died. She wasn't that old; lymphoma, I think." Hank's fingers looked like they were anxious for a cigarette to squeeze. "Al tried sailing on his own after that. Had the boat rigged to sail single-handed. See how the trimming lines all run to the aft cockpit?"

Hank pointed them out as he reached for the Camel Lights in his breast pocket.

"But I guess it just wasn't the same without his wife, so he stopped sailing ten years ago, maybe. Seriously, I doubt Big Al will sell it to you. I think he just put the sign on it to make his new wife, Barb, happy." Hank let out a stream of smoke as he glanced around the docks. "There's some other boats around here for sale, maybe—"

"No. This is the one," Adam said. "Would you introduce me to Big Al?"

Hank shrugged and smiled. "What the hay, let's give him a ring."

Despite Hank's enthusiastic endorsement of Adam over the phone, Big Al was reluctant to come down to meet him. He was especially skeptical after hearing that Adam had little sailing experience. And by the time Al pulled into the Noyo Harbor parking lot, he had already made up his mind not to sell.

It took less than 20 minutes for Al to change his mind. "I just liked the fella," Al sheepishly told Barb on the phone after agreeing to sell the boat. "I don't know why, exactly. Maybe the way he touched the railings, the mast, the lines—with respect, like he really gave a damn. He's right, Barb; I just know it."

Al did have one condition for handing over *The Blue Sea Horse*. Since Adam insisted on paying the asking price, which Al had inflated just to turn people away, Al insisted on giving Adam sailing lessons. "You aren't heading off nowhere with my baby-love until I say you're good and ready." Big Al extended a big hand, and Adam shook it.

Notorious for its rough waters, Cape Mendocino was not the ideal place to learn the finer points of sailing, but Big Al was an excellent teacher and Adam was no ordinary student. By the time Adam was ready to leave several weeks later, Al considered him a more than able seaman. "He reads wind and water as good as any old salt," Big Al bragged to Hank.

Adam was vague about where he was heading and what exactly his plans were, but Hank and Big Al never pushed him on it. They merely helped him stock the right supplies for a long journey, then wished him "fair winds and following seas" on the morning he set out from the California coast.

$$\diamondsuit$$

As dusk began to stretch across the evening sky, the winds and seas continued to settle. Adam set his wind vane and checked the autopilot before heading below deck. He loved the interior of his boat. The layout was simple and practical, every conceivable space serving a specific purpose. But the functionality of the space was balanced by aesthetic form. "During extended lengths at sea," Big Al had warned, "with no land in sight and nowhere to go other than below deck, if a sailor does not feel at home inside his vessel, the freedom of the sea will turn into a stint in solitary."

With Big Al's approval, Adam had made a few small changes to the cabin, adding touches to make the space more his own: abalone shells on the wall beside the main hatch, a collection of his favorite books stacked above the navigation station, sea glass of various colors glued onto the railing around the galley. Of course it was nowhere near as personalized as the interior of Beatrice's boat, but it was a start. The only picture inside *The Blue Sea Horse* was one that Adam had had framed and mounted on the wall in the galley—the photograph Michael had given him back at the Presidio House.

Adam placed a teapot on the stove then pulled a slab of tuna steak out of the icebox to thaw. While waiting for the water to boil, he leaned back against the counter and looked over at the picture. It was a large group shot taken in front of an academic building. At the top of the photo was printed: *EXTENDED DIMENSIONAL ATTENTION STUDIES—CAL BERKELEY 1970.*

The group was a roughly even split of men and women, most of them wearing tie-dyed shirts, paisley, and bell-bottoms. But Adam could tell that these weren't your average turned-on, tuned-in, and dropped-out hippies. These were intelligent, inquisitive faces, eyes full of optimism. Also apparent was how close they seemed to be—arms wrapped around neighbors, hands holding hands, some sitting on each other's laps. And theirs weren't just mandatory smiles for the camera. These were honest smiles. Open smiles.

At the back of the group, standing on the steps of the building and just visible above everyone else, were two slightly older men, side by side, the two sides of the brains behind the study. They were dressed more conservatively than the others. Adam, of course, recognized their faces from the first moment he had looked at the picture.

Rene Adiklein—in his midthirties with long, raven-black hair and sharp European features—stood on the left. He looked more like the bass player of a psychedelic band than a psychologist. Virgil Coates—in his early forties, his bushy, red hair and full beard unkempt, looking very much the impassioned professor—stood on the right.

The two men had their arms around each other.

There was another face in the photograph that Adam recognized, although not right away. In the third row down from the top, directly in the heart of the group, a young African-American man stood a head taller than his neighbors. His deep brown eyes were staring directly into the camera, as if he could see Adam looking back at him from the future. He wore a tight, blue tee shirt the color of Superman's costume, but instead of a giant red *S* on his chest, there was a large rainbow-colored butterfly.

Black print at the bottom of the photograph listed the names of everyone in the picture. Searching through the list, Adam had eventually found the name he was looking for. Michael Papillon.

Time you start flying, brother. For both of us.

Adam was doing just that. And before setting out, he had done a few other things on Michael's behalf as well.

Water boiling, Adam turned the stove off and fixed his tea. Unless he was dealing with severe weather conditions, his evening routine was simple. First, tea and chart work. Then, a quick peek above deck for a position and horizon check. Then prepare supper, eat, and wash up. Finally, another trip above deck for a last check, followed by reading before bed. Big Al had taught Adam to scan for possible oil tankers or other large entities he might collide with, at least every 20 minutes, day and night.

"Managing your sleep is by far your biggest challenge," Al warned. "It's not easy keeping your eyes open when all you wanna do is close 'em. Chew ice, slap your face, sing at the top of your lungs if you need to." Al had installed alarm clocks and timers below deck to help with this annoying yet obligatory task. The boat also had a radar sensor with a collision alarm meant to give Adam enough time to react if any oil leviathans did try to sneak up on him.

But the farther out to sea Adam got, the less he found the need for alarm clocks or other tricks to stay awake. He wasn't near any major shipping routes, for one thing. But there was another reason Adam felt safe spending time belowdecks. With so few distractions around, that new sensitivity of his seemed to amplify the farther out he traveled. He discovered this early on in his journey, when one evening *The Blue Sea Horse* did happen to come into range of another boat. Well before the radar sounded its alarm, Adam woke, already aware there was another vessel close by. And before he even saw the boat's lights, he was on deck, adjusting course.

Adam sat down with his tea to go over the charts and mark his daily progress. After calculating his new coordinates, Adam used a pencil to make a dot, then draw a line from yesterday's dot to today's. The 121 nautical miles was below his daily average, but it wasn't bad. On his map the jagged dotted line representing his total journey stretched out over 5,000 miles of ocean. Beatrice hadn't been exaggerating when she'd said the location was remote.

When Adam first looked at the coordinates she had provided him with, the numbers evoked an odd sense of familiarity. It was weeks later, after he had already set sail, when one night he happened to notice the symbol on the cover of *Navigations of the Hidden Domain* and understood why.

According to the coordinates she had given him, he would be arriving soon. Sometimes the thought did float through Adam's mind that this journey just might lead nowhere, since conventional charts and maps showed nothing but endless ocean in the area he was trying to reach. Or even worse, what if there was something at that final red dot, but Beatrice had already moved on? For the most part these thoughts were fleeting, and Adam did his best to stay focused on just sailing, one day at a time.

"And as long as you keep moving forward, I will keep pulling you toward me, and eventually we will meet again, and touch again, and with our hands melted together as one, we will peek behind the celestial curtain and see the new world waiting for us, just beyond the stars."

Adam put away his charts and returned to the galley to start dinner. Tonight's menu was seared tuna steak, sauerkraut, and dried fruit and nuts for dessert.

After dinner, he washed up. He was just about to sit down and relax for a bit when he felt that little tickle in his chest, tugging him to go above deck for a horizon check. At first Adam shrugged it off. *Unless it's a super-tanker ready to make The Blue Sea Horse into its hood ornament, I'd rather read for a while first.* His mind still housed that data-crunching machine that had ruled his existence back at Virtual Skies, and although tamed, it still hungered for problems to solve and puzzles to piece together. To scratch that itch he had a thick book of modern chess theory. But there was also the copy of *Navigations of the Hidden Domain* that Beatrice had left for him. And reading that book now, after his time in the hospital, Adam had discovered another, deeper layer within it that he had not been aware of before. Hidden meanings buried throughout its pages, not for his mind to digest, but placed there for the benefit of the underdeveloped boy in his chest.

Tonight, unfortunately, that boy had no interest in reading, as it continued nagging Adam to go above deck. Throwing on his big, blue parka, he headed up to investigate.

Adam stepped on deck and immediately noticed something odd. There was no wind on his face. Looking to the sails, he saw they both sagged lifelessly. Then he noticed the absence of sound. Thick and heavy silence, the kind he had not even thought possible out here at sea. But the real phenomenon for which Adam had been drawn above deck was what he saw when he looked up.

Even with the boat lights on, the view of the heavens was unparalleled to any he had experienced in his lifetime.

In all directions, without obstruction, the starry dome arched down to meet the glassy, still ocean all around him. The reflection of the stars even seemed to be dancing on the water's surface. Then to Adam's astonishment, he realized that the glow was not simply a mirror, but billions of specks of bioluminescent algae that had come out to greet their starry companions above.

Adam quickly took down the sails to give him an even more unobstructed view. Next he turned off all the lights until he was in complete darkness, his boat now just a silhouette against both sky and sea. Feeling his way up to the bow, Adam found the space between the forward hatch and front pulpit, just big enough to lie down.

There he floated in a sea of infinite space.

The experience was an affirmation of everything he had been through. To feel himself lying there, a dot suspended between two great unknowns, the questions "Who am I?" and "What am I doing here?" no longer tormented Adam. Instead it fueled him, adding to a new current inside of him, one that extended vertically out of the horizontal expanse that had once been the limits of his domain. By allowing himself to open up to this new direction, he could finally see a great truth about his life. He was not simply a meaningless speck floating between the two immense realms of heaven and earth. *He was what linked them.*

$$\diamondsuit$$

Adam flinched. Then his eyes opened. There had been a loud crash like some enormous object shattering. But for all its volume, it sounded like it had come from somewhere far away.

Lifting his head slightly, Adam looked around. It was still night, and he was still lying at the front of his boat, which now just barely rotated on the water like a pinwheel.

Then Adam saw it. Out across the ocean in the direction the sound had come from, a jagged line had formed in the night sky.

Stretching from the horizon all the way to the top of the celestial firmament, a hairline fracture had formed, splintering the distance from star to star to star.

The sky had cracked.

It was impossible. It made no sense. Yet there it was. Like standing inside a giant eggshell looking out. Adam could even feel warmth from the other side. Perhaps he was dreaming. Perhaps he was the only person in the world able to see it. Or perhaps he was just the first.

The light streaming down illuminated the ocean all around Adam's boat, and when he looked out, he noticed something in the waters directly ahead of his bow. The shores of a new land.

Adam had arrived.

FOR ALL CHICKEN
BOYS AND GIRLS

"This evening's traffic report is brought to you by Buzzworld. Buzzworld, personalizing your online presence in today's global marketplace. Be unique. Be the Buzz. Buzzworld-is-a-subdivision-of-Virtual-Skies-Media-and-Marketing-Solutions."

The white minivan rolled forward a few feet toward the toll plaza before coming to a halt. Up in front sat Robert's mother and father, their faces glowing taillight red. In the middle seat were Robert's siblings; his brother was sleeping, while his sister listened to her music. Robert sat in the way back, strapped into his booster seat. He was eight years old now; he was taking five milligrams of Adderall a day; he had his very own smartphone; and he no longer acted like a chicken.

"It's 7:26. Celebrity Watch will be starting shortly, but right now here's a special report from our Tech Times reporter Cynthia Gainsburg with a look at new developments in the Virtual Skies hacking scandal. Cynthia?"

"Thank you, John. It has been a week now since initial leaks surfaced indicating a widespread hack into Virtual Skies' MyStar network. Lips are tight around the Tower, however, several unnamed sources have confirmed that up to thirty million users could potentially be affected

by the breach. Top security analysts are speculating that this was an inside job, as leaked e-mails made multiple references to the discovery of a backdoor found deep within the proprietary code used to run recently added features of the network.

"The code in question is believed to have originated from one of Virtual Skies' subcompanies, Pixilate, which took charge of all social gaming for the company in early 2008. Pixilate founder Blake Dorsey, who many see as Rene Adiklein's potential successor, issued a statement insisting that, 'rumors of a worm spreading through the network are just that—rumors.' But as the day went on, unfortunately for Mr. Dorsey, it was the rumors themselves that continued to spread. Which brings us to this morning's importuned press conference, held by Rene Adiklein himself to address the issue."

"Very soon, we will be releasing an update," Adiklein's voice from the press conference sounded as cool and commanding as ever. *"To address whatever minor issues users may be experiencing. But let me assure you all, this is just a little blip, a little nothing. Everyone will have completely forgotten about it by tomorrow night's episode of* America's Most Popular.*"* Adiklein gave a charming laugh, before the female reporter's voice cut back in.

"All assurances aside, it was what took place while Mr. Adiklein was taking questions that has everyone now talking. Video of the moment, which has spread like wildfire across the Internet, shows Mr. Adiklein in mid-sentence, suddenly becoming visibly agitated by something he appears to notice at the back of the pressroom. Moments later, sounds of a disturbance can be heard breaking out. Eyewitnesses at the event claim the altercation occurred between an uninvited individual, described as a disheveled man in a wheelchair, and the security team attempting to remove him. It was at that point when Mr. Adiklein, known for his calm, unflappable demeanor, is seen on camera losing his temper."

The radio broadcast switched again to sounds from the press conference where a commotion could be heard, along with Adiklein's voice, just off mic, yelling, *"Out—get him out of here, now! A—a derelict like this—it's, it's a disgrace to the city! Out of my sight, now!"*

The female reporter's voice came back on, *"Needless to say, the bizarre incident did not help public confidence, or investor confidence for that matter, as Virtual Skies stock took its biggest hit to date. Requests for comments from Mr. Adiklein have so far been declined. We will keep you updated as the Virtual Skies hacking crisis continues to unfold. Back to you, John."*

"So, Cynthia, with this potential worm, what exactly does it mean for the millions of us out here that may be affected?"

"At this point, John, whatever it is that's spreading throughout the network does not appear to be malicious. However, people are still advised not to open any—"

Robert's mother reached down and switched off the radio, just as his father pressed down on the gas. The minivan rolled forward another foot in the stop-and-go traffic.

Back in the third row, Robert slouched down in his booster seat as he continued to collect the kills needed to upgrade his *Lust 4 Flesh* avatar. *Zombie Babies* was still his favorite game, even though he was a little old for it now, but like all his friends at school, he had recently moved up to *L4F*.

Just as Robert was about to hit 100,000 kills, he heard the ping of a new message coming in from the online stats board. It was from another player, a Michael something-or-other, not a name he recognized. Without thinking Robert clicked on the message. The moment he did, the game froze. Robert tapped the Attack icon. Nothing happened. He tried his Eat icon. Nothing.

And then, without warning, his screen went completely black. Robert suddenly became aware of the faint reflection of a boy's face looking back at him. It was his own face, but it somehow looked older, like a second-grader's. Then he remembered he was a second-grader. A big, square pixel suddenly appeared right on the tip of his reflected nose. After a moment, the pixel expanded into a line, and the line started wiggling around the screen, inching along like a crazy caterpillar. It made Robert smile.

The caterpillar stopped moving in the center of the screen. Then, like accelerated, time-lapse photography, it spun into a chrysalis, and then slowly pushed its way out of its encasement and emerged as an old-school, 2-D animation of a butterfly. Below the butterfly appeared the words:

What lies beyond the stars?

Robert read the message and at first it confused him. He considered the question again. *What lies beyond the stars?* It didn't make sense. *Nothing is beyond the stars. Just more stars, right?*

To make sure, he set down the electronic device he was holding and turned to the window. *What lies beyond the stars?* There was a sea of red-and-white lights all around him on the highway, but he strained to look up above it all, up at the night sky.

At first he saw nothing. But then, slowly, he began to see little points of light twinkling away. *I remember you,* the boy thought. *We used to be friends once.*

Then he noticed something else. Something that didn't make any sense, something that couldn't possibly be up there, and yet there it was. He saw it faintly at first, and then more clearly. And what he saw made Chicken Boy's body tingle all over, as his eyes filled with wonder and hope.

ABOUT THE AUTHOR

Michael Goorjian is an Emmy Award–winning actor, filmmaker, and writer. His acting credits include *Party of Five, Leaving Las Vegas,* and *SLC Punk.* As a filmmaker, he achieved widespread recognition for his first major independent film, *Illusion,* starring Kirk Douglas. Other directing credits include the Louise Hay documentary, *You Can Heal Your Life,* Wayne Dyer's film *The Shift,* and the Hay House film anthology, *Tales of Everyday Magic.* Michael lives in Oakland, California. *What Lies Beyond the Stars* is his first novel. Website: www.michaelagoorjian.com

Hay House Titles of Related Interest

We hope you enjoyed this Hay House **Visions** book. If you'd like to receive our online catalog featuring additional information on Hay House books and products, or if you'd like to find out more about the Hay Foundation, please contact:

VISIONS

Hay House, Inc., P.O. Box 5100, Carlsbad, CA 92018-5100
(760) 431-7695 or (800) 654-5126
(760) 431-6948 (fax) or (800) 650-5115 (fax)
www.hayhouse.com® • www.hayfoundation.org

Published and distributed in Australia by:
Hay House Australia Pty. Ltd., 18/36 Ralph St., Alexandria NSW 2015
Phone: 612-9669-4299 • *Fax:* 612-9669-4144 • www.hayhouse.com.au

Published and distributed in the United Kingdom by:
Hay House UK, Ltd., Astley House, 33 Notting Hill Gate, London W11 3JQ
Phone: 44-20-3675-2450 • *Fax:* 44-20-3675-2451 • www.hayhouse.co.uk

Published and distributed in the Republic of South Africa by:
Hay House SA (Pty), Ltd., P.O. Box 990, Witkoppen 2068
info@hayhouse.co.za • www.hayhouse.co.za

Published in India by: Hay House Publishers India,
Muskaan Complex, Plot No. 3, B-2, Vasant Kunj, New Delhi 110 070
Phone: 91-11-4176-1620 • *Fax:* 91-11-4176-1630 • www.hayhouse.co.in

Distributed in Canada by: Raincoast Books,
2440 Viking Way, Richmond, B.C. V6V 1N2 •
Phone: 1-800-663-5714 • *Fax:* 1-800-565-3770 • www.raincoast.com

Take Your Soul on a Vacation

Visit www.HealYourLife.com® to regroup,
recharge, and reconnect with your own magnificence.
Featuring blogs, mind-body-spirit news, and
life-changing wisdom from Louise Hay and friends.

Visit www.HealYourLife.com today!